STAR WARS

REPUBLIC COMMANDO™

HARD CONTACT

By Karen Traviss

STAR WARS: REPUBLIC COMMANDO: HARD CONTACT
STAR WARS: REPUBLIC COMMANDO: TRIPLE ZERO
STAR WARS: REPUBLIC COMMANDO: TRUE COLORS
STAR WARS: ORDER 66: A REPUBLIC
  COMMANDO NOVEL
STAR WARS: 501st: AN IMPERIAL COMMANDO NOVEL

STAR WARS: THE CLONE WARS
STAR WARS: THE CLONE WARS: NO PRISONERS

STAR WARS: LEGACY OF THE FORCE: BLOODLINES
STAR WARS: LEGACY OF THE FORCE: SACRIFICE
STAR WARS: LEGACY OF THE FORCE: REVELATION

CITY OF PEARL
CROSSING THE LINE
MATRIARCH
THE WORLD BEFORE
ALLY

GEARS OF WAR: ASPHO FIELDS
GEARS OF WAR: JACINTO'S REMNANT
GEARS OF WAR: ANVIL GATE

STAR WARS

REPUBLIC COMMANDO™
HARD CONTACT

KAREN TRAVISS

DEL REY • NEW YORK

Star Wars: Republic Commando: Hard Contact is a work of fiction. Names, places, and incidents either are products of the author's imagination or are used fictitiously.

2014 Del Rey Mass Market Edition

Copyright © 2004 by Lucasfilm Ltd. & ® or ™ where indicated. All Rights Reserved. Used under authorization.

Published in the United States by Del Rey, an imprint of Random House, a division of Random House LLC, a Penguin Random House Company, New York, and simultaneously in Canada by Random House of Canada Limited, Toronto.

DEL REY and the HOUSE colophon are registered trademarks of Random House LLC.

www.starwars.com
www.delreybooks.com

ISBN 978-0-345-47827-6
eBook ISBN 978-0-307-79590-8

Printed in the United States of America

First Edition: November 2004

30 29 28 27 26 25 24 23 22

ACKNOWLEDGEMENTS

Long ago, in a cinema far away, a film critic watched and re-viewed a brand-new movie called *Star Wars*. If she'd known she was going to end up writing this book, she'd have taken more notes . . . so my thanks go to editors Shelly Shapiro (Del Rey), Keith Clayton (Del Rey), and Sue Rostoni (Lucasfilm) for their wise advice; to the many *Star Wars* fans who made me welcome in their world; and especially to Ryan Kaufman at LucasArts—*Star Wars* oracle, polymath, wit, and all-around good bloke, who gave generously of his time and knowledge, and never ran out of patience when I asked for the umpteenth time, "Yes, but does the armor have to be white?" It was the best of times, folks. Thanks.

THE **STAR WARS** LEGENDS NOVELS TIMELINE

BEFORE THE REPUBLIC
37,000–25,000 YEARS BEFORE
STAR WARS: A New Hope

c. 25,793 *YEARS BEFORE STAR WARS: A New Hope*

Dawn of the Jedi: Into the Void

OLD REPUBLIC
5000–67 YEARS BEFORE
STAR WARS: A New Hope

Lost Tribe of the Sith: The Collected
Stories

3954 *YEARS BEFORE STAR WARS: A New Hope*

The Old Republic: Revan

3650 *YEARS BEFORE STAR WARS: A New Hope*

The Old Republic: Deceived
Red Harvest
The Old Republic: Fatal Alliance
The Old Republic: Annihilation

1032 *YEARS BEFORE STAR WARS: A New Hope*

Knight Errant
Darth Bane: Path of Destruction
Darth Bane: Rule of Two
Darth Bane: Dynasty of Evil

RISE OF THE EMPIRE
67–0 YEARS BEFORE
STAR WARS: A New Hope

67 *YEARS BEFORE STAR WARS: A New Hope*

Darth Plagueis

33 *YEARS BEFORE STAR WARS: A New Hope*

Cloak of Deception
Darth Maul: Shadow Hunter
Maul: Lockdown

32 *YEARS BEFORE STAR WARS: A New Hope*

STAR WARS: EPISODE I
THE PHANTOM MENACE

Rogue Planet
Outbound Flight
The Approaching Storm

22 *YEARS BEFORE STAR WARS: A New Hope*

STAR WARS: EPISODE II
ATTACK OF THE CLONES

22–19 *YEARS BEFORE STAR WARS: A New Hope*

STAR WARS: THE CLONE
WARS

The Clone Wars: Wild Space
The Clone Wars: No Prisoners

Clone Wars Gambit
Stealth
Siege

Republic Commando
Hard Contact
Triple Zero
True Colors
Order 66

Shatterpoint
The Cestus Deception
MedStar I: Battle Surgeons
MedStar II: Jedi Healer
Jedi Trial
Yoda: Dark Rendezvous
Labyrinth of Evil

19 *YEARS BEFORE STAR WARS: A New Hope*

STAR WARS: EPISODE III
REVENGE OF THE SITH

Kenobi
Dark Lord: The Rise of Darth Vader
Imperial Commando 501st

Coruscant Nights
Jedi Twilight
Street of Shadows
Patterns of Force
The Last Jedi

10 *YEARS BEFORE STAR WARS: A New Hope*

The Han Solo Trilogy
The Paradise Snare
The Hutt Gambit
Rebel Dawn

The Adventures of Lando Calrissian
The Force Unleashed
The Han Solo Adventures
Death Troopers
The Force Unleashed II

REBELLION
0–5 YEARS AFTER
STAR WARS: A New Hope

NEW REPUBLIC
5–25 YEARS AFTER
STAR WARS: A New Hope

THE STAR WARS LEGENDS NOVELS TIMELINE

 **NEW JEDI ORDER
25–40 YEARS AFTER
*STAR WARS: A New Hope***

 **LEGACY
40+ YEARS AFTER
*STAR WARS: A New Hope***

PROLOGUE

Okay, this is how it happened.

It's pitch black below and we're fast-roping into the crevasse, *too* fast: I can feel the impact in my back teeth when I land. I'm first down and I flood the chamber with my helmet spot-lamp.

There's a triple-sealed blast door between us and the Geonosians and I haven't got time to calculate the charge needed to blow it. A lot, then. *P for plenty,* like I was taught. Stick the thermal tape around the edges and push in the detonator. Easier said than done: the alloy door's covered with crud.

Delta Squad's CO gets on the helmet comlink. "You having a party down there, Theta?"

"Can't rush an artist . . ."

"You want to tell that to the spider droids?"

"Patience, Delta." *Come on, come on. Stick to the metal, will you?* "Nearly there."

"A *lot* of spider droids . . ."

"I hear you, Delta."

"In your own time. No pressure. None at all . . ."

"Clear!"

We flatten ourselves against the cavern walls. It's all white light and painful noise and flying dust for a fraction of a second. When we can see again, the doors are blown inward, ripped apart, billowing smoke. "Delta Squad—clear to enter. *Take take take.*"

"I thought you'd never ask." Delta Squad hits the ground and they're straight in, firing, while we stand back and cover their six. It's a warren of tunnels down here. If we're not careful, something could jump us from any direction.

My helmet's supposed to protect against high decibels, but war is noisy. *Really* noisy. I can't hear my helmet comlink through the *omph-omph-omph* of the Geonosians' sonic rounds and our own blasterfire. I can hear anti-armor going off, too. *Fierfek,* I can feel it through my boots.

Movement catches my eye up ahead, and then it's gone. I'm looking up through the DC-17's scope, checking that it was just my imagination, and Taler gestures toward another of the five tunnels facing us.

"Darman, take that E-Web and hold this position." He beckons Vin and Jay and they move almost back-to-back toward the mouth of the tunnel, checking to all sides.

And then I look up, overhead.

There's more Geonosians around than we thought. A *lot* more. I take down two above me and then more come out of the tunnel to the left so I open fire with the repeating blaster, nice and early, because if I let them get too close the blast will fry me as well.

Even so, it's knocking me back like a trip-hammer.

"Taler, Darman here, over." I can't see him. I can't see any of them, but I can hear rapid fire. "Taler, Darman here, you receiving me, over?"

Not so much silence as an absence of a familiar voice. Then a few fragmented, crackling shouts of ". . . down! Man down here!"

Who? Who's down? "Taler? Vin? Jay? You receiving, over?"

I've lost contact with my squad.

It's the last time I see them.

1

SCRAMBLE LINE ENCRYPTED
STAND BY STAND BY
GEONOSIS FORWARD CONTROL TO FLEET SUPPORT, ORD MANTELL.
PREPARE TO RECEIVE CASEVAC TRANSPORT. MED TRIAGE TEAM ESTIMATE SERIOUS INJURIES, TWELVE THOUSAND, REPEAT TWELVE THOUSAND. WALKING WOUNDED EIGHT THOUSAND, REPEAT EIGHT THOUSAND. ETA TEN HOURS. LOGISTICS PRIORITY FOR BACTA TANK SUPPORT TEAMS.
PREP FOR SEVENTY-TWO THOUSAND COMBAT-FIT TROOPS, REPEAT SEVENTY-TWO THOUSAND, PENDING REDEPLOYMENT. PRIORITY WEAPONS SUPPORT FOR COMMANDO UNITS.
THAT IS ALL. OUT.

Republic assault ship *Implacable:* inbound for extraction from Geonosis. Stand by.

Republic Commando 1136 studied every face in line waiting to board the gunships.

Some were helmeted, and some were not, but—one way or another—they all had his face. And they were all strangers.

"Move it," the loadmaster shouted, gesturing side-to-side with one outstretched arm. "Come on, shift it, people—fast as you can." The gunships dropped down in clouds of dust and troopers embarked, some turning to pull comrades inboard so the ships could lift again quickly. There was no reason to scramble for it. They'd done it a thousand times in training; extraction from a real battle was what they'd prepared for. This wasn't a retreat. They'd grabbed their first victory.

The gunships' downdraft kicked the red Geonosian soil into the air. RC-1136—Darman—took off his helmet and ran his gauntlet carefully across the pale gray dome, wiping away the dust and noting a few scrapes and burn marks.

The loadmaster turned to him. He was one of the very, very few outsiders whom Darman had ever seen working with the Grand Army, a short, wrinkled Duros with a temper to match. "Are you embarking or what?"

Darman continued wiping his helmet. "I'm waiting for my mates," he said.

"You shift your shiny silver backside *now*," the loadmaster said irritably. "I got a schedule."

Darman carefully brought up his knuckle plate just under the loadmasters's chin, and held it there. He didn't need to eject the vibroblade and he didn't need to say a word. He'd made his point.

"Well, whenever you're ready, sir," the Duros said, stepping back to chivy clone troopers instead. It wasn't a great idea to upset a commando, especially not one coming down from the adrenaline high of combat.

But there was still no sign of the rest of his squad. Darman knew that there was no point in waiting any longer. They hadn't called in. Maybe they had comlink failures. Maybe they had made it onto another gunship.

It was the first time in his artificially short life that Darman hadn't been able to reach out and touch the men he had been raised with.

He waited half a standard hour more anyway, until the gunships became less frequent and the lines of troopers became shorter. Eventually there was nobody standing on the desert plain but him, the Duros loadmaster, and half a dozen clone troopers. It was the last lift of the day.

"You better come now, sir," the loadmaster said. "There's nobody unaccounted for. Nobody alive, anyway."

Darman looked around the horizon one last time, still feeling as if he were turning his back on someone reaching out to him.

"I'm coming," he said, and brought up the rear of the line. As the gunship lifted, he watched the swirling dust, dwindling rock formations, and scattered shrinking patches of scrub until Geonosis became a blur of dull red.

He could still search the *Implacable*. It wasn't over yet.

The gunship slipped into the *Implacable*'s giant docking bay, and Darman looked down into the cavern, onto a sea of white armor and orderly movement. The first thing that struck him when the gunship killed its thrusters and locked down on its pad was how *quiet* everyone seemed.

In the crowded bay full of troopers, the air stank of sweat and stale fear and the throat-rasping smell of discharged blaster rifles. But it was so silent that if Darman hadn't seen the evidence of exhausted and injured men, he'd have believed that nothing significant had happened in the last thirty hours.

The deck vibrated under the soles of his boots. He was still staring down at them, studying the random patterns of Geonosian dust that clung to them, when an identical pair came into view.

"Number?" said a voice that was also his own. The commander swept him with a tally sensor: he didn't need Darman to tell him his number, or anything else for that matter, because the sensors in the enhanced Katarn armor reported his status silently, electronically. *No significant injury.* The triage team on Geonosis had waved him past, concentrating on the injured, ignoring both those too badly hurt to help and those who could help themselves. "Are you listening to me? Come on. Talk to me, son."

"I'm okay, sir," he said. "Sir, RC-one-one-three-six. I'm not in shock. I'm fine." He paused. Nobody else was going to call him by his squad nickname—*Darman*—again. They were all dead, he knew it. Jay, Vin, Taler. *He just knew.* "Sir, any news of RC-one-one-three-five—"

"No," said the commander, who had obviously heard similar questions every time he stopped to check. He gestured with the small bar in his hand. "If they're not in casevac or listed on this sweep, then they didn't make it."

It was stupid to ask. Darman should have known better. Clone troopers—and especially Republic commandos—just got on with the job. That was their sole purpose. And they were *lucky,* their training sergeant had told them; outside, in the ordinary world, every being from every species in the galaxy fretted about their purpose in life, searching for meaning. A clone didn't need to. Clones *knew.* They had been perfected for their role, and doubt need never trouble them.

Darman had never known what doubt was until now. No amount of training had prepared him for *this.* He found a space against a bulkhead and sat down.

A clone trooper settled down next to him, squeezing into the gap and briefly clunking a shoulder plate against his. They glanced at each other. Darman rarely had any contact with the other clones: commandos trained apart from everyone, including ARC troopers. The trooper's armor was white, lighter, less resistant; commandos enjoyed upgraded protection. And Darman displayed no rank colors.

But they both knew exactly who and what they were.

"Nice Deece," the trooper said enviously. He was looking at the DC-17: troopers were issued the heavier, lower-spec rifle, the DC-15. "Ion pulse blaster, RPG anti-armor, *and* sniper?"

"Yeah." Every item of his gear was manufactured to a higher spec. A trooper's life was less valuable than a commando's. It was the way things were, and Darman had never questioned it—not for long, anyway. "Full house."

"Tidy." The trooper nodded approval. "Job done, eh?"

"Yeah," Darman said quietly. "Job done."

The trooper didn't say anything else. Maybe he was wary of conversation with commandos. Darman knew what troopers thought about him and his kind. *They don't train like us and they don't fight like us. They don't even talk like us.* A bunch of prima donnas.

Darman didn't think he was arrogant. It was just that he could do every job a soldier could be called upon to do, and then some: siege assault, counterinsurgency, hostage extraction, demolitions, assassination, surveillance, and every kind of infantry activity on any terrain and in any environment, at any time. He *knew* he could, because he'd *done* it. He'd done it in training, first with simunition and then with live rounds. He'd done it with his squad, the three brothers with whom he'd spent every moment of his conscious life. They'd competed against other squads, thousands just like them, but not like them, because they were squad brothers, and that was *special*.

He had never been taught how to live apart from the squad, though. Now he would learn the hardest way of all.

Darman had absolute confidence that he was one of the best special ops soldiers ever created. He was undistracted by the everyday concerns of raising a family and making a living, things that his instructors said he was lucky never to know.

But now he was alone. Very, very alone. It was very distracting indeed.

He considered this for a long time in silence. Surviving when the rest of your squad had been killed was no cause for pride. It felt instead like something his training sergeant had described as *shame*. That was what you felt when you lost a battle, apparently.

But they had won. It was their first battle, and they had *won*.

The landing ramp of the *Implacable* eased down, and the bright sunlight of Ord Mantell streamed in. Darman replaced his helmet without thinking and stood in an orderly line, waiting to disembark and be reassigned. He was going to be chilled down, kept in suspended animation until duty called again.

So this was the aftermath of victory. He wondered how much worse defeat might feel.

Imbraani, Qiilura: 40 light-years from Ord Mantell, Tingel Arm

The field of barq flowed from silver to ruby as the wind from the southwest bent the ripening grain in waves. It could have been a perfect late-summer day; instead it was turning into one of the worst days of Etain Tur-Mukan's life.

Etain had run and run and she had nothing left in her. She flung herself flat between the furrows, not caring where she fell. Etain held her breath as something stinking and wet squelched under her.

The pursuing Weequay couldn't hear her above the wind, she knew, but she held her breath anyway.

"Hey girlie!" His boots crunched closer. He was panting. "Where you go? Don't be shy."

Don't breathe.

"I got bottle of urrqal. You want to have party?" He had a remarkably large vocabulary for a Weequay, all of it centered on his baser needs. "I *fun* when you get to know me."

I should have waited for it to get dark. I could influence his mind, try to make him leave.

But she hadn't. And she couldn't, try as she might to concentrate. She was too full of adrenaline and uncontrolled panic.

"Come on, you scrag-end, where are you? I find you . . ."

He sounded as if he was kicking his way through the crop, and getting closer. If she got up and ran for it, she was dead. If she stayed where she was, he'd find her—eventually. He wasn't going to get bored, and he wasn't going to give up.

"Girlie . . ."

The Weequay's voice was close, to her right, about twenty meters away. She sipped a strangled breath and clamped her lips shut again, lungs aching, eyes streaming with the effort.

"Girlie . . ." Closer. He was going to step right on her. "Gir-leeeeee . . ."

She knew what he'd do when he found her. If she was lucky, he'd kill her afterward.

"Gir—"

The Weequay was interrupted by a loud, wet *thwack.* He

let out a grunt and then there was a second *thwack*—shorter, sharper, harder. Etain heard a squeal of pain.

"How many times have I got to tell you, *di'kut*?" It was a different voice, human, with an hard edge of authority. *Thwack.* "Don't—waste—my—time." Another *thwack:* another squeal. Etain kept her face pressed in the dirt. "You get drunk *one* more time, you go chasing females *one* more time, and I'm going to slit you from here to—*here.*"

The Weequay shrieked. It was the sort of incoherent animal sound that beings made when pain overwhelmed them. Etain had heard too much of that sound in her short time on Qiilura. Then there was silence.

She hadn't heard the voice before, but she didn't need to. She knew exactly who it belonged to.

Etain strained to listen, half expecting a heavy boot to suddenly stamp on her back, but all she could hear was the swish and crunch of two pairs of feet wading through the crop. Away from her. She caught snatches of the fading conversation as the wind took it: the Weequay was still being berated.

". . . more important . . ."

What was?

". . . later, but right now, *di'kut,* I need you to . . . okay? Or I'll cut . . ."

Etain waited. Eventually all she could hear was the breath of the wind, the rustling grain, and the occasional fluting call of a ground-eel seeking a mate. She allowed herself to breathe normally again, but still she waited, facedown in ripe manure, until dusk started to fall. She had to move *now.* The gdans would be out hunting, combing the fields in packs. On top of that, the smell that hadn't bothered her while she was gripped by terror was starting to really bother her now.

She eased herself up on her elbows, then her knees, and looked around.

Why did they have to manure barq so late in the season anyway? She fumbled in the pockets of her cloak for a cloth. Now if only she could find a stream, she could clean herself up. She pulled a handful of stalks, crushed them into a ball, and tried to scrape off the worst of the dung and debris stuck to her.

"That's a pretty expensive crop to be using for *that*," a voice said.

Etain gulped in a breath and spun around to find a local in a grubby smock scowling at her. He looked thin, worn out, and annoyed; he was holding a threshing tool. "Do you know how much that stuff's worth?"

"I'm sorry," she said. Sliding her hand carefully inside her cloak, she felt for the familiar cylinder. She hadn't wanted the Weequay to know that she was a Jedi, but if this farmer was considering turning her in for a few loaves or a bottle of urrqal, she'd need her lightsaber handy. "It was your barq or my life, I'm afraid."

The farmer stared at the crushed stalks and the scattered bead-like grains, tight-lipped. Yes, barq fetched a huge price in the restaurants of Coruscant: it was a luxury, and the people who grew it for export couldn't afford it. That didn't seem to bother the Neimoidians who controlled the trade. It never did.

"I'll pay for the damage," Etain said, her hand still inside the cloak.

"What were they after you for?" the farmer asked, ignoring her offer.

"The usual," she said.

"Oh-ah, you're not that good looking."

"Charming."

"I know who you are."

Oh no. Her grip closed. "You do?"

"I reckon."

A little more food for his family. A few hours' drunken oblivion, courtesy of urrqal. That was all she was to him. He made as if to step closer and she drew her arm clear of her cloak, because she was fed up with running and she didn't like the look of that threshing tool.

Vzzzzzmmmm.

"Oh, great," the farmer sighed, eyeing the shaft of pure blue light. "Not one of you lot. That's all we need."

"Yes," she said, and held the lightsaber steady in front of her face. Her stomach had knotted, but she kept her voice under control. "I am Padawan Etain Tur-Mukan. You can try to turn me in, if you want to test my skill, but I'd prefer that you help me instead. Your call, sir."

The farmer stared at the lightsaber as if he was trying to work out a price for it. "Didn't help your Master much, that thing, did it?"

"Master Fulier was unfortunate. *And* betrayed." She lowered the lightsaber but didn't cut the beam. "Are you going to help me?"

"We're going to have Ghez Hokan's thugs all over us if I—"

"I think they're busy," Etain said.

"What do you want from us?"

"Shelter, for the moment."

The farmer sucked his teeth thoughtfully. "Okay. Come on, Padawan—"

"Get used to calling me Etain, please." She thumbed off the lightsaber: the light died with a *ffumm* sound, and she slipped the hilt back inside her cloak. "Just to be on the safe side."

Etain trailed after him, trying not to smell herself, but it was hard, nauseatingly hard. Even a scent-hunting gdan wouldn't recognize her as a human. It was getting dark now, and the farmer kept glancing over his shoulder at her.

"Oh-ah." He shook his head, engaged in some internal conversation. "I'm Birhan, and this is my land. And I thought you lot were supposed to be able to use some sort of mind control tricks."

"How do you know I haven't?" Etain lied.

"Oh-ah," he said, and nothing more.

She wasn't going to volunteer the obvious if he hadn't spotted it for himself. A disappointment to her Master, she was clearly not the best of the bunch. She struggled with the Force and she grappled with self-discipline, and she was here because she and Master Fulier happened to be nearby when a job needed doing. Fulier never could resist a challenge and long odds, and it looked as if he'd paid the price. They hadn't found his body yet, but there had been no word from him, either.

Yes, Etain was a Padawan, technically speaking.

She just happened to be one who was a breath away from building permadomes in refugee camps. She reasoned that part of a Jedi's skill was the simple use of psychology. And if Birhan wanted to think the Force was strong in her, and that there was a lot more behind the external shell of a gawky, plain girl covered in stinking dung, then that was fine by her.

It would keep her alive a little longer while she worked out what to do next.

Fleet Support, Ord Mantell, barrack block 5 Epsilon

It was a waste, a rotten waste.

RC-1309 busied himself maintaining his boots. He cleaned out the clamps, blowing the red dust clear with a squirt of air from the pressure gun. He rinsed the liners and shook them dry. There was no point being idle while he was waiting to be chilled down.

"Sergeant?"

He looked up. The commando who had walked in placed his survival pack, armor, and black bodysuit on the bunk opposite and stared back. His readout panel identified him as RC-8015.

"I'm Fi," he said, and held out his hand for shaking. "So you lost your squad, too."

"Niner," RC-1309 said without taking the proffered hand. "So, *ner vod*—my brother—you're the sole survivor?"

"Yes."

"Did you hold back while your brothers pressed on? Or were you just lucky?"

Fi stood there with his hands on his hips, identical to Niner in every way except that he was . . . *different.* He spoke a little differently. He smelled subtly different. He moved his hands . . . not like Niner's squad did, not at all.

"I did my job," Fi said carefully. "And I'd rather be with them than here . . . *ner vod.*"

Niner considered him for a while, and went back to cleaning his boots. Fi put his kit in the locker beside the bunks, then swung himself up into the top rack in one smooth motion. He folded his arms under his head very precisely and lay staring up at the bulkhead as if he were meditating.

If he had been Sev, Niner would have known exactly what he was doing, even without looking. But Sev was gone.

Clone troopers lost brothers in training. So did commandos. But troopers were socialized with whole sections, platoons, companies, even regiments, and that meant that even after the inevitable deaths and removals during live exercises, there were still plenty of people around you whom you knew well. Commandos worked solely with each other.

Niner had lost everyone he had grown up with, and so had Fi.

He'd lost a brother before—Two-Eight—on exercise. The three survivors had welcomed the replacement, although they had always felt he was slightly *different*—a little distant—as if he had never quite believed he'd been accepted.

But they performed to expected levels of excellence together—and as long as they did, their Kaminoan technicians and motley band of alien instructors didn't seem to care how they felt about it.

But the commandos cared. They just kept it to themselves.

"It was a waste," Niner said.

"What was?" Fi said.

"Deploying us in an operation like Geonosis. It was an infantry job. Not special ops."

"That sounds like criticism of—"

"I'm just making the point that we couldn't perform to maximum effectiveness."

"Understood. Maybe when we're revived we'll be able to do what we're really trained for."

Niner wanted to say that he missed his squad, but that wasn't something to confide in a stranger. He inspected his boots and was satisfied. Then he stood up and spread his bodysuit flat on the mattress and checked it for vacuum integrity with the sweep-sensor in his glove. It was a ritual so ingrained in him that he hardly thought about it: maintain boots, suit, and armor plates, recalibrate helmet systems, check heads-up display, strip down and reassemble DC-17, empty and repack survival pack. *Done.* It took him twenty-six minutes and twenty seconds, give or take two seconds. Well-maintained gear was often the difference between life and death. So was two seconds.

He closed the top of his pack with a *clack* and secured the seal. Then he checked the catches that held the separate ordnance pack to see that they were moving freely. That mattered when he needed to jettison explosive materials fast. When he glanced up, Fi was propped on one elbow, looking down at him from the bunk.

"Dry rations go on the *fifth* layer," he said.

Niner always packed them farther down, between his spare rappelling line and his hygiene kit. "In *your* squad, maybe," he said, and carried on.

Fi took the hint and rolled over on his back again, no doubt to meditate on how differently things might be done in the future.

After a while he started singing very quietly, almost under his breath: *Kom'rk tsad droten troch nyn ures adenn, Dha Werda Verda a'den tratu.* They were the wrath of the warrior's shadow and the gauntlet of the Republic; Niner knew the song. It was a traditional Mandalorian war chant, designed to boost the morale of normal men who needed a bit of psyching up before a fight. The words had been altered a little to have meaning for the armies of clone warriors.

We don't need all that, Niner thought. *We were born to fight, nothing else.*

But he found himself joining in anyway. It was a comfort. He placed his gear in the locker, rolled onto his bunk, and matched note and beat perfectly with Fi, two identical voices in the deserted barrack room.

Niner would have traded every remaining moment of his life for a chance to rerun the previous day's engagement. He would have held Sev and DD back; he would have sent O-Four west with the E-Web cannon.

But he hadn't.

Gra'tua cuun hett su dralshy'a. Our vengeance burns brighter still.

Fi's voice trailed off into silence the merest fraction of a section before Niner's. He heard him swallow hard.

"I was up there with them, Sarge," he said quietly. "I didn't hang back. Not at all."

Niner closed his eyes. He regretted hinting that Fi might have done anything less.

"I know, brother," he said. "I know."

2

Clone personnel have free will, even if they do follow orders. If they couldn't think for themselves, we'd be better off with droids—and they're a lot cheaper, too. They have to be able to respond to situations we can't imagine. Will that change them in ways we can't predict? Perhaps. But they have to be mentally equipped to win wars. Now thaw those men out. They have a job to do.
—Jedi Master Arligan Zey, intelligence officer

Secure briefing room, Fleet Support, Ord Mantell, three standard months after Geonosis

Fleet Support Base hadn't been built to accommodate tens of thousands of troops, and it showed. The briefing room was a cold store, and it still smelled of food and spices. Darman could see the loading rails that spanned the ceiling, but he kept his focus on the holoscreen in front of him.

It didn't feel so bad to be revived after stasis. He was still a commando. They hadn't reconditioned him. That meant—that meant he'd performed to expected standards at Geonosis. *He'd done well.* He felt positive.

But his helmet felt different. There was a lot more data on the HUD, the heads-up display. He flicked between modes for a while, controlling each command with rapid blinks, noting the extra systems and hardware that had been installed since Geonosis.

Sitting to his left was his new sergeant, who preferred to

be called Niner when superior officers weren't around, and RC-8015, nicknamed Fi. They, too, were the sole survivors of their squads. At least they knew what he was going through.

There was a fourth makeshift seat in the row—a blue alloy packing crate—and it was unoccupied. Jedi Master Arligan Zey, hands clasped behind his back, paced up and down in front of the screen, cloak flapping, breaking the holoprojection each time. Another Jedi, who had not been identified, was splitting his attention between Zey and the three helmeted commandos sitting absolutely still on the row of crates.

The reflective surfaces of the spray-clean alloy walls enabled Darman to discreetly observe an unusual alien—one he had never seen before. He had been trained to take in every detail of his surroundings, although it was very difficult not to notice the creature.

The alien was about a meter and a half long, and it was slinking around the walls, sniffing. Black-furred and glossy, it prowled on long delicate legs, thrusting a narrow muzzle into crevices and exhaling sharply each time it did. Earlier, Darman had heard Zey address it as Valaqil: he also said it was a Gurlanin, a shapeshifter.

Darman had heard about shapeshifters in training, but this wasn't a Clawdite. He was watching its reflection in his right-field peripheral vision when the door swung open and another commando entered, helmet tucked rigidly under his right arm, and saluted smartly.

"RC-three-two-two-two, sir," he said. "Apologies for keeping you, sir. The medics didn't want to discharge me."

No wonder: there was a stripe of raw flesh across his face that started just under his right eye, ran clean across his mouth, and finally ended at the left side of his jaw. He certainly didn't look like any of the other clones now. Darman wondered what level of persuasion it had taken to get the medical staff to skip a course of bacta.

"Are you fit, soldier?" Zey said.

"Fit to fight, sir." He sat down next to Darman and assumed the same ramrod posture, glancing at him briefly in acknowledgment. So this was their fourth man. They were a squad again—numerically, anyway. *Omega Squad.*

The other Jedi was staring at the newcomer with an expression of barely concealed astonishment. Zey seemed to notice and nudged his colleague. "Padawan Jusik is new to clone armies, as are we all." That was understandable: Darman had never seen Jedi before the Battle of Geonosis, and he was equally fascinated. "You'll excuse his curiosity."

Zey gestured at the holoscreen.

"This is your objective, gentlemen—Qiilura." He glanced at his datapad, reading intently. "This data has been obtained from high-altitude reconnaissance, so it has its limitations."

Zey went on, "Qiilura is technically neutral. Unfortunately, its neutral status is likely due to end very soon."

He had referred to them as *gentlemen.* Maybe Zey didn't know what to call commandos. It was still early days for all of them.

The image on the screen began as a blue-and-white disc, zooming in to views of chains of islands, deep river inlets, and rolling plains peppered with patches of woodland and gameboard fields. It looked pleasant and peaceful, and hence utterly alien to Darman, whose entire life beyond Tipoca City had been spent on battlefields, real or virtual.

"You're looking at farming communities, almost all of them located *here* in this region because it's the most fertile land," Zey said. "They produce barq, kushayan, and fifty percent of the luxury foodstuffs and beverages in the galaxy. There's also gem mining. The population is nevertheless living at subsistence level, and there is no government other than the law of commerce and profit—Neimoidian traders effectively own the planet, or at least the productive areas that are of use to them. They enforce their stewardship through a militia controlled by Ghez Hokan—a Mandalorian so unpleasantly violent that he was actually asked to leave the Death Squad for enjoying his work too much."

Jusik looked up from his datapad. He appeared to be following the presentation. "Scum," he said. "One of our sources calls them scum, indicating . . . a very disagreeable group of people."

Zey paused for breath as if to ensure that the last snippet of information had made its point. "Given how thinly stretched our resources are, we are unfortunately unable to justify intervening to deal with any injustice on Qiilura at this time. But we have excellent intelligence that indicates a significant military asset located there."

Darman was listening, and still watching the Gurlanin peripherally. It had moved around the room to sit upright beside Jusik, with its front paws neatly clasped before its chest. He was also observing Jusik. The Padawan still appeared riveted by the commandos. Darman was careful not to stare—even though any eye movement was disguised by his helmet—because Jedi knew things without having to see. His instructors had told him so. Jedi were omniscient, omnipotent, and to be obeyed at all times.

Darman hung on Zey's every word.

"Qiilura isn't on the main lane, so to speak," Zey said. "Ideal for hiding, if that's your intention. And there *are* things hidden there. We need you to apprehend one, and destroy the other—a Separatist scientist, Ovolot Qail Uthan, and her most recent project, a nanovirus. We have reason to believe both are at a research facility on Qiilura."

Zey paused, and Jusik filled the space. "We have a Jedi there, Master Kast Fulier, but we haven't heard from him or his Padawan in some weeks."

Zey picked up again. "And let me assure you that we've been searching diligently for them. We have a location for our targets, but no plans of the buildings. The lack of plans will make your retrieval and sabotage task more challenging, as will the communications situation. Questions?"

Niner raised a gloved hand from his lap. "Sir, what is the comm situation, exactly?"

"Neimoidians."

"Not quite with you, sir."

Zey looked blank for a moment, and then his face lit up with revelation. "The Neimoidians own and control all the infrastructure—the native population scarcely have pits for refreshers, but their overlords enjoy the finest comlink net and air traffic control that credits can buy. They like to ensure that nobody does business without their knowledge. So they monitor everything, and very little intelligence comes out— you'll have to avoid using the long-range comlink. Do you understand me, soldier?"

"Sir, yes *sir,* General Zey."

There was a pause, a long pause, and Zey looked along the row of three helmets and a damaged face as if waiting for something. The Jedi had said he hadn't worked with clones before; maybe he was expecting a dialogue. He stopped at Darman. The potential embarrassment to the Master prompted Darman to fill the silent void.

It was an obvious question to ask, really.

"What's the nature of the nanovirus, sir?"

Zey's head moved back just a fraction. "An intelligent and significant question," he said.

"Thank you, sir."

"The answer, then, should be of great interest to you personally. It appears to be specifically aimed at clone personnel."

The sleek black Gurlanin drew itself up to a greater height. "They fear you, and with good reason," it said in a deep, liquid voice. "So they wish to kill, as all ignorant beings do when they encounter something they fear and misunderstand."

It continued elongating and now appeared to be standing. It had changed shape.

"Yes," Zey said slowly, dragging the word into two syllables, and he looked away from the spectacle of molecular rearrangement. "At this time you still have an advantage—the Separatists almost certainly aren't aware of your potential as clone commandos. They have no idea what you can achieve, and perhaps we have no idea, either. But you have been created for excellence, and trained to realize that potential by the most experienced instructors in the galaxy. We have very high expectations." Zey slipped his hands into his cloak, head lowered slightly. "If you happen to find Master Fulier safe, we would be relieved, but Uthan and the facility are your main priorities. Do you understand everything I have said?"

"Yes sir." Darman nodded once and so did the others, but it wasn't quite a synchronized movement. *We'll get it right,* he thought. *A couple of days' training, that'll sort it. Train hard, fight easy.*

"I'll leave you to my Padawan, then," Zey said, and swept out, pausing briefly at the door to look back at the commandos, tilting his head as if he was either amazed or amused.

Jusik swallowed hard. The Gurlanin flowed from a column back into a four-limbed thing, and moved to sit beside RC-3222, gazing up at him. The commando didn't react.

"Ahhh," it sighed. It had a voice like running water. "My, that's indeed Fett's face. Fascinating."

Jusik gestured to the exit. "I'm your armorer," he said. "Weapons and data. Follow me and I'll show you what you'll have at your disposal."

The commandos rose as one—more or less—and followed him through the door and down a passage still strewn with victualing containers. The place smelled of stewed nerf even through Darman's filtration mask. The Gurlanin flowed before them, now a sinuous predator, now a trotting quadruped, shifting shape as it went.

Jusik stopped at a door at the end of the passage and turned to them. "I wonder if I could ask the rest of you to remove your helmets."

Nobody asked why, and they all obeyed, even though it wasn't phrased as the unequivocal order they were expecting. The helmet seals made faint *ssss* sounds as they opened.

"Oh," Jusik said, and stared for a second. Then he opened the door and they stepped into a makeshift armory.

It was a cache of treasures. There were upgrades and bolt-ons that Darman knew might fit his existing gear, and ordnance that he didn't recognize but looked like Republic issue, and there were . . . *exotics.* Weapons he recalled from his database as belonging to a dozen different species—and quite a few that he couldn't place at all—were laid out neatly on trestle tables. It was inviting, almost as inviting as a meal.

"That all looks rather *useful,* sir," Niner said.

"Delta Squad has been collecting a few things here and there," Jusik said. The commandos were focused on the weaponry, but Darman was also noting Jusik's behavior with growing interest. The Padawan stood back to let the men get a closer look at the armaments but he was watching them carefully. "You're nothing like droids at all, are you?"

"No sir," Fi said. "We're flesh and blood. Bred to be the best."

"Like Advanced Recon Commandos?"

"Not quite ARCs, sir. Not like clone troopers, either. We don't work alone and we don't work in formations. We just look the same."

"This is your unit of four, then? A squad?" He seemed to be recalling a hurried lesson. "Almost like a family?"

Niner cut in. "It is now, sir." He picked up a portable missile launcher that looked slightly different from the standard-issue plex. "Light. *Very* light."

"Merr-Sonn prototype," Jusik said. "Novel alloy, heavier payloads, extra range. It has a microrepulsorlift stabilizing unit, but they haven't resolved all the more challenging technical issues yet. So consider it shoulder-launching." He peered at 3222's face. "Is that painful?"

"Not too bad, sir," the commando said. But the wound had to hurt like fire. The abraded skin was still weeping. "I'll see to it later."

It didn't seem to be the answer Jusik was expecting, judging by the slight *uh* sound he made. Maybe he thought clones didn't feel pain, like droids. "Do you have names? I don't mean numbers. *Names.*"

Now, that was a very private thing. You kept your name to yourself, your squad, and your training sergeant. Darman was embarrassed for him.

"My squad called me Atin," the wounded commando said.

Niner glanced at Fi but said nothing. *Atin* was Mandalorian for "stubborn."

Jusik held up two reels of line that looked like matte ribbon, one black, one white. He took a ribbon of each color, twisted two short lengths together, and held up the braid in one hand and a bead-sized detonator in the other. "One meter is the equivalent yield of a thermal detonator, but it's directional. Ideal for making a frame charge. But be cautious with the quantity if you want to enter a building, rather than destroy it completely. You have some special implosion ordnance for that purpose."

"Any useful hand-thrown stuff?" Darman asked. "Stun grenades?"

"We have a few Geonosian sonic detonators, and a box of EMPs for anti-droid use."

"That'll do me fine. I'll take the lot."

Niner was watching Darman intently. "You're obviously our demolitions man," he said. Then the sergeant turned back to the Padawan. "We've been thoroughly trained, sir. You can have complete confidence in us."

That was true, Darman thought. They had been *very* thoroughly trained, day in, day out, for ten years, and the only time they weren't training was when they were sleeping. Even if they were untested as a special forces unit—apart from playing infantry three months ago—Darman had no doubt that they would perform to expected standards. He was happy to have the demolition role. He was proud of his skill in what was delicately known as rapid entry.

"What do you think happened to Master Fulier, sir?" Darman asked. He wouldn't normally have posed unnecessary questions, but Arligan Zey had seemed to approve of his curiosity, and Darman was conditioned to do whatever Jedi generals wished.

Jusik opened a case of Kamino saberdarts and held it out as if offering a tray of uj cakes. "Valaqil believes he was betrayed by a native," he said. "They've been known to do anything to earn food or a few credits."

Darman wondered how a Jedi could be taken by anything less than an army. He'd seen them fight at Geonosis. His warfare was a science; theirs appeared to be an art. "Didn't he have his lightsaber?"

"He did," the Gurlanin said. "But Master Fulier has, or had, some *discipline* issues."

Darman—a soldier able to withstand every privation in the field, and whose greatest fear was to wither from age rather than die in combat—felt inexplicably uncomfortable at the idea of a Jedi having failings.

"Master Fulier was—is a courageous Jedi," Jusik said, almost losing his composed manner for a moment. "He is simply passionate about justice."

Niner defused the moment. Darman felt reassured by his effortless authority. "Sir, how long have we got to plan the mission and attempt a few dry runs?" he said.

"Eight standard hours," Jusik replied, almost apologetic. "Because that's how long the journey to Qiilura will take. You're embarking now."

Etain emptied her bag on the straw mattress in the drying barn.

Despite appearances, this was the guest suite. Livestock wasn't allowed in the barn at this time of year because animals had a tendency to eat the barq grain, and that was an awfully expensive way to fatten merlies for the table. The animals were allowed in the main house, and in the winter they even slept there, partly to keep the place warm and partly to protect them from prowling gdans.

The house had smelled like it, too. Nothing of the merlies—not even their body heat or their pungent odor—was ever wasted. "Keeps them bugs away," Birhan had told her. "It's a *good* stink."

Etain knelt beside the mattress and tried to think her way out of her predicament. Master Fulier was probably dead: if he weren't, he would have returned for her. He was—had been—brilliant, magnificently skilled when he was focused on being so. But he was also impatient, and inclined not to walk away from matters that weren't his concern, and those were two factors that didn't mix well with a covert mission.

He'd decided one of Hokan's thugs needed to learn a lesson in how to respect the local population. All it took was for one of the Mandalorian's lieutenants to offer the same locals more than the price of a bottle of urrqal to say where and when Fulier was in town.

Town. That was a joke.

Imbraani wasn't Coruscant, not at all. The only infrastructure in the rambling collection of farmsteads was devoted to what it took to grow, harvest, and export its cash crops, and to the comfort of its commercial overlords. Etain had grown up in a world where you could travel at will and send messages easily, and neither of those taken-for-granted facilities was readily available here.

Etain needed one of two things right now: to get passage off Qiilura, or to get a data transmission out in her stead. She still had a mission to complete, if only to justify Master Fulier's sacrifice. She took a small sphere from the scattering of possessions on the mattress and opened it in two halves like a shef'na fruit.

A holochart blossomed into three dimensions in her cupped hands, then another, then another. She had layouts of half a dozen Neimoidian and Separatist buildings in the surrounding region, because Fulier hadn't been the only one who was careless. After a few bottles of urrqal, the local construction workers dropped their guard.

Etain was neither a natural warrior nor a great charmer, but she was aware of her talent for spotting opportunities. It made up for a lot.

She wasn't sure if her Master's fate was tied in to the holoschematics, or if he'd been seen as a direct threat to Uthan. She suspected Ghez Hokan might even have done something simply because he didn't much care for Jedi. *Play warriors,* he called them. He despised anyone who didn't fight with hard metal or their fists. Mandalorians were tough; but Hokan operated at a totally different level of brutality. Etain had realized that the moment she and Fulier had walked through what was left of a four-house village that must have displeased him in some way.

She would never erase those images from her mind. She meditated hard twice a day. It still wasn't helping. Settling down on her knees, she tried again, slowing her breathing, calming her heart.

The gravel outside the barn crunched.

Etain picked up her lightsaber from the mattress as she stuffed the holochart sphere in her tunic. Her thumb hovered over the controls set in the hilt. She should have sensed someone coming, but she had allowed her fatigue and despair to get the better of her. *I didn't check for another exit,* she thought. *Stupid, stupid, stupid. I might have to use this . . .*

As the plank door swung open, she flicked the button and the blue light pierced the dusty air. The merlie that wandered in didn't appear impressed. Nor did the small elderly woman who followed it.

"You're jumpy," she said. She had a covered tray in her hands and something bundled under one arm. The merlie nuzzled Etain's knees, seeking attention. They were distressingly intelligent animals, nearly a meter high at the shoulder and covered with long brown ringlets of wool; their round, green eyes were too disturbingly human for Etain's peace of mind. "Here's your dinner."

"Thank you," Etain said, watching as the woman put the tray down on the mattress and placed the bundle of brown fabric beside it.

"Quite a job getting that dung off your cloak," the woman said, eyeing the lightsaber the way Birhan had. "Still a bit damp. But clean."

"Thank you," Etain repeated. She turned off the blade and peeled the cloth back from the tray. Two rough clay plates held a couple of thin-breads and a mush of stew, on top of which whole barq grains were visible. She could smell their cloying musky scent.

That quantity of barq was a week's earnings for these people. "You shouldn't have gone to that trouble for me," Etain said, embarrassed.

"You're a guest," the woman said. "Besides, once I'd scraped the dung off, shame to waste the grains stuck to it, eh? Oh-ah."

Etain's stomach rolled but she kept a steady expression. Coruscant's food hygiene regulations certainly didn't apply here.

"Very kind of you," she said, and forced a smile.

"They're coming, you know," the woman said.

"I'll be ready," Etain lied, and indicated the lightsaber.

"No, not them Hokan thugs. Not them at all."

Etain wondered whether to press her, but decided against it for the time being. She had no idea who she'd be asking for answers.

The woman sighed and shooed the merlie out the door with impatient hands. "They're coming, all right," she said, and smiled, closing the door behind her.

3

CLASSIFIED, HIGHEST: ENCRYPTION ONLY
*You're the best in your field—the best soldiers, tacticians,
sappers, communicators, survival experts. I picked you
personally because I want you to train the best commandos
in the galaxy. You'll have everything you need, whatever
you want, except one thing—home. This is a top-secret
project. You'll not tell anyone where you're going and you'll
not leave Kamino, ever. As far as your friends and family
are concerned, you're already dead.*
—Jango Fett, recruiting his handpicked commando
instructors, the Cuy'val Dar—in the Mandalorian tongue,
"those who no longer exist"

The Neimoidians had a taste for elaborate and wholly inappropriate grandeur, and Ghez Hokan despised them for it.

Lik Ankkit's huge villa was set on top of a hill overlooking a kushayan plantation—a foolish choice given the prevailing winds, but it seemed to satisfy the Neimoidian's need to show he was boss. The location might have made sense from a military perspective, but—as Ankkit was a bean-counting coward like all of his kind—he didn't need defensibility, either.

No, the Neimoidian was a *di'kut*. A complete and utter *di'kut*.

Hokan ran up the hedge-flanked steps of the veranda spanning the entire front of the building, headdress tucked under one arm, his shatter gun, knives, and rope-spike provocatively visible in his belt.

He wasn't rushing to see his paymaster, oh no. He was just in a hurry to get the meeting over with. He ignored the servants and minions and swept into Ankkit's spacious office with its panoramic view of the countryside. Qiilura's commercial overlord was watering pots of flowers on the windowsill. He paused to flick one with his fingertip, and it sprayed a powerful, sickly scent into the air. He inhaled with parted lips.

"I do wish you would knock, Hokan," Ankkit said without turning around. "It's really most discourteous."

"You summoned me," Hokan said flatly.

"Merely checking on the progress of your conversations with the Jedi."

"Had there been any, I would have called you."

"You haven't killed him, have you? Do tell me you haven't. I need to know if his activities will affect market prices."

"I'm not an amateur."

"But one has to do the best with the staff one has, yes?"

"I do my own dirty work, thanks. No, he isn't talking. He's rather . . . resistant for a Jedi."

If Ankkit had had a nose, he would have been looking down it at Hokan. Hokan controlled an impulsive urge to cut this glorified shopkeeper, this *grocer,* down to size. For all his height, the Neimoidian was soft and weak, his only strength contained within his bank account. He blinked with passionless, liquid red eyes. Hokan almost—*almost*—reached for his rope-spike.

"Jedi do not visit worlds like this to take the therapeutic waters, Hokan. Have you confirmed that he has an associate?"

"He's a Jedi Master. He was seen with a Padawan."

"Not a very discreet Jedi Master, it seems."

Fulier couldn't have been good at calculating odds or he'd never have started on Gar-Ul in the tavern. But at least he was prepared to stand up for himself, despite all that soft mystical nonsense he spouted. Hokan admired guts, even if he rarely tolerated them. They were always in short supply.

"We'll find the Padawan, and we'll find out what intelligence Fulier has, if any."

"Make sure you do. I have a lucrative contract resting on this."

Hokan had become practiced at controlling his urge to lash out, but he saw no reason to subject his mouth to the same discipline. "If I succeed, it'll be because I take pride in my work."

"You need the credits."

"For the time being. But one day, Ankkit, I won't need you at all."

Ankkit gathered his robes a little closer and drew himself up to his full height, which had no effect on Hokan at all.

"You must learn to accept your reduced station in the galactic order, Hokan," Ankkit said. "This is no longer the hierarchy of brute force in which your warrior ancestors thrived. Today we need to be soldiers of intellect and commerce, and no amount of strutting around in that museum-piece uniform will revive your . . . *glorious* past. Alas, even the great Jango Fett succumbed to a Jedi in the end."

News traveled fast. Fett was a source of pride among the remaining handful of Mandalorians in diaspora. Even if he fought for money, he was the *best*. Ankkit must have known perfectly well how much that comment would sting.

Hokan was determined that the Neimoidian would see no evidence on his face to prove it. He'd certainly tried to keep that out of his mind when he was interrogating Fulier, much as he wanted to blame all Jedi for the humiliation of a cultural hero. He had to be clear why he was smashing the Jedi's bones. Revenge was unprofessional.

He took a careful breath. "Do you keep gdans as pets, Ankkit? I hear some offworlders do try."

"Gdans? No. Filthy little creatures. Most savage."

"But if you did keep one, and didn't feed it well, would you be surprised if it bit you?"

"I suppose not."

"Then feed me well."

Hokan turned and walked out without being dismissed, deliberately unbidden, and deliberately fast so that Ankkit couldn't have the last word. He replaced his helmet and ran down the steps of the ludicrously extravagant villa.

He didn't care if Ankkit rented the whole planet out to Separatist scientists. They weren't honorable enough to fight with real weapons, either: they got bugs to do their work for them. It was a disgrace. It was *unnatural*.

Hokan felt in his blood-red jacket for the Jedi's weapon. It didn't look like much at all. And it was surprisingly easy to activate, even though he suspected that fully mastering it might be another matter. A humming blue shaft of light, vivid as day, shot out from the hilt. Hokan swept it scythe-style along a neatly clipped tarmul hedge, cutting its height in half.

The lightsaber wasn't bad for a soft Jedi weapon.

Hokan suspected the lightsaber looked at odds with his traditional Mandalorian helmet and its distinctive T-shaped eye slit. But a warrior had to adapt.

And Fulier had questions to answer.

Docking Bay D-768, Fleet Support Air Station, Ord Mantell

The Nar Shaddaa agri-utility crop sprayer on the pad looked as if only its rust was holding it together. It was, to use Jusik's uncharacteristically colorful description, an old clunker.

And—somehow—it was taking them to Qiilura. It wouldn't attract much attention flying over farming country, unless, of course, it broke up in flight. This didn't seem out of the question.

"Well, they don't build them like that anymore," Fi said.

"That's because not even the Hutt Aviation Authority would certify this Narsh dirt-crate airworthy," Niner said, straining to prevent his pack from bending him over backward. He was laden with nearly double the twenty-five-kilo weight he was used to carrying, along with a powered emergency chute. Niner had never actually come across the HAA, but he'd absorbed every scrap of intel read, seen, or heard in his life. "Anyway, all it has to do is get us down there."

"It's making a noble sacrifice," Jusik said, suddenly right behind them. He smiled and murmured *dirt-crate* to himself as if it amused him. Niner wondered for a moment if he'd broken protocol by using the phrase. "Are you certain you can do this? I could ask Master Zey if he would allow me to accompany you."

Niner wanted to laugh, but you didn't laugh at a Jedi, especially one who seemed to care what happened to you. "We lost too many officers at Geonosis, sir. They can't grow you to order."

The Padawan lowered his eyes for a second. "It's considerate of you to think of me as an officer, Sergeant."

"You're a commander now, sir. We won't let you down. There's nobody better prepared for this than us."

"This is your first special operation, isn't it?"

"Yes sir."

"Doesn't that worry you?"

"No sir. Not at all. The six P's, sir. Proper Planning Prevents Pi . . . *Inadequate* Performance, sir."

Jusik appeared to be counting and then raised his eyebrows. "This is *real,* Sergeant."

Ah. For all their skills and wisdom, there were still some things that even Jedi didn't know. Niner hesitated to lecture Jusik.

Real. Oh yes, Niner knew what *real* was, all right.

Padawan Bardan Jusik had certainly never seen the Killing House on Kamino. He'd never stormed the building, with its twisting corridors and innumerable flights of stairs; he didn't know how many commandos died in training when the rounds were live and the terrorists—or whoever the directing staff were being that day—aimed to kill, and frequently did.

He also had no idea what it was like spending four days lying prone in a scrape in the undergrowth on observation, rifle ready, urinating where you lay because you couldn't move and give away your position. He had no idea how you learned to judge the amount of charge required for rapid entry to a building the hard way, because if you didn't get it just right, in a hurry and under fire, it could blow your head clean off. Two-Eight had learned that way.

Jusik didn't know just how far and how long you could carry a wounded comrade when you had to. He probably didn't even know how to perform an emergency field tracheotomy with a vibroblade and a clean length of fuel line.

It wasn't Jusik's fault. He had far bigger issues to worry about. There was no reason for a Jedi commander to concern himself with the details of a clone commando's life. But Niner thought he probably would, and he admired the Padawan all the more for that.

"We'll be fine, sir," Niner said. "The training is quite realistic."

Inside the shabby Narsh vessel, the tanks had been stripped out, and the bulkheads lined with securing straps and stealth sheeting that would render the ship's cargo invisible to any probe or scan.

Niner realized that four men would be pretty cramped in there with packs and weapons. A couple of BlasTech E-Web repeating blasters were already stowed, and, at Atin's request, two Trandoshan LJ-50 concussion rifles.

Atin's livid face wound was looking less alarming now, but he'd always have a scar: the bacta spray could fix plenty if you used it soon enough, but it couldn't reverse scarring. He pulled himself through the open hatch with an APC array blaster in one hand and his DC-17 strapped across his chest, just about keeping his balance under the weight of his pack. Darman, acting as loadmaster, gave him a helpful leg up and eyed the blaster.

"Got a thing for Trandoshan technology?" Darman asked.

"This'll deal with shields better than our E-Web," Atin replied. "And the LJ-fifty is a nice backup when we take out the facility. Just in case. Republic doesn't make all the best gear."

Niner wondered if Atin ever talked about anything but gear. His squad must have been a miserable bunch, with a miserable instructor. Clones might have looked utterly standardized to outsiders, but every squad was altered slightly by the cumulative effects of its experiences, including the influences of the individual trainers. Every commando battalion had its own nonclone instructor, and seemed to take on some of his—or her—unique characteristics and vocabulary.

We learn, Niner thought. *We learn fast, and unfortunately we learn everything. Like* dirt-crate.

Every squad developed its own dynamics, as well. It was part of their hardwired human biology. Put four men in a group, and soon you'd have a pecking order defined by the roles and foibles that accompanied them. Niner knew his, and he thought he knew Fi's, and he was pretty sure he knew where Darman was heading. But Atin wasn't sliding into place just yet.

Fi had a Geonosian force pike. He hefted it and smiled.

"Where'd you get that?" Atin asked, suddenly interested.

"Souvenir of Geonosis," Fi said, and winked. "Seemed a shame to waste it." He flipped it over in his hand and twirled it, arm outstretched, missing Atin by a calculated handspan. He didn't react. "You wouldn't even need to use the power setting, would you? This thing's *heavy.*" He brought it down in a slicing movement. "*Wallop.* That'll make their eyes water."

"I don't think I need any souvenirs of Geonosis," Atin said. His tone was distinctly frosty. "Indelibly etched, you might say."

"Hey—"

Niner cut in. "Chat later," he said. "Shift it, people."

Niner already knew he would have his work cut out with Atin and wondered if anything would trigger his natural urge to be one of the squad. He also wondered about his apparent negativity. *He'll shake down, sooner or later. He'll have to.*

Backing up to a convenient ledge on the port bulkhead, Niner unclipped his backpack. Forty-five kilos lighter, he eased between Fi and Atin, and peered into the cockpit.

An R5 droid was at the controls. The unit was still fueling up the vessel from a droid bowser, burbling and whistling to itself. Niner leaned across to plug his datapad into the console to confirm the flight plan and synchronize it with the vessel's actual path.

The R5 didn't take any notice. It would fly the route it was given.

Improvising, thinking on his feet, making the most of the resources at hand, were all part of operating as a commando. But so was acquiring adequate intelligence. What they had wasn't enough to plan a mission, and that meant they would either have to acquire it in the field, or fail. Niner didn't want to fail Padawan Jusik. He ejected his datapad and edged back to the hatch, trying not to clip Fi or Atin.

"Comm silence from the time you take off," Jusik said, leaning through the open hatch. "The assault ship the *Majestic* is diverting to Qiilura, and will remain on station a parsec from the planet until she receives your request for extraction. Then gunships will be at your transmitted location within the hour."

Niner almost asked just how long the *Majestic* might wait, but he feared it would look as if he doubted his squad's competence. He knew the answer: the ship would wait until Uthan was taken, even if that was several commando missions down the line. It wasn't waiting for *them*.

"We won't keep the *Majestic* waiting," Niner said.

"Anything else you need?"

Niner shook his head. "No, Commander."

Darman stood to one side of the ramp, like an honor guard, waiting for the Jedi to leave.

"Very well," Jusik said, looking hesitant, as if he wanted to walk away but thought better of it. "I hope to debrief you on your return."

Niner took that literally, although Jusik was looking at him as if it meant something else. It made sense for the Padawan commander to process whatever intel they might gain. Jusik turned and walked away, and Darman jumped inside. The hatch closed with a slight shudder, sending fine fragments of rusting metal to the deck.

It only has to land, Niner thought.

He switched on the holoprojection in his datapad and studied the three-dimensional flight path over fields, lakes, and forest. It was part real image, part simulation. Projected onto an existing chart, they were looking at an area thirty klicks north of a small town called Imbraani.

A single-story building with shabby sheet-metal roofing— ringed by an incongruously well-cut expanse of grass—nestled in a plantation of kuvara trees. Some of the image was blurred, but it was the best resolution that a surveillance remote could manage at that distance above the planet. Specks—people— wandered around an encircling path.

"It's the *capture alive* bit that complicates matters," Darman said, gazing at the image over Niner's shoulder. "Or else we could just bomb it back into Hutt space."

"That's why they created us," Niner said. "For the compli- cated jobs."

He closed his eyes for a few moments to visualize the inser- tion: he saw it from takeoff to landing, smooth and planned, every detail, or as many details as their incomplete intel could furnish and his own experience of a hundred exercises could confirm.

In this detached state, something occurred to him. He pic- tured Jusik's face and his awkward, nervous shrugs. He real- ized what the Padawan had meant when he said he was hoping to debrief them personally on their return.

He meant *Good luck.* He wanted them to survive.

Niner, who had known for as long as he could remember that he was a soldier bred to die, found that intriguing.

Gdans were about thirty centimeters long, fully grown, and it took a whole pack of them to bring down even a mer- lie calf. But at night—when they emerged from their warrens and hunted—the farmers locked their doors and stayed clear of the fields.

It wasn't so much their teeth that the locals feared. It was the deadly bacteria the animals carried; a minor scratch or a bite was almost always fatal. And Master Fulier had used their entire supply of bacta spray in administering first aid to villagers, so Etain was as housebound at night as any of her hosts.

She could hear the little predators outside, squabbling and scrabbling. She sat cross-legged on the mattress and chewed on the thin-breads, almost hungry enough to gulp down the stew, but not *that* hungry. *A few bacteria are good for your immune system,* she thought. *You've probably eaten worse without knowing.*

But she *knew* this time.

Leaving the bowl where it stood, she rolled the holochart sphere over and over in her palms, running through all the possibilities for getting the information to the Jedi Council. Stow away in a transport—possible. Transmit the data from ground? No, all transmissions were tightly controlled by the Neimoidians; any other message traffic from Qiilura to Coruscant would draw instant attention. There was always the possibility of finding the right droid courier, but that was a long shot, and it might take so much time as to be useless.

Perhaps she'd have to do the job herself.

Lightsabers were superb weapons, but right now she needed an army. The realization that she had beaten the odds to obtain valuable information but was now unable to get it to those who needed it almost crushed her.

"I'm not done yet," she said aloud. But she feared that she was, at least for the night. Her eyelids felt heavy and she braced her elbows on her knees, letting her head rest in her hands.

A good night's sleep. She might have a better idea in the morning. Her eyes closed. Images of Coruscant, her clan practicing passing a ball by thought alone, a nice hot bath, food she trusted to be clean . . .

Then, suddenly, every fiber in her body leapt at once. Heart pounding, Etain thought at first that she'd had one of those half dreams of falling that sometimes came when she was dozing off. But now she was fully awake and knew that she hadn't.

Something had changed. Something in the Force had been altered, and forever. She jumped to her feet, suddenly clear what it was; she needed no training or education to understand it. Every instinct coded in her genes cried out.

Something—*someone*—was gone from the Force.

"Master," she said.

She had *suspected* he was dead. Now she knew he was, and she knew it had happened right then. It was impossible not to wonder how and where, but she knew enough about the Neimoidians' hired muscle and their techniques to guess.

Ignoring the ever-present gdans, she went to the barn door and swung it open. It was an act of helplessness. There was nothing she could do, now or ever.

Something rustled in the grass. It was a solitary something, and it sounded larger than a gdan. She noticed for the first time that the constant snuffling and squabbling of the gdan packs had stopped. They'd gone.

Etain felt for her lightsaber, just in case.

Loud squawking and a flurry of wings made her start. A disturbed flock of leatherbacks rose into the air and scattered in the darkness, trailing sparks of light from their scales. Through the Force, she detected only small creatures with simple desires, and a male merlie wandering along the fence, armed with such fearsome tusks that not even gdans would risk approaching him.

She looked up at the night sky. It appeared unchanging, constant: but she knew it never was.

They're coming.

She thought she heard the old woman's voice. Putting it down to grief and lack of sleep, Etain stumbled back inside and barred the door.

It was just another crop sprayer hired to dress the fields after the barq harvest, laden with bug killers and soil enhancers and piloted by a droid. At least, that was what the Narsh crate's transponder had told the Qiilura traffic controller, and judging by the absence of a missile up the tailpipe, he had believed it.

Darman was still exploring the enhancements to his helmet and suit. "I used to think I wore this armor," he said. "Now I think it's wearing me."

"Yeah, they spent some credits upgrading this since last time," Fi said. "Wow. Walking weapons system, eh?"

"Two hundred klicks," Atin said, without looking up from his datapad. He'd propped his helmet beside him with the tactical beam pointed up to provide some light in the closed bay. Darman couldn't hear him over the noise of the vessel's atmosphere engines, but he could lip-read easily enough. "Let's hope everything works."

It was helmets on at one hundred klicks. The squad was prepared both for a controlled landing and an early bailout and free fall if they were picked up by Separatist ground units. Darman hoped their luck would hold. They were landing heavy, with more gear than they'd ever used in training, and they'd have to hit the drop zone accurately to avoid an impossible trek across country. Accurate, if they had to jump for it, meant high-altitude low-opening procedure. They could drift for fifty klicks if they opted for the safer, slower high-opening technique.

Darman didn't relish being defenseless in the air for that long.

Niner was studying his datapad, balancing it on his right thigh. A three-dimensional shimmering holo of their flight path played out a handspan above it. He glanced up at Darman and gave him a silent thumbs-up: *On course and on target.* Darman returned the gesture.

There was an art to loading up for a mission when carrying the firepower of a small army among four men. Darman had loaded his pack to capacity. The rest of his weapons and ordnance was in a second shockproof container that stood knee-high. The bowcaster—he loved that weapon—was strapped across his chest plate with jury-rigged webbing, to leave his hands free for the DC-17. He had an assortment of detonators, kept safely separate from the charges and other ordnance in the lower section. He was now so heavy even without the extra equipment that he had to bounce to get upright from a sitting position. He rehearsed standing a few times. It was tough. Fortunately, the squad would be inserted close to the target. He didn't have to haul it far.

"One hundred klicks," Atin said. He switched off his spotlamp. "Helmets."

The compartment was suddenly dark, and there was a collective hiss of helmet seals purging and reengaging. They could only talk to each other at very short range now: on Qiilura, anything more than ten meters risked detection. The only visible light was the faint blue glow from the heads-up display in their visors, a group of ghostly disembodied T-shapes in the gloom, and the shimmering landscape playing out from Niner's datapad. His head was tilted down slightly, watching the actual position of the utility vessel in the simulated landscape.

The sprayer started to lose height, exactly on course. In a matter of minutes, they would be—

Bang.

A shudder ran through the airframe, and then there was no engine noise at all.

For a second Darman thought they'd been hit by antiaircraft fire. Niner was on his feet instantly, moving forward to the cockpit, accidentally whacking Atin with his pack as he turned. Darman, without conscious decision, grabbed the emergency hatch handle and prepared to activate it for a bailout.

Darman could see the droid clicking and flashing, apparently engaged in a dialogue of some kind with the vessel. The ship wasn't listening.

"AA, Sarge?"

"Birdstrike," Niner said, deceptively quiet. "Atmos engine's fried."

"Can the R5 glide this thing down?"

"It's trying."

The deck tilted, and Darman grabbed at the bulkhead to stay upright. "No, that isn't gliding. That's crashing."

"Bang out," Niner said. "Bang out now."

The Narsh dirt-crate hadn't let them down. It had just succumbed to being in the wrong airspace at the wrong time, and met the local avian species the hard way. Now they were plummeting toward the kind of landing not even the latest Katarn armor could help them survive.

Darman blew the hatch, and the inrush of air sent dirt and debris whirling through the cargo bay. The door fell away through the opening. It was pitch black outside, a challenge for a free-faller even with night vision. Darman was starting to experience serious doubt for the second time in his life. He wondered if he was becoming one of those despised creatures that his training sergeant had called *cowards*.

"Go go *go*," Niner shouted. Fi and Atin eased through the hatch and stepped out. *Don't try to jump, just let yourself fall.* Darman stood back to make way for Niner: he wanted to salvage as much gear as he could. They needed the repeating blasters. He grabbed some of the dismantled sections.

"Now," Niner said. "You first."

"We need the gear." Darman thrust two sections at him. "Take these. I'll—"

"I said *jump.*"

Darman wasn't a rash man. None of them were. They took calculated risks, though, and he calculated that Niner wouldn't leave him. His sergeant was standing at the open hatch, arm held out imperiously, a clear sign to get on with it and *jump.* No, Darman had made up his mind. He lunged forward and shoulder-charged Niner out of the hatch, grabbing the door frame just in time to stop from plunging after him. It was clear from the stream of expletives that Niner was not expecting this, nor was he happy about it. The extra pack jerked out after him on its tether. Darman heard one last profanity and then Niner was out of range.

Darman grabbed a strap and peered down, but he couldn't see his sergeant falling, and that probably meant nobody else could, either. He now had a minute, more or less, to salvage what he could and get out before the utility hit the ground.

He switched on his helmet lamp. He couldn't afford the

time to listen to the rushing wind and the complete absence of reassuring engine noise, but he heard it anyway. He dropped the bowcaster and began lashing the blaster sections together with a line. It was a shame. He loved the bowcaster, but they needed those cannons more.

Knotting lines was hard enough with gloves on, but was even harder when you were seconds from crashing. Darman fumbled a knot. He cursed. He looped the line again and this time it held. He let out a sob of relief, dropped the weapon, and dragged the gear down to the hatch. Nobody could hear him at this range, and he didn't care what the droid thought.

Then he stepped out into black void. The wind took him.

There was no rushing landscape beneath him yet to take his attention from the heads-up display. He was free-falling at nearly two hundred kilometers an hour, trailing sections of heavy, heavy cannon. He maneuvered into tracking position, pack square across his back, rifle tight into his side, the remainder of his gear on the container that rested on the backs of his legs. When he deployed the canopy at eight hundred meters, he would release the container. And he'd use the powered-descent option, because that might save him from the unsupported, potentially lethal weight of cannon that was falling with him.

Yes, he knew exactly what he was doing. And yes, he was scared.

He'd never jumped with so much unsecured load in training.

The canopy deployed, and it felt like he'd slammed into a wall. The power pack kicked in, heating up the air around him. He could steer now. He counted down fifteen seconds.

Something flared into brilliant white flame beneath him, off to his right—the Narsh vessel crashing some thirty klicks short of the target zone.

Darman realized he had thought nothing of leaving the R5 on board the stricken utility. It was expendable.

And that was how he was seen, he supposed. It was surprisingly easy to think that way.

He could see the ground now. His night vision could pick out the tops of trees, right beneath.

No, no, no.

He tried to miss. He failed.

He hit something very, very hard in the air. Then he hit the ground and didn't feel anything at all.

4

This is the true art of genetic selection and manipulation.
A human is naturally a learning creature, but it is also
violent, selfish, lustful, and undisciplined. So we must walk
the knife-edge between suppressing the factors that lead to
disobedience and destroying that prized capacity for
applying intelligence and aggression.
—Hali Ke, senior research geneticist of Kamino

Niner was hauling in his canopy when the explosion jerked him upright. A column of white roiling fire shot into the night sky above the tops of the trees. He knew it was hot and bright because his helmet visor's filter kicked in to stop it from overwhelming his night vision.

Even though he knew it was coming, his heart sank. Darman probably hadn't made it. He'd disobeyed his order. He hadn't jumped when he told him to.

So maybe you've lost a brother. Maybe not. Either way, you'll lose two more if you don't get your act together fast.

Niner triangulated the position of the blast and then went on bundling up the free-fall canopy, cutting away the lengths of cord before burying it. With a breaking strength of five hundred kilos, the cord was bound to come in handy. He wound each length in a figure-eight around his thumb and smallest finger and slipped the skeins into a belt pouch, then went in search of his extra pack.

It hadn't fallen far from him. The low-opening technique worked well if you needed accuracy. Niner found the pack at the edge of a field, covered in small dark-furred animals that seemed fascinated by it and were gnawing at the soft padding strip on one side. He flashed his spot-lamp to scatter them, but they stared back up the beam, burst into angry chatter, and then turned toward him.

It was unnerving, nothing more. Their little teeth snapped impotently on his armor. He stood still, assessing them, his data bank scrolling in front of his eyes and telling him that they were gdans, and that they weren't logged as a hostile alien species. All the nonhuman life Niner had ever seen for real, other than Kaminoans and various instructors, had been on Geonosis and through a blaster sight. He was utterly dependent on the intelligence loaded into his database—that, or finding things out for himself.

All but one of the gdans gave him up as inedible within a minute and disappeared into the waist-high crop. The remaining creature worried away at his left boot, a tribute to its tenacity, if not its intelligence. Those boots were specced to withstand every assault from hard vacuum to acid and molten metal. The little animal clearly believed in aiming high.

Darman would have found it fascinating, he was sure. It was a pity to lose him. He had all the makings of a good comrade.

"Come on," Niner said, nudging the animal with the butt of his blaster rifle. "I've got to get to work. Shove off."

The gdan, teeth locked around a clamp, looked up and met his eyes, or at least it seemed like it. It could only have really seen a faint blue light. Then it let go and trotted back toward the field, pausing once to stare back at him before disappearing into a hole in the ground with all the ease of a diver.

Niner took out his datapad and calculated his position. There was no GPS he could lock in to without the Neimoidians detecting him, but he could at least use dead reckoning based on the sprayer's last position, matching features on the landscape to his chart. It was old-fashioned soldiering. He liked it. He had to be able to do the business when the tech wasn't there, even if that meant using nothing but a Trandoshan blade.

If you stab someone in the heart, they can still run. I once saw a man run a hundred meters like that, screaming as well. Go for the neck, like this. Sergeant Skirata had taught them a lot about knives. *Put a bit of weight behind it, son.*

Still, tech had its place. A speeder bike would have been handy, although they hadn't thought they'd need them. The insert was supposed to be five klicks from the target.

Never mind, he thought. *It would make me look pretty conspicuous out here anyway.* The gear would slow him on his way to the pre-agreed rendezvous point, but he'd get there. If Fi and Atin had landed safely, they'd be heading for RV Alpha, too.

He started tabbing, trying to make ten klicks an hour, avoiding tracks and open ground. In the end he had to drag the extra pack behind him on straps like a sled. Tactical advance into battle—*tabbing,* as Skirata called it—meant walking at six to ten klicks an hour with a twenty-five-kilo pack. "But that's for *ordinary men,*" the instructor would say, as if nonclones were subhuman. "You are clone commandos. You will *do* better because you *are* better."

Niner was lugging nearly three times that load now. He didn't feel better at all right then. He decided to add a portable repulsorlift to his new list of gear to request upon return.

Qiilura's moon was in its new phase, and he was grateful for that. In his light gray armor, he would have stood out like a beacon. *Hadn't the top brass thought of that, either?* He stifled the uncharacteristically critical opinion about his superiors and decided there had to be something he didn't know but they did. He had his orders.

Even so, he diverted to a narrow river shown on the holochart and stopped long enough to smear mud over his armor and gear. There was no point chancing his luck.

At four hundred meters from RV point Alpha, he slowed down, and not because he was struggling under the weight. A silent approach was necessary. He hid the pack he was dragging deep in the undergrowth and recorded its location to collect later. Fi and Atin might have been tracked. They might not have made it at all. There was always the possibility of ambush. No, he definitely wasn't taking chances.

For the last two hundred meters, he got down in the grass and crawled.

But they were there, and alone.

Niner found himself staring up into the beam from Fi's helmet and he knew that the infrared targeting was centered at the point between his filtration mask and the top of his chest plate. It was a vulnerable point, provided one got close enough and used the right caliber rounds. Not many hostiles could get that close, of course.

"You gave me a start, Sarge," Fi said, holding his blaster clear and looking him over. He killed the light and indicated his chest plate. "Great minds, eh?"

Fi's armor was no longer pristine, either. Niner wasn't sure what he'd smeared over it, but it disrupted his outline well enough. The thought had obviously occurred to all of them. Atin was daubed with something dark and matte as well.

"Shape, shine, shadow, silhouette, smell, sound, and movement," Niner said, repeating the rules of basic camouflage. If it hadn't been for Darman's absence, he would have found the situation funny. He tried. "Shame they couldn't find something beginning with S to complete the set."

"I could," Atin said. "Any contact from Darman?"

They were forty kilometers from the point where Niner had landed. "I saw the blast. He was last off."

"You saw him jump, then."

"No. He was grabbing as much gear and ordnance as he could salvage." Niner felt he needed to explain. "He shoved me out the hatch first. I shouldn't have let that happen. But I didn't abandon him."

Atin shrugged. "So what have we got, then?"

"We've got a brother missing."

"I meant by way of resources. He had most of the demolition ordnance."

"I know you meant that, and I don't want to hear it." If he

could feel concern—even sorrow—for Darman, then why couldn't Atin? But it was no time to start a fight. They had to stick together now. A four-man mission with three men: their chances of succeeding had plummeted already. "We're a squad now. Get used to it."

Fi interrupted. He seemed to have a knack for defusing situations. "All our gear's intact, anyway. We can still put quite a dent in them if we have to."

And what did they have to put a dent in, exactly? They had high-altitude drone recces of the target building, but no idea yet if the walls were just plastered blocks or if they were lined with shock-absorbing alloy plates. There could be just the thirty or so guards seen walking the perimeter, or hundreds more holed up in underground barracks. Without better intelligence, they had no way of knowing just how much gear was enough for the job.

It was a case of adding P for plenty, just to be sure. Niner liked to be sure.

"How much time are we going to spend looking for him?" Atin asked. "They know they've got company now. It wasn't exactly a silent insert."

"SOPs," Niner said. *Standard operating procedures:* that was how things should be done; how commandos expected them to be done. "We get to each RV point for the time we agreed upon, and if he doesn't show we'll go to the position of the blast and see what's left. *Then* we'll decide if we're going to consider him MIA or not."

"You'd want us to search if it was you missing," Fi said to Atin. "He can't call in. Not at this range. Too risky."

"I wouldn't expect you to compromise the mission for me," Atin said, distinctly acid.

"He's alone, for fierfek's sake. *Alone.*"

"Just shut it, will you?" Niner said. The good thing about ultra-short-range comlinks was that you could stand around and have a blazing argument inside those helmets, and nobody outside could hear you. "Finding him isn't only the right thing to do, it's the sensible thing to do. Locate him and we find his gear. Okay?"

"Yes Sarge," Fi said.

"Got it," Atin said. "But there has to be a point where we consider him dead."

"Without a body, that'll be when Geonosis freezes over," Niner said, still angry and not knowing why. "Until then, we're going to sweat our guts out to find him, provided it doesn't blow the mission. Now let's see if we can sling this gear between some poles or something. We'll never keep this pace up for tens of kilometers unless we find a better way of transporting it."

Niner set his helmet comlink to receive long-range anyway. There was no harm in listening. If Darman was out there, Niner wasn't planning on abandoning him.

The clearing hadn't been there yesterday.

Etain picked her way through flattened kuvara saplings and into a circle of blackened stubble, following Birhan's steps. The air smelled of smoke and roasted barq.

He was swearing fluently. She didn't know much Qiiluran, but she knew a curse when she heard one.

"This is your lot again," Birhan said. He surveyed the field, hands to his brow to block out the sun breaking over the horizon. Now that it was daylight, they could see the extent of the damage from last night's explosion. "What am I going to do? What's going to happen to our contract?"

It wasn't phrased like a question. The Neimoidians weren't known to be sympathetic about the host of natural disasters constantly threatening the farming communities' precarious existence. But this was no natural disaster.

The blast area spanned around five hundred meters, and the crater at the center was twelve, maybe fifteen meters wide. Etain didn't know how deep it was, but a Trandoshan and an Ubese were standing at the edge of it, peering down, blasters in hand, looking as if they were searching in the soil. They didn't take the slightest notice of her or Birhan. She must have looked suitably starved and dowdy, rough enough to pass for a farm girl.

It was probably too late to convince them the crater was

caused by a meteor fragment. But at this point Etain didn't know any more than they did.

"Why do you think it's *my lot*?" she asked.

"Obvious," Birhan said sourly. "I seen loads of speeders and freighters and sprayers come down hard. They don't leave craters. They falls apart and burns, yes, but they *don't* blow up half the countryside. This is off-planet. It's *soldiers*." He kicked around some of the charred and blackened stalks. "Can't you have your fight on someone else's planet? Don't you think I got enough problems?"

She wondered for a moment if he was considering turning her in to Hokan's men for a few credits to make up for the loss of the precious barq. She was already an extra mouth to feed at a time when money he was counting on had just gone up in a fireball with much of his crop. It was time to find somewhere else to hide, and some other plan for getting that information off Qiilura.

Etain was still considering the scorched land when the Ubese and the Trandoshan jerked upright and turned to jog away toward the dirt track beside the field. The Ubese had one hand pressed to the side of his helmet as if he was listening to something: a comlink, probably. Whatever the summons had been, it had been urgent enough to get them running. It also confirmed that this wasn't just a Narsh sprayer making an all-too-frequent crash landing.

Etain waited a moment longer, then walked forward to peer into the pit to see what had so engrossed them.

It had been a monstrous blast. The sides of the blackened crater were blown almost smooth, and there was debris everywhere. It was an enormous blast area for a small craft.

She left Birhan and walked around inspecting the ground as Hokan's men had done, not sure what she was seeking. She was almost at the kuvara orchard before she saw it.

The early sunlight caught a scraped metal edge of something embedded in the ground, rammed deep by the explosion. Etain crouched down, as casually as she could, and worked the soil loose from it with her fingers. It took her a

few minutes to expose enough to understand the shape, and
a few more to work out why the scorched colors were so familiar. It was distorted, the metal frozen in a moment of
being torn apart by enormous force, but she was pretty sure
she'd seen one intact before.

It was a plate from an R5 astromech droid—a plate with
Republic markings.

They're coming.

Whoever they were, she hoped they'd made it alive.

Darman knew it was risky moving around by day, and the
fact that his right leg seemed to scream every time he put his
weight on it didn't help matters.

He'd spent two painful hours scooping out a shallow depression in a thicket about a hundred meters from what
passed for a road. Roots and stones had slowed him down.
So had the pounding he'd taken hitting the canopies of trees
during his landing. But he'd dug in now, and he lay under a
lattice of branches and leaves on his belly, watching the road,
sometimes through his rifle sight, sometimes with the elec-
trobinocular panel that flipped down in his visor.

At least the little animals that had swarmed over him in the
night had disappeared. He'd given up trying to fend them off.
They had explored his armor for a while and then moved on
to watch him from distance. Now that it was daylight, there
were no more glittering eyes staring out from the undergrowth.

He still wasn't sure of his position, either. There was no
GPS network he could use without being picked up. He
needed to get out and about and do a recce if he was going to
have any chance of aligning landscape features with the
holochart.

He knew he was facing north: the arc of small stones
around a thin branch he'd stuck in the soil charted the sun's
progress, and gave him his east–west line. If his datapad had
calculated speed and distance correctly, he was between
forty and fifty klicks northeast of the first RV point. He'd
never cover that distance on foot in time, not with the extra

gear and not with his leg in this state. If he dragged the pack, he'd draw a neat *follow-me* line through the vegetation.

Darman eased himself over on his back, removed his leg plates, and unsealed his undersuit at the knee. It felt as if he'd torn a muscle or a tendon above the joint. He soaked the makeshift bandage with bacta again and replaced the legging and plates before rolling back into position.

It was high time he ate something, but he decided that he could wait a little longer.

He checked the dirt road through the crosswires of the DC-17's electromag scope. The first time he had worn the helmet with the built-in display shimmering before his eyes, he had been overwhelmed and disoriented by the flurry of symbols in his field of vision. The rifle scope made it seem even more chaotic. Lights, lights, lights: it was like looking from the windows of Tipoca City at night with the lamps and reflective surfaces of the refectory behind you—so many competing images that you couldn't focus on what lay beyond the stormproof glass.

But in time—that time being the short, desperate morning when the whole of Kilo and Delta squads first wore the HUD display while using live ordnance—he got used to it. Those who didn't get used to it fast didn't return from the exercise. He learned to see, and yet not see. He was constantly aware of all the status displays that told him when his weapons were charging, and if his suit was compromised, and what was happening around him.

Now he was focused solely on looking down a clear tunnel framed by interlocking segments of soothing blue, with a highlighted area to show when he had an optimum firing solution for his target. The information on range, environment, and the score of other options was still there. He could take them in without consciously seeing them. He saw only his target.

A faint rumbling sound made him stiffen. Voices: they were approaching from his right. Then they stopped.

He waited. Eventually the voices started again and two Weequays came into his field of view, too slowly for his liking. They were looking at the road's shoulders with unusual diligence. One stopped suddenly and peered at the ground, apparently excited, if his arm gestures were any indication.

Then he looked up and started walking almost directly toward Darman's position. He took out a blaster pistol.

He can't possibly see me, Darman thought. *I've done this by the book. No reflection, no movement, no smells, nothing.*

But the Weequay kept coming, right into the bushes. He stopped about ten meters from Darman and was casting around as if he'd followed something and lost the trail. Then he moved forward again.

Darman had almost stopped breathing. His helmet masked all sound, but it certainly didn't feel that way. The Weequay was so close now that Darman could smell his distinctive sweat and see the detailed tooling on his sidearm—a KYD-21 with a hadrium barrel—and that there was a vibroblade in his other hand. Right at that moment Darman couldn't even swallow.

It's okay to be scared.

The Weequay stepped sideways, looking at waist height as if browsing for discs on a library shelf.

It's okay to be scared as long as you . . .

The Weequay was right on him now, squatting over his position. Darman felt boots depress branches that were touching his back, and then the creature looked down and said something that sounded like *gah.*

. . . as long as you use it.

Darman brought his fist up hard under the Weequay's jaw, ramming his own vibroblade up into the throat and twisting his fist off to one side to sever blood vessels. He supported the deadweight of the impaled Weequay on one arm, until it stopped moving. Then Darman lowered his arm, shaking with the effort, and let the body roll to the ground as quietly as he could.

"What you find?" the other Weequay yelled. "Gar-Ul? Gar?"

No answer. *Well, here we go.* Darman aimed his DC-17 and waited.

The second Weequay began running in a straight line toward the bushes, and that was a stupid thing for him to do when he had no idea what had happened to his comrade. They'd been lording it over farmers for too long; they were sloppy. He also made the mistake of pulling out his blaster.

Darman had a clear head shot and he took it almost without thinking. The Weequay dropped, cleanly and silently, and lay crumpled, with wisps of smoke rising from his head.

"Oh, clever," Darman sighed, as much to hear the reassurance of his own voice as anything. Now he'd have to break cover and retrieve the body. He couldn't leave it there like a calling card. He waited a few minutes, listening, and then eased himself onto his injured leg to limp out into open ground.

He dragged the Weequay into the bushes, noting the smell of cooked meat. Now he could see what the first Weequay had been following: a broad path of tiny animal footprints. The curious gdans had given him away. He limped out again, checking carefully, and obliterated the drag marks with a branch.

Waste not, want not. The Weequays wouldn't be needing the blasters or vibroblades now. Darman, pulse slowing to normal, searched the bodies for anything else of use, pocketing data cards and valuables. He didn't feel that he was a thief; he had no personal possessions that weren't the Grand Army's property, and he felt no need to acquire any. But there was a chance the cards contained information that would help him achieve his objective, and the beads and coins would come in handy if he needed to buy or bribe something or someone.

He found a suitable spot to hide the bodies. He didn't have time to bury them, but was suddenly aware of movement in the undergrowth, animal movement, and gradually small heads appeared, sniffing the air.

"You again, eh?" Darman said, although the gdans couldn't possibly hear him beyond the helmet. "Way past your bedtime." They edged forward and then swarmed across the

Weequay with the shattered head, taking tiny bites as they settled on him in a dark-furred blanket of snapping motion.

Darman wouldn't have to worry about burying anyone.

The faintest of liquid sounds made him look around at the other Weequay. Darman had his rifle aimed instantly. The Weequay wasn't dead, not quite. For some reason, that upset Darman more than he could have ever imagined.

He'd killed plenty of times at Geonosis, smashing droids with grenade launchers and cannons at a distance, hyped up on fear and the instinct to live. *Survive to fight.*

But this was different. It wasn't distant, and the debris of the kill wasn't metal. The Weequay's blood had dried in a stream down his glove and right forearm plate. And he hadn't managed a clean kill. It was *wrong.*

They had drilled him to kill, and kill, and kill, but nobody had thought to teach him what he was supposed to feel afterward. He did feel something, and he wasn't certain what it was.

He'd think about it later.

Aiming his rifle, he corrected his mistake before the small army of carnivores could move on to their next meal.

5

*Think of yourselves as a hand. Each of you is a finger, and
without the others you're useless. Alone, a finger can't
grasp, or control, or form a fist. You are nothing on your
own, and everything together.*
—Commando instructor Sergeant Kal Skirata

Darman moved on fast, up a tree-covered slope a kilometer
south. He planned on spending the rest of the daylight hours
in a carefully constructed hide at the highest vantage point
he could find, slightly below the skyline.

He concentrated on making a crude net out of the canopy
cords he had salvaged. The activity kept him occupied and
alert. He hadn't slept in nearly forty standard hours; fatigue
made you more careless and dangerously unfocused than alcohol. When he had finished tying the cord into squares, he
wove grass, leaves, and twigs into the knots. On inspection,
he decided it was a pretty good camouflage net.

He also continued observation. Qiilura was *astonishing*. It
was alive and different, a riot of scent and color and texture
and sounds. Now that his initial pounding fear had subsided
into a general edginess, he began to take it all in.

It was the little living noises that concerned him most.
Around him, creatures crawled, flew, and buzzed. Occasionally things squealed and fell silent. Twice now he'd heard
something larger prowling in the bushes.

Apart from the brief intensity of Geonosis, Darman's only
environmental experience had been the elegant but enclosed

stilt cities of Kamino, and the endless churning seas around them. The cleanly efficient classrooms and barracks where he had spent ten years turning from instant child to perfect soldier were unremarkable, designed to get a job done. His training in desert and mountain and jungle had been entirely artificial, holoprojection, simulation.

The red desert plains of Geonosis had been far more arid and starkly magnificent than his instructors' imaginations; and now Qiilura's fields and woods held so much more than three-dimensional charts could offer.

It was still open country, though—a terrain that made it hard for him to move around unnoticed.

Concentrate, he told himself. *Gather intel. Make the most of your enforced idleness.*

Lunch would have been welcome about now. A *decent* lunch. He chewed on a concentrated dry ration cube and reminded himself that his constant hunger wasn't real. He was just *tired.* He had consumed the correct amount of nutrients for his needs, and if he gave in to eating more, he would run out of supplies. There was exactly enough for a week's operations in his pack and two days' worth in his emergency belt. The belt was the only thing he would grab, apart from his rifle, if he ever had to make a last-ditch run for it without his forty-kilo pack.

Beneath him, farm transports passed along a narrow track, all heading in the same direction, carrying square tanks with security seals on the hatches. *Barq.* Darman had never tasted it, but he could smell it even from here. The nauseatingly musky, almost fungal scent took the edge off his appetite for a while. If he had his holochart aligned correctly, the transports were all heading for the regional depot at Teklet. He twisted the image this way and that in his hands and held it up to map onto the actual landscape.

Yes, he was sure enough now where he was. He was ten klicks east of the small town called Imbraani, about forty klicks northeast of RV point Beta and forty klicks almost due east of RV point Gamma. They'd picked RV points along the flight path because the Separatists would expect dispersal, not a retracing of their steps. Between RVs Alpha and Beta was a stretch of woodland, ideal for moving undetected by day. If the rest of his squad had landed safely and were on schedule, they would be making their way to Beta.

Things could be looking up again. All he had to do was get to RV Gamma and wait for his squad. And if they hadn't made it, then he'd need to rethink the mission.

The idea produced a feeling of desolation. *You are nothing on your own, and everything together.* He'd been raised to think, function, even breathe as one of a group of four. He could do nothing else.

But ARCs always operate alone, don't they?

He pondered that, fighting off drowsiness. Leaves rustled suddenly behind him, and he turned to scan with the infrared filter of his visor. He caught a blur of moving animal. It fled. His database said there were no large predators on Qiilura, so whatever it was could be no more troublesome than the gdans—not as long as he was wearing his armor, anyway.

Darman waited motionless for a few moments, but the animal was gone. He turned back and refocused on the road and the surrounding fields, struggling to stay awake. *Lay off the stims.* No, he wasn't going to touch his medpac for a quick boost. Not yet. He'd save his limited supply for later, for when things got really tough, as he knew they would.

Then something changed in his field of vision. The frozen tableau had come to life. He flipped down the binoc filter for a closer look, and what he saw made him snap it back and gaze through the sniperscope of his rifle.

A thin wisp of smoke rose from a group of wooden buildings. It was quickly becoming a pall. It wasn't the smoke of domestic fires; he could see flames, flaring tongues of yellow and red. The structures—barns, judging by their construction—were on fire. A group of people in drab clothing was scrambling around, trying to drag objects clear of the flames, uncoordinated, panicking. Another group—Ubese, Trandoshan, mainly Weequay—was stopping them, standing in a line around the barn.

One of the farmers broke the line and disappeared into a

building. He didn't come out again, not as long as Darman watched.

Nothing in his training corresponded to what he was witnessing. There was not a memory, a pattern, a maneuver, or a lesson that flashed in his mind and told him how this should be played out. Civilian situations were outside his experience. Nor were these citizens of the Republic: they weren't *anyone's* citizens.

His training taught him not to be distracted by outside issues, however compelling.

But there was still some urge in him that said *Do something.* What? His mission, his reason for staying alive, was to rejoin his squad and thwart the nanovirus project. Breaking cover to aid civilians cut across all of that.

The Separatists—or whoever controlled this band of assorted thugs—knew he was here.

It didn't take a genius to work it out. The sprayer had exploded on landing, detonating any demolition ordnance that Darman hadn't been able to cram into his packs. The Weequay patrol hadn't called in when their masters had expected. Now the humans—farmers—were being punished and threatened, and it was all to do with him. The Separatists were looking for him.

Escape and evasion procedure.

No, not yet. Darman inhaled and leveled his rifle carefully, picking out an Ubese in the crosswires. Then he lined up the rest of the group, one at a time. Eight hostiles, forty rounds: he knew he could slot every one, first time.

He held his breath, forefinger resting on the trigger.

Just a touch.

How many more targets were there that he couldn't see? He'd give away his position.

This isn't your business.

He exhaled and relaxed his grip on the rifle, sliding his forefinger in front of the trigger guard. What would happen to his mission if they caught him?

In the next two minutes, reluctant to move, he targeted each Ubese, Weequay, and Trandoshan several times, but didn't squeeze the trigger. He wanted to more than he could have imagined. It wasn't the hard-drilled trained response of a sniper, but a helpless, impotent anger whose origin he couldn't begin to identify.

Don't reveal your position. Don't fire unless you can take out the target. Keep firing until the target is down and stays down.

And then there were times when a soldier just had to take a chance.

They could be Republic citizens, one day.

They could be allies now.

Darman wasn't tired anymore, or even hungry. His pulse was pounding loud in his ears and he could feel the constriction in his throat muscles, the fundamental human reflex to flee or fight. Fleeing wasn't an option. He could only fight.

He targeted the first Weequay, a clean head shot, and squeezed the trigger. The creature dropped, and for a moment his comrades stared at the body, unsure of what had happened. Darman had nothing against Weequays. It was only coincidence that this was the third one he'd killed in a few hours.

And, suddenly unfrozen, the band of thugs all turned to stare in the direction of the shot, drawing their weapons.

The first bolt hit the bushes to Darman's left; the second went three meters over his head. They'd worked out where he was, all right. Darman snapped on the DC-17's grenade attachment and watched through the scope as the civilians scattered. The grenade sent a shower of soil and shattered wood into the air, along with four of the eight militia.

He'd certainly pinpointed his position now.

When he sprang to his feet and began the run down the slope, the four remaining enemy stood and stared for a couple of seconds. He had no idea why, but they were transfixed long enough for him to gain the advantage. A couple of plasma bolts hit him, but his armor simply took it like a punch in the chest and he ran on, laying down a hail of particle rounds. The bolts came toward him like horizontal luminous rain. One Trandoshan turned and ran; Darman took him down with a bolt in the back that blew him a few meters farther as he fell.

Then the white-hot rain stopped and he was running over bodies. Darman slowed and pulled up, suddenly deafened by the sound of his own panting breath.

Maybe they'd managed to report his presence via their comlinks in time, and maybe they hadn't. The information wouldn't have been much use on its own anyway. He ran from barn to barn, checking for more hostiles, walking through the flames unscathed because his armor and bodysuit could easily withstand the heat of a wood fire. Even with the visor, he couldn't see much through the thick smoke, and he moved quickly outside again. He glanced at his arm; smoke curled off the soot-blackened plates.

Then he almost walked straight into a youth in a farmer's smock, staring at him. The boy bolted.

Darman couldn't find any more of Hokan's troops. He came to the last barn and booted the door open. His spotlamp illuminated the dim interior and picked out four terrified human faces—two men, a woman, and the boy he'd just seen—huddling in a corner next to a threshing machine. His automatic response was to train the rifle on them until he was sure they weren't hostiles. *Not every soldier wears a uniform.* But his instincts said these were just terrified civilians.

He was still trailing smoke from his armor. He realized how frightening he looked.

A thin, wavering wail began. He thought it was the woman, but it seemed to be coming from one of the men, a man just as old as Sergeant Skirata who was staring at him in horror. Darman had never seen civilians that close, and he'd never seen anyone that scared.

"I'm not going to hurt you," he said. "Is this your farm?"

Silence, except for that noise the man was making; he couldn't understand it. He'd rescued them from their attackers, hadn't he? What was there to fear?

"How many troops has Hokan got? Can you tell me?"

The woman found her voice, but it was shaky. "What are you?"

"I'm a soldier of the Republic. I need information, ma'am."

"You're not him?"

"Who?"

"Hokan."

"No. Do you know where he is?"

She pointed south in the direction of Imbraani. "They're down at the farm the Kirmay clan used to own before Hokan sold them to Trandoshans. About fifty, maybe sixty of them. What are you going to do to us?"

"Nothing, ma'am. Nothing at all."

It didn't seem to be the answer they were expecting. The woman didn't move.

"He brought them here looking for him," said the man who wasn't whining, pointing at Darman. "We've got nothing to thank him for. Tell him to—"

"Shut up," the woman said, glaring at the man. She turned back to Darman. "We won't say a word. We won't say we saw you. Just go. Get out. We don't want your help."

Darman was totally unprepared for the reaction. He'd been taught many things, but none of his accelerated learning had mentioned anything about *ungrateful civilians, rescues thereof.* He backed away and checked outside the barn door before darting from barn to bush to fence and up the slope to where he'd left his gear. It was time to move on. He was leaving a trail behind him now, a trail of engagements and bodies. He wondered if he'd see *civvies,* as Skirata called them, in quite the same benign way in the future.

He checked the chrono readout in his visor. It had been only minutes since he had run down the slope, firing. It always felt like hours, hours when he couldn't see anything but the target in front of him. *Don't worry,* Skirata had said. *It's your forebrain shutting down, just a fear reflex. You're bred from sociopathic stock. You'll fight just fine. You'll carry on fighting when normal men have turned into basket cases.*

Darman was never sure if that was good or not, but it was

what he was, and he was fine with that. He loaded his extra pack on his back and began working his way to the RV point. Maybe he shouldn't have expended so many rounds. Maybe he should have just left the farmers to their fate. He'd never know.

Then it struck him why both the militia and the civilians had frozen when they first spotted him. The helmet. The armor. *He looked like a Mandalorian warrior.*

Everyone must be terrified of Ghez Hokan. The similarity would either work to his advantage or get him killed.

"Down!" Atin yelled.

Niner flung himself flat and heard Fi grunt as he did the same, the air knocked from his lungs.

An airspeeder flew overhead with a deceptively gentle hum. Atin, squatting in the cover of a fallen tree, followed it with his rifle scope.

"Two up, camo and custom armament," he said. "Somehow I don't think the locals drive those. Not with mounted cannons, anyway."

The hum of engines faded. Niner struggled to his feet and regained his balance, wishing for the speeder bikes and an absence of armor. The squad was too heavily laden and the armor wasn't designed for blending into the landscape, although it was the difference between life and death in hostile territory: protection against blasterfire, nerve agents, and even hard vacuum. And when they got to their target it would come into its own. The armor was designed for FIBUA ops, fighting in built-up areas and inside buildings, urban warfare of the kind the galaxy now had plenty to offer. For now, they'd just have to make the best of the scenic part of the mission.

He was tired. They all were. Not even the animal panic brought on by the risk of discovery could shake that off. They needed to sleep.

Niner checked his datapad. They were still ten klicks from RV Beta and it was midday. It was much easier to move by night, so he wanted to press on and make the RV point by midafternoon, then lie up until nightfall. If Darman had made it—and maybe he hadn't, but Niner's mind was made up—they would wait for him.

"He's back," Atin said. "Everyone down."

The quiet drone of engines interrupted Niner's calculations. The airspeeder was heading south toward them again. They froze, mud-smeared, invisible from that altitude—or so they hoped.

It wasn't entirely training that produced the reaction.

Aerial surveillance was especially threatening. Niner recalled the Kaminoan KE-8 Enforcer craft cruising above the training grounds of Tipoca City, ready to pluck out and discipline any defective clone who didn't conform. They were equipped with electroshock devices.

He'd seen a KE-8 in action, just once. After that he worked extra hard to conform.

"He's on a square search," Atin said. He was turning into an excellent point man; for some reason he was slightly more attuned to his surroundings than Fi or even Niner himself. "He must be working out from the center."

"Center of what, though?" Fi asked.

Niner forgot his fatigue. *You never leave your mates behind.* "If he hasn't seen us, he's seen Darman."

"Or what's left of him."

"Shut it, Atin. What's your problem?"

"I've been Darman," Atin said.

He said nothing more. Niner didn't think it was a good time to ask for an explanation. The engines were overhead. Then the sound faded a little and dropped in pitch, but soon resumed full volume.

"He's circling," Atin said.

"Fierfek," Niner said, and all three men reached for their anti-armor grenade attachments at the same time. "What's he seen?"

"Maybe nothing," Fi said. "Maybe us."

They fell silent. The airspeeder was indeed circling. It had also dropped lower and was now about level with the tops of the trees. Niner could see its twin cannons. His helmet wasn't telling him it had locked on, but that didn't mean it hadn't. You could never count on tech.

Best piece of gear is the eyeball. It was the first piece of advice Skirata had ever given him. Accelerated learning was fine, but anything direct from the mouths of men who had fought real engagements left a bigger impression.

Niner leveled his rifle and peered through the scope, trusting to BlasTech Industries that the sight really wasn't reflective. He'd find out the hard way if it was.

He could see the sun glinting off the human pilot's goggles. The gunner was a droid. He wondered if they felt vulnerable without any armored canopy, heads conveniently skylined for a shot. He suspected that anyone looking down from that height with a cannon or two didn't feel vulnerable at all.

The fuselage banked above him and turned slowly, rising well above the trees as if the pilot was trying to get a visual fix again. It wasn't coincidence. Niner kept the DC-17 trained on the central propulsion unit.

Then a red flashing symbol went off in his visor.

The thing had a lock on him.

He squeezed the trigger. The white-hot blast kicked his visor into blackness for an instant, and the detonation was so close that the shock wave hit him like a body blow.

He scrambled to his feet and ran. How he ran with more than fifty kilos of deadweight on his back he would never know, but adrenaline could do remarkable things. His instinct was to get clear before debris rained down on him. Armor and bodysuits could withstand a lot, but the human instinct buried deep inside him screamed *get clear.*

When he stopped he had covered a hundred meters even in the tangled undergrowth of the coppice. He was panting like a mott and the suit was struggling to cool him down.

Behind him, a fire burned, with smaller flames scattered around it like seedlings around a tree. He turned to look for Fi and Atin. His first thought was that he had brought the speeder crashing down on them.

"Did you have to?"

Fi was right next to him. He hadn't heard him above the noise of his own breathing.

"He got a lock on me," Niner said, feeling relieved, and then oddly guilty, but not sure why.

"I know. I saw your Deece go up and I thought I'd better get moving or I'd be wearing a speedie."

"Atin?"

"Can't hear him."

That didn't mean anything. The close-range comm setting was only ten meters; Atin could be anywhere. Niner didn't know him well enough yet to guess his movements, and it had been enough of a close shave for him not to spend much time contemplating the issue. Now he was worried that he—the sergeant, the man they looked to for leadership—had run for it without thinking of them, and that they knew it.

"This is going to make a nice marker," Fi said, staring up at the climbing smoke. It would be visible for a long, long way.

"What did you expect me to do? Lie there and take a cannon round?"

"No, Sarge. I thought you'd manage a double tap, though." He laughed. "Better make sure nobody survived."

It was a remote chance, but speeders could be surprisingly robust. Niner and Fi walked back through the smoke, rifles ready. Droid parts were scattered across the scene of devastation, one scuttle-shaped faceplate staring up at the pall of smoke as if in surprise.

"They don't bounce much, then," Fi said, and moved it with his boot. "Atin—Fi here. You there, over?"

Silence. Fi put his left gauntlet against his ear. Niner wondered if he'd now lost two men in as many days.

"Atin here, over."

Atin stepped out of the smoke, dragging his extra pack and a scorched hunk of metal that trailed a few wires and plugs. It looked like the speeder's onboard computer. "The pilot didn't bounce either," he said. "Here, help me get this strapped on again."

It took both Fi and Niner to lift the pack and reattach it to his armor. A few days earlier, either one of them could have managed it single-handed. *We're too exhausted to be safe,* Niner thought. *Time we got out of here and got some rest.*

"I might be able to get something from this," Atin said, indicating the charred metal box in one hand. It was the first time Niner had heard him sound remotely cheerful. Atin seemed to relate to gear better than he did to people. "Worth a try."

Niner took over the point position and they struggled into denser cover. He glanced back and hoped the flames would burn themselves out; they didn't have a hope of outrunning a full-scale forest fire. But maybe that was the least of their problems. And if Darman was alive and anywhere near, he'd see their handiwork, and Niner hoped he'd recognize it as such.

The squad had now left a couple of telltale marks of combat on the sleepy rural landscape. Whether it wanted it or not, Qiilura was involved in the war.

"You're a *di'kut,*" Hokan said.

He took off his helmet. His face was centimeters from the Ubese's, and he wanted it to look him in the eye. As a species they weren't prone to trembling, but this one was doing a fine job of being an exception.

"*What* are you?" he whispered.

"A *di'kut,* sir."

"You've made me look like a *di'kut,* too. I don't like that."

Hokan had assembled his entire senior staff in the room. He reminded himself that the room was in fact a disused merlie-shearing shed, and that his lieutenants were the twenty least stupid individuals selected from the criminal detritus that had washed down society's sewer to Qiilura. It disappointed him that the Neimoidians would spend so much on secure communications and so little on personnel. A few credits more and he could have bought the small army he needed.

The Ubese—Cailshh—was standing absolutely still in the middle of the room as Hokan circled. It might have been a female, because you never could tell with Ubese, but Hokan suspected it was male. He hadn't wanted to hire Ubese. They could be unpredictable, even sly. But very few mercenaries wanted to work on Qiilura and those who did were simply unemployable anywhere else, almost always because of a criminal record even a Hutt would balk at. And here he was, paying them what he could because Ankkit wouldn't fork out for proper support.

Hokan despaired. And when he despaired of professional standards, he suspected extreme coaching was necessary to refocus the team.

"So you torched another farm," he said.

"It was a warning, sir. In case they got ideas. You know. Hiding people they shouldn't."

"No, that's not how it works." Hokan propped his backside against the edge of the table and stared into the anonymous masked face, arms folded. He didn't like people whose eyes he couldn't see. "You warn them first. If they break the rules, *then* you punish them. If you punish them before they break the rules, they have nothing to lose, and they hate you, and they will seek revenge, and so will their offspring."

"Yes sir."

"Do you understand that?" Hokan looked around at the assembled staff, and spread his arms in invitation to join the coaching session. "Does everyone understand that?"

There were some grunts.

"Does everyone *understand that*?" Hokan snarled. "What do we say when an officer asks you a question?"

"Yes . . . sir!" It was almost a chorus.

"Good," Hokan said quietly.

He stood up again. Then he took out Fulier's lightsaber, activated the beam, and sliced it through the Ubese's neck, sending the head flying—bloodless, quiet, and clean.

There was sudden and absolute silence. The staff had been quiet before, but they'd been making the marginal noises of people forced to endure a boring lesson. Now there was not the slightest swallow, cough, or sigh. Nobody breathed.

He peered down at the body and then at the legs of his dark gray uniform trousers. Perfectly clean: no blood. He rather liked this lightsaber now. He sat back on the edge of the desk.

"That," Hokan said, "was *punishment* for Cailshh. It's a *warning* for the rest of you. Now, is the difference clear? It's very important."

"Yes sir." Fewer voices joined in this time, and they wavered.

"Then go and find our visitors. And you, Mukit. Clear up this mess. You're Ubese. You understand the proper way to dispose of the remains."

The group began filing out, and Mukit edged over to the neatly sundered body of Cailshh. Hokan caught the arm of his senior Weequay lieutenant as he tried to slip through the door.

"Guta-Nay, where's your brother and his friend?" he asked. "They haven't shown up for two meals, and they haven't signed off shift."

"Don't know, sir."

"Are they making a few credits on the side with that Trandoshan? A bit of freelance slaving?"

"Sir—"

"I need to know. To work out if anything . . . unusual might have happened to them."

Guta-Nay, no doubt recalling what Hokan had done to him when he chased that farm girl, moved his lips soundlessly. Then his voice managed to surface above his fear. "I never seen, sir, not at all, not since yesterday. I swear."

"I chose you as my right-hand . . . *man* because you could very nearly express yourself in several syllables."

"Sir."

"That makes you an intellectual among your kind. Don't make me doubt my judgment."

"Not seen him, sir, honest. Never."

"Then get out on the route they were patrolling and see what you can find." Hokan reached across his desk and took out the electroshocker. It was only an agricultural instrument for herding, but it worked fine on most nonanimal species. Guta-Nay eyed it cautiously. "This is why I disapprove of undisciplined acts like thieving and drinking. When I need to be certain of someone's whereabouts, I can't be. When I need resources, they're already committed. When I need competence, my staff is . . . distracted." He pushed the shocker up into the Weequay's armpit. "There is a Republic presence here. We don't know the size of the force, but we do have a speeder down and a large black crater at Imbraani. The more data I have, the more I can assess the size of the threat and deal with it. Understood?"

"Yes sir."

Hokan lowered the shocker and the Weequay shot out the door, his enthusiasm for his career refreshed. Hokan prided himself on motivational skills.

It's started, he thought. He shut himself in his room and switched on all the comlink screens. *They're coming to take Qiilura.*

Hokan had some idea of what kind of deal Ankkit had with the Separatists. There had been a significant amount of construction work carried out to convert a grain store into the kind of building that had triple-sealed doors, and the type of walls that could be sterilized with extreme heat. Then he'd had to try to make credible bodyguards out of the rabble he employed because important Separatist scientists came and went, and the Neimoidians saw conspiracy everywhere they looked. They weren't always wrong about that.

Then the Jedi came to Imbraani, and it all fell into place, as neatly as the arrival of the Republic forces now on the planet. There was a military target here.

I'm my father's son, though. I'm a warrior. Hokan wondered if all cultures separated from their heritage were unable to move on, doomed to relive old glories. *I'd rather be fighting a worthy opponent than terrorizing farmers who haven't got the guts to stand up for themselves.*

Fighting soldiers also commanded a higher fee, of course.

And the greater the fee, the quicker he would be off this planet and heading . . . somewhere.

There was no longer a home for him, and few of his kind left. But things could change. Yes, they very well might one day.

Hokan leaned back in the chair and let the chatter of comlinks wash over him.

6

"**G**et out," Birhan yelled. "Get out and don't come back! You've brought all this on us. Go on, clear off."

The farmer shied a clod of dirt at Etain, and she side-stepped it. It broke into dust behind her. The old woman—who wasn't Birhan's wife, she'd discovered—came up from behind and grabbed his arm.

"Don't be a fool," she said. "If we take care of the Jedi, then they'll take care of us when the Republic comes."

Birhan was still staring at Etain as if he was debating whether to go and grab his pitchfork. "Republic my rump," he said. "Them's no different to Neimies when it comes to it. We'll still be bottom of the pile whoever runs the show."

Etain stood with her arms folded, wondering how the old woman, Jinart, had managed to attach herself to Birhan's sprawling family. She was an appalling cook and couldn't have been much help with heavy farm labor. Etain imagined she earned her keep spinning merlie wool like the rest of the elderly Qiilurans she'd met.

But right now, Etain doubted even Jinart's powers of persuasion. She decided to try her own again.

"Birhan, you want me to stay," she said carefully, concentrating as Master Fulier had taught her. "You want to cooperate with me."

"I rotten well *don't* want to cooperate with you, missy," he said. "And say *please.*"

She'd never quite mastered Jedi persuasion when under stress. Unfortunately, that was always the time when she needed it.

Jinart nudged Birhan roughly, no mean feat for such a short woman. "If them Jedi have landed, fool, then she'll bring them around here to sort you out," she said. "This is no time to make new enemies. And if they haven't—well, it'll all blow over and then you'll have someone who can make things grow. That's right, innit, girl? Jedi can make crops grow?"

Etain watched the display of rustic logic with growing respect. "We can harness the Force to nurture plants, yes."

That was all too true: she had heard the stories of Padawans joining the agri corps when they didn't perform well during training. That was all she needed—life on a backwater planet, talking to fields of grain. It wasn't just the intelligence data she had hidden in her cloak that made her want to get off the planet as fast as she could. Agriculture spelled failure. She didn't need further reminding of her inadequacy.

"Yah," Birhan spat, and trudged off, muttering profanities.

"We all get nervous when Hokan's thugs start burning down farms," Jinart said. She took Etain's arm and steered her back to the barn that had become her home. No, it wasn't home. There could never be *home* for her. *No loves, no attachments, no commitments except the Force.* Well, at least it wouldn't be hard to tear herself away from here. "And killing farmers, of course."

"So why aren't *you* nervous?" Etain asked.

"You're a cautious child."

"I have a dead Master. It encourages you somewhat."

"I have a broader view of life," Jinart said, not at all like a wool-spinning old woman. "Now you keep yourself safe and don't go wandering about."

Etain was developing a Neimoidian level of paranoia and wondered if even her own instincts were deceiving her. She had at least always been able to sense another's emotions and condition. "So they know where to find me?" she said quietly, testing.

Jinart stiffened visibly. "Depends on who *they* might be," she said, wafting the pungent scent of merlie as she walked. "I don't care for urrqal much, and at my time of life there's little left to covet."

"You said they were coming."

"I did indeed."

"I have no patience for riddles."

"Then you should have, and you should also be reassured, because they're here and they'll help you. But you also need to help them."

Etain's mind raced ahead. Her stomach knotted. No, she was falling for carnival fortune-teller's tricks. She was adding her own knowledge and senses to vague generalities and seeing meaning where there was none. Of course Jinart knew strangers had arrived. The whole of Imbraani had known about Master Fulier, and it was very hard *not* to know something had happened when vessels crash-landed on your farm, and when every hiding hole in the area was being searched by Hokan's militia. For some reason or another, Jinart was playing a guessing game.

"When you specify something, I'll take you seriously," Etain said.

"You should be less suspicious," Jinart said slowly, "and you should look at what you think you see much more carefully."

Etain opened the barn door and the scent of straw and barq tumbled out, almost solid. She felt suddenly calmer, and even hopeful. She had no idea why. Perhaps Jinart was naturally reassuring, as comforting as a grandmother, despite all her odd talk.

Etain couldn't actually remember a grandmother, or any of her biological family, of course. *Family* wasn't familiar or soothing because she had grown up in a commune of Jedi novices, educated and raised and cared for by her own kind, and by that she never meant *human*.

But family, even from what she had seen briefly of squabbling farmers' clans, suddenly seemed desirable. It was difficult to be alone right then.

"I wish I had time to educate you in survival," Jinart said. "That task will have to fall to someone else. Be ready to come with me when it gets dark."

Jinart was becoming much more articulate. She was more than she appeared to be. Etain decided to trust the old woman because she was the nearest she had to an ally.

She still had her lightsaber, after all.

Darman came to the edge of the wood and found himself facing an open field the size of Kamino's oceans.

It seemed like it, anyway. He couldn't see the boundary on either side of him, just straight across where the trees began again. The rows of grain—steel gray, shining, sighing in the wind—were only waist-high. He was thirty klicks east of RV Gamma, desperate to reach it and get some sleep while waiting for the rest of the squad.

Following the cover of the hedge—wherever that might take him—would cost him a lot of time. He opted to take the direct route. He removed one of the three micro-remotes from his belt pack and activated it. The tiny viewing device was about the size of a pygmy hummer, small enough to grasp in his palm, and he set it to scout the area for five kilometers around him. He didn't like using them unless he absolutely had to. On a planet like this, their shiny metallic coating was hardly geared toward stealth. They also had a tendency to go missing. And because they recorded as well as transmitted, they were one of the last things he wanted to let fall into the enemy's hands.

But he wasn't exactly invisible, either. He glanced down at his filthy armor, streaked with dried mud, wet green moss, and far, far worse, and knew he was still a big plastoid-alloy industrial object in a gentle organic environment.

He lowered himself onto all fours, adjusting his balance carefully so the packs sat squarely down the length of his back. His knee still hurt. Crawling through a field wasn't going to help it. *The sooner you get there, the sooner you rest.*

The remote soared vertically into the air, playing back a rapidly shrinking view of the field, then the wider landscape of farmland and woods, all within Darman's visor display. There were no buildings as far as he could see. That didn't necessarily mean the area was deserted.

Crawling with his packs generated a lot of heat, but the bodysuit regulated it obediently. The armor system had more pluses than disadvantages. He didn't have to worry about wildlife waiting to bite, sting, poison, infect, or otherwise ruin his entire day.

But it was slow going. He had to loop wide if he was going to avoid the little town, Imbraani. In fact, the whole day had been one of slow progress, although the only timetable he could latch on to now was that of his comrades, and how long it would take them to make RV Gamma. Then they'd move on if he didn't show by the appointed time. After that—well, after that they were off the chart, so to speak. It would be a matter of regrouping and gathering enough intel to take the target.

Darman suspected it would take longer than a few days. A *lot* longer. He had started making notes of what local flora and fauna might be edible, and the positions of springs and watercourses that hadn't shown up on the high-altitude recce. He wondered if the gdans made decent eating. He reckoned it might not be worth trying.

Every so often he paused to kneel and sip some water from his bottle. His stomach's fantasies were no longer of sizzling nerf strips but of sweet, filling, sticky, amber uj cake. It was a rare treat. His training sergeant had allowed his squad—his original squad—to try it, breaking the Kaminoan rules on feeding clones carefully balanced nutritional mixes. "You're still just boys," he'd told them. "Fill yer boots." And they had. *Good old Kal.*

The flavor was still achingly vivid in Darman's mind. He wondered what other normal civilian indulgences he might enjoy if he had access to them.

He slapped the thought down hard. His discipline was his self-esteem. He was a professional.

He still thought about that uj cake, though.

"Come on, get moving," he said, very tired of the absence of comrades' voices and seeking comfort in his own. He would be his commanding officer, just to stay sharp. "Shift it."

The remote continued to relay predictable images of bucolic peace, neat patchworks of fields punctuated by the wild tangled woods, reminders of an unsettled and untamed world. There were no giant harvester droids out yet. At one point, he thought he saw a dark form moving through the field some way to his left, but when he focused on it there was simply a gap opened by the wind.

Then there was a sudden patch of darkness in his visor.

Darman stopped dead. The thing had malfunctioned. But the image returned, glowing, red, and wet, and he realized he was looking into the digestive tract of a living creature.

Something had swallowed the remote.

A few moments later a large bird, slowly flapping four wings, sailed overhead and cast an alarming shadow before him. He glanced up. It was probably the same kind that had been sucked into the Narsh sprayer's atmos engine.

"I hope it gives you gutache, you scumbag," he said, and waited for it to dwindle to a black speck before moving on.

It took more than half an hour to reach the other side of the field, and he still had twenty-five klicks to go to the RV point. He'd decided to go north of the town, although he shouldn't have risked moving by day at all. *Get there early. Wait for them, just in case they decide I'm dead and they don't hang about.* He eased into the bushes, scattering small creatures that he could hear but not see, and considered taking off his packs just for a moment's relief.

But he knew that would make it much harder to move when he slotted them back into place again. Exhausted, he fumbled in his belt for a ration cube and chewed, willing the nutrients to hit his bloodstream as fast as they could, before he slumped into sleep and didn't get up again. Lights danced in front of his eyes. Fatigue was giving him a heads-up display of its own.

The last of the cube dissolved in his mouth. "Come on, soldier, haul it up," he said. Playing mind games could keep him going. The trick was to remember where the game ended and then snap back to reality. Right then he decided to let his commander-self shout him into action.

"Sir!" he said, and sprang up from a kneeling position in one move. He tottered slightly when his knees locked out, but he stayed upright and leaned against a tree. He made a mental note that he needed to keep better hydrated.

It was so dark in the wood that his night vision kicked in from time to time, superimposing ghostly green images on the trunks and branches. He'd grown used to the range of animal sounds, and the occasional whisper of leaves or snap of twigs blended into the pattern of what his brain was cataloging as NFQ—normal for Qiilura. From time to time a slightly abnormal snap or rustle would make him drop to a squat and turn, rifle ready; but he was clear.

He followed the river on his holochart for part of the way, although it was actually more of a stream. The faint trickle of liquid over rocks was reassuring in the way that the sound of water could be, and after an hour he came upon a break in the tree canopy that allowed sunlight to filter down on the stream in slanted shafts. Brilliantly colored insects circled and danced above the surface.

Darman had never seen anything quite like it. Yes, he knew all about geological formations and what they foretold for soldiers: sources of water, treacherous scree, risk of landslide, caverns to shelter in, high ground for defense, passes to block. Accelerated learning packaged the natural world for him and explained how he could use it to military advantage.

But nobody told him it looked so . . . *nice.* He had no words for it. Like the uj cake, it was a glimpse of another world that wasn't his.

Sit down and rest. You're too tired. You'll start making fatal mistakes.

It was weakness talking. He shook his head rapidly to clear it. *No stims, no, not yet.* He had to press on. The insects kept up a constant circuit of the stream like recce aircraft, circling, seeking.

You're hours ahead. Stop. No sleep makes you careless. You can't afford to be careless.

It did sound like common sense. It wasn't the game-voice, his imaginary commander, giving him orders: it felt deep within him, instinct. And it was right. He was making slower and slower progress and he had to concentrate on putting one foot in front of the other.

He stopped and unclipped one pack, then the other. It was a good enough place to camp. He filled his water bottle and hauled a few half-decayed logs into place to build a defensive sanger, just as Sergeant Kal had taught them. It was only a low defensive circle of rocks—or whatever came to hand— but it made a difference on a battlefield when you couldn't dig in. He sat in the walled hollow he had created, staring at the water.

Then he cracked the seal on his helmet and breathed unfiltered air for the first time in many hours.

It smelled complex. It wasn't the air-conditioning of Tipoca City and it wasn't the dry dead air of Geonosis. It was alive. Darman released all the gription panels on his armor and stacked the plates inside the circle of the sanger, set his helmet to detect movement, and left it on the makeshift wall. Then he peeled off his bodysuit section by section and rinsed it in the flowing water.

The day was surprisingly warm; he'd had no way of telling what it felt like while he was sealed in the suit, just the ambient environment data on his display.

But the water was shockingly cold when he stepped in. He washed quickly, sat in the pool of sunlight to dry off, and then replaced the panels of bodysuit. They'd dried a lot more quickly than he had.

Before he let himself nod off he put his armor back on.

There was no sense in getting used to the pleasant sensation of not wearing it. It was drilled so thoroughly into him that he was surprised he'd thought otherwise even for a second: in enemy territory, you slept in full gear with your blaster ready. He cradled his rifle in his arms, leaned back on his pack, and watched the insects dancing on the sunlit water.

They were hypnotically beautiful. Their wings were electric blues and bright vermilion and they wove a figure-eight. Then, one by one, they dropped down and floated on the surface, drifting with the current, still wonderfully vivid, but now apparently dead.

Darman reacted. *Airborne toxin.* He shut his eyes tight, puffed out the air in his lungs, and snapped his helmet back into place, drawing breath again only when the seal was secure and his filtration mask could take over. But there was no data on his visor to indicate a contaminant. The air was still clean.

He leaned out and scooped up a couple of the insects caught in an eddy. One kicked a leg a few times and then was still. When he looked up, there were none left flying. It seemed sad. What bothered him more was that it seemed inexplicable.

Curious, he fumbled for an empty ration cube container and dropped the insects into it to consider them later. Then he closed his eyes and tried to doze, rifle ready.

But sleep eluded him. His helmet detected movement and woke him every few minutes at the intrusion of small creatures no threat to him. Once or twice it picked up a gdan, and he opened his eyes to see glittering points of reflected light staring back at him.

The system picked up something larger once, but it wasn't as large as any humanoid in his database, and kept its distance before disappearing.

Get some sleep. You're going to need it, son.

Darman wasn't sure if it was his own voice or that of his imaginary commander. Either way, it was an order he was only too willing to obey.

* * *

Ghez Hokan never took kindly to being summoned, but Ovolot Qail Uthan had the gift of being charming about it. She *invited* him to meet her in the research complex. She even sent one of her staff with a speeder to collect him from his offices.

Hokan appreciated the gesture. The woman understood how to use power and influence. The Neimoidian grocer had yet to learn.

Uthan was not particularly pretty but she did have the knack of dressing well—in plain dark robes—and carrying herself like an empress. That balanced the scales. What Hokan liked most about her was that while she seemed to know that feminine charm wouldn't override his common sense, she never dropped her seductively reasonable facade. She was a professional, and mutual respect went a long way with him. The fact that she was a scientist with subtle political skills impressed him further still. He could almost forgive the unnatural act of fighting without real weapons.

The decaying exterior of farm buildings gave way to reinforced alloy doors and lengthy corridors with what appeared to be emergency bulkheads. Hokan carried his helmet under one arm, unwilling to leave it—or his weapons—with the servant. The wizened man looked local. The locals were all thieves.

"Expecting some grain silo fires, then?" he said, and prodded the recessed blast bulkheads with his forefinger.

Uthan laughed a low, tinkling laugh that he knew could just as easily switch to a commanding voice and freeze a parade ground of troops. "I'm grateful you could make the time to see me, General Hokan," she said. "Under normal circumstances, I would never bypass someone with whom I had a contract and speak directly to his . . . subcontractor. It's very rude, don't you think? But I'm a little concerned."

Ah, Ankkit wasn't part of this conversation. Hokan began to understand. And she was laying on the flattery with a trowel. "I'm merely Hokan, a citizen. Let me address your concerns . . . madam?" He felt suddenly foolish. He had no idea what to call her. "Mistress Uthan?"

"*Doctor* will be fine, thank you."

"How can I reassure you, then, Doctor?"

She steered him into a side room and indicated three shimmering beige brocade upholstered chairs, clearly imported from Coruscant. He hesitated to sit on such a conspicuously decadent seat, but he did because he would not stand before her like a servant. Uthan took the chair nearest him.

"You have some idea of the importance of the work I carry out here, I think."

"Not in any detail. Viruses. From the building specification, anyway." He'd policed the construction crews, who were also all thieves. "Hazardous materials."

If Uthan was surprised, she gave no indication whatsoever. "Exactly," she said. "And I confess I'm somewhat disturbed by the events of recent days. Lik Ankkit assures me my security is guaranteed, but I would really welcome your assessment of the situation." Her tone hardened just a fraction: still syrup, but now with gritty, sharp crystals in it. "Is this project under any threat? And can you maintain its security?"

Hokan didn't hesitate. "Yes, I believe your facility is vulnerable." He was a master of his trade. He saw no reason to lose his reputation over a restriction not of his making. "And no, I can't guarantee anything with the level and quality of staff that I have."

Uthan sat back with controlled slowness. "Last matter first. Do you not have the resources to employ them? Ankkit's contract is quite generous."

"That generosity has not filtered down to my operation."

"Ah. Perhaps we should shorten the supply chain in the interests of efficiency."

"I have no opinion on that. Ankkit's welcome to his cut as long as I have the tools to do the job."

"That wasn't quite the cut I had in mind for Lik Ankkit." She smiled. There was no warmth in it. "And you believe the recent incursions are related to this facility?"

"Circumstantial evidence. Yes." Hokan returned the smile and suspected his was a few degrees cooler. If she'd do this to Ankkit, she'd do it to him. "It's a big planet. Why the Imbraani region? Why send Jedi agents?"

"Have you located any forces?"

"No. I've identified at least two points of hard contact and one downed vessel, though."

"Hard contact?"

"Situations when soldiers actually engage each other." Not that his rabble of mercenaries rated the distinction of *soldiers*. "I can't gauge numbers."

"If I were to arrange for you to have command of Separatist droids and their officers from our nearby garrison, would that make your task easier?"

"I take no sides. I won't lie to you and pretend to support your cause."

"You have military experience, of course. There's no disgrace in being a mercenary."

"I'm Mandalorian. It's in my soul as well as part of my education. No, there's no shame in it as long as you give of your best."

Uthan suddenly melted into what seemed to be a thoroughly genuine and sympathetic half smile. "I think I should share something with you. It might be distressing." There were still hard edges in her unctuous tone. "The Republic has created an army of cloned troops. *Millions*. They have been bred to fight and serve Jedi generals without question, altered to be their willing servants. They have had no normal life and they age very rapidly—if they survive being wasted in foolish battles. Do you know whose genetic material was used to create these unfortunate slaves?"

"No, I don't." Hokan was never embarrassed to admit ignorance. That was for small men. "Tell me."

"Jango Fett."

"What?"

"Yes. The finest Mandalorian warrior of his day has been used to churn out cannon fodder for the aggrandizement of the Jedi."

If she had spat in his face, he couldn't have been more appalled. He knew she was aware of what would enrage him;

she used the emotional term *warrior,* not *bounty hunter.* She knew how much the revelation would offend his cultural pride. But she was right to tell him. It was a matter of honor, and more than his own. He would not see his heritage used in this travesty of honest war.

"I'd take the contract even if you didn't pay me," he said.

Uthan seemed to relax. "We can give you up to a hundred droids to start with. Ask if you need more. It's a small garrison because we didn't want to attract attention, but now that we have that attention anyway we can reinforce if necessary. What about your existing militia?"

"I think layoff notices might be in order. Perhaps your troops might start by helping me with the administration of that."

Uthan blinked for a second, and Hokan realized she had taken longer than usual to understand what he meant. She'd grasped the meaning: *I can be as ruthless as you.* She'd think twice before undermining him as she was undermining Ankkit.

"That might be a sensible start," she said.

Hokan stood up and held his helmet in both hands. He had always been proud of that tradition, proud that it hadn't changed in thousands of years except for a technical enhancement here and there. What really mattered was what lay under Mandalorian armor—a warrior's heart.

"Would you like to know what virus we're developing here, Major Hokan?" Uthan asked.

So he had a real rank now, not the flatteringly extravagant *General.* "Do I need to?"

"I think so. You see, it's specifically for the clones."

"Let me see. To make them proper men again?"

"Nothing can do that. This is to kill them."

Hokan replaced his helmet carefully.

"The kindest solution," he said, and meant it.

7

Bal kote, darasuum kote,
Jorso'ran kando a tome.
Sa kyr'am Nau tracyn kad, Vode an.

(And glory, eternal glory,
We shall bear its weight together.
Forged like the saber in the fires of death,
Brothers all.)
   —Traditional Mandalorian war chant

It would have been much, much easier to fight in a different environment.

Niner decided that when he got back to base he'd ask to amend the training manual on nonurban warfare, to reflect the fact that SOPs for temperate rural terrain were definitely *not* interchangeable with jungle tactics.

It was the fields. There was too much open ground between areas of cover. Niner had been sitting in the fork of a tree for so long that one buttock was numb and the other was catching up fast. And still the group of militia was sprawled in the grass at the edge of a recently mown field, passing around bottles of urrqal.

Niner didn't stir under his camouflage of leaves. It was nearly autumn, so it was a trick they wouldn't be able to rely on much longer, as almost all the woodland was deciduous. They planned to pull out long before then.

"Anything happening, Sarge?" Fi's voice was a whisper in

his helmet, even though the sound wouldn't carry. It was a
smart habit, just in case. If one precaution was good, two was
better. "Still swigging?"

"Yeah. We could always wait until they die of liver failure.
Save the ammo."

"You okay?"

"My bladder's a bit full, but fine otherwise."

"Atin's shredding that speedie's onboard computer."

"I hope he's doing it quietly."

"He's moved into the wood a bit. He reckons he's down-
loaded some high-res charts, but the rest are probably fried.
He's on the encryption files now."

"As long as he's happy."

Fi made a stifled snort of laughter. "Yeah, he's happy."

I've been Darman. Niner still had no idea what Atin had
meant by that. He'd remember to ask him at a more appropriate moment. All he wanted right then was for Hokan's men to
get up and move on so they could cross over to RV Beta, just
four klicks ahead. It would have been easy to pick them off
from here, but that would leave a nice pile of calling cards
and the squad had left too many already. Niner wanted to
avoid all the hard contact that he could.

They have to run out of urrqal soon.

And they can't be taking Ghez Hokan very seriously.

Niner was watching the group through his rifle scope,
wondering why there was a preponderance of Weequays,
when they all looked up, but not at him. They were looking
to his right.

"Five more targets approaching," Fi said.

Niner tracked right very gently. "Got 'em."

They didn't look like militia. There was an Umbaran, very
smart in a pale gray uniform that matched his skin, and four
battle droids marching behind him. Some of the militia boys
got to their feet. One of them, reclining on the ground, held
his bottle out in offering, muttering something about curing
rust.

The only words of conversation that Niner could pick up
from the Umbaran were "... Hokan asks ... any contact ..."

The breeze took the rest. *They've got reinforcements,* he thought. *They look like a different problem altogether.*

And they were, but not for him this time. The reinforcement droids raised their integral blasters without warning and simply opened fire into the group of militia. They fired a few bolts in an orderly manner and then waited, looking down at their victims as if checking. The Umbaran—commissioned officer or sergeant?—stepped forward and fired another blast at close range into a Weequay. Apparently satisfied that their job was done, they gathered up the group's assortment of blasters and sidearms, searched the bodies for something—ID, Niner suspected—and marched calmly away, back down their approach route.

Niner heard Fi exhale at the same time he did.

"Well," Fi said. "You can empty your bladder now, I suppose."

Niner slid down from the fork of the tree, and his leg buckled under him. He removed the plates and rubbed his thigh to get the circulation going. "What do you reckon that was all about, then?"

"Hokan doesn't like them drinking on duty?"

Atin appeared, a jumble of circuitry and wires in one hand. "Looks like the tinnies have shown up to take over. But why shoot them?"

"Tinnies?" Fi said.

"What did your squad call them?"

"Droids."

Niner nudged Fi. "General Zey said Hokan was violent and unpredictable. He executes his own people in cold blood. Let's remember that."

They gathered up their gear and this time it was the turn of Atin and Niner to carry the load they'd rigged underslung on a pole. Fi walked ahead on point.

"I haven't fired a shot yet," he said.

"On this sort of mission, the fewer the better," Atin said.

Niner took it as a sign that Atin was joining in. His tone wasn't as defensive. Regular people said they couldn't tell the difference between one clone and another, did they? That was what came of spending too much time looking at faces and not enough wondering what shaped people and went on inside their heads.

"Save 'em for later," Niner said. "I think we're going to need every single round."

I must be out of my mind.

Etain watched the ramshackle farmhouse buildings through a gap in the barn's planked walls. The roofs were outlined against the deepening turquoise of the dusk sky: two lamps stood by the porch of the main building to keep the gdans away from the path to the outside refresher. There were so many of the little predators nesting around the farm that one of their warrens had subsided, leaving a gaping hole in the farmyard that was now filling up every time it rained. Birhan wasn't big on maintenance.

That did make some tasks easier, though. Satisfied that nobody was approaching, she went back to working boards loose from the barn's frame at the rear of the building. There was no other exit if she were ambushed, so she was making one.

She concentrated on the boards, fixing their shape and position in her mind. Then she visualized them separating and moving aside, creating a gap. *Move,* she thought. *Just part, swing aside . . .* and the boards did indeed move. She rehearsed shifting them with the Force a few times, letting them fall back into place quietly.

Yes, she could use the Force. When she felt confident and controlled, she could master everything Fulier had taught her; but those days could be few and far between. She wrestled with a temper unbefitting a Jedi. She watched those with serene acceptance of the Force and envied their certainty. She wondered why Jedi blood had bothered to manifest itself in someone who was so fallible.

Etain hoped she could manage to use the Force to do something more momentous than moving planks if the situation demanded it. She was certain that the next few days would test her beyond her limits.

Jinart arrived just after it grew completely dark. Despite watching intently through the crack in the wall, lightsaber ready, Etain didn't see her approach, or even hear her until the door swung open.

But she *felt* her. And she wondered why she hadn't felt her before.

"Ready, girl?" Jinart asked. She was wrapped in a filthy shawl that seemed about to walk of its own accord. It was a pretty convincing disguise.

"Why didn't you tell me?" Etain asked.

"Tell you what?" Jinart asked.

"I might be less than the ideal Padawan, but I can always sense another Jedi. I want to know why."

"You're wrong. I'm not that at all. But we *are* serving the same cause."

Jinart cast around and picked up the remnants of a loaf that Etain hadn't finished. She shoved it under her shawl.

"That wasn't an explanation," Etain said, and followed her out the door. There were no gdans to be seen. If this woman was strong in the Force and not a Jedi, she had to know why. "I need to know what you are."

"No, you don't."

"How do I know you're not someone who has turned to the dark side?"

Jinart stopped abruptly and spun around, suddenly faster and more upright than an old woman should have been. "I can choose when I am detected and *not* detected. And given your competence, I'm the one who's most at risk. Now, *silence.*"

It wasn't quite the answer Etain was expecting. She felt the same authority as she had in the presence of Fulier, except that he exhibited peaks and troughs of the Force, while Jinart projected an infinite steadiness.

She was *certainty*. Etain envied certainty.

Jinart led her into the woodland that skirted Imbraani to the east. She was keeping up a punishing pace, and Etain decided not to ask any more questions for the time being. At various points along the way, Jinart deviated: "Mind the warrens," she said, and Etain sidestepped holes and depressions that told her colonies of gdans had been busy beneath the ground.

They finally paused half an hour later, having covered an arc that brought them north to the edge of the Braan River. As rivers went, it was more of a large stream. Jinart stood still, apparently looking at the water but not appearing to focus. Then she jerked her head around and stared west, taking a deep breath and exhaling slowly.

"Walk upstream," she said. "Follow the riverbank and keep your wits about you. Your soldier is still there, and he needs those plans."

"A soldier. *One?*"

"That's what I said. Come on. He won't be there much longer."

"Not a group, then. Not even a few."

"Correct. There are others, but they're a little way from here. Now go."

"What makes you think I have plans?"

"If you hadn't, I wouldn't be risking myself to direct you toward your contact," Jinart said. "I have other work to do now. When you find your soldier, I'll try to persuade Birhan to take him in for a while. He'll need somewhere to hide. Get on with it. He won't hang around."

Etain watched Jinart start away toward the town, looking back just once. The Padawan slipped out her lightsaber and tried to get a sense of what might lie west along the riverbank, and when she glanced back again Jinart was nowhere to be seen. She was aware of the scrabbling of small clawed feet around her. Whatever influence had kept the gdans at bay while Jinart was with her was gone. She kicked out occasionally and hoped her boots were thick enough.

If she went back to the farm, nothing would have changed and she would be no nearer to delivering the information. She had no choice but to go on.

The bank was overgrown in places and she stepped into the river, knowing it would be shallow. The knowledge didn't make it any more pleasant to wade in sodden boots. But it was a reliable route, and it kept the gdans from trying their luck with her.

They were wary of Jinart. Etain wondered why the Force didn't deter them from stalking her as well. It was more confirmation, if she ever needed it, that she really wasn't much of a Jedi when it came to utilizing the Force. She had to concentrate. She had to find that single-minded sense of both purpose and acceptance that had so long eluded her.

Although Etain had clearly not yet come close to mastering control of the Force, she could see and feel beyond the immediate world. She could feel the nocturnal creatures around her; she even felt the little silver weed-eels parting to avoid her before they brushed her boots on the way downstream.

Then she became aware of something she wasn't expecting to encounter in the wilds of the Imbraani woods.

A child.

She could feel a child nearby. There was something unusual about the child, but it was definitely a youngster, and there was a feeling of loss about it. She couldn't imagine any of the townspeople letting a child out at night with gdans about.

Ignore it. This isn't your problem now.

But it was a child. It wasn't afraid. It was anxious, but not *scared* as any sensible child should have been, wandering around alone at night.

Suddenly there was something touching her forehead. She put out her hand instinctively as if shooing away an insect, but there was nothing there. And still she felt something right between her brows.

It dipped briefly to her chest, exactly on her sternum, and back up to her forehead. Then she was suddenly blinded by a light of painful intensity that shot out of the darkness and overwhelmed her.

She had nothing to lose. She drew her lightsaber, prepared to die on her feet if nothing else. She didn't need to see her opponent.

There was a slight *ah* sound. The light snapped off. She could still sense a child right in front of her.

"Sorry, ma'am," a man's voice said. "I didn't recognize you."

And still she detected only a child, so close that it had to be next to the man. For some reason she couldn't sense him in the Force at all.

Red ghost-images of the light still blinded her. She held her lightsaber steady. When her vision cleared, she knew exactly who she was staring at, and she also knew Jinart had betrayed her.

She'd probably betrayed Fulier, too.

Etain could see the distinctive full-face Mandalorian helmet of Ghez Hokan.

The sinister T-shaped slit told her all she needed to know. She raised the lightsaber. Both his hands were resting on his rifle. Perhaps the child—the unseen child—had been a lure, a distraction projected by Jinart.

"Ma'am? Put the weapon down, ma'am—"

"Hokan, this is for Master Fulier," she hissed, and swung at him.

Hokan leapt back with astonishing reflexes. She didn't recognize his voice: it was younger, almost accentless. He didn't even raise his rifle. The monster was playing with her. She spun on the ball of her foot and very nearly took his arm off. Sudden rage constricted her throat. She slashed again but found only air.

"Ma'am, please don't make me disarm you."

"Try it," she said. She beckoned him forward with one hand, lightsaber steady in the other. "You want this? Try me."

He launched himself at her, hitting her square in the chest and knocking her backward into the river. *The child was still there.* Where? How? And then Hokan was on top of her, holding her under the water with one hand, and she dropped the lightsaber. She fought and choked and thought she was going to drown and she had no idea why she couldn't fight off an ordinary man with both her fists. She should have been able to muster more physical strength than this human.

He hauled her up out of the water one-handed and dumped

her on the riverbank flat on her back, holding both her arms down.

"Ma'am, steady now—"

But she wasn't finished yet. With an animal grunt she drove her knee up hard between his thighs, as hard as she could, and when she was frightened and desperate and angry that was very hard indeed. She hadn't known it until now.

Etain gasped as her knee went *crack*. It hurt. But it didn't seem to hurt him.

"Ma'am, with respect, please *shut up*. You're going to get us both killed." The sinister mask loomed over her. "I'm not Hokan. I'm *not him*. If you just calm down I'll show you." He loosened his grip slightly and she almost struggled free. Now his tone was bewildered. "Ma'am, stop this, please. I'm going to let go and you're going to listen to me explain who I am."

Her breath was coming in gasps and she coughed water. The ever-present child so disoriented her that she stopped trying to dislodge him and let him struggle to his feet.

Etain could see him—it—clearly now. She could see well in the darkness, better than a normal human. She was staring at a huge droid-like creature clad in pale gray armor plates with no face and no markings. And it had a blaster rifle. It— he—held out a hand as if to pull her to her feet.

Well, it wasn't Ghez Hokan. That was all she could tell. She took his armored hand and got to her feet.

"What in creation's name are you?" she managed to ask.

"Ma'am, my apologies. I didn't recognize you at first. This is entirely my fault for failing to identify myself correctly." He touched black-gloved fingers briefly to his temple, and she noticed the knuckle plate on the back of the gauntlets. "Commando of the Grand Army CC-one-one-three-six, ma'am. I await your orders, General."

"General?" Voices coming from things that appeared to have no lips reminded her too much of droids.

He tilted his head slightly. "My apologies. I didn't see the braid . . . Commander."

"And what's the Grand Army?"

"The Republic's army, ma'am. Sorry. I should have realized that you've been out of contact with Coruscant for a while now, and . . ."

"Since when did we acquire a Grand Army?"

"About ten years ago." He gestured to the bushes along the bank. "Shall we discuss this somewhere less public? You're presenting something of a target to anyone with a night scope. I think even the local militia can manage one of those between them."

"I dropped my lightsaber in the river."

"Let me get it, ma'am," he said. He stepped into the shallow water, and the light on his helmet flicked on. He bent down and fumbled in the illuminated water, then stood up with the hilt in his hand. "Please don't use it on me again, will you?"

Etain raked her soaking hair back from her face with chilled fingers. She took the lightsaber carefully. "I don't think I'd have much luck anyway. Look, why are you calling me *Commander*?"

"Ma'am, Jedi are all officers now. You *are* a Jedi, aren't you?"

"Hard to believe, isn't it?"

"No offense, ma'am—"

"I'd ask the same question if I were you." *Commander. Commander?* "I'm Padawan Etain Tur-Mukan. Master Kast Fulier is dead. It seems you're the soldier I have to help." She looked up at him. "What's your name?"

"Ma'am, Commando CC—"

"Your name. Your *real* name."

He hesitated. "Darman," he said, sounding as if he were embarrassed by it. "We need to get out of here. They're looking for me."

"They won't have much trouble finding you in *that* outfit," she said sarcastically.

"The dirt's rinsed off." He stood silent for a moment. "Do you have orders for me, ma'am? I have to make RV point Gamma and find the rest of my squad. "

He was talking army gibberish. "When do you have to do that? Now?"

He paused. "Within twelve standard hours."

"Then we've got time. I have plans to show you. Come back with me and let's work out what we have to do next." She took the lightsaber from him and gestured with both arms. "I'll help you carry what I can."

"It's heavy, ma'am."

"I'm a Jedi. I might not be a very competent Jedi, but I *am* physically strong. Even if you did take me down."

"A bit of training will fix that, ma'am," he said, and he eased off that terrible Mandalorian helmet with a faint *pop* of its seal. "You're a commander."

He was a young man, probably in his early twenties, with close-cropped black hair and dark eyes. And despite the hard planes of his face he had a trusting and innocent expression that was so full of confidence that it surprised her. He wasn't just confident in himself; he exuded confidence in *her.* "You're probably just a bit rusty, ma'am. We'll get you back on form in no time."

"Are you *on form,* Darman?" He had overpowered her. It wasn't supposed to be like that. "How good are you?"

"I'm a commando, ma'am. Bred to be the best. Bred to serve *you.*"

He wasn't joking. "How old are you, Darman?"

He didn't even blink. She could see the hard muscle in his neck. There wasn't even a hint of fat on his face. He looked extremely fit indeed, upright, a model soldier.

"I'm ten years old, ma'am," Darman said.

Droids didn't drink or chase women, and they had no interest in making money on the side. They weren't real warriors, soldiers with pride and honor, but at least Ghez Hokan could trust that they wouldn't be found lying in the gutter with an empty bottle the next morning.

And they did look truly magnificent when they marched.

They were marching now, along the wide gravel path that led up to Lik Ankkit's villa. Hokan walked beside them, then behind them, moving position because he was so fascinated by the absolute precision of their steps, and the complete unvarying conformity of their height and profile. They looked like bricks in a perfect wall, a wall that could never be breached.

Machines could be made to be identical, and that was good. But it was anathema to do that to men—especially Mandalorian men.

The Umbaran lieutenant raised his arm and brought the droid platoon to a halt ten meters from the veranda steps. Lik Ankkit was already standing on the top stair, gazing down at them in his fancy headdress and that *di'kutla* robe like the weak, decadent grocer he was.

Hokan walked forward, helmet under his arm, and nodded politely.

"Good morning, Hokan," Ankkit said. "I see you've finally made some friends."

"I'd like to introduce you to them," Hokan said. "Because you're going to be seeing a great deal of each other." He turned to the lieutenant. "Proceed, Cuvin."

The Umbaran saluted. "Platoon—advance."

It was all vulgar theatrics, but Hokan had waited a long time for this. It was also necessary. He had to billet some troops near Uthan's facility for rapid deployment. They would be little use in the base thirty kilometers away.

Ankkit stepped forward as the droids reached the steps. "This is an outrage," he said. "The Trade Federation will not tolerate—"

The Neimoidian stood aside just as the first rank of paired droids reached the intricately inlaid kuvara door, with its marquetry image of entwined vines.

Hokan wasn't expecting a display of heroics, and he didn't get one. "It's very good of you to allow me to billet my troops here," he said. "A noble use of all that wasted space. The Separatists are grateful for the personal sacrifice you've made to ensure the security of Doctor Uthan's project."

Ankkit walked down the steps as fast as his towering headdress and long robe would allow. Even by Neimoidian standards of anxiety, he looked terribly upset. He *shook*. He stood almost a head taller than Hokan even without the head-dress, which was rustling as if some creature had landed in it and was struggling to escape. "I have a *contract* with Doctor Uthan and her government."

"And you failed to honor the clause that guaranteed adequate resourcing for security. Doctor Uthan's notice of penalty should be on its way to your office."

"I do not take kindly to betrayal."

"That's no way to address a commissioned officer of the Separatist forces."

"An *officer*?"

"Field commission." Hokan smiled because he was genuinely happy. "I have no need of you now, Ankkit. Just be grateful you're alive. By the way, Doctor Uthan's government has paid a bonus directly to the Trade Federation to ensure I'm allowed to work unhindered. Enemy troops have landed, and this region is now under martial law."

Ankkit's slit of a mouth was clamped tight in anger. At least he wasn't pleading for his life. Hokan would have had to kill him if he had begged. He couldn't bear whining.

"And I suppose that means you, Hokan," Ankkit said.

"*Major* Hokan, please. If you see any of my former employees wandering around, don't shelter them, will you? Some of them have failed to show up to collect their severance payment. I'd like to handle their outplacement package personally."

"You're the paradigm of efficient management for us all," Ankkit said.

Hokan enjoyed the moment of revenge, then put it aside as the distracting bauble that it was. Ankkit was no threat now; you couldn't bribe droids. The Umbaran and Aqualish officers now knew what happened to negligent soldiers because they'd carried out his execution orders. Hokan was careful to ensure that everyone was clear on what happened if they left his employment under a cloud.

"And where do *I* live?" Ankkit asked.

"Oh, plenty of room here," Hokan replied. There was a

loud crash, followed by the tinkle of fragile glass hitting a hard floor. Droids could be so careless. "I'm sure you won't get in their way."

He touched his fingers to his helmet and strode off.

There were still a few of his former troops missing. One was his Weequay lieutenant Guta-Nay. He wanted to locate him very badly, as he needed to demonstrate to the new officers that he would happily do his own disciplinary work. It was an image he wanted planted in their heads should Ankkit ever attempt to bribe *them*.

He walked down the path to the waiting speeder bike. A farmer had found scraps of circuitry on his land and wanted to know if it was worth a bottle of urrqal to reveal the location.

Hokan set off to visit him personally, to show that the information was worth more than that. It was worth a farmer's life.

RV point Beta should have been a coppice at the top of a shallow escarpment west of Imbraani. When Niner got within visual range of it, there were no trees to be found.

"Coordinates are right, or else this visor is up the creek," Atin said, tilting his head one way, then the other. "No, position's accurate. Confirm no trees, though. Shall I deploy a remote to recce?"

"No," Niner said. "Let's save them for ordnance. Too conspicuous out here. We'll have to lay up as close as we can and rely on eyeballing Darman if he shows. Where's the nearest cover?"

"About one klick east."

"That'll have to do."

Atin looped back, keeping within the trees and retracing their steps to ensure they weren't being tracked. His armor was now caked with moss, and Niner was glad he wasn't downwind of him. Whatever he'd crawled through smelled authentically rural. Fi and Niner tabbed on, carrying the extra gear between them, an assortment of entry equipment including three dynamic hammers, a hydraulic ram, and a ratchet attachment for the *really* difficult doors. They had transferred all the explosive ordnance to their backpacks. If they made hard contact and had to drop the load and hurry out, Niner didn't fancy being left with a hydraulic ram and ration packs for self-defense. A pile of grenades was far more useful.

"Logging," Fi said quietly.

"What?"

"The missing coppice. It's coming up on autumn. They've been out cutting trees for winter since the recce was done."

"That's the problem with intel," Niner said. "Goes stale really fast."

"Not like exercises."

"No. It's not. This is going to be invaluable for training updates when we get back."

Fi sounded as if he had sighed. That was the funny thing about helmet comlinks. One got used to listening to every nuance of breath and tone and even the different ways his brothers swallowed. They couldn't see each other's facial expressions, and had to listen for them. It was probably like being blind. Niner had never known any blind people, but he had heard of a batch of clones whose eyesight wasn't 20/20 disappearing after their first exercise. Kaminoans were obsessive about quality control.

He might have been bred for selfless obedience, but he wasn't stupid. The Kaminoan technicians were the only things that truly terrified him, and what he felt when he obeyed their instructions was different than the feelings he had when a Jedi gave him orders. He wondered if Fi and Atin felt the same way.

"You don't think we're going to make it, do you, Fi?"

"I'm not afraid to die. Not in combat, anyway."

"I didn't say you were."

"It's just . . ."

"Ten-meter range, son. No Kaminoans listening."

"It's just so inefficient. You said it yourself. You said it was a waste."

"That was Geonosis."

"They spend so much time and trouble making us perfect and then they don't give us what we need to do the job. You remember what Sergeant Kal used to say?"

"He used to swear a lot, I remember that."

"No, he used to get upset when he'd had a few drinks and say that he could make us better soldiers if we had time to go out and live. *Data-rich, experience-poor.* That's what he used to say."

"He used to slur the words quite a bit, too. And he didn't like clones."

"That was all bluster. And you know it."

Yes, Kal Skirata said awful things about clones, but it never sounded as if he meant them, not to the clones, anyway. He got uj cake from home, no easy feat on secret, sealed Kamino, and shared it with the commando squads he was responsible for training. He called them his Dead Men, his Wet Droids, all kinds of abusive things. But if you caught him off duty in his cabin, he would sometimes fight back tears and make you eat some delicacy smuggled in for him, or encourage you to read one of his illicit texts that wasn't on the accelerated training curriculum. They were often stories of soldiers who could have done many other things, but chose to fight. Sergeant Kal was especially eager for his Wet Droids to read stuff about a culture called Mandalorian. He admired Jango Fett. "This is who you really are," he'd say. "Be proud, however much these ugly gray freaks treat you like cattle."

No, he didn't like Kaminoans much, did Kal Skirata.

Once he signed up with the Kaminoans, he said, they never let him go home again. But he'd told Niner that he didn't want to. He couldn't leave his boys now, not since he *knew.* "Brief," he'd say, gesturing with a glass of colorless alcohol, "is never glorious."

Niner was determined to work out what Kal Skirata had come to understand, and why it upset him so much.

"Nobody has all the answers," Niner said. "The trouble with getting used to being powerful is that you can forget the small details that'll bring you down."

Fi made that *ffff* sound as if he was about to start laughing. "I know who you're quoting."

Niner didn't even realize he'd said it. It was Sergeant Kal all right. He'd even started using the word *son*.

He missed him.

Then the comlink warning light in his HUD interrupted his thoughts. *Medium range.* What was Atin—

"Contact, five hundred meters, dead on your six." Atin's voice cut through. "Droids. Ten, one humanoid—confirm ten tinnies, one wet, looks like an officer." There was a loud blast behind them. "Correction—hard contact."

Niner knew this by rote and Fi didn't even exchange words with him. They dropped the gear and darted back the way they had come, rifles up, safetys off, and when they got within fifty meters of Atin's location they dropped into the prone position to aim.

Atin was pinned down at the foot of a tree. There was one droid slumped on its side with wisps of smoke rising from it, but the others were formed up, laying down covering fire while two advanced in short sprints, zigzagging. Atin was managing to get off the occasional shot. If they'd wanted him dead, they probably had the blaster power to do it.

They wanted Atin alive.

"I can see the wet," Fi said. He was to Niner's left, staring down the sniperscope. "Aqualish captain, in fact."

"Okay. Take him when you're ready."

Niner snapped on his grenade launcher and aimed at the line of droids. They were spread, maybe forty meters end-to-end. It might take two rounds to knock them out if they didn't scatter. Droids were great on battlefields. But they weren't made for smart stuff, and if their officer was down . . .

Crack.

The air expanded instantly with the release of heat and energy. That was what gave plasma bolts their satisfying sound. The Aqualish fell backward, chest plate shattered, and lumps that looked like clods of wet soil but weren't flew from him and dropped. The droids stopped for a fraction of a second, then carried on their course as if that was the best idea they had.

Fi scrambled away from his position and rolled.

No, they really weren't good at close-quarters combat, at least not without direction from a wet. But there were always a lot of them, and they could return fire as well as any organic life-form. Three of the seven remaining droids turned their attention to the direction of Fi's bolt.

The bushes where Fi had been firing exploded in flame. Niner perceived that it was all happening slowly—at heartbeat pace—but it wasn't, not at all. He aimed and fired, once, twice. The twin explosions almost merged into one. Soil and grass and metal fragments rained down around him. At close range, droids were almost as dangerous when you hit them as when they hit you: they were their own shrapnel.

The firing stopped. Smoke drifted from at least five impact points. Niner could see nothing moving.

"One tinnie intact but immobile," Fi said.

"Got it," Niner said. He fired again, just in case.

"Looks sorted out there," Fi said. He lowered his rifle. "Atin? You okay?"

"Nothing missing that I can't bolt back on."

"You're a laugh a minute," Niner said, and started to ease up on one arm. It was amazing how he could forget the weight of his pack for the few moments it took to save his life. "Now, how did they—"

"Down!" Atin yelled.

A bolt flew a meter above Niner's head and he dropped back on his belly. It sounded like two shots. Then there was silence.

"*Now* it's sorted," Atin said. "Someone help me get up, please?"

When Niner managed to get into a kneeling position he could see a thoroughly shattered pile of droid, a bit closer to him than the line. It had been two shots he'd heard: one had been aimed at him and one had come from Atin, to make sure there wasn't a second.

"Coming, brother," Niner said.

Atin's mud-smeared chest plate was a different color now, matte black with streaks radiating from the center. "I can't breathe properly," he said, utterly matter-of-fact, in the way badly injured men often were. He gulped in a breath. "My chest hurts."

Fi propped him up against the trunk of a tree and took his helmet off. There was no blood coming from his mouth: he was bone white, and his raw scar looked dramatic, but he wasn't bleeding out. His pupils looked okay: he wasn't in shock. Fi released the gription on his chest plate and eased the armor off.

The bodysuit was intact.

"Sure it's just your chest?" Fi asked. He didn't have a tally scan to check Atin's status. You didn't start removing armor or embedded objects until you knew what you were dealing with. Sometimes that was all that was holding a man together. Atin nodded. Fi peeled away the section of suit starting at the collar.

"Phwoar," Fi said. "That's going to be a monster of a bruise." There was a livid patch from his sternum to halfway down his chest. "You collecting distinguishing features or something?"

"Hit me square on," Atin said, panting. "Not a regular round. Armor works though, eh?"

Fi took his helmet off and listened to Atin's breathing with his ear pressed to his chest.

"Ow."

"Shut up and breathe."

Atin took shallow breaths, wincing. Fi straightened up and nodded. "Can't hear any pneumothorax," he said. "But let's keep an eye on him. The air trapped inside can build up. Might be fractured ribs, might just be a bad bruise." He took out a canister of bacta and sprayed the rapidly developing bruise. Atin lifted his arms slightly as if testing them.

Fi sealed the bodysuit and armor back in place.

"I'll take your pack," Niner said, and unclipped it. It was the least he could do. "I think we can skip RV Beta now. Let's leave some souvenirs around there so Darman can spot them if he shows up. You never know if more tinnies will follow. They're not original thinkers."

They probably had a few minutes, even if any of the droids had managed to call in to base. Fi sprinted off through the trees with a few pieces of debris to leave them at the RV point. Niner searched the remains of the Aqualish officer and took everything that looked like a key, a data medium, or proof of ID. Then he dragged Atin's pack behind him on a webbing strap, heading for the place they'd left the entry equipment.

It was going to be a tough slog to RV Gamma, at least until Atin could carry his pack again.

The whole engagement had lasted five minutes and eight seconds, first shot to last, including running time. He had no idea if it had been one second or half an hour. Funny thing, time perception under fire. Niner's boots crunched over droid shrapnel and he wondered how long a firefight felt to a droid.

"Is that how they see us?" Niner asked. "Ordinary people, that is. Like droids?"

"No," Atin said. "We don't have any scrap value." He laughed and stopped short with a small gasp. It must have hurt him. "I'm going to slow you down."

"Don't go gallant on me. You're coming the rest of the way because I'm not lugging all that gear around with Fi. I want a break sometime."

"Okay."

"And thanks. I owe you."

"No. You don't."

"Thanks anyway. Want to explain why you've been Darman?"

Atin was holding his rifle carefully, a handspan clear of his chest. "I've been the last man left standing in two squads now."

"Oh." Silence. Niner prompted: "Want to tell me how?"

"First squad tried to rescue me on a live range exercise. I didn't need rescuing. Not that badly, anyway."

"Ah." Niner felt instantly appalled at himself for thinking Atin didn't care what happened to Darman. He was just caring too much. "My training sergeant said there was something called survivor's guilt. He also said that in those cases, having you survive was what your squad wanted."

"They bred a lot of stuff out of us. Why not that as well?"

Niner stopped dragging Atin's pack and slung his rifle over his shoulder. He lifted the pack and was glad to carry it.

"If they had, I might not be here now," he said, and knew Darman would be waiting for them tomorrow.

Ghez Hokan surveyed the scrap heap that had been a functioning droid platoon a few hours earlier. Whatever had hit them had hit fast and hard. And—judging by the precisely placed sniper shot and the blast pattern of only two grenades—they had been taken out by experts.

It might have been one man or it might have been a platoon. You typically couldn't ambush battle droids like that with a handful of men, but that depended entirely on who the men were. It was a shame the captain hadn't called back with a sitrep as instructed: if he hadn't been killed, Hokan would have had him shot for disobeying operational procedure. He studied the droid escort lined up neatly by the speeder bikes and wondered if they felt anything when they saw dismantled comrades.

"There's no sign of a camp, sir." Lieutenant Cuvin came jogging back from the woods opposite the clearing. It was curious to see the Umbaran's deathly pallor tinged pink by the exertion. "Some broken branches at knee height and crushed grass from troops firing prone, but I honestly can't tell how many men we're dealing with."

"You can't tell much, can you, Lieutenant?" Hokan said.

"Sir, I'll check again." He was white-faced now, white even for an Umbaran.

"Sir! Sir!" Second Lieutenant Hurati was enthusiastic, no doubt keen to be elevated to Cuvin's rank. He *sprinted* to his commander, an attitude Hokan appreciated. "I've found the most extraordinary thing."

"I'm glad one of you has found something. What is it?"

"A pile of droid parts, sir."

"And this is extraordinary because . . . ?"

"No, sir, they're some way from here and they're sort of *arranged,* sir."

Hokan strode off for the speeder. "Show me."

The trees had been cut down a few days earlier because there was already klol fungus growing on them in a pale-pink mesh. One broad stump—the flattest one, almost like an altar—supported the remains of a droid.

The torn pieces of its trunk were laid flat. The arms were neatly arranged on one side of the thorax and the legs on the other. Part of the faceplate was propped up as if looking sky-ward.

"That's how the droid pilot was left, too, sir." Hurati *was* a good man. He'd obviously studied the report the militia had filed, however appallingly inadequate its presentation had been. "I think it's a sign."

It was a long way to move a dead droid from a battle. There were no drag marks leading to the stump. It was a heavy load to carry on foot; they might even have a trans-port, although he could see no signs that a repulsorlift had passed over the ground. Hokan stared at the ritually arranged debris and tried to think who would want to send the Sepa-ratists a message—and what it might mean.

"It's a trophy," Hokan said. "They're taunting us. They're showing how easy this is for them."

That made him angry. He was Mandalorian. Being an easy enemy wasn't his way. "A curfew, Hurati. Declare a perma-nent curfew on all powered vehicles until further notice. Anything moving under power is either ours or the enemy. We can track all friendly transports." He paused. "You have made sure all our vehicles have their own transponders, haven't you?"

"Yes sir."

"Why the delay, then?"

"It's—it's harvest, sir. How will the farmers get their pro-duce to Teklet for shipping?"

"I imagine they have handcarts," Hokan said. He swung

his leg over the speeder's saddle. "Ankkit will have to find an alternative means of conveyance for his crops."

Hokan pondered on the carefully arranged droid debris all the way back to his new headquarters in Ankkit's villa. He feared that moving into that vulgar Hutt bordello of a house would make him soft and decadent, too, so he set up his office in an outbuilding. He didn't care for fancy drapery and useless ornaments. It just happened to be convenient for the research facility, and close to his troops.

So who had the Republic sent to target Uthan's project? They were clearly bold men; first they made sport of an aerial patrol, now a droid platoon and its captain. They seemed to be choosing their targets casually. The clone army must have been terribly important to the Republic's strategy for these troops to land like this. Where were the conventional armies? Where were the Jedi generals? When would they come?

This was a new kind of war. He could feel it.

He hated not knowing who was out there, preparing to fight him. If he hadn't known the man was dead, he would have sworn it was Jango Fett himself.

8

You know what makes you especially effective? It's not just
that you're genetically superior and intensively trained. And
it's not just because you obey orders without question. It's
because you're all prepared to shoot to kill, every time.
Only one percent of civilians are prepared to kill, and less
than a quarter of ordinary human soldiers, even under fire.
—Sergeant Kal Skirata, from his opening lecture to
commandos on military psychology

The droid fired a volley of bolts at the sealed alloy doors
until they glowed red. And still nothing happened.

"Stop!"

The droid appeared not to hear.

Dr. Ovolot Qail Uthan ran down the flight of steps, red
and black strands of hair streaming out behind her. She was
wearing a voluminous dark blue nightgown; it looked as expensive as her day wear. Hokan saluted her politely and went
on watching the droid's progress.

"Have you gone mad?" Uthan whispered fiercely. She didn't
strike Hokan as the sort of woman who would need to raise
her voice to make her point. "There's a *biohazard* behind that
door."

"I know," Hokan said. "Just testing. It's all holding up well
indeed. Excellent safety bulkheads."

Uthan took a discreet but deep breath and glanced briefly
at the backs of her hands. "This facility has been built and

tested to the highest containment standards, Major. You needn't worry."

"But I do, Doctor." He watched the droid patiently wasting bolt after bolt on the door for a while. It paused to swap power packs. *"Stop."*

It stopped. Hokan took out the lightsaber he had taken from Kast Fulier and ran its pure blue light down the seam between the two doors. Smoke curled up from the surface, but no breach appeared. It would take even a Jedi a long time to cut through this plating.

"Forgive my insistence, but could this not wait until the morning?" Uthan asked. "I'm working around the chrono as it is to weaponize this agent. I even sleep here. I would prefer to be doing that right now."

"My apologies, Doctor, but we might not have the luxury of time."

"What's time got to do with it?"

"I think I need to relocate you."

Uthan had a way of lowering her head slightly, then straightening up as if she were a krayt dragon. It was most impressive. "This is a high-risk biohazard facility. It can't be relocated like some *tent*."

"I appreciate the inconvenience involved. I still believe it would be safer if you were to pack up your materials and staff and move elsewhere."

"Why? You have the security situation under control."

"I have it more under control than I did, that's true, but enemy troops have landed. I don't know their numbers, and I don't know what matériel and armaments they have at their disposal. All I know—all I think I know—is that this is what they've come for."

"This is a fortress. You have a hundred droids at your disposal. Let them come. You can repel them."

"All fortresses can be breached in time. I could give you a list of circumstances under which someone who's very resourceful could get past these doors, but I want you to trust my judgment and accept what I say. Let's move you and your work to somewhere less obvious until I have a more accurate assessment of the threat."

Uthan looked completely impassive, staring slightly past Hokan as if she was calculating something.

"I can remove the biomaterials and my staff," she said at last. "The equipment can be replaced if needed. I won't be able to continue working without a safe laboratory environment, of course, but if you believe the project is at risk, then idle time is a better option than wasting three months' work."

What a splendidly sensible woman she was, almost Mandalorian in her discipline and dedication. Hokan ushered the droid out. "How long?" he asked.

"Six hours, perhaps."

"Is this material that dangerous?"

She tilted her head slightly. "Only if you're a clone. If you're not, it might simply make you unwell."

"It must be strange to fight with weapons you can't see."

"War is about technology," she said.

Hokan smiled politely and walked back out into the courtyard to stand in the dim light from the doorway. There was the first hint of chill on the night air; winter was coming, and the landscape would be much easier to patrol when the leaves had fallen. When the snows came, it would be even easier. But he suspected that this conflict was going to be a rapid one. Intelligence reports were starting to come in that the Republic was now fighting on hundreds of different fronts. *Hundreds.*

Their new army would have to be millions strong to achieve that dispersal. So they were all clones. *Sad travesties of the great Jango Fett.*

Well, he knew one thing. The Republic wouldn't be sending clones to deal with this particular problem. They had to know the Separatists already had the one weapon that could stop them in their tracks. And this kind of operation was beyond the capacity of the docile infantry clones Uthan had described. This was not a game of numbers.

Hokan replaced his helmet and started visualizing the research facility as a trap. So they wanted to come and take a look, did they? He'd make them welcome.

"Droids, form up. Two ranks across this entrance."

The droids moved as one, even in the darkness, and Hokan again admired their precision. Now they were a road sign pointing the way to the target, confirming what the Republic thought it knew. But they'd be wrong. They'd be sending their best men to a decoy.

War is about technology.

"No," Hokan said aloud. The droids snapped to attention. "War isn't even about firepower." He tapped his temple. "It's about applying your brains." Then he touched his chest. "And it's about courage."

He didn't expect the droids to understand that. Clones probably didn't understand it, either.

The straw stank of something awful, but Darman was too exhausted to care. It looked like it might be soft enough to sink into. That was good enough for him.

But first he walked around the walls of the barn and checked for an exit if he needed one in an emergency. There were several loose boards in one wall that would do fine. The rickety building looked as if he could actually punch an escape hole through any fragile plank he chose.

Reassured, he dropped everything he was carrying and tried to sit on the bales, but it turned into more of an uncontrolled slump. He didn't even take his helmet off. He sat back and let out a breath.

The Padawan commander leaned over him. "Are you all right, Darman?" She held her hand out, palm down over him, as if she was going to touch him but didn't.

"I'm fit to fight, Commander." He started to sit up, and she held her hand in a slightly different gesture that clearly meant *Stay where you are.*

"I didn't ask that," she said. "I can feel you're in some distress. Tell me."

It was an order. It came from a Jedi. "I injured my leg

when I landed. Apart from that I'm just tired and a bit hungry." *Bit hungry?* He was ravenous. "Nothing at all, Commander."

"Landed?"

"I free-fell from a vessel."

"With all that equipment?"

"Yes ma'am."

"You astound me." He couldn't tell if that was good or bad. "Two things, though. Please don't call me *Padawan* or *Commander*—I don't want to be recognized as a Jedi. And I'd rather be called Etain than *ma'am*." She paused, no doubt thinking of some other failure on his part. "And please take your helmet off. It's rather disturbing."

So far Darman had met three Jedi and they all seemed to find him distracting in some way, with or without his helmet. All his life he had been taught that he and his brothers were created for the Jedi, to help them fight their enemies; he'd expected some recognition of that bond, or at least an expression of satisfaction. He removed his helmet and sat feeling confused, torn between the absolute clarity of his military expertise, and the confusion of dealing with the civilian world he had been thrust into for the first time.

The Padawan—no, *Etain,* she'd made her orders clear— took a small sphere out of her cloak and opened it in both hands. Layer after layer of holographic images spilled out of it, stacking neatly like plates.

"Plans," she said. Her voice had changed completely. She radiated relief. "Plans of all the Separatist and Neimoidian buildings in this region. Floor plans, utility layouts, wiring diagrams, drainage, ducts, specifics on materials used— every detail of how the contractors built them. This is what you need, isn't it? What you are looking for?"

Darman wasn't tired anymore. He reached out and broke the beam of the projection, flipping a plan vertically so he could read it. He looked through them all and heard himself let out an involuntary breath.

Etain was right. It was nearly every bit of intelligence they needed, apart from more fluid details such as personnel numbers and routines. With these plans they knew how to cut power to the buildings, where to insert nerve agents into air ducts or water supplies, and exactly what they would see and where they would have to go when they gained entry. The plans showed the construction of walls, doors, bulkheads, and windows, so they knew precisely what size of charge or type of ram would be needed to breach them. This was a set of clear instructions for achieving their objective.

But Etain didn't seem to know that objective. "What are you going to do with this?" she asked.

"We've come to abduct Ovolot Qail Uthan and destroy her research facility," Darman said. "She's developing a nanovirus intended to kill clones."

Etain leaned closer. "Clones?"

"I'm a clone. The whole Grand Army is composed of clones, millions of us, all commanded by Jedi generals."

Her face was a study in blank surprise. It was also fascinating in a way he couldn't define. He had never seen a human female this close, this *real*. He was astonished by the dappling of small brown dots across the bridge of her nose and her cheeks, and the different strands of colors in her long, unkempt hair—light browns, golds, even reds. And she was as thin as the locals. He could see blue veins in the backs of her hands, and she smelled different from anyone he'd ever shared space with. He wasn't sure if she was pretty or downright ugly. He just knew she was utterly alien and utterly fascinating, as alien as a gdan or a Gurlanin. It was almost stopping him from concentrating on the job.

"All like you?" she said at last, blinking rapidly. She seemed unsettled by his scrutiny. "What have I said?"

"No ma'am—sorry, *Etain*. I'm a commando. We're trained differently. Some people say . . . that we're *eccentric*. I realize you haven't received much by way of intelligence."

"All I knew—all my Master would tell me—was that Uthan was here and that the plans were critical to the Republic's safety. Clones didn't come into the conversation." She was staring at him just as Jusik had. "There's an old woman who told me you were coming, but she didn't tell me much else. How many of there are you on Qiilura now?"

"Four."

"*Four?* You said there were millions of you! What use is four going to be?"

"We're commandos. Special forces. You understand that term?"

"Obviously not. How are four ten-year-olds going to storm Uthan's complex?"

It took him a few moments to realize she was being sarcastic. "We fight differently."

"You're going to have to be very different indeed, Darman." She looked absolutely crushed, as if he'd let her down simply by showing up. "Are you really ten years old?"

"Yes. Our growth is accelerated."

"How can we possibly train competent soldiers in that time?"

"It's very intensive training." He was finding it hard not to say *ma'am* each time. "They created us from the best genetic stock. From Jango Fett."

Etain raised her eyebrows, but said nothing else. Then she stood up, reached for a basket balanced on a low beam, and handed it to him. It was full of odd round items that smelled edible, but he thought he'd check anyway.

"Is this food?"

"Yes. The local bread and some sort of steamed cake. Nothing exciting, but it'll fill you up."

Darman bit into a lump that yielded slightly in his fingers. It was glorious. It was strongly flavored and chewy and among the most satisfying meals he had ever eaten: not quite on the scale of uj cake, but so far from the odorless, tasteless, textureless field rations that it might well have been.

Etain watched him carefully. "You *must* be starving."

"It's wonderful."

"That doesn't say much for army food."

Darman reached into his belt and pulled out a dry ration cube. "Try this."

She sniffed it and bit into it. The expression of vague disbelief on her face changed slowly into one of revulsion. "It's appalling. There's nothing in it."

"It's the perfect nutritional profile for our requirements. It has no smell, so the enemy can't detect it, and no fiber, so we excrete minimal waste products that would enable us to be tracked, and—"

"I get the idea. Is that how they treat you? Like farm animals?"

"We don't go hungry."

"What do you like doing?"

He really didn't know what answer she was after. "I'm a good shot. I like the DC-seventeen—"

"I meant in your free time. Do you get free time?"

"We study."

"No family, of course," she said.

"Yes, I've got squad brothers."

"I meant—" She checked herself. "No, I understand." She pushed the basket of bread closer to him. "My life hasn't been that much different from yours, except the food was better. Go on. You can finish the whole lot if you want."

And he did. He tried not to watch while Etain wrung water from her robe and shook out her boots. She made him feel uncomfortable but he didn't know why, apart from the fact that she wasn't quite the Jedi commander he had been so thoroughly trained to expect.

The only females he could recall were Kaminoan medical technicians whose quietly impersonal tones intimidated him more than a yelling drill sergeant. And his platoon had once experienced an unpleasantly memorable lecture in encryption techniques from a female Sullustan.

He feared females. Now he feared his Jedi officer and was also agitated by her in a way that he didn't even have a word for. It didn't feel *acceptable*.

"We need to move on," he said. "I have to make the RV point. I've been out of comm contact with my squad for nearly two days, and I don't even know if they're alive."

"This gets worse by the second," she said wearily. "First we have four. Now we might be down to one."

"Two. Unless you have other duties."

"You've seen me fight."

"You're a Jedi. A commander."

"That's a title, not an assessment of my ability. I'm not exactly the best of the best."

"You must be. I know what Jedi can do. Nobody can defeat you as long as you have the Force."

She gave him a very odd smile and picked up the holochart sphere. She seemed to be struggling to find her thread again. She swallowed a few times. "Show me where your RV point is—that's right, isn't it? RV? Show me where it is on this chart."

Darman took out his datapad and linked his mission charts with the image projected from the sphere. He pointed to the coordinates.

"It's here," he said. "Before we set out on exercises or missions, we agree where we'll meet up if anything goes wrong. We had to bail out when our transport crashed, so we're scattered, and the procedure is that we go to an RV point for a set time window."

He zoomed in on the area northwest of Imbraani. Etain tilted her head to follow.

"What's this?" she asked.

"Primary target. Uthan's facility."

"No, it's not."

"Intel said—"

"No, that's the Separatist base. Their garrison." Her eyes darted back and forth, scanning the chart. She pointed. "*This* group of buildings is the facility. You can see. Look." She superimposed the floor plans of the facility with the layout of the farm buildings and shrank the image to fit. They lined up perfectly.

Darman's stomach knotted. "My squad will be heading for the Separatists, then."

"We'd better make sure we intercept them," Etain said. "Or they'll run smack-bang into a hundred droids."

Darman was suddenly on his feet in one move, even before he'd realized that he'd heard someone coming.

"I don't think so," a woman's voice said. "Because the droids are all heading for Imbraani."

Darman's sidearm was out of his belt and aimed before Etain could even turn her head.

9

*There is something very touching about them. They look
like soldiers; they fight like soldiers; and sometimes they
even talk like soldiers. They have all the finest qualities
of the fighting man. But behind that is nothing—
no love, no family, no happy memory that comes from
having truly lived. When I see one of these men killed,
I weep more for him than for any ordinary soldier
who has lived a full and normal life.*
—Jedi General Ki-Adi-Mundi

Darman had flattened Jinart's face against the wall and put
his blaster to her head in the time it took Etain to jump to her
feet.

"Steady there, boy," Jinart said quietly. "I mean you no
harm."

He had her pinned securely. The expression on his earnest
face was entirely benign, so far divorced from the potential
violence he was ready to mete out that Etain shuddered.

"Let her go, Darman," she said. "She's a fellow Jedi."

Darman stood back instantly and let Jinart go.

"I'm not a Jedi, I tell you," Jinart said irritably. She looked
up into Darman's face. "So you'd shoot an old woman, would
you?"

"Yes ma'am," Darman said. Etain stared, horrified.
"Threats come in all guises. Not all soldiers are young
males, and not all soldiers wear uniforms."

Etain waited for Jinart to aim a kick at his groin, but the old woman broke into a satisfied grin. "There's a sensible boy," she said. "You'll do well. Trust this one, Etain. He's very good at his job." She peered at the blaster, still firmly in his grip. "DC-seventeen, I see."

"There are *four* of them," Etain said, expecting Jinart to react with the same disappointment she had.

"I know." The woman handed Etain a bundle of rags. "A complete squad of clone commandos. Here, dry clothing. Nothing chic, but at least it's clean. Yes, I know all about them. I've been tracking the other three."

"They're okay?" Darman was all anxiety again, still emitting that same sense of *child* that Etain found hard to bear. "I've got to rejoin them. Where are they?"

"Heading north."

"To RV Gamma."

"Whatever you say, lad. You've all led me on something of a dance. You're a challenge to track."

"That's how they trained us, ma'am."

"I know."

Jinart was still staring at Darman's face. "You really *are* a perfect copy of Fett, aren't you? In his prime, of course." Her voice had become lower, with less of the hoarse cracking typical of the very old, and Etain wondered if this was the moment at which she would reveal that she was a Sith. The Padawan slid her hand slowly into her sodden cloak.

Jinart suddenly became black as Coruscant marble, and then devoid of texture and hair and fabric and wrinkles, as if she were wax poured into a crude mold. Her form began flowing.

Darman's incongruously innocent face broke into something like a familiar smile. Etain was ready this time. She was focused; she visualized the lightsaber as part of her arm. She was prepared to fight.

"You're the Gurlanin," Darman said. "We weren't told you were on this mission. How did you manage that?"

"I'm not Valaqil," said a soothing liquid voice. "I'm his

consort." Jinart, now a four-legged, black-furred creature, sat up on her haunches and seemed to simply extend upward like a column of molten metal. "Girl, you do look surprised."

Etain couldn't argue with that. Even if you'd encountered the full diversity of nonhuman species—and she certainly had, even within her own Jedi clan—seeing a shapeshifter metamorphose before your eyes was mesmerizing. On top of that, even this naïve clone soldier knew what this creature was. She didn't.

"You're quite a revelation, Jinart. But why can I sense something about you that feels like the Force?"

"We're telepaths," the Gurlanin said.

"Oh . . ."

"No, I'm not delving into your mind. It doesn't work like that. We communicate only with each other."

"But I heard your voice that night, in my mind."

"I was standing near you, actually. Not in any shape you'd notice, of course."

"And me, ma'am?" Darman asked, seeming totally absorbed by the conversation.

"Yes, I told you to get some sleep. I make a convincing fallen tree, don't I?" Jinart flowed and changed and reassembled herself into the epitome of a crone again. "I know, stereotypical, but effective. Old women are invisible. Like you, Darman, we go where others won't and do what others can't. The communications network here is totally controlled by the Trade Federation, and in practice that means a single relay and monitoring ground station at Teklet. And while my kind cannot transmit details over interstellar distances, we *can* communicate broad ideas and notions to each other. My consort and I are your comlink. Not perfect, but better than silence."

The Gurlanin made a liquid sound like water boiling. "I've spent the last two days running myself ragged to gather this intelligence, and it's as much for this young man as it is for you. Ghez Hokan now has command of the armed forces here, such as they are, and he's no fool—he realizes Republic troops are here for Uthan's box of tricks. Darman, he's tracking your comrades."

"We're pretty good at evasion."

"Yes, but they do tend to leave bodies and parts behind them. He admits he doesn't know how many of you there are, and that troubles him."

"You're privy to his concerns, then?" Etain said. She trusted nobody now. She still didn't know who had betrayed Master Fulier, and until she did she would keep an open and cautious mind. Although her Master hadn't told her about the clones, he must have known if he had discovered Uthan's activities. But he hadn't trusted her. For all his kind words, when it came down to it he simply confirmed—even from the grave—that she was not fit to become a Jedi Knight.

"I know Hokan's concerns because I can make a very convincing old man as well as an excellent grandmother," Jinart said. The reply made no sense. "I'll catch up with Darman's comrades and try to direct them to somewhere safe. They have no reliable *intel,* as you call it, a finite amount of ordnance, and no advantage of surprise any longer. Hokan knows what you have come to do and he has enough firepower and droids to stop you. That makes your mission next to impossible without some change of plan or intervention."

Darman considered her carefully. Jinart's news hadn't dented that tangible confidence: Etain saw not a flicker on his face. "It could be worse. I quite liked the sound of a single transmitter."

"Might I also add that the locals will turn you in for one chance to get disgustingly drunk."

Darman looked at Etain. She squirmed. "Out of ideas, soldier?" she asked.

"I await your orders, Commander."

It was the final straw. Weeks of fear, hunger, and fatigue on top of years of doubt and disillusion suddenly brought Etain's fragile edifice crashing down. She had done all she could do, and there was nothing left in her to give.

"Stop it, stop calling me *Commander.*" She felt her nails dig into her palms. "I am *not* your blasted commander. I haven't a clue what to do next. You're on your own, Darman. *You're* the soldier. *You* come up with a plan."

Jinart said nothing. Etain felt her face burn. She had lost all dignity. A lifetime of careful training in the art of control and contemplation had come to nothing.

Darman changed before her eyes. He transformed not in the physical sense that the Gurlanin had, but the change was just as startling because the sense of the child that Etain detected so clearly simply evaporated. Its place was taken by calm resignation and something else, a rather forlorn feeling. She couldn't pin it down.

"Yes ma'am," he said. "I'll do that right away."

Jinart jerked her head in the direction of the door. "Get some air, Darman—I need to talk to *Commander* Tur-Mukan."

Darman hesitated for a moment and then slipped outside. Jinart rounded on Etain.

"Listen to me, girl," she whispered, all harsh sibilants. Droplets of fine saliva glittered briefly in the dim light. "That soldier may think a Jedi's every word is a divine pronouncement, but I don't. You'd better sharpen up *fast*. The commandos and I are all that stands between maintaining some kind of order in the galaxy and its fragmentation, because if the clone army can be wiped out, then the Separatists will *win*.

"You can either help us or stand aside, but you will *not* be an obstacle, and that's what you are if you can't lead those men. They've been bred to obey Jedi without question. Sadly, in this case that means *you*."

Etain was used to feeling worthless. There was no lower place that Jinart could cast her. "I didn't ask for that responsibility."

"And neither did Darman." Jinart flashed back into a mass of seething black sinews for a terrifying second. "That's the nature of duty. It calls and you give your all. He will. So will his comrades, every single one of them. They need you to help them do their job."

"I'm still learning how."

"Then learn fast. If those soldiers weren't conditioned to

obey you I'd consider cutting you down now and have done
with it. My kind have nothing to thank Jedi for, nothing at
all. But we share a common enemy, and I want to see Valaqil
again. Think yourself lucky."

Jinart swept out. Etain sank down on her knees in the hay
and wondered how she had come to this. The barn door
creaked open slowly, and Darman peered around.

"Don't mind me," she said.

"You okay, ma'am?" He winced visibly. "Apologies.
Etain."

"You probably think I'm useless as well, don't you?"

"I came up with a plan, as you ordered."

"Bred for diplomacy, too, eh?"

"If Hokan has set the facility as a decoy, then we need him
to think that we believe it's still the genuine target. So we
split—"

"I'll take that as a yes."

Darman lapsed into silence.

"I'm sorry," she said. "Carry on."

He knelt down, facing her, and swept the floor clear with
his hand, creating a clear space on which to demonstrate
something. He reached for some crusts of bread and a lump
of insect-eaten wood.

"What do you think I am?" he asked quietly.

"From what Jinart says, a clone soldier bred to obey." She
watched him break the wood and the crusts into separate
chunks and place them in a row like game pieces. "No
choice."

"But I do have a choice," he said. "A choice in how I inter-
pret your orders. I'm intelligent. I've seen Jedi fight, so I
know what you're capable of. Once you're exposed to situations that call on your skills, you'll be the same."

He was all contradictions. She wondered for a moment if
he wasn't a clone soldier at all but another Gurlanin playing
spiteful games with her. But she could feel a combination of
quiet desperation and . . . faith. Yes, *faith.*

He was the only person in many years who had shown any

degree of confidence in her, and the first since Master Fulier who had shown her real kindness.

"Very well," she said. "This is your overriding order. Whatever happens, you are to intervene if anything I do or say compromises your mission. No, don't look at me like that." She held up her hand to stifle the protest she could see forming on his lips. "Think of me as a commander in training. You must train me. That might mean showing me the correct way to do things, or even saving me from my own lack of . . . experience." She could hardly bring herself to say it. "And . . . and that's an order."

He almost smiled. "This is why I have confidence in obeying a Jedi commander. Your wisdom is unequaled."

Etain had to think about that for a few seconds. If Jinart had said it, she would have seethed. Darman meant it. And perhaps he meant it in a number of ways.

Yes, he was intelligent and subtle, not a droid at all. How did a ten-year-old get that way? Disturbed, she concentrated on the comfort of believing that he had seen things that she never had, and so knew best. "Go on," she said. "You had a plan."

RV Gamma, laying-up point, nightfall

"How do you feel now?" Niner asked.

Atin moved his arms, bent at the elbow in a swimming motion, testing his pectoral muscles. "Nearly good as new. No breathing problems, either. No, just a hard smack on the plate."

Fi's disembodied voice spoke up in their helmet comlinks. He was tucked under a bush on the edge of the ridge, keeping watch on the track below. "I'm such a good field medic. Wait till you see me do a tracheotomy."

"I'll pass if that's all right with you," Atin said, easing off his helmet. "Dinner?"

"What do you prefer," Niner asked. "Dry rats, dry rats, or maybe dry rats?"

"Let's go with the dry rats for a change." Yes, Atin was definitely feeling better, and not just physically. "Who used to say that, then?"

"Uh?"

"The dry rations thing."

"Oh. Skirata. Our old instructor sergeant."

Atin took a bite out of the white cube and washed it down with a gulp of water from his bottle. "He never trained us. Heard a lot about him."

"Trained Fi and Darman, too. Our squads were all in the same battalion."

"We had Walon Vau."

"That explains where you get your cheery outlook."

"Sergeant Vau taught us the importance of planning for the worst scenario," Atin said, all loyalty. "And maximizing your tech. *Being hard is good, being hard with superior tech is better.*"

"I'll bet."

"I'd heard everyone loved Skirata, though. Even if he was a bad-tempered drunk."

Niner had never been drunk and he didn't even know what alcohol tasted like. "He cared what happened to us. He *was* one of us, pretty much. Not just there because he couldn't cope with not being in the army anymore, or had to disappear. No, he was a good man." Niner would have given a great deal to have seen Skirata come limping through the trees right then, demanding to know what they were doing lounging around like a bunch of Kaminoan nahra artists. "No idea where he is now, not since we left Kamino. Best covert ops and sabotage man ever."

"You'd know, of course."

"We'll all know soon. I'm relying on what he taught us to get this mission completed."

Niner ate the perfectly balanced, sensibly designed, and utterly tasteless cube, and sat silently, still waiting for Darman. They couldn't even trap something and cook it: the smell of roasting meat and the light of the fire would betray their position.

With Fi on watch, he could shut his eyes and sleep for a couple of hours. He put his helmet back on, partly to be ready to move fast if they had enemy contact, and partly to keep the temperature up in his suit. It was getting chilly. He allowed himself one comfort that he didn't really need, *for morale.*

You scare me. You just absorb everything I tell you. Don't you ever forget?

"No, Sarge," Niner said.

He had no idea how long he'd been asleep. He woke with a start at the sound of Fi's voice.

"Possible contact, due east, range forty klicks. Looks like it's centered on Imbraani."

Even through the visor, it wasn't clear exactly what Fi had spotted, but Niner could see it now, too. A glow marked the horizon like a false sunrise. It was constant, the gentlest graduation from amber to deep red: it wasn't an explosion.

Niner switched between visor modes, main spectrum to infrared to full spectrum, and then back again. The glow was hot, too. The infrared long-range picked it up.

"I reckon that's one big fire coming," Fi said.

They waited, watching: Niner could hear Atin a few meters away, gathering up equipment and assembling it, ready to pull out. With the binocs on full distance, they could see that the fire was being eclipsed in places by billows of smoke. Eventually, Atin joined them, and all three observed the distant blaze in silence.

"They're not burning crop stubble at night," Fi said. "They haven't even finished harvesting that stinking barq stuff yet. They've found something."

"I know."

"Either they've found Darman, and they're teaching the locals not to shelter the enemy, or they haven't found Darman and they're trying to flush him out."

Niner thought it was relatively good news. "But it means he made the landing," he said. "So we wait here right up to the last second, and maybe a little longer just to be sure."

Atin laid the gear down again. He was too professional

and disciplined to slam it on the ground, but Niner picked up on the slight sag of his shoulders. "And if he doesn't show by then?" he asked, with a level tone that suggested he didn't want to show dissent any longer. "Next plan?"

"We take another look at the whole area from Teklet to Imbraani," Niner said. "We start from scratch."

"This isn't to scale," Darman said. He scraped marks in the loose soil on the exposed dirt floor of the barn and placed pieces of stale bread carefully on the crude chart. "This is the river. These three crusts are RVs Alpha, Beta, and Gamma." He snapped the wood into more pieces and placed them. "This is the droid base . . . and this is Uthan's lab."

Etain held out her cupped hand. He dropped two chunks of wood into it. "This is Lik Ankkit's residence," she said. "He's the Neimoidian overlord, for want of a better word. He runs the agricultural produce export business, and that near enough makes him an emperor here."

"Okay. What else have we got?"

Etain crumbled her remaining lump of wood into smaller pieces and scattered them carefully in patches. "Imbraani itself, and Teklet, which is the spaceport, and its storage and distribution depot."

"And *this* was the last known position for my squad."

Etain stared at the worm-eaten wood and the moldy crusts that might help them save the Grand Army from destruction. "Why are we scraping maps in the dirt when we've got perfectly good holocharts?"

"That's what Sergeant Skirata used to do," Darman said. "He didn't like holos. Too transparent. He also thought that feeling the texture of dirt focused your mind."

"And you don't need any technology to do it."

"He was a great believer in intuition."

Darman drew his blaster and turned suddenly. The barn door opened. He relaxed and dropped his arm to his side. Jinart held more drab fabric bundled in her arms. "You have to go," she said breathlessly. "Take a look out there to the east. They're burning the fields to flush you out and deny you cover. There's somewhere you can lie low, but you have to pass for farmers—that's not going to be easy for you, lad. You're too big and well fed."

Etain didn't rise to the bait. She knew she'd fit in fine with the undernourished, shabby locals.

"I have to take my gear," Darman said. "I can lay up somewhere with it if I have to."

"Can't you leave any of it?"

"Not if we're going to blow up that facility. I've got all the implosion ordnance to deal with the nanovirus, as well as the E-Web cannon. We need it."

"Then take a cart. There's a curfew on powered vehicles." Jinart tossed one of the bundles to Darman. "And get out of that armor. You couldn't be more conspicuous if you were wearing a wedding gown."

"We can try to make RV Gamma."

"No, go to the first safe house you can find. I'll reach your squad and let them know, then I'll return to you."

There was an assortment of barrows and handcarts stored in the barn, all in various states of disrepair. They'd attract no attention: the network of dirt roads was well traveled by people trying to get their quota of barq and other crops to Teklet on foot or with merlie-carts.

Loading the sections of the blaster cannon on the sturdiest barrow they could find made Etain realize just how heavy a burden Darman had carried. When she tried to heave one of the gray packs into the cart, it nearly wrenched her shoulder from the socket, so she decided to enlist a little assistance from the Force. She hadn't expected it to be so heavy. She wasn't the only one with deceptive physical strength.

"This is all weapons?" she asked.

"Pretty much."

"Not enough to take a hundred droids, though."

"Depends how you use it," Darman said.

Etain wondered if he looked more conspicuous out of his sinister gray armor than in it. The armor had made him look much bigger, but even without it he was so solidly built that it was obvious he'd spent his life training for strength, eating adequate protein. Subsistence farmers didn't have that distinctive slope from neck to shoulder formed by overdeveloped trapezius muscles. Even the youngsters bore the marks of constant exposure to the elements; Darman simply looked strikingly healthy and unburned by the sun. He didn't even have callused hands.

And then there was that ramrod parade-ground posture. He looked exactly like the elite soldier he was. He would never pass for a local. Etain hoped the farmers would be more terrified of him than they were of Hokan.

The night horizon was amber like the urban skies of Coruscant, but it was flame, not the light of a million lamps, that caused the reflection from the clouds. It looked like rain might follow; they could cover the cart with a tarpaulin and not cause any curiosity. Layers of barq stalk, sacks of barq grain, and strips of dried kushayan buried Darman's "gear," as he kept calling it. His language swung from slang and generality to highly educated subbtlety, from *gear*—his catchall noun for any artifact—to DC-17s and DC-15s and a whole slew of numbers and acronyms that left Etain befuddled.

"Look at that," Darman said, assessing the skyline. "That flame front must be four klicks, at least."

"That's a million or more credits' worth of barq going up in smoke. The farmers are going to be furious. The Neimoidians are going to be even angrier."

"So will Birhan," Jinart said. "That's a fair whack of his barq you're using for camouflage, girl. Get going." The Gurlanin took Darman's datapad and inserted a mem-stick. "These are all the relatively safe homes I could chart. Don't advertise your identity, either of you. Even if the master of the house you call on knows who you are, do him the favor of not compromising him by admitting it."

Etain had covered her distinctive Jedi cloak with an Imbraani ankle-length tunic. Jinart indicated her hair. "And that," she said.

"The braid, too?"

"Unless you want to advertise what you are."

Etain hesitated. She had once heard someone say they could never remove their betrothal ring, not until they died. Her Padawan's braid felt equally permanent, as if her soul was woven in with it, and that removing it after so long— even temporarily—would rend the fabric of the universe and underscore her belief that she was not Jedi material. But it had to be done. She unfastened the single thin braid and combed the strands of wavy hair loose with her fingers.

She felt less like a Jedi than ever, and not even remotely close to a commander.

"I imagine you never thought a Jedi commander would run away from a fight," she said to Darman as they made their carefully unhurried way up the track.

"Not running away," Darman said. "This is E and E. Escape and evasion."

"Sounds like running to me."

"Tactical withdrawal to regroup."

"You're a very positive man." The child was almost completely absent now. She could mainly sense focus and purpose. He shamed her without intention. "I'm sorry that I lost my composure earlier."

"Only in private. Not under fire, Commander."

"I said not to call me that."

"Where we can be overheard, I'll obey your order." He paused. "Everyone loses it now and then."

"I'm not supposed to."

"If you don't crack sometimes, how do you know how far you can go?"

It was a good point. For some reason he was far more reassuring than Master Fulier had ever been. Fulier, when not getting caught up in putting the galaxy right, was all effortless brilliance. Darman was expert at his craft, too, but there was a sense of hard-won skill, and there was no randomness or mystery to that.

She liked him for being so pragmatic. It crossed her mind that she might be saving clone soldiers from death by biological agent so they could die from blaster and cannon round. It was a horrible thought.

She didn't like having to kill, not even by another's actions. It was going to make life as a commander exceptionally hard.

The droids advanced along the edge of the wood with flamethrowers borrowed from the same farmer whose fields they were burning. Ghez Hokan and his lieutenants Cuvin and Hurati stood in the path of the blaze, staring back at it from three hundred meters.

"We'll have to burn a great deal of land to deny all cover to the enemy, sir," Cuvin said.

"That isn't the point," Hurati said. "This is as much to create the impression of protecting the facility as it is to flush out troops."

"Correct," Hokan said. "There's no point alienating the natives, and I can't afford to compensate them all for lost production. This is sufficient. We'll use droids on the remaining boundaries."

Cuvin seemed undeterred. "May I suggest we use hunting strills? We could bring in a pack with their handlers in two days. The Trade Federation won't welcome the disruption to the barq harvest, and a shortage of the delicacy will be noticed by some very influential people."

"I don't care," Hokan said. "The same influential people will be even more inconvenienced by the arrival of millions of Republic clones on their homeworlds."

Hokan was in full Mandalorian battle armor now, not so much for protection as to convey a message to his officers. Sometimes he had to indulge in a little theater. He knew that the glow of the flames illuminating his traditional warrior's armor made a fine spectacle, calculated to impress and overawe. He was at war. He didn't have to prostitute his martial skills as an assassin or bodyguard for weak and wealthy cowards any longer.

Cuvin was right about the strills, though. It didn't mean he wouldn't have to deal with his dissent, but finding the Republic troops wouldn't be easy.

"How many do you estimate now, Hurati?" he asked.

Hurati flicked a holochart into life and a fly-through image shimmered in the dark. "Vessel downed *here,* confirmed Republic R5 military droid." He pointed. "Remains of two Weequay militia found here, here, and here—but gdans had dismembered and dragged the cadavers over a five-klick range, so the exact location of the kill is estimated. The airspeeder was brought down *here.* The speeder circuitry was found dismantled *here,* but as it was at the entrance to gdan burrows, there's no telling where they might have found it to start with. The engagement with the droid patrol was *here,* because we deployed the patrol based on that finding."

"That's pretty much all in a five-klick corridor spanning forty klicks. Looks obvious to me that they're heading for Teklet, probably to take the port before targeting the facility."

"It would look that way, sir."

"Numbers?"

"I would have said no more than ten, sir. We have reports from farmers who've found evidence of movement across their land. They're very protective of their crops, so they notice these subtle signs—unlike droids, sir."

"And what does that suggest, then?"

"Multiple tracks crossing an area forty klicks by thirty klicks, sir. Expertly done, too—the locals thought it might be wildlife, but these tracks are not random. I'd say we're being decoyed."

Ten troops. Ten—pathfinders, special forces, saboteurs? Were they preparing the ground for more troops, or were they tasked to complete the mission on their own? Hokan wished he had a few Mandalorian mercenaries, not droids and career officers. He kept his concern well hidden behind his full-face helmet. He also wished he had more airspeeders; he'd never needed more than one to police farms, and it would take days to have any shipped to Qiilura. "Farmers can be pretty cooperative, can't they?"

"Remarkably so, ever since that one found the circuitry, sir."

Hokan turned and started walking back toward the research facility that was now empty but lavishly and conspicuously guarded. He beckoned Hurati to follow him. Cuvin started to follow, too, but Hokan held up his hand to motion him to stay put.

"Lieutenant," he said quietly. "Any sign of my former employee, Guta-Nay?"

"Not yet, sir. Patrols have been briefed."

"Good, and keep an eye on Cuvin for me, won't you? I don't think he's going to make captain."

Hurati paused, but briefly. "Understood, sir."

It was amazing what the unspoken promise of an extra rank insignia could do. Hokan wondered what had happened to the code of conduct.

So there were perhaps ten commandos operating in the region. Hunting them down would be enormously time-consuming. Barring luck, Hokan would never catch them, not with droids and these young academy theorists. Sooner or later, the enemy would need to resupply; sooner or later, they would show themselves.

The Republic was playing decoy games with him, and he with them. It was looking better all the time. They didn't appear to be adopting their usual tactic of landing infantry in force. It was a game of wits, and if need arose he could sit tight and force the Republic to come to him.

If he wanted to bring the Republic close enough to shoot, then he might need an even more compelling bait.

Dr. Uthan would understand. She was a pragmatic woman.

Fi was getting edgy. It wasn't like him. Niner had only known him a matter of days, but you made quick judgments on small detail if you were a clone commando, especially among your own.

He didn't sleep when Niner relieved him on watch, and after fifteen minutes Fi came forward to the observation position and settled down beside him. The fires seemed to have stopped; the glow was still visible, but it was static. It had probably reached one of the streams and was burning itself out.

"They know we're here anyway," Fi said. Niner needed no telepathy to know he was worrying about Darman. "We could try the comlink at longer range."

"They'd get a fix on positions."

"They'd have to get lucky."

"And we only have to be unlucky once."

"Okay. Sorry, Sarge."

He lapsed back into silence. Niner adjusted his infrared filter to remove the distracting light of the fire. Suddenly, it was abnormally silent, and that meant the gdans had stopped their incessant prowling, which was *not good*.

Niner looked down his rifle scope one-handed to get a narrower focus on the bushes in front of him. As he panned across 180 degrees, he caught sight of little paired reflections, the alert eyes of gdans huddled in uncharacteristic stillness to avoid something.

Movement. His scope flashed blue in one quadrant, warning him. Maybe whatever it was could see infrared. He killed the targeting, switching to image intensification and the Mark One Ear'ole, as Skirata called it. *You got eyes and ears, son, good ones. Don't rely on the tech too much.* Something was coming, something slow, stealthy, smaller than a man, more sly than a droid.

Niner put his hand on Fi's shoulder—*Stay down*—not daring to speak, even on comlink.

It was ten meters away, coming straight at them, making no attempt to stalk. Maybe it didn't know what they were. It was going to get a surprise, then.

Niner flicked on his tactical spot-lamp, and the blinding beam caught a shining black shape. He cut the beam immediately, muscles relaxing. The creature was so flat to the ground now that it looked as if it were flowing water. It was only when it was right in front of them that it sat up and became Valaqil.

"I thought I'd let you see me coming, given your armaments," said a voice that wasn't Valaqil's but was equally liquid and hypnotic. "I make it a rule never to startle a humanoid with a rifle."

"Just as well that we've seen a Gurlanin before," Fi said, and touched his glove to his helmet politely.

"I didn't seem to surprise your colleague, either. I've come to brief you. I'm Jinart. Please don't call me *ma'am* every two seconds like Darman does."

Niner wanted to ask a hundred questions about Darman, but the Gurlanin had used the present tense and so he was *alive*. Niner was glad he had his helmet in place. Displays of emotion weren't professional, not to outsiders, anyway.

"You're heading for the wrong target," Jinart said. "You're on a course for the Separatist base. Normally you'd be knocking on the door of a barracks with a hundred droids inside, but they've moved half of them to defend the research facility and patrol the area. Neither Uthan nor her nanovirus is at the actual facility any longer."

"So it's all going just great," Fi said cheerfully.

"Your targets are at a villa just outside Imbraani, despite what evidence you might see of the facility being defended. It's a trap."

"What's Darman doing?" Niner asked.

"He has your special ordnance and detailed plans of your targets. I've sent him into hiding with the Jedi."

"General Fulier? We thought—"

"You thought right. He's dead. The Jedi is his Padawan, Tur-Mukan. Don't get your hopes up. She isn't commander material—not yet, perhaps never. For the time being, this is still your war."

"We weren't planning on a frontal assault, not without infantry," Niner said. "Now that we've lost the advantage of surprise, we're going to have to get it back again."

"You do have one element—Ghez Hokan has no accurate idea how few of you there are. I've made sure there are many, many obvious signs of movement through the woods and fields."

"You've been busy."

"I can do a good impersonation of a small army, or at least its movement." Jinart glanced at Atin and Fi as if checking them. Maybe she was working out how she would mimic the form of a commando. "Not thinking of shooting and eating any merlies, are you?"

"Why?"

"That armor isn't looking such a tight fit on you as it should."

Fi nodded. "She's right. Expending about thirty percent more calories than planned, Sarge. They didn't calculate for us carrying gear overland."

"You'll exhaust your rations soon," Jinart said. "Merlies are delicious. Just *never* shoot one, please. If necessary, I could hunt them and leave them for you."

"Why?"

"The one you shoot might be me."

It was one more angle they hadn't covered on exercises. Not even Kal Skirata had dealt with Gurlanins, it seemed, or if he had he hadn't mentioned it. Niner liked them. He wondered what world they came from. It was bound to be a fascinating one.

"Where will you head now?" Jinart asked. "I need to let Darman know where you are."

"I'd have said RV Gamma, but that's going the wrong way, from what you've told us."

"I can give you the location of a suitable area nearer Imbraani, and when I return to Darman I will give him the same coordinates."

Atin cut in. "They mine gems here, right?"

"Zeka quartz and various green silicates, mainly, yes."

"Picks and shovels or mechanized?"

"Mechanized."

"They'll have explosives for blasting, then. And remote detonators with nice, safe, long-range settings."

Gurlanins chuckled just like a human. She might have been amused. On the other hand, she might have been thinking Atin was a madman. But Niner liked the direction that Atin's inventive mind was taking.

"Get your holocharts," Jinart said. "Let me give you a virtual guide to the gem industry of the Imbraani region."

10

A thin, cold drizzle started falling almost as soon as the sun came up. It felt like Kamino; it felt like home, and that was at once both reassuring and unpleasant.

The moisture beaded on Darman's cloak, and he shook it off. Merlie wool was full of natural oils that made it feel unpleasantly clammy next to the skin. He longed to get back into the black bodysuit, and not only because of its ballistic properties.

Etain was pushing the rear of the cart. Darman was pulling it, walking between its twin shafts. There were times on the rutted track when she had the worst of it, but—as she kept telling him—Jedi could summon the Force.

"I could help," he said.

"I can manage." Her voice sounded like she was straining it through her teeth. "If this is lightweight gear, I'd rather not see the regular variety."

"I meant I could help with martial skills. If you want to train with your lightsaber."

"I'd probably end up slicing off something you'd miss later."

No, she wasn't what he was expecting at all. They walked on, trying hard to look downtrodden and rural, which wasn't so much of a challenge when you were hungry, wet, and tired. The dirt road was deserted: at this time of year there should have been visible activity at first light. Ahead of them was the first safe house, a single-story hut topped by a mixture of straw thatch and rusting metal plates.

"I'll knock," Etain said. "They'll probably run for their lives if they see you first."

Darman took it as a sensible observation rather than an insult. He pulled his cloak up across his mouth and pushed the cart out of sight behind the hut, looking around slowly and carefully as if he were casually taking in the countryside. There were no windows at the rear, just a simple door and a well-worn path in the grass leading to a pit with an interesting aroma and a plank across it. It wasn't an ideal location for an ambush, but he wasn't taking chances. Stopping in the open like this made you vulnerable.

He didn't like it at all. He wished he could feign invisibility like Sergeant Skirata, a short, wiry, nondescript little man who could pass completely unnoticed, until he decided to stop and fight. And Skirata could fight in a lot of ways that weren't in the training manual. Darman recalled all of them.

He pressed his elbow into his side to reassure himself that his rifle was within easy reach. Then he slipped his hand under his cloak and felt for one of the probes in his belt.

When he reached the front again, Etain was still rapping on the doorpost. There was no response. She stood back and seemed to be looking at the door as if willing it to open.

"They're gone," she said. "I can't sense anyone."

Darman straightened up and walked casually toward the rear of the house. "Let me check the regular way."

He beckoned her to follow. Once around the back, he took a probe and slid the flat sensor strip carefully under the gap beneath the back door. The readout on the section that he was holding said there were no traces of explosive or pathogen. If the place was booby-trapped, it would be very low tech. It was time for a hands-on check. He pressed on the door with his left hand, rifle in his right.

"It's empty," Etain whispered.

"Can you sense a tripwire that'll send a row of metal spikes swinging into you?" he asked.

"Point taken."

The door swung slowly open. Nothing. Darman took a remote from his belt and sent it inside, picking up low-light images from the interior. There was no movement. The room appeared clear. He let the door swing back, recalled the remote, and stood with his back to the entrance for one final check around him.

"I go in, look again, then you follow me if you hear me say *in, in, in,* okay?" he said, almost under his breath. He didn't meet her eyes. "Lightsaber ready, too."

As soon as he was inside, he pulled his rifle, stood hard up in the corner, and scanned the room. *Clear.* So clear, in fact, that last night's meal was still half eaten on the table. There was a single door that didn't appear to open to the exterior. A cupboard, a closet—maybe a threat. He trained his rifle on it.

"In, in, in," Darman said. Etain slipped through and he gestured her to the corner opposite, then pointed: *Me, that door; you, back door.* Etain nodded and drew her lightsaber. He walked up to the closet and tried to raise the latch, but it didn't open, so he took two steps back and put his boot to it, hard.

They didn't build well around here. The door splintered and hung on one rusted hinge. Behind it was a storeroom. It made sense now: in a poor country, you locked away your food supply.

"They left in a hurry," Darman said.

"Are you wearing your armored boots?" Etain said.

"I wouldn't be kicking down a door without them." He'd covered them in tightly wound sacking. "No boots, no soldier. As true as it ever was." He stepped through the gap into the store and studied the shelves. "You're just learning the first step in clearing a house."

"What's that?" Etain reached past him for a metal container marked GAVVY-MEAL.

"Who's watching the door? Who's watching our gear?"

"Sorry."

"No problem. I expect it never occurs to you when you have Jedi senses to rely on." There: he hadn't even tried to call her *ma'am* this time. "If we knew why the occupants left in such a hurry, this might have made a decent place to lay up. But we don't. So let's grab some supplies and move on."

He took dried fruit and something that looked like cured leathery meat, making a mental note to test all of it with the toxin strip in his medpac. It was too kind of the locals to leave all this. There was, of course, every chance they had fled in terror from the same violence that he had witnessed looking down from his observation point just after he landed.

Etain was filling a couple of water bottles from a pump outside.

"I've got a filter for that," Darman said.

"Are you sure you weren't trained by Neimoidians?"

"You're in enemy territory."

She smiled sadly. "Not all soldiers wear uniforms."

She'd catch on. She *had* to. The thought that a Jedi might be unable to offer the leadership he had been promised was almost unbearable. His emotions didn't have names. But they were feelings that had memories embedded in them— finishing a fifty-kilometer run thirty-two seconds outside the permitted time, and being made to run it again; seeing a clone trooper fall on a beachhead landing exercise, weighed down by his pack and drowning, while no directing staff paused to help; a commando whose sniping score was only 95 percent, and whose whole batch disappeared from training and were never seen again.

They were all things that made his stomach sink. And each time it did, it never quite regained the same level as before.

"Are you all right?" Etain asked. "Is it your leg?"

"My leg's fine now, thank you," he said.

Darman wanted his trust back, and soon.

They resumed their path along the dirt track that was gradually liquefying into mud, the rain at their backs. By the time they got to the next farm the rain seemed to have set in for the day. Darman thought of his squad making their way through sodden countryside, perfectly dry in their sealed suits, and he smiled. At least this made it harder for anyone to track them.

A woman with a pinched expression like a gdan stared at them from the front step of the farmhouse. It was a grander building than the last one: not by much, but the walls were stone and there was a lean-to shelter along one side. Etain walked up to her. Darman waited, looking, aware of an outdoor refresher to the right that might contain a threat, keeping half an eye on a group of youngsters tinkering with a large machine on rollers.

They all looked so different. *Everyone was so different.*

After some conversation, Etain beckoned him and indicated the lean-to. So far, so good. Darman still didn't plan on relinquishing his ordnance. He reached into the barq for his helmet and detached the comlink, just in case Niner tried to contact him.

"Are you coming?" Etain asked.

"Just a moment." Darman took out a string of AP micromines and trailed them around the front of the house as far as the cable would stretch. He set them to run off a remote signal and tucked the transmitter section of the detonator in his belt. Etain watched him with an unspoken question, perfectly clear from her expression. "In case anyone gets any ideas," Darman said.

"You've played this game before," Etain said.

He certainly had. The first thing he checked when he entered the farmhouse, one hand against his rifle, was where the best observation point might be. It was a perforated airbrick that gave him a good view of the road. There was a large window in the far wall with a brown sacking sheet tied across it. Reassured—but only slightly—he sat down at the table that dominated the front room.

The family that took them in consisted of the thin gdan-faced woman, her sister, her even thinner husband, and six youngsters ranging from a small boy clutching a piece of grubby blanket to the nearly full-grown men working outside. They wouldn't give their names. They didn't want a *visit,* they said, as if a visit was much more than it seemed.

Darman was riveted. These people were humans like him; yet they were all different. But still they had features that looked similar—not the same, but similar—to others in the group. They were different sizes and different ages, too.

He had seen diversity in training manuals. He knew what different species looked like. But the images always came to mind with data about weapons carried and where to aim a shot for maximum stopping power. This was the first time in his life that he had been in close contact with diverse humans who were in the majority.

To them, perhaps, he also looked unique.

They sat around the rough wooden table. Darman tried not to speculate on what the stains in the wood might be, because they looked like blood. Etain nudged him. "They cut up the merlie carcasses here," she whispered, and he wondered if she could read his mind.

He tested the bread and soup placed in front of him for toxins. Satisfied that it was safe, he dug in. After a while he was aware that the woman and the small boy were staring at him. When he looked up, the child fled.

"He doesn't like soldiers much," the woman said. "Is the Republic coming to help us?"

"I can't answer that, ma'am," Darman said. He meant that he would never discuss operational matters; it was an automatic response under interrogation. *Never just say yes, never just say no, and give no information except your ID number.* Etain answered for him, which was her prerogative as a commander.

"Do you want the Republic's help?" she asked.

"You any better than the Neimies?"

"I'd like to think so."

The table fell silent again. Darman finished the soup. Politics was nothing to do with him; he was more interested in filling up on something that had flavor and texture. If all went according to plan, in a few weeks he'd be far from here and on another mission, and if it didn't, he'd be dead. The future of Qiilura was genuinely of no relevance to him.

The woman kept refilling his bowl with soup until he slowed up and eventually couldn't manage any more. It was the first hot food he'd had in days, and he felt good; little perks like that boosted morale. Etain didn't seem so enthusiastic about it. She was moving each chunk cautiously around with her spoon, as if the liquid contained mines.

"You need to keep your strength up," he said.

"I know."

"You can have my bread."

"Thanks."

It was so quiet in the room that Darman could hear the individual rhythm of everyone's chewing, and the faint scrape of utensils against bowls. He could hear the distant, muffled sound of merlies nearby, an intermittent gargling noise. But he didn't hear something that Etain suddenly did.

She sat bolt upright and turned her head to one side, eyes unfocused.

"Someone's coming, and it's not Jinart," she hissed.

Darman flung off his cloak and pulled his rifle. The woman and her relatives jumped up from the table so fast that it tipped despite its weight, sending bowls tumbling to the floor. Etain drew her lightsaber, and it shimmered into life. They both watched the entrance; the family scrambled through the back door, the woman pausing to grab a large metal bowl and a bag of meal from a sideboard.

Darman doused the lamps and peered out through a hole in the air-brick. Without his visor, he was completely dependent on his Deece for long-distance vision. He couldn't see anything. He held his breath and listened hard.

Etain moved toward him, gesturing at the far wall, indicating *seven*—a whole hand then two fingers.

"Where?" he whispered.

She was marking something on the dirt floor. He watched

her finger draw an outline of the four walls and then stab a number of dots outside them, most around the one she'd been pointing to, and one dot near the front door.

She put her lips so close to his ear it made him jump. "Six there, one here." It was a breath, barely audible.

Darman indicated the far wall and pointed to himself. Etain gestured to the door: *Me?* He nodded. He gestured *one, two, three* quickly with his fingers and gave her a thumbs-up: *I'll count to three.* She nodded.

Whoever was outside hadn't knocked. It didn't bode well.

He clipped the grenade attachment to his rifle and aimed at the far side. Etain stood at the door, lightsaber held above her head for a downward stroke.

Darman hoped her aggression would triumph over her self-doubt.

He gestured with his left hand, rifle balanced in his right. *One, two—*

Three. He fired one grenade. It smashed through the sack-covered window and blew a hole in the wall just as he was firing the second. The blast kicked him backward, and the front door burst open as Etain brought her lightsaber down in a brilliant blue arc.

Darman switched his rifle to blast setting and swung his sight on the figure, but it was an Umbaran and it was dead, sliced through from clavicle to sternum.

"Two," Etain said, indicating the window, or at least where it had been seconds earlier. Darman sprang forward across the room, dodging the table and firing as he came to the hole smashed in the wall. When he stumbled through the gap there were two Trandoshans coming toward him with blasters, faces that seemed all scales and lumps, wet mouths gaping. He opened fire; one return shot seared his left shoulder. Then there was nothing but numb silence for a few moments, followed by the gradual awareness that someone was screaming in agony outside.

But it wasn't him, and it wasn't Etain. That was all that mattered. He picked his way across the room, conscious of the growing pain in his shoulder. It would have to wait.

"It's all clear," Etain said. Her voice was shaking. "Except for that man . . ."

"Forget him," Darman said. He couldn't, of course: the soldier was making too much noise. The screams would attract attention. "Load up. We're going."

Despite Etain's assurance that there were no more waiting outside, Darman edged out the door and kept his back to the wall all the way around the exterior of the farmhouse. The wounded soldier was an Umbaran. Darman didn't even check how badly hurt he might be before he shot him cleanly in the head. There was nothing else he could do, and the mission came first.

He wondered if Jedi could sense droids as well. He'd have to ask Etain later. He'd been told Jedi could do extraordinary things, but it was one thing to know it, and another entirely to *see* it in action. It had probably saved their lives.

"What was that?" she asked when he returned to the lean-to. She already had the extra pack slung on her back, and he realized she'd actually moved the micromines even though they were still live. Darman, swallowing anxiety, disabled the detonator and added it to the list of things he needed to teach her.

"Finishing the job," he said, and pulled on his bodysuit section by section. She looked away.

"You killed him."

"Yes."

"He was lying wounded?"

"I'm not a medic."

"Oh, Darman . . ."

"Ma'am, this is a war. People try to kill you. You try to kill them first. There are no second chances. Everything else you need to know about warfare is an amplification of that." She was horrified, and he really wished he hadn't upset her. Had they given her a lethal lightsaber and not taught her what it really meant to draw one? "I'm sorry. He was in a bad way, anyway."

Death seemed to shock her. "I killed that Umbaran."

"That's the idea, ma'am. Nicely done, too."

She didn't say anything else. She watched him attach the

armor plates, and when he finally replaced his helmet he knew he didn't care how conspicuous he looked in it, because he wasn't going to take it off again in a hurry. He needed that edge.

"No more safe houses," Darman said. "There's no such thing."

Etain followed him into the woodland at the back of the house, but she was preoccupied. "I've never killed anyone before," she said.

"You did fine," Darman told her. His shoulder was throbbing, gnawing into his concentration. "A *clean* job."

"It's still not something I would care to repeat."

"Jedi are trained to fight, aren't they?"

"Yes, but we never killed anyone in training."

Darman shrugged and it hurt. "We did."

He hoped she got over it fast. No, it wasn't enjoyable, killing: but it had to be done. And killing with lightsaber or blaster was relatively clean. He wondered how she'd handle having to stick a blade in someone and see what ran out. She was a Jedi, and with any luck she'd never have to.

"Them or us," he said.

"You're in pain."

"Nothing major. I'll use the bacta when we reach the RV."

"I suppose they turned us in."

"The farmers? Yeah, that's civilians for you."

Etain made a noncommittal grunt and followed silently behind him. They moved deeper into the woods, and Darman calculated how many rounds he'd expended. If he kept engaging targets at this rate, he'd be down to his sidearm by nightfall.

"It's amazing how you can sense people," Darman said. "Can you detect droids, too?"

"Not especially," she said. "Usually just living beings. Maybe I can—"

A faint whine made Darman turn in time to see a blue bolt of light streaking toward him from behind. It struck a tree a few meters ahead, splitting it like kindling in a puff of vapor.

"Obviously not," Etain said.

It was going to be another long, hard day.

A warning siren sounded: three long blasts, repeated twice. Then the peaceful fields northwest of Imbraani shook with a massive explosion, and terrified merlies bolted for the cover of the hedgerows.

"Blasting today, then," Fi said. "Lovely day for it."

Niner couldn't see anything but droids—industrial droids—moving around the quarry. He ran his glove across his visor to clear the droplets of rain and tried several binoc magnifications, flicking between settings with eye movements. But if there were organic workers around, he couldn't see any.

The quarry was a massive and startling gouge in the landscape, an amphitheater with stepped sides that allowed droid excavators to dig out rock for processing. The depression sloped gently at one side; it was a towering cliff on the other. A small site office with alloy-plated walls and no windows sat beside a wide track at the top of the slope. Apart from the steady procession of droids laden with raw rock for the screening plant, the area was deserted. But someone—something—was controlling the detonations. They had to be in the building. And structures with solid alloy walls like that tended to have interesting contents.

The all-clear siren sounded. The droids moved in to scoop up the loose rock, sending spray and mud flying as they rumbled up the slopes.

"Okay, let's see what we can liberate from the hut," Niner said. "Atin, with me. Fi, stay here and cover."

They darted out of the trees and across a hundred meters of open land to the edge of the quarry, dodging between giant droids that took no notice of them. One droid, its wheels as high as Niner was tall, swung its bucket scoop unexpectedly and struck his shoulder plate a glancing blow. He stumbled and Atin caught his arm, steadying him. They paused, waiting for the next droid to return up the slope, then jogged alongside it until level with the site building.

They were now exposed, pressed close to the front wall.

The building was only ten meters wide. Atin knelt at the door and studied the single lock.

"Pretty insubstantial if this is where they store the explosives," he said.

"Let's take a look."

Atin stood up slowly and placed a scope on the door to listen for movement. He shook his head at Niner. Then he slid a flimsi-thin flat endoscope around the jamb, working it back and forth, slowly and carefully. "Now that's a tight fit," he said. "Can't get it in."

"We could always just walk in there."

"Remember, we're probably heading into a store full of explosives. If I could get a probe through it could at least get a sniff of the air and test for chemicals."

"Okay, let's walk in *carefully,* then."

There was no handle. Niner stood to the hinge side, Deece in one hand, and pressed silently on the single plate that made up the door. It didn't yield.

Atin nodded. He took out the handheld ram, ten kilos that had seemed like dead, useless weight in their packs until now. He squared it up to the lock.

Niner raised one finger. "Three . . . two . . ."

It applied a force of two metric tons.

"Go."

The door fell open, and they both leapt back as a stream of blasterfire shot out. It stopped suddenly. They squatted on either side of the entrance. Usually this was simple: if someone inside didn't want to leave, a grenade coaxed them out, one way or another. But with a high chance of explosives being inside, that method was a little too emphatic. Niner shook his head.

Atin moved the endoscope carefully, getting a glimpse of the building's interior. Then he edged the probe into the doorway, drawing another stream of blasterfire.

"Two moving around," he said. "Light's out. But the probe got a sniff of explosives."

"Spot-lamp and rush them, then?"

Atin shook his head. He took out a grenade and locked it

in the safety position. "How nervous would you be if you were sitting on enough stuff to put this quarry into orbit?"

"Drink-spilling nervous, I'd say."

"Yeah." Atin hefted the grenade a few times. "That's what I thought."

He bowled the disabled grenade into the doorway and jerked back. Three seconds later, two Weequays rushed out. Niner and Atin fired simultaneously; one Weequay dropped instantly, and the other's momentum carried him on a few meters farther, until he fell in the path at the top of the ramp. The quarry droids trundled on, oblivious. If the shot hadn't killed him, the advancing droid did.

"Sarge, you need some help down there?"

Niner motioned Atin inside. "No, Fi, we're set here. Keep an eye out in case we get company."

The building reeked of cooking and unwashed Weequay. A small droid, lights blinking on standby and caked in dried mud, stood by a console. The rest of the space—three rooms— was taken up by explosives, detonators, and various spare parts and stenciled crates.

"There's your demolitions man," Atin said, tapping the droid on its head, and retrieved his grenade. He wiped it with his glove and put it back in his belt pack.

"I'd rather have Darman," Niner said. He studied the inert droid, which seemed to be waiting for the dislodged rock to be cleared. It jerked suddenly into life, made its way toward a crate of explosives, opened the safety lid, and took out several tubes. Then it turned toward the room where the detonators were kept. Niner reached out and opened its control panel to deactivate it. "Take some time off, friend," he said. "Blasting's over for the day."

It didn't appear that the Weequay had been employed here. The droid sorted all the charges and oversaw the blasting. On an upturned crate were the remains of a meal, eaten off makeshift plates fashioned from box lids. It looked like the Weequays had been hiding out here, and Niner was pretty sure he knew who they had been avoiding.

Atin checked the various charges and detonators, select-

ing what appeared to take his fancy and piling it in a clear
space on the muddy floor. He was a connoisseur of technology, especially things with complex circuitry. "Lovely," he
said, with genuine satisfaction. "Some dets here that you
can set off from fifty klicks. That's what we need. A bit of a
pyrotechnics show."

"Can we carry as much as we need?"

"Oh, there's some beauties here. Darman would think they
were pretty basic, but they're going to work fine as a diver-
sion. Absolute *beauts*." Atin held up spheres about the size
of a scoopball. "Now this baby—"

Crash.

Something fell to the floor in one of the rooms off the
main one. Atin held his rifle on the doorway and Niner drew
his sidearm. He was edging toward the door when a sudden
voice almost made him squeeze the trigger.

"Ap-xmai keepuna!" The voice was shaking, and judging
by the accent it probably belonged to a Weequay. "Don't kill!
I help you!"

"Out. *Now.*" Projected from his helmet, Atin's voice was
intimidating enough without a rifle to back it up. A Weequay
stumbled out from behind a stack of crates and sank to his
knees, hands held up. Atin pushed him down flat with his
boot, Deece aimed at his head. "Arms behind your back and
don't even breathe. Got it?"

The Weequay appeared to have got it very quickly. He
froze and let Niner cuff his wrists with a length of wire.
Niner did a sweep of the rooms again, worried that if they'd
missed one target they might have missed more. But it was
clear. He walked back and squatted down by the Weequay's
head.

"We don't need a prisoner slowing us down," he said.
"Give me a good reason why I shouldn't kill you."

"Please, I know Hokan."

"I'll bet you know him pretty well if you were hiding out
here. What's your name?"

"Guta-Nay. I were *right-hand man*."

"Not anymore, though, eh?"

"I know places."

"Yeah, we know places, too."

"I got key codes."

"We've got ordnance."

"I got codes to Teklet ground station."

"You wouldn't be messing around, would you, Guta-Nay? I don't have time for that."

"Hokan kill me. You take me with you? You Republic guys nice, you *gentlemen*."

"Steady, Guta-Nay. All those syllables might burn you out."

Niner looked at Atin. He shrugged.

"He'll slow us down, Sarge."

"Then we either leave him here or kill him."

The conversation wasn't designed to scare Guta-Nay, but it had that effect anyway. It was a genuine problem: Niner was reluctant to drag a prisoner around with them, and there was no guarantee the Weequay wouldn't try to buy back favor from Hokan with intelligence on their strength and movements. He was an unwelcome dilemma. Atin clicked his Deece, and it started to power up.

"I get you Neimie boss, too!"

"We definitely don't need him."

"Neimie's really mad at Hokan. He put droids in his nice shiny villa. Floors messed up."

Guta-Nay's breathing rasped in the silence of the room. Niner weighed the extra baggage against the prospect of some edge in gaining access to Uthan.

"Where's Uthan now?"

"Still in villa. Nowhere else to hide."

"You know a lot about Hokan, don't you?"

"Everything." Guta-Nay was all submission. *"Too much."*

"Okay," Niner said. "You got a reprieve."

Atin waited a couple of seconds before powering down his rifle. He seemed doubtful. Niner couldn't see his expression, but he heard the characteristic slight exhalation that was Atin's silent *oh-terrific*.

"He'll leave a trail a worrt could follow."

"Ideas?"

"Yeah." Atin leaned over Guta-Nay, and the Weequay turned his head slightly, eyes wide with terror. He seemed more terrified by the helmet than the gun. "Where do the droids take the raw rock?"

"Big place south of Teklet."

"How far south?"

"Five klick maybe."

Atin straightened up and indicated with a pointed finger that he was going outside. "Technical solution. Wait one."

His predilection for gadgets was becoming a blessing. Niner was tempted to take back the unkind thoughts he'd had about the man's training sergeant. He followed him outside. Atin jogged alongside one of the excavation droids, matching its pace before jumping up scrambling onto its flatbed. The machine rumbled inexorably up the slope as if nothing was going to divert it from its progress to the screening plant. Then it stopped and swung around, narrowly missing the droid bringing up its rear. It paused a couple of meters from Niner; Atin, kneeling on the flatbed, held up two cables.

"You can't get it to do tricks," he said. "But you can start, steer, and stop it now."

"Brain bypass, eh?"

"I've seen a few people with those . . ."

"So we ride it into town?"

"How else are we going to move all this explosive?"

They couldn't pass up the chance. Niner had plans for the charges, places to lay them all around the Imbraani countryside. They also had a temptingly neat window of opportunity to take out the ground station at Teklet, and rendering Hokan's troops deaf to what was happening around them would double their chances of pulling off the mission. It meant they could use their own long-range comlinks at last.

"Tell you what," Niner said. "I'll take this one to Teklet. You hotwire another and take Fi and our friend as far back down the road to Imbraani as you can get with as much as you can carry." He took out his datapad and checked the chart. "Lay up *here* where Jinart suggested, with the droid if you can, without it if you can't."

A bulldozer droid on a steady path to the screening plant would attract no attention. It just had to overshoot by a few kilometers. It would be dusk soon, and darkness was their best asset when it came to moving around.

Niner hauled Guta-Nay out of the building. "Is the ground station defended in any way?"

Guta-Nay had his head lowered, looking up from under his brows as if blows to the head normally accompanied questions. "Just fence to stop merlies and thieving. Only farmers around, and they scared anyway."

"If you're lying to me, I'll see that you get back to Ghez Hokan alive. Okay?"

"Okay. Truth, I swear."

Niner summoned Fi from his cover position, and they loaded two droids. One carried enough explosives to reduce the ground station to powder several times over, and the other took everything they could lay their hands on, except for some detonators and explosives to keep the blasting droid busy for a few more hours. There was no point letting the quarry's silence advertise the fact that they had liberated some ordnance. It would spoil the whole surprise.

They loaded Guta-Nay last, bundling him into the huge bucket scoop with his arms still bound. He protested at being stuck on top of spheres of explosive.

"Don't worry," Atin said dismissively. "I've got all the dets here." He bounced a few detonators up and down in his palm; Guta-Nay flinched. "You'll be fine."

"Jinart's quite an asset," Fi said. He took off his helmet to drink from his bottle, and Guta-Nay made an incoherent noise.

"She could be right behind us now and we'd never know. I hope they stay on our side." Niner removed his helmet, too, and they shared the bottle before handing it to Atin for a last swig. "What's that Weequay whining about now?"

"Dunno," Atin said, and took his helmet off as well. He

paused, bottle in hand, and they all stood and stared at Guta-Nay, loaded in the scoop of the droid like cargo.

His mouth was slightly open and his eyes were darting from one commando to the next. He was making a slight *uh-uh-uh* sound, as if he was trying to scream but couldn't.

"It's Atin's face," Fi said. "Don't stand there being so ugly, man. You're scaring him."

Niner gave the Weequay a quick prod with his glove to shut him up.

"What's the matter?" he asked. "Haven't you ever seen commandos before?"

They were *here*.

The break that Ghez Hokan had been waiting for had come: a farmer had rushed to notify the authorities that Republic soldiers—one man, one woman, both very young—were at a house on the Imbraani–Teklet road.

Hokan studied the dripping foliage at the side of the farmhouse. The maze of footsteps in the mud and the crushed stalks were no different from those on any farm, and they were disappearing fast in the rain. Behind the ramshackle collection of sheds and stone walls, the land sloped away to the Braan River.

"It's a mess in there, sir," Hurati said. "One wall nearly blown out. All dead. And that was just two enemy commandos."

"One," Hokan said.

"One?"

"Only male clones in the front line. The other had to be a Jedi." He turned over the body of an Umbaran with his boot and shook his head. "That wound was made by a lightsaber. I know what a lightsaber wound looks like. Two people. I wouldn't even have that information if it hadn't been for informants. Do I have to rely on dung-caked *farmers* for intelligence? Do I? *Do I?*"

He regretted having to shout. But it seemed necessary. "Why can't anyone manage to *call it in* when they make an enemy contact? Think! Use your *di'kutla* heads, or I'll show you how to recognize a lightsaber wound the hard way." Two droids began lifting the Umbaran's body onto a speeder. "Leave that thing where it is. Get after your comrades and find me some enemy."

Hurati put his hand to the side of his head. "Droids have found something else in a house up the road, sir." His expression fell blank as he listened to his comlink. "Oh. *Oh.*" He turned to Hokan. "I think you should see this for yourself, sir."

Hurati didn't strike him as an officer that would waste his time. They mounted the speeder and worked their way back up the road to another small, dilapidated hovel set among the trees. Hokan followed Hurati into the farmhouse, where a couple of droids had illuminated the rooms with spot-lamps.

For some reason he would never fathom, the first aspect of the chaos that caught his eye was the soup tureen lying on its side on the filthy floor. It was only when he turned his head that he saw the bodies.

"Ah," Hokan said.

Soldiers used blasters. In a pinch, they would use knives or blunt objects. But he had never known anyone in uniform, not even his ragtag militia, who used *teeth*. The three adults were ripped and torn as if a large carnivore had attacked them. All had crush injuries to what was left of their throats. One woman had so little intact tissue in her neck that the head was bent over at almost ninety degrees. Hokan found himself staring.

"There are others outside in the shed," Hurati said.

Hokan had never considered himself easily disturbed, but this worried him. It was an act by something he didn't recognize and couldn't comprehend, beyond the scope of a sentient creature's simple revenge. It might have been coincidence, an animal attack on someone who happened to be an informer— but he couldn't think of any species on Qiilura that could or would bring down humans.

Hurati studied the bodies. "I didn't think killing civilians was the Republic's style."

"It's not," Hokan said. "And commandos wouldn't waste time on work that wouldn't aid their effort."

"Well, whoever killed them wasn't motivated by robbery."

Hurati picked up a large metal bowl from the floor, dusted it with his glove, and set it on a shelf. "This is probably our informer. I wouldn't count on much assistance from now on. Word will get around fast."

"You're certain there are no blaster wounds?" It might have been simple predation. He knew in his gut that it wasn't. But what had done this?

"None," Hurati said.

Hokan didn't like it at all. He beckoned Hurati to follow him and walked out briskly to summon two droids. "I want a ring around Imbraani. Pull all the droids back. I'd rather lose Teklet than risk Uthan's project."

"We could arrange for Doctor Uthan to be evacuated."

"Moving her and her entourage is going to be slow and conspicuous. We're better off defending a position than moving. I want half the droids blatantly visible at the facility and the other half around the villa—but discreetly, understand?"

There was a rattle of metal in the distance, and Hokan spun around to see droids swarming toward the riverbank.

"Have they found anything?"

Hurati pressed his hand to his head, listening to the comlink. "Two enemy sighted five klicks west of here, sir. The droids have engaged them."

"That's more like it," Hokan said. "I'd like at least one alive, preferably both if the girl's a Jedi."

He swung onto the speeder bike and motioned Hurati to sit up front and drive. The speeder zipped down the track heading west as Hurati confirmed coordinates with the droid patrol.

Hokan hoped the droids could manage an instruction like *take them alive*. He needed real troops for this, actual soldiers who could get into awkward places and see subtle things. He now had just thirty organic officers remaining and slightly under a hundred droids: ideal for a small set-piece battle, but next to useless for countering a commando force spread over terrain with plenty of cover.

They'd definitely have to come to him. Just this once, though, he'd humor them and join the pursuit.

11

*Owing to shortages, we regret to inform you that we have
been forced to increase the price of the new season's barq.
Shortages are due to local difficulties at source.
We will of course be giving preference to our most
favored regular customers.*
—Trade Federation notice to wholesalers

Darman had taken down quite a few tinnies on Geonosis,
and one thing he'd learned was that they were built for conventional infantry combat on nice, flat ground.

They weren't so clever on treacherous terrain—or without
an organic officer calling the shots.

He could see a group of trees a hundred meters away that
appeared to be skylined against nothing, and he hoped that
meant there might be an escarpment on the other side.
"Down there," he yelled to Etain, pointing. "Come on, and
get ready to *jump.*"

He'd almost forgotten the pain in his shoulder. He
clutched his rifle tight to his chest and sprinted for the tree
line. It took him ten seconds. The land sloped away below, all
thorn bushes and muddy soil right down to the river, broken
only by a natural back-sloping terrace that formed a small
gully. When he looked back, Etain was right behind him—
and he wasn't expecting her to be.

"Keep going!" she panted. "Don't keep looking back."

The blasterfire of the advancing droids was hitting branches
far too close for comfort. When they got to the edge he sim-

ply shoved her. She tried to right herself for a second before falling and rolling down the slope. He launched himself and rolled after her.

Darman had the protection of Katarn armor, but she didn't. When they came to a halt at the bottom of the gully, Etain was minus her outer cloak and plus a lot of scrapes. But she still had two sections of the E-Web cannon strapped to her share of the pack. She was clinging to them with grim determination.

"Next time, let me jump, will you?" she hissed. "I'm not completely helpless."

"Sorry." He checked his grenades. "I'm going to run short of ammo soon. I'm going to have to sacrifice some demolition ordnance."

"Tell me what you're planning."

"Bringing down the slope. With them on it." He paid out the line of micromines and scrambled a few meters back to string them horizontally between the trees. "Can you dig out some of the bore-bangs from that pack, please? Four should do it."

"What are they?"

"The long red sticks. Custom ordnance."

He heard her gasping her way up the slope behind him. When he turned his head she was gripping a bush with one hand, and holding out tubes of explosive in the other. Her fingers were covered in blood. He felt suddenly guilty, but he'd have to worry about that later.

"Thanks, ma'am," he said automatically. He balanced precariously, feeling the strain in his calves, and scrambled from bush to bush. He held each bore-bang perpendicular to the slope and twisted the end cap; the cylinder whirred and burrowed deep into the ground. He spaced them at five-meter intervals.

The chinking noise of droids on the move was getting closer, carrying on the still, damp air.

"Run!" Darman hissed.

Adrenaline was a wonderful thing to see in action. Etain grabbed her pack and bolted along the gully. Darman followed. Fifty meters—a hundred—two hundred. He paused to look back and saw one thin metal faceplate peer over the edge.

"Down!" he yelled, and squeezed the detonator in his palm.

A chunk of Qiilura blew apart at approximately eight thousand meters a second. Darman heard it and regretted not seeing it, but his head was shielded by his crossed arms and he was facedown in the dirt. It was pure instinct. He should have told Etain to cover her ears, although it wouldn't have helped her much. He should have made her run a lot sooner. He should have done a lot of things, like ignoring Jinart, and instead stayed on the mission.

He hadn't. He'd deal with it.

The noise of the blast overloaded his helmet for a few moments; there was a crackling silence. Then sound rushed back in again and he could feel clods of soil plopping against his back like heavy rain. When he got to his knees and turned around, there was a brand-new landscape to be seen. Trees jutted out from a sharp cliff of packed mud at bizarre angles. Some had intact branches, and others were snapped off and splintered. A single metallic leg protruded from the debris. Dirt was crumbling away from the face of the cliff like wet permacrete, and one tree was sliding slowly downward.

Darman looked around for Etain. She was a few meters ahead, kneeling back on her heels with her hand to one ear. When he drew closer he could see a thin trickle of blood running down the side of her face.

"Okay?" he asked.

Etain stared at his mouth. "I can't hear you," she said. She nursed her left ear, face contorted with pain.

"You've blown an eardrum. Take it easy." Stupid: she couldn't hear, and she couldn't see his lips with his helmet on. It was reflex reassurance. He was about to look for his bacta spray when she looked past him and pointed frantically. He turned. A droid was peering over the edge of the crater. It didn't appear to have seen them.

Darman didn't know how many there might be. He debated whether to deploy a remote, then wondered what he'd do if it showed him a hundred more tinnies coming. He wasn't sure where else to run. He estimated that he could hold them off for about an hour, and then they'd be out of everything except his vibroblade and Etain's lightsaber.

Then he heard a shout.

"Droids, report!"

Darman flattened himself into the side of the slope beside Etain. He could hear the voices, even if she couldn't. She stared up at the cliff and squeezed her eyes shut. For a moment Darman thought it was plain terror, and he wouldn't have blamed her. He'd blown away half a hillside and still hadn't stopped the droids. He was starting to feel a gnawing emptiness in his gut as well.

He concentrated on the voices, trying to guess numbers. Two humans, two *men*.

". . . they've booby-trapped . . ."

". . . can you see anything?"

". . . there's nothing else down there."

Darman held his breath.

"No, they're gone. Must have speeders."

"Droids, form up and return . . ."

The metal face pulled back and the clinking gait faded on the air, along with the whir of a speeder engine. Then there was silence, broken only by the occasional creak of a splintered tree being pulled slowly apart on its journey down the shattered slope.

Darman glanced at Etain. Her eyes were still shut, and she was breathing hard.

"I didn't think I could do that," she said.

"Do what?" She stared at him. He took off his helmet so she could see his mouth. "Do—what?" Darman mouthed, exaggerating the syllables. Her gaze fixed on his lips.

"Influence them. Both of them."

"Was that some sort of Jedi thought trick?"

She looked baffled. She obviously wasn't used to lip-reading. "It's sort of a Jedi thought trick," she said.

Darman stifled an urge to laugh. It wasn't funny at all.

She'd achieved something he found almost magical. At that point in the crisis, it was the best military option, better than letting loose with all the ordnance at his disposal, and something even Kal Skirata couldn't do.

They were alive. They could move on.

"Nice job, commander," he said. "Very nicely done." He touched his glove to his forehead and grinned. "Let's get ourselves sorted, eh?"

Darman took out his medpac and removed two sharps of painkiller and the bacta spray. He fixed his own shoulder first, jabbing the needle hard into the blue vein in the crook of his left elbow so that the drug dispersed faster. But it still made his eyes water when he sprayed the blaster burn.

Etain watched with grim resignation and swallowed visibly.

"Come on, Etain," Darman said. "Hold still."

He aimed the spray like a pistol into her left ear.

Darman had no idea that Jedi could curse fluently in Huttese, but he was learning more about them every minute. A *lot* more.

The excavation droid rattled down the road, managing to find every pothole and rut between Imbraani and the screening plant. Niner bounced each time, too. Buried in the scoop under a layer of loose rubble, with enough explosives to level everything within half a kilometer, he was . . . *anxious.*

The detonators were disabled. He kept checking that.

Now that night had fallen and the rain stopped, he could ease himself into a position where he could see ahead. Blue navigation lights picked out the droid's front fender, and an amber hazard light whirled on its canopy, illuminating the trees on either side of the track. It was a lumbering thing that wouldn't get out of anyone's way. Behind it, a convoy of identical droids followed. They were an intimidating procession.

Even the column of tinnies marching toward Niner moved to one side of the road.

He picked them out in his night-vision visor, although the

sound alone identified them. *Clink-rasp-clink-rasp.* It was
the knee joints. Nothing but battle droids marched that regu-
larly, not even clone troopers. There were no voices, not even
the occasional command to form single file, or *shut it back
there.* It was all grim mechanical purpose.

Niner closed his fingers around the grips of the DC-17. He
really didn't want to engage them. It was going to be hard
enough to direct the excavator to the target and get away in
one piece without pausing for skirmishes along the route.
Walk on, will you? Just walk on. He didn't want to test the
manufacturer's assurance that a few blaster bolts wouldn't
set off the charges. He was sprawled on top of them. Proximity made you skeptical.

There were fifty battle droids in the column heading for
Imbraani. If he managed to knock out the ground station,
that would be the first message he'd send on his long-range
comlink.

The *chunk-chunk-chunk* of their feet drew level with him
and he froze.

Chunk-chunk-chunk-chunk-chunk.

It began to fade behind him. He breathed again. Once the
excavator droid was coaxed past its logical destination of the
screening plant, it would be that much more conspicuous. At
least the tinnies looked busy. The worst part was having a
pretty good idea about what orders they'd been given.

Just ten klicks. He was minutes away from the point where
the droid would attempt to deliver its load. At that moment,
he'd divert it toward Teklet itself, through the center of the
town and into the ground station compound. At least the aerial recce appeared to have been right about that. Teklet was a
sprawl of storage silos and shipping facilities for getting pro-
duce off the planet, and not much else.

The worst that the Trade Federation had ever anticipated
dealing with was a band of angry farmers. It was going to
make his job a good deal easier.

Just ahead, the droid's flashing light bounced off a sign
pointing left: ALL CONTRACTOR TRAFFIC—NO ENTRY VIA MAIN
GATE. The excavator knew its way and began slowing for the

turn. Niner took Atin's jury-rigged cables and unplugged one strand. *Go on. Go on. Go . . .*

The droid was almost at the turn. It was moving at around twenty-five klicks now, threatening to veer off. But it carried on, past the sign, past the slip road, and on toward Teklet. "That's my boy," Niner said. The sweat prickled between his shoulder blades, despite his suit's environment controls. "Couldn't speed up a bit, could you?" Maybe that was asking for trouble. When he eased his head clear of the layer of rubble and peered around the side of the scoop, he could see a procession of droids strung out behind him along the curve of the road, neatly line astern like battle cruisers, each flashing an orange hazard light with its outline picked out in blue.

It was actually pretty, all things considered. Then the nearest droid slowed and peeled off down the slip road, the light show behind Niner fading, then disappearing altogether. He was on his own. He settled back under the rubble with his head tilted so that he could see ahead through a channel in the debris.

Teklet had little in the way of street lighting, and there were few people about. As architecture went, this wasn't tasteful, elegant Tipoca. It was a service depot and it looked like one. A couple of Trandoshans were sitting under an awning outside a hut, blasters across their laps; they stared at the droid with vague curiosity but didn't appear to move. Niner was almost past the ribbon of huts when the thought struck him that a five-hundred-meter blast zone would take out a lot of Teklet, and people with it. Not all of them were Separatists.

Once you make that your concern, they'll always have a weapon to use against you. Skirata said they had to get used to it. Achieving your objective sometimes had a high price.

A bonded cargo transporter with red security straps sealing its containers crossed in front of him. The droid missed it by two seconds. If the driver was cutting it that close, then they hadn't taken much notice of the machine. So far, so good . . . and getting better. As the droid pressed on, Niner was checking his escape route. It was a good two-hundred-meter sprint to the nearest cover from any part of the road. It was going to be tight.

He had to get the droid to halt right alongside the ground station. If it kept going, the blast would be centered elsewhere. He could set the dets now, slide out of the scoop, and run for it, but that meant observing the droid up to the last second, and that meant he'd probably be too close when it blew.

But he was committed now. The ground station had to go. It would put a serious dent in the Separatists' defenses for a few critical days, maybe even weeks, and that was an edge they needed.

Working some rubble aside with his finger, Niner could see the lights of the compound. He flicked to night vision, and the green image showed him flimsy mesh fencing and a waist-high retaining wall. The excavator would roll right over it on its path to the building itself.

They'd know he was there, all right.

He'd left the dets until last. The charges were linked by cord in series, just waiting for the final connection to the three detonators that—in theory—Niner could trigger remotely. He clamped the cords together and shoved them into the aperture of the det housings, snapping them shut.

The explosives were now live. He wasn't just sitting *on* a bomb; he was sitting *in* one. The charges, dispersed among the rubble, were up to his neck. He began to ease his legs clear, ready to jump.

If he didn't walk away from this, then that was the way it had to be. For a moment Niner felt a cold spasm in his gut that he recognized from a dozen all-too-real exercises. He was probably going to get killed. He was *possibly* going to get killed. If anyone thought intensive training wiped out the fear of dying, they were wrong. He was as afraid as he was when live rounds had flown past him for the first time. It never went away. He just learned to live with it, and tried to learn well enough that he could use it to work for him, and get him out of trouble faster.

Niner fumbled with the cabling. He steered the droid in a gentle arc so that it was square-on to the fence. It wasn't the best course he'd ever steered, but with a five-hundred-meter blast zone, it was going to be good enough. He ducked. The wire mesh loomed in his face at the edge of the scoop, then strained and vibrated, tearing up posts with it as the droid pushed through, oblivious.

It was nearly at the wall. The building was five meters high; flat roof, no windows. They didn't seem to like windows here. He heard a single shout, something like *chuba,* and he had to agree. This was going to fierfek someone's watch with a lot of reports.

Niner yanked the cables apart and cut the droid's power. Its momentum carried it on a few more meters, and metal twanged and squealed as the chain-link fence was stretched to the breaking point. The wires finally snapped back like a bowstring under the excavator's wheels.

One, two, three . . .

The droid was at a dead stop hard against the wall. The blocks were beginning to crack, and gaps were opening between them. He had a sudden vision of finding himself buried in collapsing masonry and unable to move, and a combination of animal panic and a lifetime of training propelled him out of the rubble and over the edge of the scoop. He fell flat from two meters and struggled to right himself. Then there was shouting and, fifty-kilo pack or not, he executed the fastest bugout of his career, Deece in one hand and the remote det control in the other.

There was one way out and that was through the gap he'd smashed in the fence.

It wasn't covert. A human in an overall was standing open-mouthed in his path, and Niner knocked him flat on his back as he ran full-tilt for the hole in the mesh.

He had about a minute to put distance between himself and the ground station before he blew the charges. At twenty klicks an hour, that meant he'd be about —

Fierfek, just do it.

Niner was past the first line of trees and into long grass when he dropped and pressed the remote det in both hands.

Teklet was a sudden ball of light. Then the roar of air and the shock wave shook him. He crouched as debris rained down on him, hoping—really *hoping*—that Katarn armor was all that it was cracked up to be.

Ghez Hokan was the first to admit that it was taking a lot less to get him irritated lately. He'd waited long enough. He tapped the comlink console impatiently.

"I asked to be out through to CO CISCom ten minutes ago, *di'kut*."

"I realize that, Major. He'll be with you as soon as he's free."

"Enemy forces have infiltrated and I need to speak to your commanding officer. Do you understand what we have on Qiilura? Could you possibly shift your *di'kutla shebs* long enough to find out why this is so vital to the war?"

"Sir, we have Republic troops infiltrating more places than I care to name right now, so—"

The screen flickered and broke up in noise. Hokan switched to another channel and got the same crackling, shimmering display. It was the same for every channel he tried. His first thought was that someone had disabled his receiver. They were closer than he'd thought, and a lot more daring. He put on his helmet and edged cautiously down the passage to the exterior door, his Verpine shatter gun in one hand and a hunting vibroblade in the other.

The droid sentry stepped aside to let him pass. On the roof, the comm relay was intact. Hokan took out his personal comlink and called Hurati.

All Hokan could hear was the chatter of static. It struck him that the Republic troops might well have done what he would have, faced with the same target.

"Droid, can you make contact with your fellows?"

"Affirmative sir."

The droids had their own comlink system. They could

communicate instantly on any battlefield. What they didn't need was the main relay at Teklet in order to do it.

"Can you contact Lieutenant Hurati?"

The droid paused for a few moments. "I have him, sir."

"Ask him if he has any news of Teklet."

Pause. A much longer pause.

"Large explosion seen in the direction of Teklet, sir."

It's what I'd do if I was preparing an assault, Hokan thought. *I'd render my enemies blind and deaf.*

There was nothing he could do on the ground to deal with an invasion, if one was coming. There was a Republic assault ship in Qiilura space, and that didn't bode well.

He had two options for his immediate task. He could defend Uthan's project—the technical knowledge invested in her and her staff, and the nanovirus itself—or, if he was overrun, he could prevent it falling into enemy hands to be studied and neutralized.

It was a big planet. If he had to run, they'd have to find him. In the meantime, he'd sit tight and wait for them to come.

"Tell Hurati I want every functioning droid back here now," Hokan said. "We're digging in."

12

Coruscant Command to Republic Assault Ship *Majestic*,
Qiilura Sector
Cruiser *Vengeance* will RV with you at 0400. You have clearance
to intercept any vessel leaving Qiilura space, prevent landing by
non-Republic vessels, and engage any vessel failing to comply. Have
biohazard containment standing by.

Niner struggled to his feet and stared back at the ground station.

It wasn't there anymore. Neither were the few small huts scattered along the approach road. There was billowing smoke and fires burning, including one that looked as if it were a blowtorch. Another explosion made him shield his head, and more debris peppered his armor.

Apart from that, the area was silent. He set off through the trees again, feeling as if he'd been picked up and shaken hard by someone really angry. A small pack of gdans began chasing him, snapping on his leg armor, but they caught on fast that he was going to be impossible to eat and fell back. He opened his long-range comlink for the first time in days.

"Niner here, anyone receiving?"

He could hear his own breath rasping as he ran. He was down to a stumbling jog now and feeling the reality of his exhaustion. He'd take a stim or two later. He had to.

"Sarge? Fi here. Target acquired, then."

"Wow. P for plenty."

"You sound busy."

"On my way to the RV."

"You're running."

"You bet. Sitrep?"

"Had to dump the droid and cache a lot of stuff. But the Weequay can carry a surprising amount if you ask him nicely. ETA an hour or so."

"Call Darman, in case Jinart hasn't caught up with him yet."

"Copy that. ETA?"

"Depends. Looking for transport right now."

"You sure about that?"

"You can do fast or you can do covert. Right now fast looks good to me. Out."

Niner kept close enough to the road to hear vehicles. He needed a speeder. The mangled chassis of a personal transport of some kind was upended at the side of the road, testimony to the force of the blast.

Eventually, someone would show up to take a look at the damage. Then he'd have his chance.

After a few minutes Niner was starting to see intact buildings through the trees. He was nearing the farthest edge of the blast zone. Farther ahead he could see lights coming toward him, and his visor told him they were approaching fast. He dropped down into the cover of the grass. As they got nearer, he could pick out one landspeeder and a speeder bike.

Niner couldn't face walking back into the blast zone to take one. He'd have to stop them here. And he'd have to stop them with minimum damage, or else he'd still be hiking back to the RV point.

He aimed his rifle on sniper setting and waited until the landspeeder was within three hundred meters. It didn't surprise him that it wasn't an emergency vehicle. He could see the driver clearly: a Trandoshan. They didn't have a record in humanitarian public service. He was probably rushing to see if his slave traffic had been affected by the blast. The speeder was carrying a Trandoshan as well.

Niner squeezed gently, and the bolt shattered the landspeeder's screen. The vehicle veered right off the road, spraying mud and gravel in the air, and the speeder bike swung left and pulled up dead. For a moment the rider hesitated, instinctively looking around in the dark as if unsure what had happened, but then he appeared to work it out just as Niner's second bolt caught him full in the chest. The speeder bike hung motionless a meter above the ground.

There was a lot to be said for night-vision visors.

Niner ran from cover and swung onto the speeder, catching his pack on the back of the seat. He savored the moment. Taking the weight off his feet ranked near the top of the list of primeval human needs, along with a long drink of ice-cold water. The relief was wonderful.

A good night's sleep and a decent hot meal would have rounded it off perfectly. The sooner he got back to his squad and finished the job in hand, the sooner he'd be able to indulge. He steered the speeder into the woods and headed south with newly uplifted spirits.

Pinpricks of light formed a small constellation ahead of Etain. They might have been a kilometer away, or they might have been within arm's reach: she couldn't tell by sight alone.

But she could certainly smell their breath. It was a cloying, sickly scent of raw meat. She swiped her lightsaber across the entrance to the shelter, and the gdans scattered. She had tried using the Force to persuade them to bother someone else, but it only succeeded in making them more curious, although they had stopped trying to take bites out of her.

How do you do it, Jinart? How do you keep them at bay? She sat huddled under the covering Darman had constructed and listened to the water working its way down through the leaves. The rain had stopped, but the runoff was still trickling through and plopping on the sheet of plastoid above her head. She could hear again, at least in one ear.

She could also see very clearly. What she saw was the face

of the Umbaran she'd almost decapitated with her lightsaber. Panic and fear had pushed the event from her mind, but now that she was quiet and tired, it flooded back and wouldn't go away.

Etain tried to meditate for the first time in days, shutting out the irritating drip of water on her head. Darman prowled around outside, silent and unnerving. She could feel him ebbing and flowing; anxious, even a little scared, but focused and devoid of violence or inner conflict.

She wanted to ask him how he achieved that balance. They had both been raised in complete isolation from the everyday world, with their own set of values and disciplines, not because they had been chosen to be different but because they had been *born* that way. Their calling was random, genetic— unfair. He'd obviously succeeded brilliantly; she had failed in equal measure. She let the sensation of his clarity wash over her.

It was almost soothing. Then it was suddenly gone and a wave of pure exhilaration hit her like a body blow. Darman thrust his head through the entrance to the shelter.

"They're coming," he said. "My squad's on its way." He paused as if he was listening to something, his glove held against the side of his helmet. It was odd to watch someone so obviously delighted without having the slightest idea of his facial expression. "An hour or so. Niner's taken out the comm station at Teklet. Fi and Atin have acquired a bit more gear that'll come in handy. Plus a prisoner." He paused again. His head was moving as if he was talking. He appeared to be able to switch back and forth between being audible and in-audible to her, as if his helmet was a separate environment into which he could retreat at will. "A *Weequay,* of all things. Oh well, they've got their reasons."

He was utterly still for a few moments before nodding vig-orously. He eased off his helmet and his face was one broad grin, aimed at nothing in particular.

"They're all right, I take it," Etain said.

"They're fine."

"I'm glad. You're brothers, right?"

"No, not really."

"All right, you're clones."

"They're not my original squad," Darman said. His expression was still all delight and good humor. "My brothers were all killed at the battle of Geonosis, and so were theirs. We didn't even know each other before this mission. But three of us had the same training sergeant, so I suppose we feel like family. Except Atin, of course."

It was an extraordinary statement. Darman showed not the slightest sign of being wounded by his recent loss. Etain knew little of biological families, but she knew that losing Master Fulier would still hurt badly in three months' time, and even in three years. Perhaps they'd bred grief out of clones, too.

"You don't miss your brothers, then."

Darman's grin slowly relaxed. "Of course I do," he said quietly. "Every day."

"You seem to be taking it . . . calmly."

"We know we're likely to get killed. If we dwell on that, we won't be any use to anyone. You just get on with it, that's what our old training sergeant used to say. We're all going to die sometime, so you might as well die pushing the odds for something that matters."

Etain wanted to ask him what mattered to him about the Republic's cause. She was almost afraid to, but she needed to know.

"What do you think you're fighting for, Darman?"

He looked blank for a moment. "Peace, ma'am."

"Okay, what do you think you're fighting *against*?"

"Anarchy and injustice." It was a rote response, but he paused as if considering it for the first time. "Even if people aren't grateful."

"That sounds like your training sergeant, too."

"He wasn't wrong, though, was he?"

Etain thought of the locals who had betrayed them to Hokan's men. Yes, she'd learned a lot about the reality of conflict in the last few weeks. But it still wasn't enough.

"It's getting light," Darman said. He sat down cross-legged in the hide, armor plates clacking against something. "You look cold. Need any more painkillers?"

Etain had achieved a consistent level of dampness and pain that she could live with. She was too tired to think of doing anything else. She'd even stopped noticing the persistent odor of wet merlie wool. "I'm okay."

"If we light a fire we'll be a magnet for half the Separatist army." He rummaged in his belt and held out a ration cube to her, still that incongruous amalgam of fresh naïveté and utterly clinical killer. She shook her head. He pulled out a bag. "Dried kuvara?"

She realized from the way he had put the fruit carefully in his belt and not in his pack that he prized it. He lived on rations with all the taste appeal of rancid mott hide. The sacrifice was rather touching; she'd have plenty of time to gorge herself on the galaxy's varied foods, provided she got off Qiilura alive, but Darman wouldn't. She managed a smile and waved it away. "No. Eat up. That's an order."

He didn't need encouraging. He chewed with his eyes closed and she felt desperately sorry for him; yet a little envious of his delight in ordinary things.

"I know a good way to warm up," he said, and opened his eyes.

Etain bristled. Maybe he wasn't as naïve as he seemed. "You do?"

"If you're feeling up to it."

"Up to *what*?"

Darman made a *wait-and-see* gesture with one raised finger and got up to go outside. No, Etain thought, he wouldn't have meant *that* at all. She was suddenly embarrassed that she'd even imagined he might. She stared at the backs of her hands, suddenly appalled at their abrasions and broken nails and general ugliness. A roughly trimmed pole was thrust into the shelter. She jumped. She didn't need any more surprises.

"If that's supposed to be funny, Darman, I'm not laughing."

"Come on, commander." He peered down the length of the pole. "Lightsaber drill. Let's do it now before you have to for real."

"I just want to rest."

"I know." He squatted down and stared at her. "I don't know much about swords, either, but I'm trained in hand-to-hand combat."

He didn't move. His persistence annoyed her. Actually, it suddenly *angered* her; she'd had enough. She was exhausted, and she wanted to sit numbly and do absolutely nothing. She jumped to her feet, snatched the pole, and ran at him.

He sidestepped her, but only just.

"Relatively safe way to perfect your lightsaber skills," Darman said.

"Relatively?" She held the pole two-handed, furious.

"Relatively," Darman said, and brought his own mock lightsaber around sharply on her shin.

"Ow! You—"

"Come on. Do your worst." Darman leapt back out of the range of a savage and uncontrolled lunge. "That's it. Come at me."

That was the point at which she always stumbled—the fine line between giving maximum effort and being blinded by angry violence. *You have to mean it. It's not a game anymore.* She came at him with a two-handed sweep from right to left, cracking hard against his weapon and feeling the impact in her wrists and elbows, forcing Darman onto his back foot. Three more rapid sweeps, right, right, left—and then one immediately downwards, unexpected, hitting him so hard between neck and shoulder that if the pole had been a real lightsaber she would have sliced him in half.

She heard the sickening *thwack*. It was the first time she'd seen him in pain. It was a split second of a grimace, no more, but she was instantly appalled at herself.

"Sorry—" she said, but he came straight back at her and sent the stake flying from her hand.

"You have to press home your advantage," Darman said, rubbing his neck. "I've never used an energy blade and I don't have the Force to call on. But I do know when to go all-out."

"I know," Etain said, inspecting her shin and catching her breath. "Did I do any damage?"

"Nothing serious. Good move."

"I don't want to let you down when you need me most."

"You've done fine so far, Commander."

"How can you do all this, Darman?"

"Do what? Fight?"

"Kill and remain detached."

"Training, I suppose. And whatever was in Jango Fett that made him . . . detached."

"Were you ever afraid in training?"

"Almost always."

"Did you ever get hurt?"

"All the time. Others died. It's how you learn. Getting hurt teaches you to shoot instinctively. That's why our instructors began training us with simunition that would hurt us without causing permanent damage. Then we moved on to live rounds."

"How old were you then?"

"Four. Perhaps five."

She hadn't known that. It made her shudder. She couldn't recall any Jedi dying in training. It was another world. She picked up her pole and made a few slow passes with it, her gaze fixed on its tip. "I find this accelerated growth difficult to comprehend."

"It's a Kaminoan industrial secret."

"I mean that it's hard for me to reconcile what you appear to be and what you can do, with—well, with someone who's had less experience of the profane world than even a Padawan."

"Sergeant Skirata told us we *perplexed* him."

"You talk about him a lot."

"He trained my squad and also Niner's and Fi's. That might be why they put us together for this mission when our brothers were killed."

Etain felt ashamed. There was no self-pity in him whatsoever. "What will they do with you in thirty years, when you're too old to fight?"

"I'll be dead long before then."

"That's rather fatalistic."

"I mean that we'll always age faster than you. We've been told decline for clones is mercifully swift. Slow soldiers get killed. I can't think of a better time to die than when I'm no longer the best."

Etain really didn't want to hear anything more about death right then. Death was happening all too easily and frequently, as if it didn't matter and had no consequences. She could feel the Force being distorted around her; not the regular rhythm of life as it was meant to be, but the chaos of destruction. She felt she could neither accept it nor influence it.

"We're supposed to be peacekeepers," she said wearily. "This is ugly."

"But war always is. Calling it peacekeeping doesn't change anything."

"It's different," Etain said.

Darman pursed his lips, looking slightly past her as if rehearsing something difficult in his mind. "Sergeant Skirata said that civvies didn't have a clue, and that it was all right for them to have lofty ideas about peace and freedom as long as they weren't the ones being shot at. He said nothing focuses your mind better than someone trying to kill you."

That stung. Etain wondered if the comment were just an unguarded recollection, or a subtle rebuke of her principles. Darman appeared equally capable of either. She still hadn't come to terms with his duality, killer and innocent, soldier and child, educated intelligence and grim humor. Undistracted by a normal life, he seemed to have spent more time in contemplation than even she had. She wondered how much the intense experience of the outside world would change him.

She'd killed just one fellow living being. It had certainly changed her.

"Come on," he said. "Sun's coming up. Might dry out your clothes."

It was definitely autumn. A mist had blanketed the countryside like a sea. A puddle had formed in the sheeting stretched over the top of the shelter, and Darman went to scoop it out but stopped.

"What *are* these things?" he asked. "I saw them on the river, too."

Ruby- and sapphire-colored insects were dancing above the surface of the puddle. "Daywings," Etain said.

"I've never seen colors like it."

"They hatch and take flight for a day, and they die by the evening," she said. "A brief and glorious . . ."

Her voice trailed off. She was appalled at her own insensitivity. She began assembling an apology, but Darman didn't appear to need one.

"They're amazing," he said, completely absorbed by the spectacle.

"They certainly are," she said, and watched him.

Lik Ankkit's villa had been splendid. It was still splendid in its unnecessary way, but the polished kuvara floors, with their intricately inlaid flower motif borders, were now scuffed and gouged by the metal feet of droids.

Ankkit hovered in the doorway while these four droids screwed alloy sheets across the window frames, shutting out the sunrise. Ghez Hokan watched the progress of the conversion from mansion to fortress.

"You'll split the *wood*," Ankkit hissed. "Careful! Do you know how long it took to have those panels carved?"

Hokan shrugged. "I'm not a carpenter."

"They were not made by *carpenters*. They were made by artists—"

"I don't care if Supreme Chancellor Palpatine carved them himself with a dinner fork. I need to secure this building."

"You have a perfectly adequate purpose-built facility not three kilometers from here. You could defend *that*."

"And I have."

"Why? Why ruin my home when Uthan is no longer here?"

"For a devious and treacherous little bean counter, Ankkit, you show a surprising lack of tactical creativity." Hokan walked over to the Neimoidian and stood close to him. He would *not* be intimidated by this grocer's height. He didn't care if he had to crane his neck to look him in the eye; *he* was the bigger man. "I know she's no longer here. The enemy might believe she is. If I observed *my* enemy making lavish preparations to defend an installation, I might assume it was a bluff and investigate an alternative target. If I found that alternative target discreetly prepared against intruders, I would make an educated guess that it was the real objective, and attack it."

Ankkit appeared unconvinced. He glared at Hokan with half-lidded red eyes, which was a rare show of courage for him. "And how will they spot this discreet reinforcement?"

"I've made sure that supplies have been seen arriving here with an accompanying degree of security procedure. Movement by night, that sort of thing. Given the nobility of the local population, I'm sure someone will trade that information for some bauble or other. It always worked for me."

"This reinforcement will not save my home from destruction."

"You're right, Ankkit. Wooden structures don't bear up well to cannons. That's why I've moved Doctor Uthan back to the facility. If I have to, I can actually defend metal and stone more successfully."

"So why did you move her here in the first place?"

"I'm surprised that you even have to ask. To keep everyone guessing, of course."

It had seemed like a sensible idea at the time: he hadn't known what he was dealing with. Now he was fairly sure that he was facing no more than ten men. Had an army landed, he'd have known by now. Moving Uthan—not a task he could achieve in complete secrecy anyway—had helped thicken the fog of confusion.

Hokan was leaving nothing to chance. He was laying a

trail of clues that would lead the enemy commandos to one conclusion: that Uthan and the nanovirus were barricaded in Lik Ankkit's villa.

A droid dragged a heavy alloy joist through the salon, plowing a furrow in the golden floorboards. Ankkit let out a muffled squeal of frustration. The droid's comrades lifted the joist and aligned it with a horizontal beam, knocking over a fine Naboo vase and smashing it. Droids weren't programmed to say *Oops* and sweep up the fragments. They simply crunched through them, oblivious.

Ankkit was shaking again. He screamed for a servant. A sullen-looking local boy appeared with a brush and swept the debris into a pan.

"Oh dear," Hokan said. He didn't think it was the right time to mention that the labyrinth of wine cellars and secure vaults beneath the villa was now packed with explosives. He didn't know how to revive a Neimoidian who had fainted, and he had no intention of learning.

Lieutenant Hurati was waiting outside the front door. Even when not under scrutiny, Hurati stood with military composure. Hokan had never caught him sneaking a drink from a flask or scratching himself. Hurati didn't straighten up when he saw Hokan, because he was already at attention.

"Sir, Doctor Uthan is getting irritated about the disruption," the lieutenant said.

"I'll talk to her. How is our droid signal chain working out?"

"It's adequate, sir, but I would feel more secure if we had comm monitoring online."

"My boy, there was a time when we had no listening stations, and we had to fight wars by observation and our own wits. It can be done. What have the droids spotted?"

"The incursions appear to be limited to Teklet and the area to the south, sir, and quite specific in nature. At least we know why they attacked the quarry office. I have to say I haven't encountered an excavator bomb before." Hurati licked his lips nervously. "Sir, are you sure you don't want any patrols to search the Teklet road? I'd be happy to do it myself, sir. It's no trouble."

Hokan took it for the genuine concern it was rather than a criticism. "No, we could be chasing gdan trails all over the region. Our enemy is obviously good at diversionary tactics, and I'm not going to take any bait. I'll wait for them to take mine." He patted Hurati's back. "If you're anxious to be busy, keep an eye on Ankkit. I don't want him interfering. Restrain him by any means you consider necessary."

Hurati saluted. "Will do, sir. Also—Lieutenant Cuvin . . . I don't think he will make captain, as you said."

Hokan liked Hurati more every day. "Has his removal from the promotion list been noted by your fellow officers?"

"It has, sir."

"Good. Well done."

Hurati was proving to be a loyal aide. He was eager to obey. Hokan decided he would have to watch him. He promoted him anyway. There was nothing to be gained by willfully ignoring excellence in another.

13

"Turned out nice again," Fi said, somewhere ahead of the column.

"You been on the stims?" Niner asked.

"I'm just naturally cheerful."

"Well, I'm not, so where did you get it from?"

Niner didn't like being tail on a patrol. He walked backward, scanning the trees, wondering why he was this close to Imbraani without a sign of enemy contact since Teklet.

Tinnies couldn't climb trees. It was the wets he was worried about.

"Want to swap?" Fi said.

"I'm fine."

"Just say the word."

Fi was about a hundred meters ahead on point. Atin walked behind Guta-Nay. The Weequay was carrying a fair share of the ordnance and equipment they'd had to load on their backs since abandoning the excavator droid and the speeder bike.

"Very quiet, all things considered," Atin said. "Mind if I send up a remote?"

"Might as well," Niner said. "Patch visual through to all of us, will you?"

"We there yet?" Guta-Nay asked.

"Soon." Niner hadn't found the Weequay much use so far except as a pack animal. All he seemed to know about Hokan's tactics was that they *hurt bad*. "Now, are you going to be cooperative, or am I going to return you to your boss?"

"You not do that! It *cruel* it is!"

"He'll probably just give you a big kiss and tell you how much he's missed you."

"He gonna cut my—"

"I'm sure he will. Want to tell us more about the droids?"

"A hundred."

"Any SBDs?"

"What?"

"Super—battle—droids." Niner indicated the bulky shape with his arms held away from his sides, letting his rifle hang on its webbing. "Big ones."

"No. I seen none, anyway."

"I told you we should have slotted him," Fi said. "Still, he carried a bit of gear. I suppose we ought to cut him some slack for that."

The metallic sphere of the remote rose just above the level of the trees and shot off. Niner's field of vision was interrupted in one quadrant by an aerial view of the countryside. As the remote tracked along paths and swooped among branches, it was clear that nobody was about, a worrying thing in itself. Then it dived in to show a familiar figure, stripped to the waist, bending over a makeshift basin of soapy water fashioned from a section of plastoid sheet.

The remote hovered above Darman as he reached for his rifle, not even raising his eyes.

"Sarge, is that you?"

Niner was staring into the business end of Darman's Deece. It was a sobering close-up. "We're about ten minutes from the RV. Going anywhere nice?"

The rifle disappeared from the frame and Darman, half shaved, stared back. "Knock first, will you?"

"I'm glad to see you, too. Where'd you get that wound?"

"This one? Or *this* one?"

"The burn."

"A Trandoshan. Ex-Trandoshan, actually. We've had a little more attention than we'd have liked."

"The commander's still in one piece?"

"Well, *this* bruise is hers. I'm teaching her to fight dirty. She's catching on."

"Get the kettle boiling, then. We're bringing a guest."

Darman's faintly impatient expression dwindled below the remote and was replaced by an open view over Imbraani. It wasn't so much a town as a scattering of farms, with a few knots of industrial-looking buildings dotted among them. Atin sent it higher and a few more remote buildings were visible.

"Take it in over the villa," Niner said.

"Open country, Sarge. Bit risky."

"I think we've lost the element of surprise."

"Okay. Long lens, though."

"What you doing?" Guta-Nay asked. To him, they were traveling in silence. He couldn't hear the conversations going on between helmet comlinks. Niner switched channels with a couple of deliberate blinks.

"Taking a look at that villa."

"I know about villa."

"We all know about the villa."

Niner would have welcomed a visit from Jinart. They hadn't seen the shapeshifter since yesterday. She could have been anywhere, of course, but she hadn't made herself visible. He hoped she hadn't run into problems.

Five minutes now. No time at all. They'd be a squad again, and they'd have a commander. They'd be at the RV, and then they could rest up, eat, have a wash, and generally clear their heads. It began to feel like good news.

There was just the matter of taking Uthan and the nano-virus, then getting out in one piece.

* * *

Etain had almost grown used to thinking of Darman's armored anonymity as a friendly face. Then three more exactly like him emerged from the trees and disturbed that fragile equilibrium.

And then they took their helmets off.

It was rude, she knew, but all she could do was stare, and she found herself slowly putting her hand to her mouth in an attempt to disguise her shock.

"Yes, sorry about the Weequay, Commander," one of them said. He had Darman's voice and Darman's face. "He's a bit ripe, I know. We'll have him clean himself up."

They were utterly identical, except for one with a terrible scar across his face. The other two seemed like different moods of the same man, one serious, one pleasantly calm and unconcerned. They were all staring at her.

"I can't tell you apart," she said.

"I'm CC—"

"No, you have proper names. I *know* you have names."

"It's—it's not policy, Commander."

Darman lowered his eyes. "It's a private thing."

"Everyone calls me Fi," said the calm one, clearly not bothered by policy. "And this is Atin."

"Niner," the serious one said, and saluted. Etain couldn't sense a great deal from either of them, but the scarred Atin exuded a sense of loss that was almost solid. She could feel its weight. She tried to concentrate on the Weequay. She didn't need to tap into the Force to tell that he was terrified. He was bent over as if about to drop to his knees, staring up at her.

Weequay didn't all look the same. She *knew* this one. He had chased her across a barq field. He was a rapist and a murderer, not that the descriptions set him apart from any other of Hokan's thugs. She reached for her lightsaber.

"Whoa," Darman said.

"Girlie?" Guta-Nay said.

"I'll give you *girlie*," she said, but Darman caught her arm and she was instantly ashamed of her reaction. Again, it was anger. It was what stood between her and making sense of her calling. She had to get the better of it. If Darman could exercise force without venom, then so could she.

"What's he here for?" she asked, thumbing off the blade.

"We thought he might have useful information," Niner said.

Etain was desperate to be useful. She felt as if she were only capable of performing conjuring tricks: enough skills to distract, but not enough to be a functioning soldier. She also wanted Darman to stop treating her as if she were merely in need of a little more instruction. She wanted him to tell her how much he despised all that potential power wasted on a girl with no discipline or focus. He wasn't stupid. He *had* to be thinking that.

"What do we need to know, Niner?"

"How Hokan thinks, Commander."

"Give me some time with him."

Guta-Nay straightened up and took one step back, shaking his head. He was expecting Hokan-style treatment.

Fi chuckled. "Guta-Nay thinks you're going to cut off his . . . er, braids, ma'am."

Braids. She'd forgotten. She pulled a section of hair free of her collar, plaited it as fast as she could, and fumbled in her pocket for a piece of cord to fasten it. *This is what you are. Live up to it, if only to justify Darman's faith in you.*

"We're going to have a little chat," she said. She let her braid fall back inside her collar. "Sit down . . . Guta-Nay."

It wasn't easy for him to settle down on the ground with his hands still tied, but Etain wasn't taking any chances. He knelt and then fell sideways in an undignified sprawl. She hauled him into a sitting position and they sat outside the shelter in silence. She wanted him to calm down before she attempted to influence him.

A sudden clack of armor made her glance over her shoulder, and she was astonished to see Atin giving Darman an awkward hug, slapping him on the back. She caught Darman's eye: he looked bewildered.

Whatever had given Atin his huge emotional burden had

been slightly relieved by finding Darman well. Then the two men parted as if nothing in particular had happened. Etain turned back to Guta-Nay, suddenly very aware that for all their calm manner and unnatural appearance, these soldiers were every bit as painfully human as she was.

Bred to fight.

A new doubt was growing in her. She shook it off and turned to Guta-Nay, who wouldn't meet her eyes.

"You're not afraid," she said quietly, and visualized the gentle trickle of water from the fountain of her clan home on Coruscant. "You're relaxed and you want to talk about Ghez Hokan."

He certainly did.

"Haven't seen Jinart?" Darman said.

"Not since yesterday." Niner cleaned his armor. It didn't matter how visible they were now, and he hated scruffy rig. Darman had stripped down his Deece and was wiping the ignition chamber more than it needed it. Fi wandered around the temporary camp, cradling his rifle, keeping watch.

"Well, whether she's here or not, I think we go in sooner rather than later."

"The villa or the facility?"

"Latest intel we have from Jinart indicates the villa."

"But . . ."

"Yeah, but. I'd find it hard to walk away from a place I could defend, too. That villa's nothing but firewood." He put down the shoulder plate he was cleaning. "Show me that plan again."

Darman clipped the DC-17 back together and reached into his belt for the holochart sphere. "She did okay to get this."

"Our commander? Jinart seemed dismissive of her."

"C'mon, Niner. She's a Jedi. She's an *officer.*"

"Well? What do you think?"

Darman rubbed the bridge of his nose. "She's got a lot of fight in her."

"And?"

"She's . . . well, she's not exactly Skirata. But she's learning fast. And you should see the Jedi stuff she can do. There's more to it than just the fighting skills."

Niner occasionally had his doubts about nonclone officers. They all did. They never admitted it publicly, but Skirata had warned them, quietly, privately, that outside officers sometimes needed help, and while you always obeyed *orders,* you needed to be able to make *helpful interpretations* if the officer was less than specific. Officers could unintentionally get you killed.

"*Nobody's* Skirata," Niner said. He was watching the commander discreetly. Whatever she had done to Guta-Nay had transformed him into a true conversationalist. She was actually looking bored, as if she'd been cornered by someone who really, really wanted to explain every engineering detail of a repeating blaster.

"You have to admit that's quite a skill," Darman said.

Niner tried not to think about it. It made him uneasy, not knowing how many of his actions were his own choice. He didn't like the other conflicts she created in him, either. He had never been this close to a human female before, and he was relieved that she was emaciated, unkempt, and generally less than appealing. The proximity still made him feel edgy, though, and from the way Darman was looking at him, it seemed they shared the realization.

They both watched Guta-Nay unburdening himself to the commander until she seemed to tire of it and got up from her cross-legged position. She walked over and looked at both of them uncertainly.

"I'm sorry, Darman," she said to Niner. Then she gave an embarrassed shrug. "Sorry. Of course—you're Niner. I got a little detail out of him, but he isn't the analytical type, I'm afraid. I can tell you that Hokan carries a Verpine shatter gun and a custom KYD-twenty-one blaster. He's got a lot of Trandoshan equipment, and as far as any of the militia knew, there were no more than a hundred battle droids at the garrison. Hokan is also apparently something of a game player—he likes to bluff and double-bluff."

Niner considered the information. "That's useful, Commander. Thank you."

"I was going to see if I could summon Jinart. She could probably see what's happening down there at the villa."

"Can you do that?" Darman asked.

"I can sense her, when she wants me to. I'll see if she can sense me." She stared down at her boots. "And please don't call me *Commander*. I haven't earned the rank. Until I do—if I ever do—I'm Etain. Darman knows that, don't you, Darman?"

He nodded. Niner didn't feel comfortable with that. He liked to know who stood where in the hierarchy of things. "Whatever you say. Can I ask you a question?"

"Certainly."

"Why did you say *of course you're Niner*?"

She paused. "You feel different. All of you. You might look the same, but you're not. I don't normally identify individuals by their effect on the Force, but I can if I concentrate."

"We seem different to you?"

"You know you are, surely. You know you're Niner and he knows he's Darman. You're as self-aware as I am, as any other human."

"Yes, but . . ."

"All beings are individuals, and their essence in the Force reflects that. The act of living makes us different, and in that way you're like twins, only more so. Atin's *very* different. What happened to him to make him so burdened?"

The answer stunned Niner. He was used to being a product. His squad and his sergeant had treated him like a man, but the Kaminoans certainly hadn't. This was the first time that a Jedi, a commander, had confirmed the clone commandos' intensely private suspicion that they were no less than normal men. It was no longer a secret dissent that had to be hidden.

"Atin was the only survivor of his first squad, then he was reassigned and lost all three brothers in action again," Niner said. "He feels guilty."

"Poor man," she said. "Does he talk about it?"

"Not much."

"Perhaps I could help him see he has nothing to feel guilty about. Just a little encouragement. Nothing like the influence I used on the Weequay, I promise."

"That's kind of you."

"We have to look out for each other."

Right then Niner didn't care if she had less idea of guerrilla warfare than a mott. She possessed one fundamental element of leadership that you couldn't teach in a lifetime: she cared about those she led.

She had earned her rank on the strength of that alone.

"Contact, five hundred meters," Fi said.

The squad abandoned their impromptu meal of stewed dried meat and put their helmets back on. Etain was again surprised at how fast they moved. They were lying prone in the undergrowth, rifles trained, in the time it took her to turn and check where the Weequay was.

You're not going to make a sound, Guta-Nay. You want to be totally silent.

He was. But she felt what was approaching. She scrambled into the bushes on her hands and knees and leaned close to Darman. "It's Jinart," she said. "Relax."

Darman, Fi, and Atin sat back on their heels. Niner stayed prone, still lined up on his sights, and held his hand away from the trigger in a conspicuous gesture.

"Niner likes to be sure," Darman said. "No offense."

The grass shook visibly, and then a living oil slick flowed past the kneeling commandos. It seemed to be carrying something horrific in its black swirls. The slick resolved itself into Jinart's natural form, and she had a huge lump of raw meat in her jaws. She laid it on the ground.

"I gave you plenty of warning," Jinart said, staring at Niner. She sniffed the air and appeared to follow an invisible beacon with her long snout. Her gaze settled on Guta-Nay, dozing against a tree, bound hands in his lap. "What possessed you to collect *that* souvenir?"

"We thought he might come in handy," Fi repeated.

"You can't even eat Weequays," Jinart said, and metamor-phosed into her human form. "Better not let the creature see me for what I am, just in case. Have you eaten? Would you like some merlie?"

Fi took his helmet off and grinned. "We've got time for that, have we?"

"You might as well fight on a full stomach," Jinart said. "You have a tough job on your hands."

Fi picked up the leg of merlie and rinsed it with water from his bottle. "Dar, you got any of that dried fruit left?" He ejected the vibroblade from his knuckle plate and began cut-ting the leg into chunks. Etain wondered how he had devel-oped his relentless good humor; she couldn't imagine him shooting anyone. One thing she had discovered in the last few days was that professional soldiers were neither habitu-ally angry nor violent.

They didn't even talk tough. They were a mass of contradic-tions. They washed their clothing and they shaved and cooked and generally conducted themselves like well-behaved, well-educated Padawans. Then they went out and blew up instal-lations and killed total strangers and cracked bad jokes. Etain was getting used to it, but slowly.

While Atin kept an eye on Guta-Nay, the rest of them sat listening to Jinart in the shelter.

"I have been observing," she said. "Hokan has made much of reinforcing the Neimoidian villa under strict security, and he does indeed have most of his hundred droids there. The whole building is packed with explosives, most of them in the wine cellars. But he has also moved Uthan back to the in-stallation."

"Our fragrant Weequay friend was right about the double bluff, then," Etain said.

Niner shrugged. "It's what I'd do. Defend the strongest po-sition."

"So we go for the installation, then," she said.

"We'll have to deal with both targets. They're only two or three kilometers apart. Once we start on the main facility, the droids from the villa will pop over for a visit in a matter of minutes."

Etain rubbed her forehead. "If they followed the plans when they built the facility, then the only way in will probably be through the front door."

Darman shrugged. "We can make our own doors. That's what frame charges and water cuts are for."

"Sorry?"

"We blow holes in the walls. But I'd rather avoid that if we're dealing with hazardous materials. Don't want to break any bottles, I reckon."

"There isn't even a fire exit. One door, no windows, no large ventilation shafts."

"Doesn't look like anyone enforces building regulations around here." Darman shrugged. "Front door, walls, or drains. Walls would be best, but how we can get into position unnoticed is another matter."

Niner looked at Darman as if waiting for a suggestion. "A split attack could divert them if it's noisy enough."

"Well, if Hokan's been kind enough to load up the villa with things that go bang, it would be a shame for them to go to waste." Darman studied the holochart plan of the villa. "They won't fall for a droid bomb again, but we do have a lot of explosives we could introduce to the mix."

"You make it sound as if it's going to be relatively easy," Etain said.

"No, it's going to be hard. But that's what we're trained for."

"I'd rather have you effecting rapid entry to the main facility," Niner said.

"But we should place our own explosives inside the villa, in the cellars if we can," Darman said. "A high-energy explosion will set off the rest of their charges. If we can place one, it'll direct the blast upward, and if the droids are on top of the pile, it'll solve that problem, too."

"Okay, in real terms, there's a layer of solid droid on top of the cellars. Can't free-fall in. So it's through the front door, the wall, or the drains. And the drains look like thirty-centimeter diameter."

"Bore-bangs?" Fi said.

"They won't drill far enough into the ground to penetrate the cellars, and they're not powerful enough anyway." Darman's gaze was fixed on the holographic plan. "Although they might be if Atin modified them and packed in a bit of the thermal tape. I was saving it for the blast doors in the facility, but I could spare a meter. That'd be ample."

"How about a remote?" Atin said. "If we can direct it into the building, that is. If you took out the recording components, you could pack in the thermal tape—about a couple of meters, easily."

"They'll be able to spot anything that's flying."

Jinart, in aged crone mode, looked from face to identical face. "What size is this device?"

Darman formed a fist. "About this big. I'll show you one."

"I could carry that to the villa, right to the walls, if you can direct it from there."

Niner pointed into the shimmering image of the building. "Down the roof vent, which would put it in the main hall running front to back."

"Or maybe along the main drain from this culvert about two hundred meters behind the house. I like that better."

Etain joined in the communal ritual of staring at the holographic display as if an answer would eventually emerge on its own. "The only point in blowing up the villa is if you could hit as many droids with it as possible."

"Then we have to convince them we're going all out for the villa," Niner said. "That means a feint of some sort, which would be fine if we had more men. But we don't."

Then Etain did have an idea, and it was one that she wasn't proud of.

"How about sending Hokan a direct message?" she said. "What if Guta-Nay were to escape and tell him we were planning to attack the villa?"

"But he knows there are only four of us," Darman said. "Sorry, five."

"Six," Jinart said sourly.

"We could convince the Weequay that we have another squad or two in the area," Etain said. "At this point, he'll believe anything I tell him. But I'll be sending him to his death."

Fi nodded. "Yeah, if Hokan skewers him without waiting to hear what he's got to say, we're stuffed."

He was cheerfully, benignly callous. Etain was briefly appalled before letting the reality wash over her. Given the chance, Guta-Nay would have abused and killed her without a second thought. Aside from that, the squad's target was effectively a weapons factory, a weapon that would kill millions of men just like Niner, Fi, and Atin. *And Darman.* If they didn't kill, they would be killed.

It didn't take her long to move from her reverence for all living things to thinking *waste the Weequay.* She wondered if that was the true nature of corruption.

"I'll do my best to give him a good opening line," Etain said.

"He's scum," Jinart said suddenly. "If his death can help remove the Trade Federation and all their minions from my world, then it is a cheap price to pay."

My world? Etain obviously had the same thought as the commandos, because they all reacted, looking at the shapeshifter expectantly.

"We didn't realize this was your homeworld," Niner said.

"It is," Jinart said. "I'm among the last of my kind. Various invaders have driven us from our habitat without even seeing us—and now I doubt they would have done any differently had they known we were here. Yes, we'll help you rid this world of Neimoidians and every other hostile alien species that's here. That's our bargain with the Republic. You help us; we help you. That's why we risk our lives. It is *not* for the greater glory of your cause."

"Nobody told us," Etain said. "I'm sorry. I can't speak for the Republic, but we'll do our best to see that they keep their word."

"Mark that you do," Jinart said. She indicated the commandos with a swing of her fine black head. "Like your young friends here, we are few, but we have no problem inflicting a great deal of damage."

Etain could only nod. At least Jinart was brutally honest. Perhaps telepaths, deprived of secret thought, had no other style of interaction. The creature was staring at her, all unblinking orange eyes, and she could see for the first time that the four fangs protruding over the Gurlanin's lower lip each ended in a double point.

"I'll place scent marks around this camp," Jinart said stiffly. "The gdans won't bother you tonight." She slipped away and merged with the land, leaving a trail of rustling noises as she moved through the bushes.

"Okay, let's see what Guta-Nay can manage," Niner said. "If we don't see signs of movement toward the villa by midday tomorrow, we'll go in anyway, and that'll mean splitting the squad and taking both groups of droids. We really don't want to do that if we can help it."

"This has the makings of a diverting evening," Fi said. "Anyone for supper?"

It was an elaborate charade, and the bizarre thing was that it needed no rehearsal. Guta-Nay was entirely unquestioning: Etain had begun to see him as a monstrous and sadistic child, unable to comprehend the feelings of others, or control his own. They sat around and ate the merlie stewed with dried kuvara, talking about leaving enough for the "other squad" when it showed up. They discussed in hushed tones about how "the villa" was their target. If this was the misinformation game, it was an easy one.

Even so, Etain definitely didn't feel proud of her subterfuge when she cut the ties around the Weequay's wrists, ostensibly an act of kindness so that he could eat. It was designed to send him to his death. At least she felt some relief that as soon as it was dark, and they made a show of turning their backs on him and being preoccupied, Guta-Nay would try to escape, and vindicate Jinart's judgment that he was *scum*.

The decision still sat heavy on her.

Fi and Darman were asleep, judging by the position of their heads. It was impossible to tell with their helmets on, but they were sitting against a tree, chins resting on their breastplates and arms folded over the rifles clutched to their chests. She had no doubt that if she walked over to them, they'd wake and be on their feet in a second.

She glanced up. Niner was on watch, perched in the fork of a tree with one leg dangling, occasionally peering down his rifle scope at something.

"What can he see?" she asked.

Atin, cross-legged with an array of wires and detonators spread around him, looked up. He'd taken off the armor section that protected his backside and was using it as a convenient plate for components while he worked.

"Line of sight? Up to thirty kilometers in good viz. Connected to a remote ship system? Well, you name it, Com— sorry, *Etain.*" He pointed to his rifle, and then went on packing tight-coiled black and white ribbons of explosive into the remote. "Have a look through the Deece. Safety's on, but don't press anything."

Etain shouldered the rifle. It was a lot lighter than it looked, and the view through the scope was startlingly vivid despite the failing light. She found it difficult to shut out the display that was superimposed on her field of vision. It narrowed the view to a tight focus on the target. "Is this what you see through that visor?"

"Sort of."

"Can I try the helmet? I want to know what it's like to be inside it."

Atin gave her a dubious look and shrugged. "You won't get all the readouts without the rest of the armor system, but you'll see enough. It's top shelf. They upgraded it just for this mission."

She lifted the helmet and held it above her head, a bizarre coronation. As she lowered it into place, the feeling of confinement and stifling heat almost made her nauseous, but she steeled herself to tolerate it.

"Hot," she said.

"It's fine when it's sealed to the rest of the suit," Atin said. He got to his feet and loomed in her field of vision. "See the red light in the top corner?"

"Mm."

"Look at it and blink twice, fast."

She did. It unleashed chaos. All she could see now was a riot of lines and numbers and flashing symbols. She was aware of a normal view beyond it, but the rest of the data dancing before her eyes was overwhelming.

"That's the HUD," Atin said. "Heads-up display. Real life-saver. The proverbial eyes in your backside."

"It's distracting. How do you cope with it?"

"You get used to it fast. We've used these systems all our lives. You can filter the information out, like listening to a conversation in a crowd."

Etain lifted the helmet off and inhaled cool evening air. "And you can communicate without any audible sound outside the helmet?"

"Yes, and even without Command and Control hearing us on certain frequencies. I don't think ordinary troopers can do that, but we're different."

"Separate specialized training?"

"They're trained from day one to be more obedient than us. And we're more obedient than ARC troopers. They're pretty well raw Jango."

He was talking about himself as if he were a commodity. Etain found it uncomfortable: yes, these young men were odd because they were externally identical, but they were still individual men, and not exotic houseplants or strains of grain. She understood that the Republic faced desperate times. She just wondered how many desperate measures that could justify. Somehow it seemed an affront to the Force to do this to fellow humans, even if they seemed remarkably sanguine about it.

She handed him back his helmet. "We use you, don't we, Atin? All of you."

"No soldier has it easy." He fumbled with a length of wire, clearly embarrassed, brow furrowed in mock concentration.

The fresh scar from cheek to chin was all the more shocking etched into fresh young skin, and not a battle-hardened, wrinkled face that indicated a full life. "But I like this job. What else would I do?"

It was a painfully good question. What would any of them do if they were discharged from the Grand Army? She reached out and squeezed his arm instinctively, but all she grasped was plastoid-alloy plate.

"I know what happened to you," she said. She concentrated, a precision job: just enough to influence him to see what was true and reasonable, but not to make mockery of his natural grief. "What happened to your brothers wasn't your fault. You're a good soldier. Sometimes the odds are too far against you."

He stared down at his boots. Eventually, he looked up and shrugged. "I'll do my best to make sure this bunch stays alive, then." There was little indication on his face that the gentle push toward acceptance had worked, but Etain felt less of a jagged tear in the Force around him. He might heal, in time.

And time was something none of the clone commandos would have. It made her ashamed.

"Can I help with anything?" Etain said.

"You could help me put some remote dets into these. I told Dar I'd finish them for him." Atin indicated small packs of mining explosive, and handed her something that looked like a packet of steel toothpicks. "Slide these between the ribbon and the main charge. Makes any party go off with a bigger bang."

"What are they?"

"IEDs," he said. "Great for planting down drainage systems and air-conditioning ducts."

"Not more acronyms."

"Improvised explosive devices. Be sure you make them look neat. Dar's fussy about his devices."

It was a relatively simple but fiddly task: Etain was a quick learner. They sat in silent concentration, making bombs as casually as if they were shelling qana beans. *This is how it happens,* she thought. *This is how you slide from peace-keeper to soldier to assassin.*

"Can I ask you a favor?" Atin said, not looking up from the bomb in progress.

"Of course."

"May I look at your lightsaber?"

Etain smiled. "Well, you've shown me yours, so it's only fair I should show you mine." She took out the hilt and held it up to him. He wiped his palms on his bodysuit and took the saber carefully. "*That's* the dangerous end, and *this* is the control."

He showed no inclination to activate it. He seemed absorbed by the hilt and its markings.

"Go on," Etain said.

The lightsaber flared into blue light with a *vzzmmm.* Atin didn't even flinch. He simply stared down the length of the blade and seemed to be checking it for true.

"It doesn't feel like a weapon," he said. "It's a beautiful thing."

"I made it."

That changed his expression. She had struck a chord with him, one builder of gadgets to another. "Now that *is* impressive."

Etain enjoyed the respect. Being treated with deference as an officer made her squirm, but this felt good. *So I think I'm pretty good at something. And someone else thinks I'm good at it, too.* It was a boost that she sorely needed.

Atin thumbed off the blade and handed the hilt back to her with suitable reverence. "I'd still rather have plenty of distance between me and the enemy," he said. "This is a close-in weapon."

"Maybe I need to practice my more remote skills," Etain said. "You never know when telekinesis might come in handy."

They went on bundling explosives with ribbon charges and stacking the packages in a heap. She heard and felt Darman relieve Niner on watch: their respective presences ebbed and flowed, merging at one point as they crossed paths.

Through the night Etain alternated between dozing and checking on Guta-Nay. She was careful not to give him the idea that she was watching him, and instead concentrated on sensing whether he was still there, sitting in the lee of a tree with his knees drawn up to his chest. Sometimes he slept; she could feel the absence of mental activity, almost like sensing a plant. Other times he woke and felt more vivid and chaotic, like a predator.

It was getting light again. It had been a long and restless night.

And still Guta-Nay sat there. He'd made no attempt to escape.

Of course he won't. Etain felt her stomach knotting. *He's terrified of Hokan. He wants to stay with us. We're the good guys, the civilized guys.*

Once again she was horrified by her ruthless and almost involuntary calculation of benefit against evil. She wandered past the shelter made of leaves, tarpaulin, and a camouflage net that seemed to be handmade. Niner, now clearly asleep, still wearing full armor, was curled up on his side, one arm folded under his head. Atin was reading his datapad; Fi was finishing the cold remains of the merlie stew. He glanced up at her and held out the mess tin.

"I'll pass, thanks." Fat had congealed in unappetizing yellow globules on the surface. It seemed soldiers could sleep anywhere and eat anything.

This couldn't be a moral dilemma. It was obvious. These men had become her responsibility, both as an individual and as a Jedi: she owed it to them to see that they survived. She liked them. She cared what happened to them, and she wanted to see Atin live long enough to overcome his demons.

And she could do something that even they couldn't.

"Guta-Nay," she said, putting her hand on the Weequay's shoulder. He opened his eyes. "Guta-Nay, you're not afraid. You want to go to Ghez Hokan and tell him what you know. You want to offer him information about the Republic forces in exchange for your life. You want to tell him that they plan to attack the villa because they think the forces at the facility are a decoy."

Guta-Nay stared past her for a moment, and then stood up. He picked his way through the bushes and headed east toward Imbraani.

Etain knew she had now taken a second life.

She pinched the bridge of her nose, eyes screwed shut, and wondered what had happened to her, what Master Fulier would have thought had he been alive. Then she was aware of someone watching her.

She looked up. Darman, perched in the same fork of branches as Niner had been, stared down.

"It's hard to send someone to their death," she said, answering his silent question.

His expression was hidden behind the visor of his helmet. She didn't need to call on any of her abilities as a Jedi to know what he was thinking: one day she would do the same to men like him. The realization caught her unawares.

"You'll get used to it," he said.

She doubted it.

14

*There is nothing wrong with fear. You need never be
ashamed of it, as long as it doesn't stop you functioning.
Fear is your natural warning system; it keeps you alive so
that you can fight. Show me a man who isn't afraid,
and I'll show you a fool who is a danger to his entire ship.
And I do not tolerate fools in my navy.*
—Admiral Adar Tallon, addressing the new intake at a
Republic academy

Hokan stood on the veranda of Ankkit's villa and stared out
at a bright autumnal morning. There were still too many
leaves on the trees for his liking.

They were out there somewhere. Republic forces. A handful.

But they were not an army.

He walked to Uthan's laboratory complex, a comfortable
fifteen-minute stroll. It occurred to him that he was a good
target for a sniper, if a sniper had been able to penetrate
Mandalorian armor. Even so, he decided to divert via a coppice. His path took him along a dry-stone wall to the rear of
the installation, and he made a complete circle of the farm
building before walking up to the single entrance at the front.

As a lure, this was a good one. The line of droids across the
entrance was spectacular. Hokan made a point of inspecting
them at a leisurely pace and then engaged them in conversation about their cannons. If anyone was observing—soldier,
spy, or talkative farmer—they would get the message.

Inside, though, Dr. Uthan was losing her glamorous cool.

"Is this the last time you're going to move me?" she said, tapping her nails against the polished metal of her desk. Her files and equipment were still in packing crates. "My staff members are finding this extremely stressful, as am I."

Hokan took out his datapad and projected a holochart of the installation above the surface of the desk. The place was a cube within a cube: below ground level, the accommodations, storage, and offices lay in a ring around a central core. The core contained a square of eight small laboratories with one more—the secure room—nestled in the center. The rest of the complex had bulkheads that could be brought down and sealed to isolate a biohazard escape. It could be defended.

But it wouldn't come to that. He'd laid a careful trail to Ankkit's villa and a greeting from fifty droids, along with cannons and powerful explosives.

He wanted to get it over with.

"Yes, Doctor, this is the last time I'll move you," he said. "Try to understand why I've done this, Doctor. I believe I'm facing a small commando force. Rather than chase them, which could be diversionary, I've decided to bring them to me. This means they'll be facing a conventional infantry and artillery battle that I don't think they're equipped to fight. Those are battles of numbers."

"I'm not sure if I do see your point, actually."

"We can defend this installation. I have the numbers and the firepower. Sooner or later, they'll take casualties."

"You're certain about this?"

"Not certain, but everything I see suggests they have landed a minimal amount of troops—for example, no evidence of large-scale transport. They hijacked explosives from a quarry to destroy the Teklet ground station. If they had the matériel, they wouldn't have bothered."

"And then again, maybe that's a diversionary tactic, too."

Hokan looked up from the holochart. "Nobody has perfect knowledge in battle. No plan survives contact with the enemy. Yes, I'm making an educated guess, as every commander in history has had to do."

Uthan considered him with cold black eyes. "You should have evacuated my project from the planet."

Hokan folded his arms. "When you move, you're vulnerable. You're vulnerable crossing the countryside between here and the spaceport. You're even more vulnerable attempting to leave Qiilura with a Republic assault ship on station. And now we have no communications beyond runners, and a bunch of droids relaying messages. No, we sit tight."

Uthan indicated the warren of rooms behind her with one hand. "If this comes to a pitched battle, what about my project? What about my staff? Those five scientists represent the best microbiologists and geneticists in the CIS. In many ways, they're more important than the biomaterial we hold. We can start again, even if the work so far is lost."

"It's as dangerous for them to leave as it is for you."

"I see."

"You specified a very secure layout when you had this facility built. You must know it's defensible."

Uthan seemed suddenly fixed on the holochart in front of her. It showed hydraulic emergency bulkheads and chambers within chambers. It showed ventilation systems with triple filters. It could be sealed as tightly as a bottle.

"It's not secure enough to stop anything getting *in*," she said carefully. "It's to stop anything getting *out*."

"You said the nanovirus was only lethal for clone troops."

There was a pause, the sort of pause Hokan didn't like. He waited. He stared at her, and he was disappointed to see for the first time that she was nervous. He waited for her to continue. He would wait all day if necessary.

"It will be," she said at last.

"You said that it might make other organisms merely— what was the word—unwell?"

"Yes."

"How unwell, then, if you go to all this trouble to contain it?"

"Very unwell."

"*Dead* unwell?"

"Possibly. Depending on whether the exposed subject has certain sets of genes . . ."

Hokan experienced a rare moment of uncertainty. It wasn't because he was closer to a dangerous virus than he supposed. It was because someone had lied to him, and his instinctive way to deal with that was a violent one. The fact that he was dealing with a woman was the only thing that made him hesitate.

But it was only hesitation. He leaned forward, seized her by her elegant designer collar, and heaved her sharply out of her seat across the desk.

"Never lie to me," he said.

They were eye-to-eye. She was shaking, but she didn't blink. "Get your hands off me."

"What else haven't you told me?"

"Nothing. You didn't need to know the details of the project."

"This is your final chance to tell me if there's anything else I should know."

She shook her head. "No, there isn't. We're having some problems isolating the parts of the virus that will attack only clones. They're human. All human races share the majority of genes. Even you."

He held her for a few more seconds and then let go, and she fell back into her chair. He really should have shot her. He knew it. It would have made her staff more compliant. But she was a significant part of the asset. He hadn't gone soft because she was a woman, he was certain of that.

"Understand this," he said, feeling suddenly very uncomfortable. "This means we're sitting on a weapon that might destroy us as easily as it will destroy the enemy. It places constraints on how we fight." He went back to the holochart and indicated various features of the installation with his forefinger. "You're sure it can't escape into the environment?"

Uthan was staring at his face, not at the chart. It was as if she didn't recognize him. He snapped his fingers and pointed at the chart.

"Come on, Doctor. Pay attention."

"That's—that's the biohazard containment area. Impregnable, for obvious reasons. I was thinking we might retreat in there for the time being."

"I would prefer to keep you and the biomaterial separate. In fact, I would prefer also to keep you separate from your staff. I dislike having all my eggs in one box—if the enemy ever breaches this facility, then they won't be able to destroy the project in one action. If they eliminate one part, we can still salvage the other components, be they personnel or materials."

"These rooms aren't as secure in biohazard terms."

"But they *are* relatively secure in terms of stopping someone from getting at them. The hazardous materials can stay in the central biohazard chamber."

"Yes," she said. "I concede that."

"Then get your people moving."

"You think it'll come to that? To a battle?"

"No, not here. But if it does, this gives me the best chance of succeeding."

"You're prepared to fight while sitting on a bomb, effectively."

"Yes. Your bomb. And if we're both sitting on it, it'll motivate us to prevent its detonation, won't it?"

"I think you're a dangerous and foolhardy man."

"And I think you're a woman who's lucky that she has relative immunity through her value to the Separatist cause." Hokan straightened up. Maybe she wanted an apology. He saw no reason to give one. A scientist, expecting half the relevant facts to be acceptable in the solution of a problem? It was sloppy, unforgivably sloppy. "I'll have a droid help you if you like."

"We'll do it ourselves. I know how careful they are with fragile objects."

Hokan closed the holochart and walked out into the corridor.

Outside, a droid approached him. "Captain Hurati is bringing a prisoner and a visitor," he said. "He says he disobeyed your orders on both."

Maybe promoting the man hadn't been such a good idea. But Hurati was smart. He'd taken them alive when he should have taken them dead, and that was significant. The young officer wasn't squeamish.

Hokan decided to give him the benefit of the doubt. When the droids at the entrance parted to let him pass, Hurati was waiting, and he had two others with him.

One was a Trandoshan mercenary. He carried his distinctive tool of the trade, an APC repeating blaster.

The other was no stranger at all. It was Guta-Nay, his former Weequay lieutenant.

"I got information," the Weequay said, cowering.

"You better have," Hokan said.

With one pair of shoulders missing, Niner had some hard choices to make about what equipment they could take with them. He stared down at the various weapons and piles of ordnance laid out on the ground, astonished by what they had managed to carry as well as in consideration of what they couldn't take into battle.

"We could always cache some stuff near the target," Fi said.

"Two trips—double the risk."

Atin picked up one of the LJ-50 concussion rifles. He had been most insistent on saving those. "Well, I'm taking this conk rifle and the APC array blaster if I'm going into that facility."

"Don't trust Republic procurement, then?" Fi said.

"No point being a snob about gear," Atin said.

"Don't get stuck in any confined spaces."

It was a fair point: with a backpack, Deece, rifle attachments, and sections of cannon, there wasn't a lot of room left to load much else. Niner didn't want to say it aloud, but they were trying to do two squads' work. Something had to give.

"Come on, you know I can carry equipment," Etain said.

She didn't look like she could even carry a tune: battered, disheveled, and ashen, she seemed about to drop. "Ask Darman."

"That right, Dar?" Niner said on the helmet link.

Darman glanced down from his observation point in the tree. "Like a bantha, Sarge. Load her up."

They could split the E-Web across five of them. That meant an extra piece and a decent supply of extra power cells and ordnance.

"Okay, plan A," Niner said. He projected a holochart from his datapad. "The nearest suitable laying-up point is just under one kilometer from the facility in this coppice *here.* We tab down there now and deploy two surveillance remotes to give us a good view of both the facility and the villa. Depending on the situation, we can try to come back for the spare gear during the day. It's two klicks each way. Not a lot, but it's daylight, and if Guta-Nay did the business, we'll have a lot of attention."

"I'm up for it," Atin said. "We're going to need it."

"Go on with plan A," Etain said.

"As we agreed—get a remote loaded with ribbon charge into the villa and do what damage we can, while Fi lays down fire at the rear of the facility, Darman blows the main doors, and I go in with Atin. If we can't get the remote into the villa, then we have to tie the droids down with a split attack—plan B."

Etain chewed her lower lip. "That sounds almost impossible."

"I never said we had good odds."

"And I'm not that much use against droids."

"You would be if you had one of these," Atin said, and offered her the Trandoshan array blaster. "Lightsabers are all very well, but we don't want to get too intimate with the enemy, do we? It's got a good close-range spread so you don't even have to be an expert marksman to use it." He made a gesture with his hands. "Bang. *Serious* bang."

She took the weapon and examined it carefully, then

shouldered it like a pro. "Never used one of these. I'll get the hang of it fast."

"That's the spirit, ma'am."

"You should also know that I can move things, too. Not just carry them."

"Move?"

"With the Force."

"Handy," Fi said.

Niner slapped a clip of plasma bolt rounds in Fi's hand to shut him up. "We might need you to keep Doctor Uthan co-operative, too. Worse comes to worst, we've got sedation for her, but I'd really rather have her walking than as a dead-weight."

"Is there a plan C?"

"The nice thing about the alphabet, ma'am, is that it gives you plenty of plans to choose from," Fi said.

"Shut up, Fi," Niner said.

"He has a point," Etain said. She spun around to face the undergrowth. "Jinart?"

The Gurlanin slipped out of the bushes and wandered among the selection of weapons, a glossy black predator again, picking her way between the equipment with careful paws. She sniffed at it.

"Show me what I need to carry," she said.

"Can you manage three remotes?" Atin asked.

"All bombs?"

"No, two holo-cams, one bomb."

"Very well. You can explain to me what you want done with them when we reach your . . ."

"Laying-up point," Niner prompted. "LUP."

"You enjoy not being understood, don't you?"

"Part of our mystique and charm," Fi said, and strapped more webbing onto his armor.

They followed the line of the woods, a route that took them a couple of kilometers out of their way, but offered the shortest distance over open terrain. Etain—Niner still struggled with first-name familiarity, even in his mind—kept close to Darman. She seemed to like him. She was polite and sympathetic to the rest of them, but she certainly *liked* Darman. Niner could see it on her face. She exuded concern. He heard snatches of conversation.

"How did you ever carry all the E-Web sections alone?"

"No idea. Just did, I suppose."

She was a Jedi. Skirata said they were fine people, but they didn't—and couldn't—care about anyone. But you got close very quickly under fire. He wasn't going to ask Darman what he was playing at. Not yet.

They reached the edge of the woodland and came into a hundred-meter stretch of waist-high grass. Fi went forward as point man. Sprinting and dropping was now beyond them, but there appeared to be nothing around to spot their gray armor anyway, so they walked at a crouch. Niner's back was screaming for a rest. It didn't matter how fit you were when you pushed yourself this hard: it hurt.

When they reached the coppice, it was painkiller time. Niner stripped off his arm plate and peeled back a section of suit. He didn't bother finding a vein. He stabbed the needle into muscle.

"Know the feeling," Darman said. He dropped his pack and sat down, legs outstretched. "Anyone taken any stims so far?"

"Not yet," Niner said. "I reckon we should all dose up one hour before moving, just to make sure we're a hundred percent." He glanced at Etain, wondering how she might appear after a week of normal meals, unbroken sleep, and clean clothing. She looked worryingly frail now, even though she was doing a valiant job of keeping up. "You, too. *Especially* you. Can Jedi take stimulants?"

"What exactly do they do?"

"The equivalent of ten hours' good, solid sleep and four square meals. Until they wear off."

"I ought to draw on the Force to sustain my stamina," she said. "But the Force could do with a bit of help right now. Count me in."

She sat down and rested her head on her folded arms. Maybe she was meditating. Niner switched to helmet comms.

"Dar, she's not going to collapse on us, is she? We can't carry anything else."

"If she drops, it'll be because she's dead," he said. "Trust me, she's tougher than she looks. Physically, anyway."

"She'd better be. Let's get those remotes deployed."

Jinart had identified a couple of high points to place the cam remotes. One was on the gutter of a farm building overlooking the entrance to the facility; the other was a tree whose canopy gave a good 270-degree view of the villa. The third remote—the one loaded with ribbon charge—needed more careful placement. She sat up on her hind legs and a pouch formed on her stomach like a cook's apron.

"Normally I would carry my young around in this," she said. She placed the three spheres in the pouch, giving the impression that she'd swallowed some particularly lumpy prey. "But if I don't help you, my chances of raising another litter are remote. So I consider it an appropriate act."

Niner was as fascinated as ever by the Gurlanin. The more he saw of the creatures, the less he knew about them. He hoped he might have the chance to find out more one day.

In an hour it would be midday. Atin took out his ration pack and mess tin, a flat sheet that snapped into shape. He placed his remaining ration cubes in it and held it out. "How much have we got among us?"

"I'm down to half a day's worth," Fi said.

"Me, too," Niner said.

Darman reached into his pack and pulled out a carefully wrapped brick-sized bag. "A day's worth of cubes and this dried kuvara and jerky. Let's pool this and have two meals before we go in. If we pull this off, we'll be running too fast to have lunch. If we don't, it'd be a shame to die hungry."

"Gets my vote," Atin said.

Niner was going to ask Etain, but she was sitting cross-legged with her eyes shut and her hands in her lap. Darman put a finger to his lips and shook his head.

"Meditating," he mouthed silently.

Niner hoped she emerged from it transformed. He was still one squad short of an adequate force for this job.

* * *

"You have ten seconds to live," Ghez Hokan said. He took out Fulier's lightsaber, and the blue shaft of energy buzzed into life. He wondered what made the blade a consistent, finite length each time. "Speak."

Guta-Nay, looking more bemused than he recalled, ignored the lightsaber. "I been captured by soldiers. I get away."

"Republic troops? Human?"

"Yes. They catch me, they make me carry stuff."

Hokan sheathed the blade. "They obviously spotted your talents. How did you get away?"

"They were sleeping. They not care. I go."

"How many soldiers?"

"Four. And girlie."

"Girlie?"

Guta-Nay pointed at the lightsaber. "She got one like that."

So the woman with them *was* a Jedi. "Just four?"

"They got another lot." He pursed his lips, grappling with a new word. *"Squad."*

"Very well, so we have two squads. Eight men. That would fit." Hokan turned to Hurati. "And our Trandoshan friend?"

"He says he's highly irritated about his business being interrupted, sir, and he offers himself and three colleagues to help you deal with the inconvenience."

"Thank him and accept his offer." Hokan turned back to Guta-Nay. "I want you to think very hard. Did they say what they were going to do? Where they were going?"

"The villa."

How predictable people were. The locals would tell you anything for money, sell you their daughters, inform on their neighbors. Hokan had half expected the ruse to be almost too obvious. "You're doing well. Tell me what equipment they have."

"Blasters. Explosives." The Weequay made an indication of great width with his hands. *"Big* gun. They got armor with knives in gloves."

"Describe."

"Like yours."

"What do you mean, like mine?"

Guta-Nay indicated his head and made a T-shape with his fingers. "Your helmet."

It was difficult to take in. Guta-Nay was an inarticulate brute, but there was no ambiguity in his description. "Are you saying they were wearing *Mandalorian armor*?"

"Yeah. That it."

"You're sure about that."

"Sure."

"Anything else?" Hokan wondered how he expected this creature to be able to assess intelligence. "Anything else unusual?"

Guta-Nay concentrated on the question as if his life depended on it, which it did not; Hokan would kill him anyway. "They all look the same."

"They were wearing uniforms?"

"No, the men. Same faces."

Children could be unerringly accurate in their observation of detail, and so could stupid adults. Guta-Nay was describing something that Dr. Uthan had told him about: soldiers, identical soldiers, mindlessly obedient soldiers—*clone* soldiers.

Hokan couldn't believe that clone troopers could operate like this. And the one weapon that would work against them was denied him, because in its present state it would kill everyone, Uthan and her team included.

But there were probably only eight of them. He had nearly a hundred droids. He had weapons.

"Hurati? Hurati!"

The young captain came running and saluted. "Sir?"

"I think we face a two-pronged attack. There are two squads, and I find it unlikely to imagine that they would *not* have one squad attack the villa, while the other made an attempt on the most obvious target. Divide the droid platoons between the locations."

"That's what you would do with two squads, sir? Not concentrate your forces?"

"Yes, if I weren't sure my objectives were consolidated in one place. They can't know who and what is in which building. And they'll attack at night, because while they're bold, they're not stupid." He shook his head, suddenly interrupted by his own preoccupation. "Who would have thought clones could carry out this sort of operation? Uthan said they were no more than cannon fodder."

"Commanded by Jedi, sir. Perhaps our tactician is the woman."

It was an interesting idea. Hokan considered it for a moment, then realized that Guta-Nay was waiting expectantly, oddly upright and apparently unafraid.

"Well?" Hokan said.

"I tell you stuff. You let me live?"

Hokan activated the lightsaber again and held it out to his side, just above the level of his right shoulder.

"Of course not," he said, and swung the blade. "It would be bad for morale."

15

So how do we justify what we are doing now? Breeding men without choice, and without freedom, to fight and die for us? When do the means cease to justify the end? Where is our society heading? Where are our ideals, and what are we without them? If we give in to expedience in this way, where do we draw the line between ourselves and those we find unacceptably evil? I have no answer, Masters. Do you?
—Jedi Padawan Bardan Jusik, addressing the Jedi Council

Etain jerked involuntarily, as if falling in a dream. She opened her eyes and stared straight ahead.

"He's dead," she said.

"Who is?" Darman had been watching her meditate, worrying what might happen to her in the coming battle, afraid both for her and because of her. She could be either a liability or an unimaginable asset. "What's wrong, Etain?"

Niner caught his eye with a look that suggested he thought Darman was being too familiar with an officer, whatever she had ordered. Then he went back to checking his datapad.

"Guta-Nay." She rubbed her forehead and looked defeated. "I felt it in the Force."

Fi looked about to say something, and Atin silenced him with a frown. Darman gave both of them a *shut-up* look. There was a way of saying unpalatable things to people, and Darman thought it would be better coming from him than from his comrades.

"Hokan would have found him sooner or later," he said.

"If the Weequay's managed to mislead him about our true target, he's at least redeemed himself a little."

"Dar," she said. It was shockingly familiar, the squad nickname for him. "I killed him as surely as if I'd cut him down."

"You told us yourself that he was a rapist," Fi said, sounding irritated. "The world won't miss him."

"Shut up, Fi." Darman tried again. "It'll save lives in the end."

"Yeah, ours," Fi said.

Darman twisted around, angry. "I said shut up, didn't I?"

Niner stepped in. "You can *both* shut it," he said. "We're all tired and we're all testy. Save it for the enemy."

Darman swallowed a sudden and unexpected desire to tell Fi to lay off Etain, and in no uncertain terms. Fi knew nothing about her, *nothing*. Darman was ambushed by a split second of protectiveness and was immediately embarrassed by it.

He turned back to her. "He's right. It's one life for many."

"Means justify the end, right?" Etain stood up from her cross-legged position in one movement. "And what about you? What happens if I send you or Fi or any of you into a situation where you're going to die?"

She was genuinely upset. He could see it in her face, and in the way she held one thin, scratched, bony hand clenched tightly into a fist. He stood up as well, walking after her as she headed for the edge of the coppice.

"We were all made for this," Darman said. It was true, wasn't it? He wouldn't exist at all if it hadn't been that someone needed soldiers, utterly reliable soldiers. But it didn't feel that way right then. Her reaction told him he was wrong, and suddenly he saw Kal Skirata, in tears, a drink in his hand. *You poor boys. What sort of life is this?* "Etain, we all do what we have to. One day you really *will* have to give an order that's going to get some of us killed."

"Us?"

"Soldiers, troopers. Whatever."

"Perhaps, but the day I can accept that without being diminished by it is the day I'm not fit to be a Jedi."

"Okay," he said. "I understand that."

"How do *you* feel when you kill?"

"I never had time to think about it. On Geonosis, they killed my brothers and they were trying to kill me. They weren't like us."

"So what if it was someone you knew?"

"But you didn't know Guta-Nay, and he isn't like you. Or me, come to that." Darman hadn't a clue what she was going on about. She was new to killing. It was inevitable that she'd have a few problems dealing with it. "Etain, this squad needs you to be sorted and alert. Think about that."

He turned and walked back to where Niner and the others were sitting. It seemed too obvious to replace their helmets and discuss privately whether the commander was going flaky on them. She wasn't giving orders anyway. But a simple glance could convey a great deal. Darman hoped Fi understood that his fixed stare meant *Lay off.*

Apparently, he did. Fi made a quick palms-out movement with his hands as if in submission. The subject was dropped.

Niner was right. They were all frayed by the last few days, hovering on short fuses. They busied themselves checking and rechecking weapons.

We've never fought as a squad before.

They were probably all thinking the same thing. Darman took the hydraulic ram apart and reassembled it, then checked the hand pump for pressure. It came with an assortment of claws, and at least having the original plans and specs of both buildings meant he knew which ones to leave behind. It could exert eight metric tons, so if the charges didn't get them through the door, the ram would. The hand-operated ram was lighter to carry, but packed less than half the punch.

He'd have liked cutting equipment, too, but he'd opened steel blast doors on Geonosis with thermal tape charges, and the ribbon version was even more powerful. Explosive moved at eight thousand meters a second, enough to slice through steel: rapid entry didn't get much more rapid than that.

This wasn't a silent job. It was an application of force against an enemy who knew they were coming.

"Whoa, receiving," Niner said. He shoved his helmet back on his head in a hurry. Darman could hear the *blip* of the alarm from where he was sitting. "Jinart's got the remote cams in place." He was looking at something only he could see, and judging by his quick head movements, it was interesting. Darman and the others followed suit.

"What are they doing?" A platoon of tinnies was marching down the track from the villa and into the facility. There appeared to be some urgency in their pace. "It looks like they're going back to the laboratory."

The remote was looking down on the scatter of small structures around the former farmhouse. It didn't have a complete view of all the approaches to the building, but it did look out on both the front path and the land to the rear. It had no view of the rear slope of the roof or the land immediately at the back.

There was a man in armor very similar to their own, standing with a familiar helmet tucked under one arm. He was middle-aged and his hard face and confident attitude said clearly that he was a Mandalorian. It had to be Ghez Hokan.

Darman heard the collective holding of breath in his helmet comlink. Hokan was talking to a Trandoshan mercenary, making short stabbing gestures with a finger pointed at nothing in particular. He was agitated but in control. He was marshaling troops.

"Yeah, Dar, I think that's *exactly* what they're doing. Looks like he's making some last-minute changes."

"Why would they be doing that?" Darman said, but he had an unpleasant feeling that he knew.

"Because we've been too clever by half," Niner said. "*Fierfek.* Guta-Nay did his job, all right. Too well. What would you do if you thought you were really facing two squads?"

"Assume two separate attacks were really possible."

Atin made a noise that sounded like a controlled exhalation. "Oh well. We were going to meet the whole tinnie family sooner or later. Plan C, anyone?"

They waited, standing in an awkward group. Within half an hour they would know if Jinart had managed to get a remote cam close to the Neimoidian villa as well.

Darman felt a hard rap on his back plate and jerked around to see Etain standing with her hands on her hips, looking anxious. "What's got everyone upset?" she asked. "Come on, I felt it. What's gone wrong?"

Darman took off his helmet. "Guta-Nay did a pretty good job of convincing Hokan we were targeting the villa. But we overplayed our hand by hinting that we had another squad."

"Why?"

"It looks as if Hokan thinks one squad will be going after each target. So our chances of getting most of the droids in one location have taken a bit of a tumble."

Etain raked her fingers through her hair and shut her eyes. "Time for a rethink, then."

Darman replaced his helmet to watch the feed from the remote. Then the second cam came online. There was a shaky but clear view of the Neimoidian villa and its outbuildings, seen from the branches of a swaying tree. A wide path stretched away out of shot from the front of the house.

At least they could now see the size of the problem facing them. If Hokan tried to move Uthan, they had a high chance of spotting her.

But whichever remote view Darman switched to, there were an awful lot of droids.

"Okay," Niner said. "Fi, you take the first watch on the remotes. I'm going to see if we can get some backup. *Majestic* should be on station by now."

"We were ordered to keep comm silence until we needed extraction," Darman said, looking at Etain.

"Commander?" Niner said. "We've taken out the comm station. They can't intercept our signal."

Etain didn't even pause. "Sergeant, you go right ahead and call up *Majestic*," she said. "Ask for whatever help you think we need."

Fi held up one hand. "Hey, we might have a break here. Check out the remote at the villa."

Darman switched channels with a double blink. The display in his HUD showed him a shot of a young boy in a scruffy smock walking around to a side door at the villa, a fruit-laden basket clutched in both arms. He knocked, and the door was opened by a droid. The youngster went in. There was something familiar about him, even though Darman had never seen him before.

He had a very characteristic walk.

"Tinnies wouldn't have sent out for fruit, would they?" Fi said.

The kid's gait reminded Darman of an old woman he'd recently slammed up against a barn wall.

"You've got to hand it to Jinart," he said. "She's certainly got guts."

"Let's hope she manages to get that fruit into the cellars."

"Let's hope she comes back out," Etain said.

Dr. Uthan appeared to have forgotten that Hokan had hauled her across a desk by her collar, at least for the time being. She sat in one of the beige brocade chairs that really didn't match her utilitarian office, listening to him with apparent patience.

"This is an unprecedented opportunity," she said at last.

Hokan agreed completely. "I realize that you haven't managed to create a delivery system for the nanovirus yet, but I think we might be able to help with that. Inhalation will work, yes? Could we introduce it into a sealed room?" He had ideas for ambush and entrapment. "Can that be done?"

"It's one of several vectors," she said. "And skin contact, too. But that isn't quite what I had in mind."

"Which was?"

"A live subject. I would like you to take one of the clones alive."

"That wasn't quite what *I* had in mind. I tend to have problems with the *alive* bit. Not my forte."

"You can't simply spray this agent around, Major. I told you we haven't ironed out the genome specificity."

"I have droid troops. While rust might be a health issue for them, I suspect that viruses aren't."

"Having a live test subject would almost certainly enable us to achieve weaponization faster."

"If you allow me access to the nanovirus, I'll do what I can to save one for you."

Uthan shook her head. Her vivid red-and-black-streaked hair was scraped up in a tight bun on the top of her head, giving her an even more severe appearance. Not a wisp of hair escaped the topknot. "I can't do that. While you might be an expert in combat, you're not a microbiologist, nor used to handling hazardous substances. This is far too dangerous a pathogen for you to use at this stage of its development. I'm also not prepared to expend what limited samples we have on a risky counterassault."

Hokan knew he could have taken it by force. But it would have been pointless. She was right; if the virus wasn't in a state that could be weaponized, it was a long shot compared to the proven weapons he had at his disposal.

"Pity," he said. "I'll endeavor to learn more about this technology after we've dealt with the current difficulty."

"So what happens now?"

"Sit tight. Stay in this suite of rooms with your staff until further notice."

"What do we do if shooting starts?"

"The same."

"What if they get through your defenses?"

"They won't, but if it makes you feel safer, I'll provide you with hand weapons for your personal protection."

Uthan gave him a regal nod of the head and reached for a pile of notes. Then she went on reading, pausing occasionally to write something in the margins of the papers. Despite the brief showdown earlier, she didn't seem afraid of him in the least: perhaps working with deadly organisms on a daily basis gave her a different perspective on threats.

"Something highly effective, please," she said as he turned to leave.

"Commanding Officer *Majestic,*" the voice said. "That was fast. Position?"

Niner couldn't get a video image on his HUD, but the sound was crystal clear. "That's a negative on the extraction for the time being, *Majestic.* Requesting gunnery support."

"Say again?"

"We'll be needing gunnery support. It might get a bit hectic down here. A hundred droids."

There was a second or two of silence. "Omega Squad, be aware that it might get busy up here, too. We have a Techno Union vessel standing off our port bow."

"Is that a negative, *Majestic*?"

"No. If we cease firing, though, it may be because we're repelling an attack ourselves."

"Understood. Coordinates uploading now. On receipt of code Greenwood, direct cannon at *this* location. On receipt of code Boffin, *this* location. Enemy now has no comm apart from droid networks, repeat comm disabled. Knock yourselves out."

"Received. My, you've been busy boys. Standing by, Omega."

Niner shut his eyes and felt the relief flood through his stomach. He wasn't exactly sure how they were going to deploy *Majestic*'s massive firepower, but at least they had it to fall back on.

"Are you making this up as you go along, Sarge?" Fi asked.

"You got a better idea?"

"I meant the code names."

"Yes."

"Classy."

"And I meant it about the better idea."

Fi drummed his fingers on the thigh plate of his armor. "I wish Skirata was around. What was it he always said? *Turn the problem upside down.* See it from the enemy perspective."

Etain glanced up, now a sure sign that Jinart was approaching. They seemed to share a kind of radar. The Gurlanin slunk into the laying-up point and swung her head around. Darman and Fi gave her a mute round of applause and a show of thumbs up.

"Nice job, ma'am," Darman said. "Amazing deception."

"Thank you, gentlemen," she said. "Uthan is definitely not in the villa. And your device is now sitting in Ankkit's wine cellars, between a case of vintage Naboo tarul wine and a crate of thermal detonators. When you're ready, you can give Qiilura its own asteroid belt."

"That'll make their eyes water," Fi said.

"And ours if we're too close," Niner said.

"So what now?"

"Let's do what Skirata taught us. Turn it upside down."

The holochart plans of the facility once again hung in midair as the squad, Etain, and Jinart sat around it, seeking inspiration.

"Is this how you plan operations?" Etain asked.

"It's not meant to be like this, no. You gather intel and then you plan and execute. This is what Skirata called a *self-adjusting screwup.* When the problem actually provides the solution to another problem. It's there. All we have to do is work it out." Niner didn't mind admitting it was more guesswork than anyone should have indulged in. But then he'd been on two real missions now, and they'd both been the same. They hadn't known what they were going into until it was too late. *Intel.* It was all about having reliable intelligence. "There's three things you should never believe— weather forecasts, the canteen menu, and intel."

Skirata said soldiers always complained. Niner was not given to complaining, but he was definitely not satisfied with the situation. This wasn't what special forces were best designed to do. They should have been there to gather intel themselves, identify the target, call in air strikes, and maybe recover hostages or data. They might even carry out assassi-

nations. They weren't meant to be artillery and infantry as
well.

If the Republic hadn't wanted Uthan alive, they needn't
have been here at all. *Majestic* could have targeted the facility from orbit, and everyone would have been home in time
for supper. Nobody would have needed to get their backside
shot at, or spend days hauling forty-five-kilo packs across
farmland.

"I'm glad you're not just accepting this," Etain said.

Fi shrugged. "If you can't take a joke, you shouldn't have
joined."

"I *didn't* join," Atin said.

At least they all managed to laugh. It was the first time that
anyone had found any humor in the situation, apart from Fi,
of course.

"What do we normally do?" Darman said suddenly. "How
do we normally take a target? Break it down."

Niner concentrated. "We isolate a target, go in, and neu-
tralize it."

"Okay, say we *don't* fight our way in."

"Not with you."

"We're expected to pull off a rapid entry and fight our way
in. What if we fought our way *out*?" Darman prodded his finger into the hologram. "Can we get in under the facility to
this central room?"

"This plan only shows drains. The bore's too narrow to get
a man down there, and this really isn't a job for Jinart."

The Gurlanin twitched visibly. "I wasn't offering, but if
there was anything I might do—"

"You've done more than enough already." Darman tilted
his head this way and that, studying the plans. "The main
drain chamber is nearly a hundred centimeters wide here,
though. It only tapers to thirty centimeters at the wall. Is
there any other way of getting into that main?"

"Short of walking up to the wall and digging under it like
a gdan, in full view of the droids, no."

Jinart sat upright. "Gdan warrens."

"They tunnel, don't they?"

"Everywhere. They even cause subsidence."

"Are there tunnels around there? Could we locate them? Would they be wide enough?"

"Yes, there are warrens, because it was once a farm site and gdans like eating merlies. The tunnels can be quite wide. And I can certainly locate them for you. In fact, I will lead you through the warrens. You might have to excavate some of the way, though."

"Basic sapper procedure," Darman said. "Except we don't have proper equipment, so we'll be digging with these." He took a folding sharp-edged trowel from his belt. "Entrenching tool. Also used for 'freshers. Apt."

"What is it between you and the gdans?" Etain asked. "Why do they avoid you and your scent?"

"Oh, we eat them," Jinart said casually. "But only if they try to approach our young."

"That's it, then," Darman said. "Get me into that central chamber from below, and I'll work my way out through the facility."

"Take Atin with you," Niner said. He didn't want to say *in case you get killed,* but he wanted another technically minded man in there to lay charges and blow doors. "Fi and I can lay down fire out front and deal with any droids we see. When you bring Uthan out, Etain can help us get her clear and then you blow the place. Then we do a runner for the extraction point."

"Gets my vote," Atin said. "You okay with that, ma'am?"

Etain nodded reluctantly. "If that's plan C, it sounds as impossible as plans A and B." She patted Darman's arm, not quite focusing, as if she was lost in thought about something. "But I don't have a better suggestion."

"Okay," Niner said. "Everyone take a stim now. Be ready to move out at nightfall. We've got four hours to prep for this. I'll notify *Majestic.*"

"What if this fails?" Etain asked.

"They'll send in another squad."

"And lose more men?" She shook her head. "If it's down

to me, I'll happily give the order for *Majestic* to pound this facility to dust, with Uthan inside or not."

"Do you think we're going to fail?"

Etain smiled. There was something mildly unnerving about the way she was smiling. "No. I don't. You're going to pull this off, believe me."

Niner kept a tight grip on his breathing. If he gave the slightest hint of a sigh of doubt, they'd pick it up. It was crazy. But, as Skirata said, they went where others wouldn't, and did what nobody else could.

And fighting your way out from the heart of an alloy-plated, heavily guarded facility designed to be impregnable to any life-form certainly lived up to that boast. For some reason he felt fine about it all.

You're going to pull this off, believe me.

He wondered if his thoughts were actually his own. If Etain was influencing his mind to improve his confidence, that was okay by him. Officers were supposed to inspire you. Right then he didn't much care how she did it.

16

What do I think about it? I don't know, really. Nobody's
ever asked me for my opinion before.
—Clone Trooper RC-5093, retired, at CF VetCenter,
Coruscant. Chronological age: twenty-three.
Biological age: sixty.

An autumnal mist had settled over the countryside. It wasn't
dense enough to provide cover, but it did give Darman a
sense of protection. He tabbed behind Atin as Jinart led the
way.

He was a walking bomb factory. Why was he even worried
about being spotted? The ram and its attachments clunked
against his armor and he adjusted them, fearing discovery.
Atin walked ahead, Deece held in both hands with his finger
inside the trigger guard, a small but significant expression of
his anxiety level.

"Matte-black armor," Darman said. "First thing we ought
to slap in for when we get back. I feel like a homing beacon."

"Does it matter?"

"Does to me."

"Dar, it's one thing for the enemy to spot us coming. It's
another thing entirely for them to do anything about it." Atin
was still checking all around him, though. "I was knocked
flat by a round and it didn't penetrate the plates."

Atin had a point. The armor might have been conspicuous,
but it worked. Darman had taken a direct hit, too. Maybe in
the future the sight of that armor alone would deter enemies,

a touch of what Skirata called *assertive public relations.*
Myth, he said, won almost as many engagements as reality.

Darman was all for a little help from the myth department.

They were four hundred meters southeast of the facility.
Jinart stopped in front of a gentle slope and thrust her head
through a break in the foliage. Her sniffing was audible.

"We enter here," she said.

There didn't even appear to be a hole. "How do you know
what's in there?"

"I can detect solid surfaces, movement, everything. I don't
need to see." She sniffed again, or at least Darman assumed
she was sniffing; it occurred to him that she might have been
echolocating. "Do you want to stand here and present a target all night?"

"No ma'am," Darman said, and got down on all fours.

Jinart might not have needed to see, but he did. He could
have relied on the night-vision visor, but he felt the need for
real, honest light. He switched on his tactical spot-lamp. He
switched it off again, fast.

"Uh . . ."

"What's wrong?" Atin asked.

"Nothing," Darman said. It was natural not to like confined spaces, he told himself. With the light projected forward, he could see just how suffocatingly small a space he
was in. With his night vision in place, he was simply looking
down a narrow field of view, safe inside his armor, cocooned
from the world in a way he was not only used to, but actually
needed.

Get a grip.

He could hear the sound of scurrying farther ahead, but it
was moving away from him. His pack caught the roof of the
tunnel, occasionally scraping loose soil and stones. The warren had been excavated by thousands of small paws, circular
in section because gdans obviously didn't need as much floor
space as a tall human male. Darman almost felt that his
hands and knees were against the sides of the tunnel because
of the curvature of the floor, like negotiating a chimney when
rock climbing. At times he felt he was losing his orientation

and had to shut his eyes and shake his head hard to regain accurate proprioception.

"You okay, Dar?" Atin asked. Darman could hear labored breathing in his helmet and he thought it was his own, but it was Atin's.

"Bit disoriented."

"Let your head drop and look at the floor. The pressure on the back of your neck is going to make you feel giddy anyway."

"You, too, eh?"

"Yeah, this is weird. Whatever we inherited from Jango, it wasn't a love of caving."

Darman let his head hang forward and concentrated on putting one hand in front of the other. He switched to voice projection. "Jinart, why do such small animals dig such big tunnels?"

"Have you tried dragging a whole merlie or vhek home for dinner? Gdans work as a team. That's what enables them to take prey that's many times their size. A point, I think, that would not be lost on men such as yourselves."

"On the other hand," Atin said cautiously, "you could say that sheer numbers overwhelm strength."

"Thank you for that positive view, Private Atin. I suggest you select the interpretation that inspires you most."

They didn't talk much after that. As Darman progressed, sweating with the effort, he was aware of a particular scent. It was getting stronger. It was sickly at first, like rotting meat, and then more bitter and sulfurous. It reminded him of Geonosis. Battlefields smelled awful. The filtration mask was active against chemical and biological weapons, but it did nothing to stop smells. Shattered bodies and bowels had a distinctive and terrifying stench.

He could smell it now. He fought down nausea.

"Fierfek," Atin said. "That's turned me off my dinner for a start."

"We're near the facility," Jinart said.

"How near?" Darman said.

"That odor is seepage from the drainage system. The pipe work is local unglazed clay."

"Is that all we can smell?" said Darman.

"Oh, I imagine it's also the gdans. Or rather their recent kills—they have chambers where they amass their surplus. Yes, it's an unpleasant stench if you're not accustomed to it." She stopped unexpectedly, and Darman bumped into her backside. She felt surprisingly heavy for her size. "That's good news, because it means we're near a much larger chamber."

Darman almost felt relief that it was simply rotting meat, although that was bad enough. It wasn't *his* meat. He crawled farther, encouraged by the promise of a bigger space ahead, and then his glove sank into something soft.

He didn't need to ask what it was. He looked down despite himself. In the way of men exposed to memory triggers, he was immediately back in training, crawling through a ditch filled with nerf entrails, Skirata running alongside and yelling at him to keep going because this was *nothing, nothing compared to what you'll have to do for real, son.*

They called it the Sickener. They weren't wrong.

Fatigue made nausea inevitable. He almost vomited, and that wasn't something he wanted to do in a sealed suit. He fought it, panting, eyes shut. He bit the inside of his lip as hard as he could, and tasted blood.

"I'm okay," he said. "I'm okay."

Atin's breathing was ragged. He had to be feeling it, too. They were physiologically identical.

"You can straighten up now," Jinart said.

Darman flicked on his spot-lamp to find himself in a chamber that wasn't just larger; it was big enough to stand up in. The walls were lined with what looked like tiny terraces spiraling up around the chamber from the floor. There were scores of twenty-centimeter tunnels leading off them.

"This is where the gdans retreat if rain floods the warren," Jinart said. "They're not foolish."

"I'll thank them one day," Atin said. "How close are we to the drain? Can you locate it?"

Jinart put a paw against the wall where there were no tiny escape tunnels. "The gdans know there's a solid structure behind this." She paused. "Yes, there's water trickling back there. The soil feels a meter thick, perhaps a little more."

Darman would have removed his helmet, but thought better of it, and settled for letting his pack drop off his shoulders. He took out his entrenching tool and made an exploratory stab at the chamber wall. It was about the consistency of chalk.

"Okay, I do five minutes, then you do five," he said to Atin.

"And me," Jinart said, but Darman held up his hand to stop her.

"No ma'am. You'd better go back to Niner. We're on our own now, and if this all goes wrong he'll need your assistance even more."

Jinart hesitated for a moment, then raced back up the tunnel without a backward glance. Darman wondered if he should have said good-bye, but good-bye was too final. He planned on coming out that front door with Atin and Uthan.

He scraped out a guide circle with the tip of the tool and hacked into the hard-packed soil. It felt like slow going and he was surprised when Atin tapped him on the shoulder and took over. A man-sized hole began to emerge.

"Should we shore this up?" Darman said, wondering what he might have to sacrifice as a pit prop.

"We should only be going through it once. If it collapses after that, it's too bad."

"If we have to blast our way in, it might collapse. Alternative exit?"

"You want to be pursued through those tunnels? They'd fry us. One flamethrower volley and we'd be charcoal."

Atin was slowing. Darman took the other side of the opening and they worked together, removing progressively damper and darker soil, flattening out the sides of the excavation so that they had access to drill through without having to lean through a short tunnel. It was weakening the integrity of the soil wall: Darman willed it to hold together until they were through.

Maybe he should have brought Etain. She could have held

the wall with that Jedi power of hers. Suddenly he realized that he missed her. It was amazing how fast you could form a bond with someone when you were under fire.

Atin's tool hit something that made a distinctive *chink* noise.

"Drain," he said. "Drill time."

A few quick rounds from the Deece would have blown a good-sized hole in the thickest clay pipe. It would also have brought down the chamber roof, Darman suspected, and summoned a lot of droids. It was time for the slow, quiet route. A hand drill was part of their basic rapid entry kit, and they each took half the rough circle, drilling at five-centimeter intervals around the circumference, starting from the top. It wasn't until they got down to the bottom that the ooze started appearing from the holes.

It had taken them an hour to excavate and drill. Darman couldn't stand the sweat trickling down his face any longer and took off his helmet. The stench really was worse than ever. He shut his mind to it.

Atin took a swig from his water bottle and held it out to Darman. "Hydration," he said. "Five percent fluid loss stops you thinking straight."

"Yeah, I know. And above fifteen percent kills you." Darman drank half the bottle, wiped the sweat away, and scratched his scalp vigorously. "Another thing to tell Rothana's geeks when we get back—up the temperature conditioning in these suits."

He lifted the ram and took a side-on stance to the disc of clay pipe visible through the soil. He gripped hard, fingers tight around each handle. He had to swing carefully this time or he might collapse the pipe. "Ready?"

"Ready."

One, two—

"Three," Darman grunted. The ram hit with a couple of metric tons of force and the perforated section fell inward as a waterfall of stinking dark slime shot out and splashed across Darman's legs and boots.

"Oh, that's just great," he sighed. "Definitely matte black next time, okay?"

Atin took his helmet off and Darman realized he was struggling not to laugh. Now that the drain was open to the air, it was a perfect conduit for sound to the building above. Atin put his hand to his mouth, bent over slightly, and appeared to be biting down hard on the knuckle plate. He was actually shaking. When he straightened up, tears were streaming down his face. He wiped them away and gulped, then bent over again.

Darman had never even seen the man smile. Now he was in hysterics because Darman was spattered with the accumulated waste of total strangers. It wasn't funny.

Yes, it was, actually. It was *hilarious*. Darman felt his stomach begin to shake in a completely involuntary reflex. Then he wasn't certain that it *was* funny, but he still couldn't stop. He shook in painfully silent laughter until his abdominal muscles ached. Eventually, it subsided. He straightened up, inexplicably exhausted.

"Shall I let Niner know we're through?" he said, and they both managed to stay completely calm for a count of three before the hysteria overtook them again.

Once you knew what laughter really was, and what primitive reflex triggered it, it wasn't funny at all. It was the relief of danger passed. It was a primeval *all-clear* signal.

And that wasn't the reality of their situation at all. The real danger was just starting.

Darman, suddenly his usual self again, replaced his helmet and opened the comlink.

"Sarge, Darman here," he said quietly. "We're into the drain. Ready when you are."

Niner and Fi set up the E-Web repeating blaster half a kilometer from the front of the facility. That was pretty close. If anyone had spotted them, they weren't reacting.

"Copy that, Dar." Niner checked the chrono on the forearm of his left gauntlet. "Can you see the drainage cover yet?"

The comlink crackled. Niner was yet again faintly pleased with himself that he'd decided to take that trip to Teklet. They'd never have stood a chance of pulling this off in comm silence. There were too many unknowns to do it by op order and chronosynch.

"I just followed the trail of crud and there it was," Darman said. "Want a look?"

Niner's HUD flashed up a grainy green image of huge dripping tubes that could have been a klick wide or just a centimeter. Come to that, it could have been an endoscopic view of someone's guts. It didn't look like fun, either way.

"What's above you?"

"Dirty square plate and it's not a drain. The water's feeding down here from other pipes." The image jerked as Darman's head lowered to look at his datapad. It threw up eerie ghost images of the building. "If they stuck to the blueprints, then this is a hazmat filter and the maximum containment chambers are above it." There was a scraping noise. "Yeah, the serial numbers match the schematic. If they had to hose down after a mishap in there, this is where the screened water or solvent would come out."

"Are you going to need to blow it?"

"Well, it doesn't look as if I can unscrew it with a hairpin. It's permacreted in place. It's not the sort of thing you want coming loose, I suppose."

"Good timing for a spot of pyro at the villa, then. Let's sync that up."

"Okay. Give me a couple of minutes to set the charges."

Two minutes was a long time. Niner counted it down in seconds. He was aware of Etain pacing up and down behind him—but you didn't tell a commander to pack it in and stop fidgeting. He focused on Fi, who was kneeling behind the E-Web tripod, checking the sights, utterly relaxed. Niner envied him that ability. His own stomach was churning. It always did on exercise: it was much worse now. His pulse was pounding in his ears and distracting him.

Darman responded eleven seconds late. "All done. I'll count you down. We're moving back out of the drain now. If we bring the outer chamber down, then we might take a little time to work our way back in."

"What's *a little time* in your book?"

"Maybe forever. It might kill us."

"Let's avoid, that, shall we?"

"Let's."

Etain was hovering at Niner's shoulder. He glanced at her, hoping she'd take the hint.

"You've never worked as a complete team before, have you?" she said unhelpfully.

"No," Niner hissed, and withheld the *ma'am*.

"You're going to do fine," she said. "You're the best-trained, most competent troops in the galaxy and you're confident of success."

Niner was close to responding with a few words of pithy Huttese, but he suddenly saw her point. His stomach settled into a peaceful equilibrium again. He could hear Darman clearly. His drumming pulse had faded. He was perfectly content not to think how she had achieved that reassurance.

"In ten," Darman said. He still had his forward helmet cam patched through to Niner's HUD. He was scrambling through a tunnel. Niner had a sensation of rushing down a flume and half expected to splash into a deep pool at the other end.

"Five . . ." It went dark. Darman had his head tucked into his chest. "Three . . ." Niner felt for the remote detonator. "Two . . . *go go go.*"

Niner squeezed the remote.

For a fraction of a second the landscape was picked out in brilliant, gold, silent light. Niner's antiblast visor kicked in. Then the ground shook, and even at two klicks the roar was deafening. It seemed to go on for several seconds. Then he realized he was hearing two blasts—one at the villa and one below the facility.

As the fire blazed and clouds of amber-lit smoke roiled into the air, the droids on watch outside the facility started reacting.

"Hold, Fi." Niner swallowed to clear his ears. "Dar, Atin, respond."

"Was that us or you?"

"Both. You okay, Dar?"

"Teeth are a bit loose, but we're fine."

"Nice job with the custom ordnance, you two. I think the villa's got a new indoor swimming pool."

"The chamber's holding down here, just about. Going in."

Silence had fallen on the countryside. It was as if everyone was waiting for the next move. Fi moved the five-pack of energy cell clips a little closer to him. Niner aimed his Deece to get a better view of the front of the villa, and saw droids milling around and an Umbaran officer with binocs scanning left to right across the fields.

"Ready, Sarge."

"Wait one."

A few more droids came out of the farmhouse door. If Niner hadn't seen the plans, he would never have believed what was concealed inside and beneath the convincingly shabby wooden siding. Etain stood to one side of him.

"Ma'am, you might want to duck and cover."

"I'm all right," she said. She looked longingly at the Trandoshan concussion rifle. "Let me know when I'm needed."

Darman's voice cut in on the comlink. "We're about to enter the drain cover," he said. "Time for distraction, Sarge."

"Got it." He knelt beside Fi and touched him on the shoulder. "Put a couple down a little short of that barn. Just to say hello. Then fire at will."

Fi hardly moved. The characteristic *whoomp* of the energy cell was followed by a ball of fire and a fountain of splintered wood. The barn rained back down, burning as it fell.

"Oops," Fi said.

It got the droids' attention, all right. Six formed a line and began marching down the field.

Fi opened up. Niner could feel the roar of noise in his chest as droid shrapnel rained down on them and incoming fire whisked over their heads. A large chunk of metal flew in an arc: Niner heard it fizzing in the air as it cooled while it fell. He didn't see where it landed, but it was close. His night vision saw the sprays of shrapnel as brilliant white irregular raindrops. A few tinnies were getting through. Niner picked off two with the grenades.

The next rank of droids advanced. Fi was firing in short bursts; Niner picked off whatever was still standing. Hot metal shrapnel continued to rain down on them. At the E-Web's rate of fire he was going to run out if he simply hosed them, and they were only minutes into the engagement. They'd dropped around twenty droids. That meant twenty more inside the facility, at least. Then the tinnies stopped coming.

The field fell silent, and it rang in Niner's ears as loudly as the cacophony of battle.

"I hate it when they work out what's happening," Fi said. He was panting from the effort.

"They'll sit tight."

"If it's just twenty or so in there, I say we go in now."

"Let's make sure we haven't got guests arriving." Niner opened the long-range comlink. "*Majestic,* Omega here, over. *Majestic*—"

"Receiving you, Omega. That was some fireworks display. Got trade for us?"

"*Majestic,* extra target for you. Have you got a visual between targets Greenwood and Boffin?"

"If you've got a remote you can patch us into."

Niner slipped off his pack and took out a remote, releasing it into the air. "Droids, estimated strength no more than fifty. If they're heading toward us, do me a favor and spoil their day, will you?"

"Copy that, Omega. Sitrep?"

"We've breached the facility and we've got twenty or thirty droids and an unknown number of wets holed up in there."

"Say again?"

"Two of our squad are inside. Ingress via the drainage system."

"You guys are off your repulsors."

"The thought did cross our minds."

"Okay, some fireworks coming your way, Omega. Be advised we still have a Techno Union vessel standing off, and we're expecting a response when we train the lasers."

"Watch how you go," Niner said. "Omega out."

Apart from the ticking of cooling metal, it was silent. Even the chatter and whistling of Qiilura's nocturnal species had stopped. Smoke was billowing across the field from the wrecked barn.

"You okay, ma'am?" Fi said.

Niner glanced around and expected to see Etain in some state of distress, but she wasn't. She was kneeling in the grass, alert, as if listening to something. Then another huge explosion shook the ground to their north.

She closed her eyes.

"Ma'am?"

She gave a little shake of her head as if loosening stiff neck muscles.

"It's fine," she said. "It just took more out of me than I imagined."

"What did?"

"Diverting all this debris. Droids make a terrible mess when they explode."

Niner hadn't a clue what she was talking about. It was only when he turned around that he saw the meter-long jagged sheet of metal right behind him. It had almost given him an unwanted haircut. Etain managed a grin.

"Can you open doors as well, ma'am?" Niner asked.

Darman and Atin looked around the plastoid-lined chamber and decided not to remove their helmets.

"This is one way to find out if a nanovirus can breach our filtration masks," Atin said.

Darman checked the cupboards, looking for booby traps and other surprises. "I don't feel dead yet. Anyway, they don't leave this stuff lying around. It'll probably be sealed in something."

He checked the room. It was exactly like a medic's station on Kamino, except it was completely constructed from plastoid ceramic. Some of the cupboards had transparent fronts; he could see racks of vials in them. In the middle of the room there was a separate sealed booth, running floor-to-ceiling, with a glove box in it. It was empty. There was also a refrigerated cabinet full of flasks and small boxes. He had no idea what might be live virus and what might be the lab technician's lunch, and he wasn't going to open everything to find out. This was another case of using P for plenty.

"Seeing as they're not helpful enough to label this stuff with a skull and crossbones, I'm going to set an implosion device in every room, to be on the safe side." He ran his hands over the walls, testing for signs of metal substructures that might block his signal. The HUD showed zero from his glove sensors. He checked his comlink to be sure that he could get a signal outside. "Darman here. Anyone receiving, over?"

"Fi here."

"The inner chamber's clear. I'm setting charges and then we're going to move out into the rest of the building."

"We're approaching the front. It's gone quiet out here and we think you've still got up to thirty tinnies for company."

"Is that you shaking the ground?"

"Majestic."

"Good to know the navy's here."

"Leaving the helmet comlink channel, by the way. Make sure you leave us your visual feed."

"We'll let you know if it spoils our concentration. Darman out."

He gave Atin a dubious thumbs-up and took the implosion charges out of his pack. He could improvise most devices, but these were special, guaranteed to create such a high-temperature fireball and shock wave that they would destroy not only everything standing in a half-klick radius, but also every microorganism and virus as well. They were disappointingly small for such massively destructive power, a little smaller than the average remote.

Darman still had two. It was overkill, and overkill made him feel safer. He picked up the lidded boxes in the refrigeration unit and tested each for weight—very carefully—before finding a lighter one that suggested it was half empty. He set it on the table, held his breath, and eased the lid off.

It held a few metal tubes with sealed caps, and enough space for one of the devices. He placed the thermal carefully inside and replaced the container.

"Go careful," Atin said, indicating the boxes.

"I will." He found another lightweight box and peered inside. "There. And if they get to searching, they might even stop after they find one device." He closed the refrigerator door.

"That won't reduce the blast any, will it?" Atin asked.

"Not so you'd notice, believe me."

"Time for the tour of the building, then."

There were status panels to the right of the door, set to warn some monitoring system if the chamber was opened, and a hand-sized button marked EMERGENCY CLOSE, a smart precaution if you were handling deadly viruses. Opening the door would advertise the fact that they had gained entry to the building. Atin moved in and carefully unclipped the control plate. He took out a disruptive device about the size of a stylus and held it just clear of the exposed circuits. It was much the same technology as a mini EMP, only with a less powerful electromagnetic pulse. Nobody wanted a full-strength EMP going off a few centimeters from their HUD, hardened or not.

"Next big bang," Atin said. "Then they might think they've just taken a hit."

The ground shook again, and Atin touched the mini EMP against the control panel. Status lights winked out; the door gave a sigh as it lost its safety vacuum seal. A thin vertical gap opened in the smooth ceramic. Sound now filtered in from outside: explosions, shouts from officers, the occasional monotone responses of tinnies. He stood back and gestured to Darman.

The gap was big enough to admit a flat endoscope, as well as the claws of the ram. He slid the probe cautiously through and checked the image it was receiving. The corridor lights were flickering. There was no movement.

"I'll force the doors and you stand by. I'll be ready to lob in an EMP grenade and a flash-bang."

"Both?" Atin said.

"Yeah, I don't want to waste any, either, but we've got wets *and* tinnies out there somewhere."

Darman wedged the ram's claws into the gap and locked the bars in place. It was more awkward to configure it as a spreader than as a simple ram, but he didn't want to blow it open. He pumped the ratchet handle furiously. An eight-metric-ton force slowly pushed the doors apart.

Atin checked outside with the endoscope again, then stepped through the opening with his Deece raised. "Clear."

Darman dismantled the ram and hurriedly hooked it back into his webbing. "Room by room, then. Killing House time."

That was something they'd done many, many times before. Each time they entered the Killing House on Kamino for an exercise, the walls and doors had been reconfigured. Sometimes they knew what they were going to find, and sometimes it was like a real house clearance, a sequence of nasty surprises that they had to take as they came.

But there was a lot more at stake now than their individual lives.

Atin gestured left. The inner corridor was a ring with doors leading off it and a single passage to the front entrance. At least there were no stairs or turbolifts to cover. They moved almost back-to-back, pausing at the corner to slide the endoscopic probe out far enough to check.

"Oh boy," Atin said, just as the first droid swung around and blasted. Darman heard the clatter of metal feet from exactly the opposite direction, and for a frozen moment he found himself staring down his scope at a very surprised Umbaran officer.

Darman fired. So did Atin. They both kept firing down their respective ends of the corridor.

"Okay, plan D," Atin said. "Niner, we're pinned down here, over."

"We're concentrating fire on the front." Niner's voice cut back in with a background of explosions both near and farther away. That was why Darman didn't like a having a four-way open comlink during an engagement. The noise and chatter were overwhelming. "They've pulled back inside. But nobody's coming out."

"We haven't located Uthan yet."

"Can you hold the position?"

"Can you see where we are? West side corridor, left of the entrance."

Atin emptied a clip into two droids that came around the corner. Then there was no noise except for their respective panting.

"Dar?"

"Still here, Niner." Back-to-back with Atin, he waited and stared down the polished hallway twenty meters ahead. There were two doors on the right, unconventional hinged doors. He glanced up at the ceiling to locate the emergency bulkheads: one was on the other side of Atin, and the next was between them and the inner chamber. If those were activated, they'd be cut off on both sides, boxed in and waiting to be picked off. And then anyone could easily enter the biohaz chamber and defuse the implosion device.

It seemed that someone had the same idea at the same time, because there was an *uh-whump* noise and then the quiet whine of a small motor.

The bulkheads were descending from their housing.

"Atin, chamber, *now*!" Darman yelled, even though he didn't need to, and they both sprinted back toward the chamber. The bulkhead was down to waist level when they reached it and skidded under on their knees.

It sealed with a *clunk* behind them. It was suddenly so silent that Darman knew another bulkhead had closed somewhere along the ring, sealing them in. There was the sound of a door unlocking manually, a real *clunk-click* noise, and then nothing.

"Start again," Darman sighed. "Let's see what's around there."

Atin moved forward and edged out the scope. He paused. He sat back on his heels and shook his head.

"Show me," Darman said, and switched his HUD to the scope view, expecting disaster.

"I think it's called irony."

Darman crawled up to him and patched the endoscope into his own helmet.

Yes, *irony* was a good word for it. He almost laughed. Between the corner and the next bulkhead, he could see two doors, one closed and one partly open. Someone—someone humanoid—was peering around the edge of it.

"Women don't half look different, don't they?" Atin said. "That's the most amazing hair I've ever seen."

Darman agreed. They hadn't seen a lot of females in their lives, but this one would have been memorable even if they had seen millions. Her blue-black hair was streaked with brilliant red stripes. They were trapped with Dr. Ovolot Qail Uthan.

And she was clutching a Verpine shatter gun.

17

CO *Majestic* to Coruscant Command
Techno Union vessel is now drifting. Damage assessment is incomplete but it is no longer returning fire. *Vengeance* is standing by
to dispatch a boarding party. Will continue to provide turbolaser
gunnery support to Omega Squad.

"Who activated the emergency systems? Which *di'kut* hit
the button? Tell me!" Ghez Hokan found himself shouting.
He had abandoned dignity. "Open this *di'kutla* bulkhead!"

Captain Hurati's voice was strained. They were both on
the wrong side of the first safety bulkhead, in a single unfor-
giving corridor that led to the entrance, and the main doors
were jammed shut. It was a very secure building: and, as
Uthan had said, it was designed to stop anything from getting
out if things went wrong. It was doing that well.

"We've been infiltrated, sir."

"I worked that out for myself, *di'kut*." He was interrupted
by a grenade exploding against the front wall. "How in the
name of—"

"I don't know yet, sir, but the bulkheads activated because
the containment chamber doors weren't registering on the
system as closed, and it triggered the emergency systems."

"Stuck open, in other words."

"Yes."

Hokan swung around on the nearest droid. "Anyone up on
the surface see signs of entry?"

A pause. "Negative."

Oh, how he longed for decent communications again. He could guess from the strength and direction of some of the explosions that the area was coming under laser cannon fire, which meant the Republic assault ship had finally showed its hand. It could even be landing more troops.

But that wasn't his immediate concern. The bad news was that somebody had already managed to get in, and not through the front door. They couldn't have come in through the drains. They *shouldn't* have been there. But there was firing, and droids were reporting casualties.

There were Republic commandos inside the facility.

Hokan had never thought himself infallible, but he had at least imagined he was exceptionally competent. He'd locked down the facility and they'd still found a way in. His first thought was that Uthan had wanted a live subject so badly that she was prepared to lure them in and trap one, but that was ludicrous: she hadn't the means or the opportunity to bypass security.

The nanovirus was out of Hokan's reach behind bulkheads that wouldn't yield. Droids patiently fired blasters into the face of the alloy. But, as in his earlier test, they were making no impression beyond heating the sealed corridor to tropical temperatures.

"Do we know if all the bulkheads are down?" he asked the droid. Its comlink with its peers made it suddenly a lot more useful than Hurati. "All of them?" Hokan was trying to work out if he had any way of getting to Uthan or the nanovirus. The control board in the office off the main corridor was showing red throughout, but he didn't know whether to believe it or not.

"All of them. Droids trapped in sections four, five, seven, and twelve."

It felt like being in the middle of a brawl and then finding yourself dragged off your opponent. The enemy couldn't get at him, but now he couldn't get at them, either. And if the biohazard chamber doors were open, then both the nanovirus and Uthan were on the commandos' side of the barrier. If they had managed to get in, they could probably get out the same way.

The front wall shuddered.

Even if any droids had survived the assault on the villa, how would reinforcements help him now?

Hokan turned to Hurati. "Can you get into the system and override the safety controls?"

"I'll do my best, sir." Hurati's face said that he doubted it, but he'd die trying. He retreated to the office with Hokan, and they rummaged through the cabinets and drawers looking for operating instructions, tools, anything that might be used to release the bulkheads. In one cabinet Hokan found a crowbar. But its edges were too thick to get any purchase in the flimsiplast-thin gap between the two sections of the front door or the lower edge of the bulkhead. He flung it to the floor in frustration, and it clattered across the tiles.

The doors needed a blast of some magnitude. And he didn't have the ordnance.

Hurati removed the cover from the alarm panel and began poking the tip of his knife experimentally into the maze of circuits and switches. Hokan took out the lightsaber and took a swipe at the bulkhead, more out of frustration than any expectation of success.

Vzzzmmm.

The air took on an oddly ozonic smell, almost irritating in its intensity. He stared at the bulkhead's previously smooth surface. There was a definite depression.

He made another pass with the blade, more slowly and controlled this time. He pressed his face close to the cooling metal at one edge and squinted across the flat surface, one eye closed. Yes, it was definitely warping the alloy.

But at this rate it would take him hours to cut through. He suspected time was a luxury he couldn't afford.

Something thudded into the wall of the corridor.

Darman didn't even hear the shatter gun fire. The Verpine projectile was never in danger of hitting anyone, but he suspected they'd have known all about it if it had.

"Wow, that's some dent," Atin said. "I don't think the good doctor is going to come quietly, though."

"Niner, are you picking this up?" Darman said. "Found her. Just like that."

There was a faint sound of movement in his earpiece. He'd switched off the video feed. Niner sounded almost relaxed. "That's the first bit of luck we've had."

"Yeah, but she's got a Verpine on her."

"They're fragile weapons and they don't bounce. Give her a fright."

"I've got a few frighteners ready."

"If you need a hand, we're going to have trouble getting in. I reckon *all* the emergency doors have shut tight."

"All quiet out there?"

"Apart from *Majestic* getting too on-target for comfort, yes. We don't want to take the whole building out with you still inside."

"Can you go back for the other ram and try to force the front doors?"

"Do you need us to?"

"We'll try getting Uthan out via the drains. If we can't, it's plan D."

"Cheer up, still got E through Z plans," Fi's voice said.

"One day, Fi, I'm going to give you a good slap." Darman said.

Atin held up his hand for silence. Darman heard the faint sibilance of whispered conversation, and then the door slammed and the lock clunked. So it wasn't an automatic safety door. Uthan had company.

"She really doesn't know me, does she?" Darman said, and peeled off a few centimeters of thermal tape. He checked around the corner with the probe, loath to test his armor against a Verpine. "It's going to take more than a lock to keep me out, sweetheart."

He hugged the wall. He was nearly at the door when it opened and he found himself face-to-face with two Trandoshans who seemed pretty surprised to see him. Maybe it was the armor. It seemed to have that effect.

There was nowhere to run.

There were times when you could pull your rifle and times

when you couldn't, and Deeces weren't much good at point-blank range unless you used them as a club. Darman aimed an instinctive punch before he thought about what he would do with the explosives in his hand. Even with an armored gauntlet, it was like hitting a stone block in the face. The Trandoshan fell back two paces. Then his comrade came at Darman with a blade. There was a frozen second or two of bewilderment as the Trannie looked at his knife, and then at Darman's armor.

"Atin, want to give me a hand here?" Darman said quietly, taking one step back with vibroblade extended.

"What do—oh."

"Yeah. *Oh.*"

The nice thing about a fixed vibroblade was that nobody could knock it out of your hand, not unless they took your arm off with it. The Trannie seemed to be considering that as an option before taking a huge lunge, the blade of his weapon skidding off Darman's arm plate.

Darman ran at the Trannie headfirst and cannoned into him, throwing him against the wall and pinning him there while he tried to drive the vibroblade into soft tissue. He tried for the throat—big blood vessels, quick effect—but the Trannie had his wrist clamped tight. It was taking Darman all his strength to keep the enemy's blade from his own throat. It seemed like deadlock.

The bodysuit was stabproof. Wasn't it? He couldn't see Atin. He had to concentrate on his own predicament, and he wasn't getting anywhere fast with the Trannie. It was time for one of those bar-brawl tactics that Skirata made sure they all learned. Darman scraped his boot along the Trannie's shin and brought it down hard on his instep. It gave him the split second of loosened grip he needed, and he plunged the vibroblade in up to its hilt, over and over, not sure what he was hitting, but noting that the Trannie was shrieking and that the shrieks were gradually getting fainter.

Skirata was right. Stabbing someone was a slow way to kill them. He pressed his forearm against the Trannie's neck and held him pinned while he slid down the wall. Darman followed him all the way down and finally knelt on his chest to make sure he didn't move while he jammed the blade up under his jaw and across his trachea.

He waited for him to stop moving, then scrambled to his feet to see Atin standing over the other Trandoshan, still cursing. There was a lot of blood, and it didn't look like Atin's.

"I could have done without that interruption," Darman said.

"Ruins your concentration," Atin said. "Where were we?"

"About to use my universal key." Darman retrieved the ribbon charge from the floor, wiped it on his sleeve, and set it with its detonator against the lock. They moved quickly to the hinge side, and Atin drew the Trandoshan array blaster he'd been so unwilling to abandon.

"Atin, it's *capture alive,* remember?"

"She's got company."

"You make sure you need to use it, then. If they'd wanted her disintegrated they'd have said." Darman took out the stun grenade and the mini EMP: she might have droids in there, too. He juggled both spheres in one hand. "Okay, I blow the lock, and in these go. They're down for five seconds. I take Uthan and you shoot anything else still moving."

"Got it."

"Cover."

Whump. The door exploded, showering kuvara splinters, and Darman leaned forward and threw in the surprises. A blinding three-hundred-thousand-candlepower white light and 160 decibels of raw noise flooded the room for two seconds, and Darman was inside before he realized it, pinning Uthan flat to the floor as Atin pumped the array blaster across the room.

The dust and smoke settled. Darman had cuffed Uthan. He didn't actually recall doing it, but that was adrenaline working. For some reason he had expected a fight, but she was simply making an odd incoherent groan. He'd become used to Etain's resilience. Uthan was a regular human, untrained, unfit, and—apart from her intellect—nothing special.

Darman picked up the Verpine and aimed it at a wall. It

made the faintest of whirring noises, then jammed. Niner was right. Verpines didn't bounce, or maybe the mini EMP had temporarily fried its electronics.

"Darman here. We have Uthan, repeat, we have Uthan."

Fi's whoop hurt his ears. Niner cut in. "Are we done here?"

"Let's check we haven't missed anything. Atin?" He glanced over his shoulder. Atin was cradling the array blaster, staring down at four bodies on the floor. It was all a bit of a mess, as Fi would say.

Three of the dead were Trandoshans, and the fourth was a young red-haired woman who wasn't pretty any longer, or even recognizable. Darman wondered if the girl was Uthan's daughter. Then he had another thought.

"How many staff do you have here, ma'am?" He took his helmet off and rolled her over so they were face-to-face. "How many?"

Uthan seemed to be regaining her composure. "You murdered my assistant."

"She had a blaster," Atin said, almost to himself.

Darman shook her. "Ma'am, I'm going to detonate an awful lot of ordnance under this building very soon, and your staff, if you have any, will be dead anyway."

She was staring up into his face, seeming totally distracted by him. "Are you really a clone?"

"I'd like to say the one and only, but you know I'm not."

"Amazing," she said.

"Staff?"

"Four more. They're just scientists. They're civilians."

Darman opened his mouth, and Kal Skirata's voice emerged unbidden again. "Not all soldiers wear uniforms, ma'am. High time those scientists took responsibility for their role in the war effort."

Yes, it was personal. War didn't get much more personal than a virus aimed specifically at you and your brothers. "Darman here. Sarge, Uthan's staff members are somewhere in the building, too. What do you want to do? Retrieve them as well?"

"I'll check with *Majestic*. Wait one." Niner's link went dead for a few moments and then crackled into life again. "No, not required. Get her clear and let us know when you're going to detonate."

"They were just following orders," Uthan said.

"So am I," Darman said, and trussed, gagged, and hooded her with salvaged parasail cord and a section of sheeting. He replaced his helmet and heaved her over his shoulder. It was going to be a tough job getting her down those tunnels. Atin followed.

They slipped back down the drain. Darman hoped that they could find their way back to the surface without Jinart as their guide.

Hokan could feel the sweat stinging his eyes. He withdrew the lightsaber and examined the substantial dent in the bulkhead.

It wasn't deep enough or fast enough, and he knew it. This was displacement activity. He was little help to Hurati, so he vented his frustration on the alloy and all he seemed to succeed in was making the stale atmosphere even hotter and more suffocating.

Then he heard a hiss of air, and he wondered if it was the seal breaching: but it wasn't.

It was Hurati.

Hokan ran the few steps along the corridor to the office. He feared that the young captain had electrocuted himself, and whether he wanted to admit it or not, he actually cared what happened to him. But Hurati was intact. He was leaning over the desk, both hands braced on the surface, head down, shoulders shaking. Then he looked up, and his face was a big, sweaty grin. A bead of perspiration ran down his nose and hung there for a moment before he batted it away with his finger.

"Check the status board, sir."

Hokan swung around and looked for the board. The unchanging pattern of red lights had now become a pattern of red and green.

"Bulkheads two, six, and nine, sir," he said. "Now I can clear the rest. I had to try every sequence. That's a lot of permutations." He shook his head and went back to carefully prodding a piece of circuit board with the tip of his knife. "They'll be jammed open, though."

"Better than jammed shut."

As Hokan watched, the lights changed from red to green, one by one, and a cool draft hit his face.

The front doors had opened.

Hokan expected a missile or blaster volley to punch through them, but all that entered was the silent, refreshing, fire-scented night air.

"Hurati," Hokan said, "Right now, I couldn't love you more if you were my own son. Remind me I said that one day." He drew his blaster and raced down the corridor, past droids, stumbling over shattered metal plates and the body of an Umbaran, and into the room where he had left Uthan with her Trandoshan guards.

He had half expected to see her lying dead on the floor with them. In a way he had hoped for it, because it would mean the Republic hadn't stolen her expertise. But she was gone. He picked up the Verpine and tested it for charge: it made a faint whir and then ticked. Either Uthan hadn't managed to get a shot off or they'd used an EMP grenade.

Hokan worked his way down the passage to the biohazard chamber, pausing on the way to check inside prep rooms and storage cupboards, wary of booby traps. As he opened one door, he heard whimpering in the darkness. He switched on the light.

The remaining four members of Uthan's research team—three young men and an older woman—were huddled in the corner. One of the men held a blaster, but its muzzle was pointed at the floor. They blinked at Hokan, frozen.

"Stay here," he said. "You might be all that's left of the virus program. Don't move." There seemed little chance that they would.

When Hokan reached the central chamber, the only sign that anything untoward had taken place was that the concealed drain in the center of the floor was now a charred, gaping space.

He looked around the walls, shelves, and cupboards. *A mistake.* He'd made a mistake, a terrible oversight. He hadn't taken the time to check what the virus containers looked like, or how many there had been. He could see gaps on shelves through the transparent doors; he pulled on the handles, but they were still locked.

He ran back up the corridor and grabbed one of the young men from Uthan's team. "Do you know what the nanovirus looks like?"

The boy blinked. "It has a structure based on—"

"Idiot." Hokan jabbed fiercely toward his own eye, indicating *look.* "What does the *container* look like? How many? Come on. Think."

He hauled the scientist to his feet and dragged him down the corridor to the biohazard chamber.

"Show me."

The boy pointed to a plain-fronted cabinet. "Fourteen alloy vials in there, inside their own vacuum-sealed case."

"Open it and check."

"I can't. Uthan has all the security codes and keys."

"Is it conceivable that the enemy could have opened it and simply shut it again?"

"Normally I'd say that was impossible, but I also remember thinking that it was impossible for anyone to breach this building."

The hole where the drain had been was now a jagged fringe of scorched, broken tiling and twisted metal frame. Hokan looked down into the void and saw debris.

For a moment he wondered if he was actually dealing with human beings and not some bizarre, unknown life-form. He knew where they'd gone. Now he had to hunt them down and stop them from taking Uthan off the planet with whatever was left of the nanovirus project.

If this was what a handful of clone soldiers could achieve, he was almost afraid to think what millions might do.

18

*You never have perfect knowledge in combat, gentlemen.
It's what we call the fog of war. You can either sit around
worrying what's real and what's not, or you can realize the
enemy hasn't got a clue either and fire off a few rounds of
psychology. A truly great army is one that only has to
rattle its saber to win a war.*
—Sergeant Kal Skirata

"**O**mega to *Majestic. Check check check.* Cease firing."

Niner waited several minutes before moving. There had been trees to the northwest of the facility that weren't there anymore. You couldn't stake your life on the accuracy of gunnery support. He edged forward on his stomach and propped himself on his elbows to check the area, first with his binoc visor and then through the scope of the DC-17.

Nothing was moving, although nothing with any sense would present itself in a bright-lit doorway anyway.

The facility was now stripped completely of its wooden farmhouse shell, and its alloy doors were wide open. For a few seconds, Niner almost expected to see Darman and Atin walk out into the yard, and for Kal Skirata to shout *Endex, endex, endex*—end of exercise. But there were no more exercises, and this night wasn't over, not by a long shot.

Behind him, Fi switched to his Deece and trained the sniper attachment on the entrance, waiting to pick off anything insane enough to walk out. Niner wasn't sure if Fi would pause for thought if anyone did come out, even with raised hands.

"Dar, Atin, can you confirm your position?"

Niner waited.

"Somewhere pitch black and smelly, and dragging a semi-conscious woman behind me," Atin said.

"Sounds like happy hour at the Outlander," Niner said, although he had no idea what a nightclub was really like, and probably never would. The comment sprang from his subconscious. "Is Uthan injured?"

"Dar got fed up with her struggling and sedated her."

"How long before you can detonate?"

Muffled noises filled Niner's helmet. It sounded as if Atin was conferring with Darman without the comlink. Maybe he'd removed his helmet to sip some water. A woman was making incoherent noises, and Niner heard Darman's voice clearly: "Shut up, will you?" He didn't need a medic to check Dar's stress levels.

Atin was back on the link. "At this rate, half an hour."

"Fi, how fast could you cover one klick right now?"

"Unladen and suitably motivated? 'Bout three minutes."

Now it was the timing that was giving them grief. They needed to keep whoever was in the facility right where they were until Darman was in position to detonate the implosion device. Niner wondered how long *Majestic* could wait, and how long it would be before they had more company. He decided to ask.

"Omega here, Majestic. What's that Techno warship doing?"

"Listing to port and smoking a bit, Omega."

"You've been busy."

"If we get busier, we'll let you know. We're dispatching the gunship now. It'll be waiting when you reach the extraction point."

Niner crawled back to Fi's position and nudged him. "You might as well make a move for the EP now with Etain. I can hold this position."

"No."

"Can I give you an order?"

"I might call you Sarge, but right now I'm ignoring you."

Etain appeared on the other side of Fi, with Jinart. "What's happening?"

"The gunship's on its way. I suggest you and Fi head out and meet it."

"Where's Darman?"

"About fifty meters down the tunnel. It's heavy going."

"It's still the quickest path through the warren," Jinart said. "Short of digging them out."

"Digging through five meters of soil without power tools or explosives is going to take a long time." Niner turned to Etain. "Is there anything you can do, ma'am?"

Etain pushed her tangled hair back from her face. "If Jinart can find the shallowest point of the tunnel, I can try to part the soil. If you explain to me what needs to happen, I can picture it. The more accurately I can picture it, the better my chances of bringing the Force to bear. I have to *see* what's happening in my mind."

"I can find their position," Jinart said.

"By all means bring your lightsaber, ma'am," Fi said. "But only use it if you miss with this." He handed her his blaster.

Etain shoved it in her belt. "You persuaded me."

Jinart was fast. Etain had trouble keeping up with her when she was running on all fours, her snout to the ground. The Gurlanin's rhythmic sniffs were in counterpoint to Etain's gasping breath.

They were moving in a square search pattern across the field to the east of the facility, trying to locate the exact section of tunnel that Darman and Fi had taken. Etain could sense Darman now. They were close.

"Are you following scent?" Etain panted.

"No, I'm listening for echoes."

"With your nose?"

"Where I keep my ears is my own business." Jinart stopped

dead and pressed her snout into the soil with a few short, strong snorts. "Here. Dig here."

"I hope they know we're right above them."

"We aren't. They're about ten meters back up the tunnel. If you excavated where they are you could bury them completely."

Etain wasn't sure if Jinart was making a general point about rescue procedure, or commenting on her competence. She didn't care. Darman was down there and he needed her help. Atin was down there, too, but the thought of Darman focused her because . . . because he was a *friend*.

She could almost imagine him advising her that sentimentality was a luxury that a commander could never afford.

"Here we go," she said, more to herself than to Jinart.

Etain knelt to one side of the line of the tunnel and placed her hands flat on the ground. When she closed her eyes, she visualized the warren, seeing its uneven walls with tree roots emerging from them like knotted rope. She saw small stones and seams of amber clay.

Then her focus became more intense. She saw smaller roots, and then the individual grains of mineral and veins of organic material. She felt her breathing slowing, changing, as if her lungs weren't moving within her but rather the air outside her body was pressing and relaxing, pressing and relaxing, slowly and rhythmically.

And she finally saw the space around each microscopic grain. It wasn't empty. It was invisible, but it was not a void. Etain felt it. She had control of it at a fundamental, subatomic level. She could feel the pressure throughout her body.

Now all she had to do was shape it.

At the sides of the tunnel, she pictured the space thinning and reducing, compacting the walls, strengthening them against collapse. Overhead—and she now felt like she was lying flat on her back looking up at the vault above her—she saw the space expand.

The grains moved farther apart. The space flowed in to

displace them. The space flowed upward to lift them. And then the space was suddenly all there was.

Etain was aware of something cold and slightly damp across the backs of her hands and opened her eyes. She was kneeling in fine, friable soil. It looked as if a patient gardener had sieved it to prepare for planting seeds.

She was looking down into an open trench. There was a domed line of soil along both sides, as neat and regular as if an excavator had done the job.

"That," said Jinart's voice beside her, "was quite extraordinary." The Gurlanin's tone was almost reverent. "*Quite* extraordinary."

Etain knelt back on her heels. Instead of the exhaustion she normally felt after using the Force to shift objects, she felt refreshed. Jinart slipped down into the trench and disappeared. A few moments later, a familiar blue-lit, T-shaped visor popped up from the darkness below, and it didn't alarm her at all.

"There's always a career for you in the construction industry, Commander," Darman said.

He scrambled out of the trench, and Etain threw her arms around him without thinking. Her blaster clunked against his armor plates. It was odd to hug something that felt like a droid, but she was overwhelmed by relief that he'd made it. She let go and stepped back, suddenly embarrassed.

"Yeah, I've been in a sewer," he said, all guilt. "Sorry."

Atin's voice carried from the trench. "Dar, are you going to stand there all night posing for the commander, or are you going to help me lift this?"

"As if I could forget," Darman said.

After some grunting and cursing, the two commandos managed to lift a thoroughly trussed body onto the edge of the trench. Etain pulled off the hood and stared into the half-closed eyes of Dr. Uthan. She was drifting in and out of consciousness.

"How much did you give her?" Etain asked.

"Enough to shut her up," Darman said.

Etain hoped the woman didn't vomit and choke to death.

It was always a risk with heavy sedatives. They hadn't come this far to lose her. Atin leaned forward, and Darman heaved Uthan onto his back.

"Ten-minute shifts," Atin said. "And I'll be counting."

"I hope she's worth the effort," Etain said.

"So do I," Jinart said. "You must make your own way now. I've done all I can. Remember us, Jedi. Remember what we have done for you, and that we expect your help in reclaiming our world. Honor that promise."

Jinart looked the Padawan up and down as if measuring her, and then the Gurlanin lost her outline and became black fluid again, vanishing into the undergrowth.

"To think I nearly shot her," Darman said, shaking his head. They moved off toward the extraction point across country remarkably empty of gdans.

Ghez Hokan lined up the young scientists on the other side of the door. He gestured to Hurati.

"On my mark," he said. "Kill the lights."

"Sir, if the speeders have been destroyed, what are we going to do?"

Hokan thought it an unusually stupid question for such a fine officer, but perhaps he was thinking about just how far untrained civilians might get on foot before falling to the enemy.

"Run," he said. "Just run."

He turned to the four biologists, hoping terror would speed them up, as it often did. "What's your name?" he asked the woman.

"Cheva," she said.

"Well, Cheva, when the lights go out, hang on to me and run like crazy, understand?"

"Yes."

"And if the captain or I shout *drop,* you drop down flat. Got that?"

"I can assure you I have."

"Hurati, you take the rear. Don't lose any of them."

Hokan was expecting more laser bombardment. It was

quiet outside, but he felt that it would begin again as soon as they emerged. He couldn't defend a facility with its doors jammed open. There was at least one squad of enemy commandos still out there. His last chance was to make a run for it with the remnants of Uthan's team and hide them somewhere. Then he would look for Uthan.

One way or another, he would salvage what he could of the nanovirus program. Beyond that, he hadn't made plans.

"Ready, Hurati?"

"Ready, sir."

Hokan slid on his Mandalorian helmet, as much for comfort as protection.

"Lights!"

19

CO *Majestic* to Coruscant Command

Standing by to retrieve LAAT/i from Qiilura. Be aware we have detected two Trade Federation warships approaching from the Tingel Arm to reinforce Qiilura. *Vengeance* is moving to protect our flank.

"**W**e're almost at the one-klick line," Darman's voice said. "Ready when you are."

Niner clapped his glove to the left side of his helmet. He feared it was becoming a nervous tic. "Good. See you at the EP."

"Give me a few minutes."

Fi made a casual thumbs-up gesture and adjusted his shoulder plate. Five minutes felt like forever right then.

"Whoa, what's happening here?" Niner said. "Dar, hold off. Wait one."

The light from the front doors had died, and his night-vision visor kicked in.

He thought he saw Darman or Atin, another odd flashback now that the stims were wearing off, but then he realized the T-slit visor coming out the door was Hokan's. He opened fire. The hesitation had cost him half a second, an eternity, and he didn't see anyone fall.

Fi laid down a burst of plasma bolt rounds, and they waited. Nothing. Then there was another flurry of movement and someone yelled "Drop!" but the three shapes didn't, at least not until the plasma rounds hit them.

It was silent again. Niner paused. As he and Fi began edging forward to check, someone got up from the blast-cratered ground and sprinted around the far side of the building.

Niner and Fi sprayed more rounds and paused again. But there was no more movement.

"If there's more inside that lobby, Sarge, can I put a bit of anti-armor in there? I don't fancy running with droids behind us."

Standard grenades wouldn't trigger the thermal detonator. "Lob in six," he said. "And then set the E-Web to self-destruct."

Fi lined up the blaster, easing it a little on its tripod. Niner heard a high-pitched noise like a repulsorlift drive starting up, but then it was drowned out by the *whump-whump-whump* of the first three grenades launching and exploding.

The doorway of the facility belched black, rolling flames and smoke.

"Now that's *endex*," Niner said, and they ran. They ran over rutted fields and crashed through two hedges and were into the trees before Niner managed to open his comlink and gasp out the *take-take-take* command to Darman.

The white flash illuminated the track before them a second or two before the shock wave smacked Niner hard in the back. It threw him forward. His mouth smashed against the interior of the visor and he tasted blood. When he turned his head and tried to get up, Fi was also flat on his chest, arms out in front, head turned toward him.

"No, Sarge," Fi said, still seeming totally pleased with life. "*That* was endex."

Ghez Hokan found himself on the ground with his speeder bike upended, its drive still running. The blast was ringing in his ears. He froze, head covered, waiting for incoming cannon fire. But only silence followed.

He struggled to his feet and managed to heave the speeder upright again. A steering vane was slightly bent, but it was serviceable. He dusted himself down and then swung back into the rider's seat.

He could see his hands gripping the bars. The tan glove on

his left hand looked black; it was still wet. Cheva had hung on to him. She'd run, as he'd told her. Her blood had sprayed over him when she was hit. It was the closest he had come to feeling pity in many years.

Enough of this. You're going soft, man. Concentrate.

"Sir." It was hard to identify the voice from a single shout. Hokan turned to check, but there was really only one man who would have struggled to stay with him. "Sir!"

Hurati rode up from behind and stopped his speeder level with his. He had no second rider. Hokan didn't need to ask.

"I'm sorry, sir," Hurati said. "They froze when the shooting started. They didn't even drop."

"Civilians tend to do that," Hokan said wearily.

"That blast was the facility. Judging by the color, that was a high-temperature implosion. Not laser cannon."

"Does it matter?"

"Nothing could have survived that, even in a blastproof container. If there were any samples of the nanovirus, they're gone now."

So there was now no nanovirus in Separatist hands, and no scientists with any degree of expertise in the program, either. That made it imperative to retrieve Uthan.

Given the blast area of an implosion device, they were using sensitive remote detonators. Hokan was relieved that he had some EMP grenades in his cargo pannier.

"Find them," Hokan said.

He couldn't even trace their route from the drainage system now. Where would he start? The enemy would need to leave Qiilura. They would have a vessel somewhere. If intelligence from Geonosis was any guide, they would have gunships to extract them and evacuate wounded.

It was a quiet, backward, rural planet. You could hear motors and drives for kilometers, especially at night.

Hokan powered down the speeder and waited, listening.

Etain could feel it long before she saw or heard it.

She hadn't been able to detect droids, or so she thought, but she could feel something *big* disturbing the Force, and it was getting nearer. She wasn't sure if it was mechanical or organic. And it didn't communicate any sense of threat beyond a mild anxiety.

Then she heard the rushing air and steady drone of a vessel's propulsion drive. She stopped and craned her neck. Atin and Darman stopped, too.

"Oh, I love that sound," Darman said.

"What is it?"

"The sound of us getting out of this cesspit in one piece. A *larty*. A gunship."

The sound was practically right overhead. As Etain scanned the night sky she picked out a silhouette against the stars. The vessel wasn't showing any navigation lights. It dipped slightly, its drive changing pitch, and Darman reacted as if someone were talking to him. He gestured and nodded. Then he waved. The gunship picked up speed and lifted higher before shooting away.

"They tracked us by our comlink transponder," Darman said. "Good old Niner. Bless him for knocking out Teklet."

Atin jerked his shoulders to heave Uthan a little higher on his back. "Your carriage, princess," he said to her, far more cheerful than Etain had imagined him capable of being. His presence felt almost healed, but not entirely. "Want to sit up front?"

Uthan had recovered from the sedation enough to squirm. Etain realized that the scientist was the only person she had ever seen who could convey such rage just by writhing. She didn't envy the soldier who had to untie her.

"Your turn, Dar," Atin said.

"Okay." He seemed elated as well as edgy. Etain could feel it. It was nearly over: they'd pulled it off. She wanted to ask him what he was going to do when he got back to base, but she could guess that it involved a lot of sleep, a hot shower, and food. His dreams were modest. She thought that was a fine example to set, even for a Padawan.

She just hoped that she could become a competent officer. She wanted Darman's respect.

"Come on, Dar," Atin said irritably. "Uthan's starting to weigh a ton. Your turn."

"Try this," Etain said, and *lifted* with the Force. Atin half turned to check what was relieving the weight on his back. Darman had almost caught up with him.

Crack. Atin pitched forward.

Etain thought he had merely tripped, but Darman was now down on the ground, and she followed suit. He was sprawled across Atin with his rifle raised. Atin wasn't screaming, but he was making a rhythmic *ah-ah-ah* noise as if he was trying to gulp air. Uthan was lying in a heap on the grass.

"Man down," Darman said, unnaturally calm. Etain heard him clearly: he still had the voice unit open. "Sarge, Atin's hit."

Whatever Niner's response was, Etain didn't hear it. Darman fired rapidly and she saw the brilliant rounds fly over her head.

Why hadn't she felt anyone behind her? Because she'd been distracted. *This was her fault.* If Atin died, she would have him on her conscience for the rest of her life.

The firing stopped. It was over inside thirty seconds. The world had somehow gone back to the way it was before, except for Atin.

Darman could obviously see something through his rifle sight that Etain could not. She watched him get up, run forward, and aim at an object on the ground. He switched on his helmet lamp.

"One of Hokan's officers," Darman said. "A captain."

"Is he dead?"

A single shot. "He is now," Darman said.

This time Etain wasn't quite as appalled as she had been when Darman had dispatched the wounded Umbaran. She was wrapped up in concern for Atin. Her perspective had shifted radically.

Atin was now worryingly quiet. When Darman turned him carefully onto his side, there was a shattered hole in his armor plate about twenty centimeters below his right armpit that was leaking blood. Darman took a small, gray oblong container with rounded edges from his belt and emptied the contents on the ground. He shoved what looked like a field dressing in the gaping hole and taped it to the armor.

"Get on," Atin said. His voice was shaking. "Go on. Leave me."

"Don't go all heroic on me or I'll smack you one."

"I mean it. Get Uthan out of here."

"Atin, shut up, will you? I'm not leaving anyone anywhere." Darman was working with all the precision of someone who'd been drilled repeatedly in combat first aid. He nodded at Etain. She grasped Atin's hand and squeezed it hard. "That's what a Verpine projectile can do to Katarn armor . . . easy, brother. I've got you." He removed one of Atin's thigh plates, peeled back the section of bodysuit, and exposed the skin. He held two short single-use syringes in his hand. "It's going to hurt a bit, okay? Steady."

Darman stabbed both needles into Atin's thigh in quick succession. Then he scrawled something on Atin's helmet with a marker and replaced the thigh plate.

Etain stared at the letters P and Z now written on the forehead of the helmet.

"P for painkiller," Darman said. He laid Atin flat on his back. "And Z for blood-loss control agent, because B looks too much like P when you're in a hurry. It's for the medics, just in case they don't scan him, so they know what I've dosed him with. Now, this is going to look really odd, but trust me . . ."

Atin was flat on his back, breathing heavily. Darman slid on top of him, back-to-chest, then slipped his arms through Atin's webbing and rolled both of them over so he was lying underneath. Raising himself on his arms, he drew his legs to a kneeling position and then stood up with Atin secure across his back. He tottered slightly. But he didn't fall.

"Easiest way to lift and carry a heavy man," Darman said, his voice sounding a little strained.

"I could have done that for you," Etain said.

"Yeah, but he's my brother. Besides, you're going to carry Doctor Uthan."

Etain felt momentary guilt for not checking on her. But the scientist was still lying there trussed, quite silent, and no doubt bewildered. Etain leaned over her.

"Come on, Doctor," she said. She went to lift her, but her hands touched something cold and wet. There was a jagged sliver of pale gray plastoid alloy protruding from just under her ribs. It was shrapnel from Atin's armor. The doctor was bleeding heavily.

"Oh no. Not this. Look. Darman, *look*."

"*Fierfek*. After all this rotten—"

"No, she's alive."

"Just get her to the extraction point. They better have a medic on board."

The disappointment was sudden and crushing. Etain felt it. It almost made her stop in her tracks, too overwhelmed by the unfairness of it all to move, but it didn't stop Darman, and so she was determined to go on. His absolute discipline was tangible. In a few days she had learned more from him than she had ever been able to learn from Fulier. Being seconds from death so many times drove the lessons home that much harder.

Etain also knew it had forged a bond that would cause her enormous pain in years to come. It was worse than falling in love. It was a totally different level of attachment: it was shared trauma. Master Fulier said you could fall out of love, but Etain knew you could never fall out of *this,* because history could never change.

She lifted Uthan across her back by her own arm and jerked her forward until she was comfortably across her shoulders.

"Let's move it, Darman," she said, and hardly recognized her own voice. For a moment, she didn't sound like a Jedi at all.

Hokan was still on the loose. Niner knew it. He'd seen him—or at least someone in his armor—come out of the facility. The officer whom Darman had shot had just been a young captain. And Hokan was probably doing what the dead captain seemed to have done, and tracked them by the gunship. Their salvation might also prove to be their undoing.

"About one more klick," Fi said. "Any word on Atin?"

"Haven't you got your long-range switched through?"

"No. It's one more distraction I can't face right now."

Niner was beginning to understand how Fi coped: the man just switched off, sometimes literally. He wondered who or what had taught him to do that, because it wasn't Skirata. Kal Skirata *felt,* all too visibly sometimes.

"I hope we get an urban deployment after this," Niner said. *Stay positive. Look ahead.* "A nice, noisy, confusing city with places to hide and lots of running water. Surveillance. Data extraction. Easy Street."

"Nah, jungle."

"You're sick."

"Jungle's like a city. Lots going on."

"You're worried about Atin."

"Shut up, Sarge. I'm just worried about me, okay?"

"Of course you are."

"Why didn't we just pound this whole region from space?"

"No intel. Virus could have been at several locations. We might not have hit them all and we'd never have known until it was too late."

"Just when we were making a good team."

"He's still alive, Fi." Niner began walking backward, playing the tail role. "He's still alive. Jedi can heal. Darman's done all the right first aid—"

Niner never did like being tail on patrol, especially at night. He liked it even less when the point man shouted, "Down!"

He dropped flat in the grass and looked where Fi was aiming his Deece.

"Speeder," Fi said. "Guess who. Crossing right-to-left ahead. It's got to be Hokan."

"Can you take him?"

"Clear shot when he passes the trees."

"Don't hang about, then."

Niner counted the seconds, following the speeder bike with his rifle scope. The speeder's movement behind the avenue of kuvara created a strobe effect. A flare of energy lit up his night vision and the rider was thrown off the vehicle in a cloud of vapor.

"That's the way to do it," Niner said.

They waited the mandatory few seconds to check that Hokan was truly down. There was no movement at all. Niner could see the glint of gdans' eyes in the grass, a sign that at least someone thought the fighting was over and that it was safe to come out again.

Niner was on his feet and Fi was up on one knee when Hokan rose from the grass like a specter. He staggered a few steps and raised his weapon.

Niner didn't hear him fire. But he heard a projectile whistle pass him and hit something with a loud *crack*. Verpine shatter guns were silent, and they were accurate. If Hokan hadn't been winded by Fi's round, then Niner would have had the same hole blown in him as Atin. "Sarge, when I kill him, can I have his armor?" Fi asked.

"You get to take it off him personally."

"I needed that motivation. Thanks."

"Still see him?"

"No . . ."

A blaster round hit the grass a meter in front of Fi and sent sparks swirling. Their enemy wasn't a mindless tinnie or a stupid Weequay. He was a Mandalorian, a natural-born fighter, dangerous even when wounded.

He was very much like them.

"You think that gunship's going to wait?" Fi asked.

"Not once they have Uthan."

"Fierfek." Fi snapped on the grenade attachment and aimed. "Maybe we shouldn't have ditched the E-Web." The night lit up with the explosion. Fi raised his head a little and blasterfire flowed back, a meter farther off target than before. "You go right of him while I keep him busy."

Niner edged forward on his elbows and knees, Deece crooked in his arms. He'd moved about ten meters when the air above him made a frying noise and a blaster bolt took the seed heads off the grass above him.

If it hadn't been for that Verpine, things would have been a lot simpler.

Majestic wouldn't wait much longer. The stims had worn off fully now, and Niner was feeling the impact of days of hard tabbing, little sleep, and too much noise. He made himself a promise there and then. If he and Fi weren't getting off Qiilura, then neither was Ghez Hokan.

But Mandalorian or not, Hokan was just one man, and he was facing two men who were at least his match. Niner didn't underestimate him, but the end result was almost certain: sooner or later he would deplete the power cells. Still, time wasn't on their side right then.

"Not good at all," Niner said. "Darman, Niner here. What's your position?"

He sounded out of breath. "Slow going, Sarge. About ten minutes from the EP."

"Ask them if they'll keep the meter running, will you? Just saying good-bye to Ghez Hokan."

"I'll drop Atin off and—"

"Negative, Dar. We can handle this once we crack his armor. Stand by."

Fi was edging forward looking for a clear shot. Niner, running out of patience, looked about for some cover he could use to get a position to the side of Hokan. The flash of a weapon discharge caught his eye but he didn't hear anything except Fi beginning to say something over the comlink and then a very brief searing peak of high-pitched noise.

Then everything went silent and black.

For a moment Niner thought he'd been hit. He couldn't hear Fi and he couldn't see the data from his HUD. There was no green image of the field and the trees behind it in his night-vision visor. But he could feel his elbows squarely braced in the soil and he could feel his Deece still in his hands. No pain—but if you were hurt badly enough you sometimes didn't feel a thing.

It took him several slow seconds to realize his helmet's

systems were totally dead. His face felt hot. He wasn't getting air.

He pulled off the helmet and squinted through the scope of his DC-17. The night-vision scope picked up his image; Fi had taken his helmet off, too, and had his hand inside it, pressing controls frantically.

EMP grenade, Niner thought. *Hokan's droided us.*

You used electromagnetic pulse charges against droids. But they were equally effective against delicate electronics attached to wets. The enhanced Katarn helmets, three times the price of an ordinary trooper's version, were packed with sophisticated prototype systems, *vulnerable* systems.

Niner crawled slowly and carefully toward Fi. A couple of blaster bolts went wide. He lay flat, head-to-head with him.

"He's fried our helmets," Fi whispered. "Don't they test these things properly?"

"I bet some civvy thought nobody would use EMPs against wets."

"Yeah, I might look him up when we get back."

"They should reset."

"How long?"

"No idea. Deece still works, though."

"As long as he puts his head up."

"I could do with one of Dar's flash-bangs."

"Doesn't fit the Deece anyway."

"Can you see him at all?"

"No . . . no, wait. There he is."

Niner had to track back and forth a couple of times before he spotted Hokan through the scope. "Got any of the IEDs in easy reach?"

"Six."

"How far can you throw?"

"Far enough."

"Wide as you can. Scatter them across him."

Niner laid down suppressing fire while Fi bounced up and down, lobbing the little makeshift bombs and dropping flat again. Niner took the detonator control.

"When I hit this, you go wide that way and try to get side-on to him."

Fi rolled slightly to one side, bracing on his right arm for a quick start. Niner hit the det. Fi bobbed up.

Nothing happened. A blaster round seared the grass between them, and Fi threw himself down again.

"We really must talk to procurement about hardening our electronics," Fi said mildly.

"I fear we might be back to old-fashioned soldiering."

"I'm fresh out of bayonets."

"Sergeant Kal would have an idea."

"You got his number on you?"

"I'm going to scream."

"What?"

"Don't laugh. This man's a nut. If he thinks I'm down and badly injured, he won't be able to resist coming over and slitting my throat."

"And then I give him a surprise party?"

"Anything that resolves this *fast*."

"Okay, kid. Off you go."

Niner suddenly realized he didn't actually know how to scream. But he'd heard enough terribly wounded men to make a fair stab at it.

He threw back his head and let go.

20

I don't know who the good guys are anymore. But I do know what the enemy is. It's the compromise of principles. You lose the war when you lose your principles. And the first principle is to look out for your comrades.
—Kal Skirata

The gunship was the most beautiful craft Darman had ever seen.

It came into view as he staggered through the line of bushes and into the newly plowed field. Its cockpit bubbles gleamed like a holo of Cloud City, and its cannon turrets had the symmetry of the finest Naboo architecture. He even loved its rust and the dents in its wings.

"Look at that, Atin," he said. "Sheer art . . . Atin?"

". . . yeah."

"Nearly there."

". . . uh."

White trooper armor came running toward him with a Gran in a medic's uniform just behind them. Atin's weight lifted from his back, and he struggled to pull his arms free of the webbing. He followed the stretcher, trying to talk to the medic.

"Verpine projectile, right side of his chest," he said. "Painkiller, five ccs of—"

"I can see," the Gran said. "Neat job, Private. Now get in that ship."

When he looked around, troopers had taken Uthan from

Etain and she was walking toward the gunship, stopping to look over her shoulder every few steps. General Arligan Zey stepped down from the troop cabin and bowed his head very slightly in her direction. She slowed down and stopped to return it.

It struck Darman as a remarkably formal greeting under the circumstances. Behind this tableau of Jedi etiquette was a scene from a nightmare, with medics working on both Atin and Uthan, removing armor, cutting garments, hooking up transfusion lines, calling for more dressings. It was like watching two parallel worlds, each wholly oblivious to the other.

Zey didn't look at Darman at all, but the ARC trooper who jumped down beside the general took off his helmet and simply stared at him in silence. Something black moved in the shadows of the ship and then emerged slowly to sniff the air with a long glossy snout.

It was Valaqil. He had come home. Darman could hardly say that he recognized the Gurlanin, because this one looked indistinguishable from Jinart. But he could guess.

"Private Atin is still collecting scars, I see," Valaqil said. "And my consort is impatient and waiting for me. I have to go."

"Jinart?" Darman shrugged, embarrassed. "She's been an extraordinary help to us, sir. A fifth—a sixth member of the squad, in fact."

"I'm sure she will tell me all the details of what has made her so very excited for the past few days."

And then he was gone, loping across the field and into the bushes. Darman hoped the Republic wouldn't disappoint the Gurlanins. They'd served as well as any soldier.

"You've done remarkably well, Padawan," Zey said. "Especially without the guidance of a Master. Quite exceptional, in fact. I think that this may hasten your progress toward your trials as far as the Council is concerned. With the supervision of a Master, of course."

Darman expected delight or embarrassment or something equally positive to soften Etain's expression. He knew she believed she was unfit to be a Jedi Knight, or even a Padawan at times. He knew it was the one thing she lived for.

But the elevation didn't appear to move her at all. She didn't even appear to hear what Zey had said.

"Master, where are Niner and Fi?" Etain asked.

Zey looked bemused. "Who?"

"Sorry, Master. The two other men from Omega Squad."

Darman felt the scrutiny of the ARC even more keenly now. He'd only seen ARCs a couple of times before, and they came as close to scaring him as anyone supposedly on his side ever could. Zey shook his head. "You're the first to make it here."

"They'll be here, sir," Darman said. He flicked open his helmet-to-helmet comlink. If the ARC was listening in, it was too bad. "Sarge? Fi? Time to get a move on."

There was no sound at all in his ear, not even static. He switched to the alternative frequency, and still there was nothing. "Niner, Fi, are you receiving?" He checked the diagnostics mode of his HUD: his helmet was fully functional. He could see the crevasse on Geonosis again, standing behind the cooling, ticking E-Web, trying to raise Taler, Vin, and Jay. He couldn't see the biometric data from their suits on his HUD.

No, not again. Not again, please . . .

"Ma'am, I'm not getting any response."

"What does that mean?"

He could hardly bear to say it. "Their helmets are offline. I don't think they made it."

"They're dead?" Zey asked.

"They're *not dead,*" Etain said firmly.

"Ma'am, I can't raise them at all."

"No, I don't care, they're alive. I know they are."

"You have to go," Zey said. "If you don't go now, you could be flying straight into a battle with Trade Federation vessels. We've attracted a lot of attention." The general turned back to the two medics working on Uthan. "Is she going to survive?"

"She's in a very bad way, sir. We need to move her."

"Keep her alive any way you can. Prepare to lift off. Etain—"

"Master, there are two men still out there."

"They're dead."

"No, I can feel them. I know them, sir, I know where they are. They're not even hurt. We *must* wait for them."

"We must also save Uthan and get you two out of here."

"They've destroyed the virus. Isn't that what matters? You can't abandon them now."

Darman could see she was at that point where she would either collapse or do something extreme. Her face was drawn tight, and her pupils were dilated. It was an expression that scared him. He'd seen it a few times in the last few days.

The gunship's drives were throbbing now. Etain still had one boot on the platform and the other firmly on Qiiluran soil.

Etain swallowed hard. *Oh,* Darman thought. *Just bite your tongue, ma'am. Don't react.* But he felt what she was feeling. All that sweat and terror and pain for nothing. All that, when they could have bombed the facility and gone home. All that—and Atin fighting for his life, and Niner and Fi either dead or marooned here.

"I will *not* leave without them," Etain said. "I regret disobeying you, Master, but I must."

Zey registered visible annoyance. "You will do as I order," he said quietly. "You're compromising the mission."

"We need these men. They are *not* expendable."

"We are *all* expendable."

"Then, sir, I'm expendable, too." She lowered her head slightly, looking up at Zey, more challenging than coy. "An officer's duty is the welfare of her men."

"I see that Master Fulier taught you little about obedience but a great deal about sentimentality—"

Darman dared to interrupt. He couldn't stand seeing Jedi Masters arguing. It was painfully embarrassing. "Look, I'll stay, ma'am," he said. "Go with Atin. See he's okay."

Despite Skirata's frequent assurances that their lives had meaning, Darman had accepted the hierarchy of expendabil-

ity: it was not only natural in the Grand Army, but also necessary and inevitable. His life was a more valuable defense
asset than a clone trooper's; the ARC's life was more valuable than his. But the mirror that Etain's loyalty and care held
up in front of him had made him see himself as a man. Yes,
Niner and Fi deserved better. They all did.

Zey ignored Darman. "You must go. More Separatist vessels are heading this way, and I know how this pains you,
but—"

Etain bounced off her back heel into the troop cabin in one
move. For a moment Darman thought she had changed her
mind, but that wasn't Etain at all. She took out her lightsaber
and held the glowing shaft a handspan away from the power
conduit running along the spine of the airframe. She could
ground them with one move. Zey's jaw was set. Nobody else
moved except for the Gran medic working on Atin, who
seemed oblivious to the drama, a quality Darman suspected
was honed by working under fire.

"Master," Etain said, "either *all* of Omega Squad leaves
Qiilura or *nobody* does."

"This is a foolish act, Etain." His tone was very calm.
"You must see the necessity of this."

"No, Master. I don't."

He's going to do some of that Jedi stuff on her, Darman
thought. *No, no, please . . .* He couldn't see the ARC's expression but he could guess it was one of astonishment.

"Etain, this is precisely why you must resist attachment."

Oh, he doesn't know her at all, Darman thought. *If only
he'd—*

Her lightsaber was still ready to slice through the conduit.
"As Jedi we say we revere all life. Are we prepared to *live*
that belief? Are these soldiers' lives worth any less than ours
because we had them created? Because we can *buy more of
them* if these are destroyed?"

"They are *soldiers,* Etain. Soldiers die."

"No, Master, they're men. And they've fought well, and
they're *my* responsibility, and I would rather die than live
with the knowledge that I abandoned them."

It was so silent that time seemed to have frozen. Zey and Etain were locked in a wordless argument. Then Zey shut his eyes.

"I feel your certainty has its roots in the Force," he said. There was a sigh in his voice. "What's your name—*Darman*? So you have names, do you? Darman, go where she directs you. She values your lives more than she values becoming a Jedi Knight."

Etain made as if to follow him. "You stay, ma'am. Please."

"No," she said. "I won't leave you, *any* of you." She was holding her lightsaber as if she were part of it now, not like something she feared would bite her. "I realize this is gross disobedience, Master Zey, but I really don't think I'm ready to become a Jedi Knight yet."

"You're completely right," Zey said calmly. "And we do need these men."

Darman followed her, looking back for a second at the general.

He looked as if he was smiling. Darman could have sworn he seemed almost proud.

Ghez Hokan had expended almost every round he had. He was down to his vibroblade, the lightsaber, and the last two projectiles in his Verpine now. He pressed his glove hard into his thigh and checked again to see if the wound was weeping fluid.

He couldn't feel any pain. His glove came away wet: the blaster burn had gone deep through skin, nerves, and fat, cauterizing blood vessels but exposing raw tissue that wept plasma.

He wondered what kind of injury was making the commando scream like that, a high-pitched, incoherent, sobbing scream that trailed off and then started up again.

Hokan couldn't see the man's comrade. He knew he had one because he had been hit from two separate positions. Maybe the other was dead. He listened a little longer. He'd heard many men die. Whatever their species, whatever their age, they almost always screamed for their mothers.

Clone soldiers didn't have mothers as far as he knew. So this one was screaming for his sergeant. The sergeant was called Kal or something like it. It was hard to tell.

For some reason that made it unbearable. For once, Hokan could not despise weakness. Whatever he thought of the Republic and the loathsome, sanctimonious Jedi, this was a Mandalorian warrior out there, used and discarded.

He would finish him. It was the decent thing to do. A wounded man could also return fire, so he wasn't going soft, not at all. He was simply ending the battle.

Hokan knelt and looked around. It was clear. Even so, he struggled to crawl with his head down toward the direction of the screams.

They were quieter now, a series of gulping sobs.

"Sarge . . . don't leave me . . . Sargeant Kal! *Sarge!* Uhhh it hurts it hurts it hurts . . ."

How dare the Republic use Jango Fett to create this abomination. How had Fett let this happen? Hokan edged closer. He could see a body in the grass now. He could see light-colored, dirt-caked metallic armor very similar in design to his own, but bulkier and more complex.

And now he was close enough to see the face with the mouth wide open. The man had his arms folded tight across his chest. He was sobbing.

It was Jango Fett, many years before.

Hokan drew himself up on his knees and knelt a couple of meters from the wounded commando, absolutely astonished.

"I'm sorry, my brother," he said. The lightsaber would have been fast, but it was a disgrace to use a Jedi weapon to kill a Mandalorian man. It was too much like reenacting Jango's fate at Geonosis. Hokan drew his vibroblade instead. "It's not your fault. They made you like this."

The commando opened his eyes and focused at a point just past him, as Hokan had seen many dying men do. They all seemed to see ghosts at the final moment.

It was only then that Hokan heard the sound of a lightsaber. And it was too late.

* * *

"You cut that fine," Niner said.

It was the only time Darman had ever seen him look shocked. He wiped his face with the palm of his glove.

"And where were you, Fi? Thanks a bunch. I could have been filleted. You were suppose to slot him."

Fi searched through the decapitated Hokan's jacket. "Ah, I could see Dar and Commander Etain behind him. I knew you were probably okay." He paused, and the rifling grew more vigorous. "Here you go, ma'am. I think you ought to have this." Fi handed a short cylinder back to Etain. It was Master Kast Fulier's lightsaber. It was a matter of honor to return it. "They do work well against Mandalorian armor, don't they?"

Etain didn't seem remotely triumphant. She took the hilt and turned it over in her hand before placing it in her pocket. Darman wondered how long it would be before she sheathed her own lightsaber. She was still clutching it in one hand, its blue blade humming and shimmering as she trembled. She wasn't focusing. Darman willed Fi not to make the obvious comment that killing someone with a lightsaber was nice and clean, no guts, no mess. For once he kept his gallows humor to himself, and simply walked a few paces away to recover the genuine Mandalorian helmet he had decided to appropriate.

"You want to put that away now, ma'am?" Darman said gently. "We're done here."

Niner got to his feet and saluted her in best formal parade fashion. "Thank you, Commander. You don't mind me calling you that now, do you?"

She seemed to come back to the here and now. The shaft of blue light vanished.

"It's an honor," she said.

Darman called back on the comlink: General Zey had kept his word. The gunship was still waiting. They set off in column, picking up speed until they broke into a trot.

The gunship was surrounded by a skirt of billowing dust. Its drive had been idling so long that the heat of the downdraft had dried the top layer of soil.

Etain didn't care if the ship had taken off. She hadn't abandoned her squad. Nothing else mattered after that. And although she knew it had been a deliberate decoy, the sound of Niner screaming would haunt her forever. He must have heard that for real at least once in his life to have mimicked it so horribly well. She felt sick, and it was not because she had killed Ghez Hokan, and that filled her with shame.

She understood fully now why attachment was forbidden to Jedi.

The ARC trooper was pacing a slow, regular square, hands clasped behind his back, head down, and Etain would no longer make the assumption that he was lost in thought. He was probably listening to comm traffic in the private world of his helmet.

General Zey was sitting patiently on the ship's platform. "Are you ready now?"

She held out Master Fulier's lightsaber to him. "Omega Squad recovered it. I felt I should return it to you."

"I know what you're going through, Padawan."

"But that's no comfort, Master."

"A concern for those under your command is essential. But it carries its own pain if you identify too much with your troops." Yes, it did sound as if Zey had known that dilemma. "There are always casualties in war."

"I know. But I also know them now as individuals, and I can't change that. No clone trooper, no commando, not even an ARC trooper will ever be an anonymous unit to me now. I'll always wonder who's behind that visor. How can I be a true Jedi and *not* respect them as beings, with all that entails?"

Zey was studying his hands a little too carefully. "Every good commander in history has had to face that. And so will you."

"If I'm a commander, then may I accompany them on their next mission?"

"I suspect that would not be for the best."

"And what do *I* do now? How can I go back to everyday duties after this?"

"There *are* no everyday duties now we're at war. I will not be leaving. I have come to do what work I can here."

"Work?"

"What will happen to our allies—the Gurlanins—if we abandon them now, with enemy forces in the area? I'm here to operate with them, and try and make Qiilura as inhospitable to Separatists as we can."

"I'm glad we're honoring our commitment, Master."

"You know this land better than anyone now. You would be a valuable asset here."

"And when will more troops join you?"

"I'm afraid we'll have to continue the covert work for the time being. We would need to *disappear.*"

We. Etain could think of nothing worse than staying on Qiilura, with its terrible memories and uncertain future. The nearest she had to friends was a squad of commandos who would be deployed on another mission within days. She would be working with a Master she didn't know. She was alone again and scared.

"Etain, you have duties," Zey said quietly. "We all have. We talk about duty when it's easy, but living it is hard." And he didn't need to add what she knew he was thinking—that she needed to be separated from the object of her recent and desperate wartime attachment. She needed to let her squad go.

It was no different from what was asked of soldiers every day.

"I—I would like to play a useful role in the future of Qiilura, Master." She hoped Darman wouldn't think she was turning her back on him and that he was after all just a glorified droid to her, an asset to be used in battle and expended if necessary. "But I would still find it a comfort one day to know how Omega Squad is faring."

"I understand," Zey said. "The choice is yours, though. You can go with Omega Squad. Or you can stay. You might even request that one of the squad remain here."

One of the squad. Maybe he thought she was just a girl who'd become too attached to a young man when neither of them would ever be able to take the relationship farther. He was testing her, challenging her to make the choice a proper Jedi Knight should make. Yes, she had become close to Darman: he'd been the making of her. But she cared at an inexplicably fundamental level about all of them.

"I don't think caring about your troops is a weakness," she said. "The day we stop caring is the day we turn our back on the Force."

She dug her nails into her palms. Zey was right, though. And it was going to hurt. She sat on the platform beside Zey in silence, eyes closed, composing herself.

The ARC trooper suddenly jerked his head up. "General, sir, we absolutely *must* go now."

"General Zey," Niner said, and touched his glove to his temple. "Sorry we kept you. Are we ready to lift?"

"We don't have time for a mission debriefing, but perhaps you'd like a moment with your commander," Zey said, and beckoned the ARC trooper to follow him. It was a gracious gesture. Etain watched him walk to the rear of the ship to offer her some privacy, apparently supervising the offloading of equipment. She wondered if they had managed to land Zey's starfighter somewhere.

She'd worry about that later. She beckoned the commandos to her.

"What's going to happen to you now?" she said.

"Next mission. Have they assigned us to you?"

She wondered whether a lie might be in order. She looked at Darman. "Not exactly," she said. "I'm staying here with General Zey."

Darman and Niner both averted their eyes, looking at the ground, nodding as if in agreement. Fi raised his eyebrows. "I'm really going to miss you, Commander. Just when we were shaping up. Typical of the army, eh?" He rapped his knuckles on Niner's back plate, pushing him a fraction toward the gunship. "Make a move, then, Sarge."

"Hope to serve with you again, Commander," Niner said, and saluted her. "And don't ever think you didn't earn that rank, will you?"

Etain wished they hadn't left her alone with Darman. She wanted a quick exit with no time to think and make a stupid, emotional comment.

"I chose to stay," she said. "I really would have liked to have stayed part of the team, but I'm not the officer you need."

Darman said nothing. Of course: how could he ever have learned how to take his leave of a friend? All his brief life had been spent among his own kind, immersed in warfare real or virtual. This was where he became a ten-year-old child again. His embarrassment and confusion were palpable.

"You could remain here with me and General Zey," she said. *And I'd know you were safe.* "You have that choice."

He really was a child now. His eyes were fixed on the ground. He was flicking one of the switches on his rifle, back and forth, over and over.

"Just me, ma'am?"

She felt she was testing him now. "Yes."

The gunship's drive rose in frequency, a high whine: the pilot was more than impatient to leave.

"I'm sorry, Commander," Darman said at last. For a moment, he really did seem to be considering it seriously. "I have a job to do."

"I can't pretend I won't miss you," she said.

Darman's gaze didn't flicker. "I've got about ten years left. But I'll be with my brothers, doing what I do best. It's all I've ever known—like going home, really." He bent his head and snapped on his helmet, becoming one of the faceless again. "You take care, Commander."

"And you," she said, and watched him run to the platform and grasp Fi's outstretched arm to be hauled inboard.

The drive roared into higher gear, and the gunship shook slightly.

Etain turned and walked away in a crouch to steady herself against the downdraft. She speeded up into a hunched run until she found a tree and sat down in the lee of it with her back to its trunk.

And she let the tears run down her face.

All that she was, and all that she would be in the future, was because a clone soldier had put such undeserved faith in her that she had become that Jedi he imagined she was. She could now harness the Force in a way she had never been able to at Fulier's side.

She thought of that look of complete faith. She thought of his stoic acceptance of his duty and of the fact that his life would be brief and bright, whatever happened. He had never known a moment of self-pity. She had learned the most important lesson of all from him.

She wiped her eyes with the heel of her hand and hoped Zey wasn't watching.

Etain didn't know if she would ever see Darman or Omega Squad again. She did know, though, that in days to come, every clone trooper or commando or ARC that she might have to order into battle would be neither anonymous, nor meaningless, nor expendable. Under that grim helmet was a man, someone just like her, a human being, but one without the freedom or the life span afforded to her.

Etain Tur-Mukan stood up and walked back into the clearing at the edge of the field to watch the gunship lift into the early-morning sky.